THE POWER
AND THE GLORY

Nov. 17, 1970

For Gerald,
    Who made it a little better
than it was.

           Peter

THE VIKING CRITICAL LIBRARY

GRAHAM GREENE

The Power and the Glory

TEXT AND CRITICISM

EDITED BY R.W.B. LEWIS

YALE UNIVERSITY

and PETER J. CONN

UNIVERSITY OF PENNSYLVANIA

NEW YORK THE VIKING PRESS

Viking Critical Library Edition:
First published in 1970 by The Viking Press, Inc.,
625 Madison Avenue, New York, N.Y. 10022.

SBN 670-56980-1 (hardbound)
670-01806-6 (paperbound)

Library of Congress catalog card number: 79-104160

Printed in U.S.A.

The editors would like to acknowledge the assistance of
David Cohen and Reginald Hyatte in the preparation of this book.

CONTENTS

INTRODUCTION
by R. W. B. Lewis

The Power and the Glory was published simultaneously in England and the United States in the spring of 1940. In this country it appeared as *The Labyrinthine Ways* since another book bearing Greene's original title (a historical tale about Roundheads and Cavaliers by Phyllis Bentley) came out here at the same time. The novel underwent another title change when it was made into a film starring Henry Fonda on muleback and called *The Fugitive*. The film was simplistic in its treatment and not very good; but both alternative titles were entirely cogent. *The Power and the Glory* does indeed have to do with a fugitive—almost, one might say, with man himself *as* fugitive, that fugitive human condition being represented by a nameless Mexican priest, the last of his breed in a region of Mexico where the Church has been outlawed. And the phrase "labyrinthine ways," taken from the opening lines of Francis Thompson's poem "The Hound of Heaven," suggests the real domain through which the priest flees and is pursued: and in context it identifies the force pursuing.

> I fled Him, down the nights and down the days;
> I fled Him, down the arches of the years;
> I fled Him, down the labyrinthine ways
>   Of my own mind; and in the midst of tears
> I hid from Him, and under running laughter.[1]

Of my own mind. The flight—from and eventually toward God and personal salvation—is essentially psychological and spiritual; and Greene's achievement is to objectify such a flight in a solidly concrete and engrossingly melodramatic adventure.

---

[1] The complete poem is printed on pp. 515-20 of this volume.

Nor has he failed to include both the tears and the running laughter.

The novel was well enough received in both countries, though one Protestant periodical commented a bit grumpily that it was designed mainly "as an illustration of doctrine," to which a Catholic reviewer replied that he was at a loss "to determine just what doctrine of the Church the book does illustrate." (We shall have more to say on Greene and the Catholic press.) But there was much praise for Greene's mastery of the art of storytelling—an art somewhat in disrepute in these literarily permissive days—and most reviewers recognized without undue difficulty, even if they did not all relish, the novel's central paradox: that a sinful, boozy, unshaven priest may quite possibly—by keeping faith, and as against the pious and morally pure human beings whom he encounters—have arrived at sainthood.

The book did not, however, gain a large audience—thirty-five hundred copies were sold in England and only about two thousand copies here, according to Greene himself. It was not until the 1950s that *The Power and the Glory* became established as Greene's most compelling work of fiction and as one of the finest English-language novels of its generation. Critics still appear reluctant to grant it authentic greatness; but greatness in a work of literature, at least during the first century or so of its life, is almost as difficult a matter to be quite sure of as, in Greene's view, the issue of individual salvation or damnation. It was, in any case, the emergence of *The Power and the Glory* as at least a major imaginative accomplishment that led to the widespread critical and scholarly attention which that novel and Greene's work as a whole have received in the past couple of decades. The editors of this edition, before making their selections, gathered a sizable trunkful of critical material: books, dissertations, full-scale essays, articles, reviews, interviews, and the like. And apart from the numerous translations of his writings, Greene has been the object of study in eight or nine foreign languages and countries, above all in France where he was sponsored by the exceedingly influential Catholic novelist and pundit François Mauriac (and where the French, speaking aloud of Greene with sometimes awed respect, refer to him as *"Grum Grin"*).[2]

We offer here a representative range of criticism, some of it chiefly informative, some closely analytic, some general and comprehensive—and all of it, we hope, helpful to the reader as he takes hold of this deceptively readable and actually very subtle and complex novel. Several of the discussions, as well, raise questions about the modern novel and its relation to what might be called the contemporary vision of life, and these suggestively transcend the immediate occasion.

Some of the informative material is provided by Greene himself, in the selections we have made from his unorthodox travel book *The Lawless Roads* (titled *Another Mexico* in the United States), his account of a journey through Mexico in the winter of 1938. Greene drew adroitly on *The Lawless Roads* for many phases of *The Power and the Glory*, and the juxtaposition of journalism and fiction pushes into view some interesting questions about the difference between the two modes of writing. Several of Greene's literary essays—a genre in which he is an unassuming master—have also been included as lending another perspective on his work, in particular upon his notion about the relation between religious thought and the literary imagination: a matter of immediate importance for understanding *The Power and the Glory*.

Among the more purely critical inquiries, Karl Patten argues for not one but two structures in the novel: a "radiant" structure, the mobile pattern of mutually illuminating characters; and a chronological structure, the evolving pattern of the action (a pattern of flight and return). Elsewhere, we notice the makings of a stimulating critical debate. Dominick P. Consolo, for example, gives an appreciative study of Greene's strongly accented, highly individual, and nearly indefinable style —the word "style" being large enough to include tone and

---

[2] For further comment on French critical studies of Greene, see the bibliographical note at the back of this book.

point of view as well as Greene's well-known verbal techniques (for example, his affection for the oxymoron or seeming contradiction, as in the phrase "merciless compassion"). But Richard Hoggart, examining somewhat the same thing, hands down a relatively unfavorable judgment. The sparseness of Greene's characterizations, he says in effect, along with his ingenious and often startling similes, result in caricature, in rather faceless figures like those in a comic strip rather than in the fully fleshed and richly individuated "real" men and women Hoggart believes we should always look for in a novel. The issue raised here will recur in different terms, and we shall have more to say about it.

Morton Dauwen Zabel presents a typically deft and perceptive general evaluation of Greene in an essay that is the more impressive since it was written before much of the evidence (the more recent novels and plays) was in. It is refreshing, moreover, to see a critic of Zabel's distinction—he was one of this country's most acute students of the fiction of Henry James and Joseph Conrad—writing with such intelligent admiration about one of Greene's "entertainments," *The Ministry of Fear*. Greene, who has a Gallic taste for making distinctions, has tended to alternate between what he calls "entertainments" (most recently, *Our Man in Havana*) and works he regards as genuine novels; and his entertainments, closely bound though they are to the novels proper, have rarely gotten the critical consideration they deserve.

Laurence Lerner, meanwhile, is the author of what the editors consider the most valuable of the comprehensive essays on Greene's writing up through *A Burnt-Out Case* (1961). Lerner charts Greene's imaginative world by discerning the four main character-types that inhabit it and the perhaps surprising "rank" accorded each by Greene: the pious, whom he detests; the sinners, whom Greene feels for and identifies with, and for whom alone he seems to hold out some hope of salvation; the innocents, who do the most harm in human affairs (as Greene sees it) by their blundering interference; and the humanists, a varied group but on the whole lying outside the only domain that really counts for Greene, the domain of good and evil. Lerner contends that Greene is not and has never intended to be a realistic writer, but rather the writer of modern-day versions of the medieval morality plays. This thesis obviously adds another element to the debate implicitly started by Consolo and Hoggart.

Graham Greene is usually, and no doubt correctly if vaguely, identified as a "religious novelist." Most of his serious writings, certainly, have to do with matters normally thought to be related to religious experience: prayer, confessionals and priests, sin and righteousness, meditations on the mystery of God's mercy, literal miracles and actual resurrections from the dead. Just as one might say that Hawthorne writes as a New Englander of Puritan descent, so one can say that Greene writes as a Christian Englishman and a convert to Roman Catholicism. One of the beguiling puzzles in Greene's broad appeal to contemporary readers is that the majority of them are surely *not* professing Christians and fewer still Catholics; questions about damnation and sainthood are hardly part of their daily concern.

This puzzle has been touched on by various commentators, some of whom view Greene's popularity with the gravest suspicion. But a good many essays have been directed to the curious structure of Greene's religious thought, insofar as one can make it out from his novels and plays, and with the help of some of his own critical writings. Barbara Seward offers a searching exploration of the theme of guilt—the most powerful emotion felt by Greene's protagonists, Miss Seward believes, the one that quickens them into life and renders them unexpectedly eligible for redemption. Sean O'Faolain, on the other hand, writing as a Catholic and exerting his always captivating prose, finds Greene far too obsessed with guilt and the human potential for evil, with the incurable ugliness of the human condition. Greene, he says, "is not primarily interested in human beings, human problems, life in general as it is generally lived." O'Faolain makes a specific exception of *The Power and the Glory,* for which he has nothing but praise; but his argument adds yet another significant voice to the expanding debate about

Greene's "realism" and his fundamental literary purpose. The French Catholic voice of François Mauriac perhaps rounds out that debate, as it tells us in a tender tribute that he is always taken aback at first when he reads a new novel by Graham Greene, since he finds himself entering what he thought to be territory quite familiar to him—human experience seen in Catholic perspective—as "through a secret . . . door hidden in the ivy-covered wall."

Other Catholics have been no less perplexed, and Catholic periodicals have discovered much to dispute in Greene's work. A fascinating summary of these discussions, though too long for us to include, was compiled by Donald P. Costello in *Renascence* (published by the Catholic Renascence Society) in its Autumn 1959 issue. Costello remarks that, though Greene has been a challenge and a source of uneasiness for many Catholic readers and critics, the division of opinion has not followed predictable lines. It has been more often the laity that have attacked Greene, and the clergy that have defended and supported him. The proportion of articles favorable to Greene as against those unfavorable—there have been many more of the former than the latter—is not much greater in Catholic periodicals judged "liberal" than in those rated "conservative." And while *The Heart of the Matter* was banned in Ireland in 1948, *The End of the Affair* (which might be thought to make more Catholic hairs stand on end) was given the Catholic Literary Award in the United States in 1952.

The Power and the Glory fared pretty well with Catholic commentators, one reviewer (in *Commonweal*) calling it "a modern classic," another able critic venturing that it might be an "even great book," and a third declaring flatly that it was "a very great novel." It was with *The Heart of the Matter* and the oddly motivated suicide of its hero Major Scobie that the Catholic controversy over Greene flared up. It is worth pursuing for a moment.

Evelyn Waugh, another distinguished English Catholic novelist, announced that the idea of Scobie willing his own damnation by suicide out of nothing other than his love of God was "a mad blasphemy," and the British critic Martin

Turnell accused Greene of an "inartistic and unworthy use of religion to give a specious glamour to sin" (a similar charge has been leveled by the American writer Mary McCarthy). Paul Dinkle in *The Catholic World* came by a different route to the conclusions reached by Sean O'Faolain. Greene's religious vision, Dinkle said, was so unnecessarily glum because it excluded the crucial element that Dinkle called "Christian joy . . . *sancta hilaritas*, the happiness that is more than reconciliation and peace." The religio-critical principle is probably very sound, but when applied to Greene it might arouse a *hilaritas* somewhat less than *sancta* at least among non-Catholic readers. Even so, the mild hilarity that does bubble occasionally in *The Power and the Glory*—the sense of honest joy, as it were, amid the ordure—may be one reason why that novel was more acceptable to certain Catholics than its successors.

Greene and *The Heart of the Matter* were defended with spirited acumen by Catholics in both hemispheres, and particularly on the ground that Greene is a novelist and not a theologian. Harold C. Gardiner, S.J.—an American scholar with a broad knowledge of literary history and a superior grasp of theological subtleties—ruled out the whole question of Scobie's alleged damnation as a critical concern. Greene, Father Gardiner insisted, does not say whether Scobie is damned or not; "nor should he, because it is not within the province of an author (save in fantasies, which his book definitely is *not*) to follow his characters beyond the limits of mundane time and space." Others were less critically urbane. Letter-writers to *The New World*, the archdiocesan paper of Chicago, fell to condemning Greene's "crude and nude naturalism," and one declared that the novel was anything but "a real contribution to the all-important work to built a CHRISTIAN world." It was less the heresy than the sex that offended many correspondents (one letter proclaimed that reading *The Heart of the Matter* was like "submerging one's head in slime"). Sex—never an insignificant phase of literature or experience—was again the source of rancor and dismay when *The End of the Affair* appeared in 1951. In that milder debate, Evelyn Waugh, himself skilled in the narration of sometimes perverse sexual conduct, sided entirely with Greene. The Catholic press has on the whole, as we have said, displayed great admiration for Greene over the years and has taken a sort of attractive pride in him. Still, the Catholic discussions of Greene's work constitute a curiously revealing aspect of our contemporary culture.

The editors have included among the selections some of their own interpretations of *The Power and the Glory*; no further analytic comment is here necessary. Let me instead take up some of the points raised by our assembled contributing critics, as a way of suggesting the "relevance" (to use a much-vexed word) of this novel. For why, in all honesty, should young American readers in 1970 be concerned with an obscure Mexican priest who stumbled to his death through the wilds of Tabasco some forty years ago?

We can begin with a question about the genre of *The Power and the Glory*. At the time it was written, it had a kind of newspaper immediacy, and indeed Greene has regularly drawn upon contemporary history for the settings and many of the ingredients of his stories: Tabasco under the sadistic Governor Tomas Garrido Canabal, as here; gang warfare in Brighton (*Brighton Rock*); London during the blitz in World War II (*The End of the Affair*); Haiti under the terror (*The Comedians*). Reading a new novel by Greene, one has a first impression of the vividly here-and-now, of headlines turning effortlessly into fictional characters and occurrences. Yet nothing, of course, loses its relevance more rapidly than a journalistic novel about current events. And the fact is, *The Power and the Glory* is not a realistic novel at all. Through that meticulously described atmosphere move figures in an ancient allegorical and to some extent apocalyptic drama. And it is, I believe, in its very evasion of realism that the novel assumes a profound relevance to ourselves.

Richard Hoggart claimed that Greene presents us not with characters but with caricatures. Hoggart is a shrewd critic, and in a sense he is quite right. But Laurence Lerner (rather like Dominick Consolo) makes the same point more sympathetically, and in my opinion more tellingly. Greene's characters,

Lerner says, "tend to simplify into Humours," into moral and theological "types"; for Greene's fiction carries back to the medieval universe of Heaven, Hell, and Purgatory, and to the religious dramas that enacted man's destiny as hovering between those grand alternatives. Now this is just what Sean O'Faolain opposes. Greene, according to O'Faolain, seems scarcely aware of the postmedieval humanistic tradition and the long English tradition of the realistic novel that grew out of it. One has, of course, only to read Greene's literary essays to know that he is steeped in the modern novel. But he has found the conventions of literary realism unsuited to his talent and, more important, to his vision of reality, of the way things really are. The force of his writing, as Lerner insists, comes in good part out of his conscious rejection of the realistic tradition, and out of his going back behind the trappings of "realism."

Greene's vision is in a way an infernal one. Lerner quotes from the second part of *The Power and the Glory*:

Down a slope churned up with the hoofs of mules and ragged with tree-roots there was the river—not more than two feet deep, littered with empty cans and broken bottles. Under a notice which hung on a tree reading: "It is forbidden to deposit rubbish . . ." all the refuse of the village was collected and slid gradually down into the river. When the rains came it would be washed away. He put his foot among the old tins and the rotting vegetables and reached for his case.

The details there are no doubt recalled from personal memory and described with perfect accuracy, but Lerner properly calls the scene "a landscape of Hell—a parody of some innocent rural scene." By the same token, one might also call the scene apocalyptic; for in the apocalyptic vision, the world appears as a grotesque parody of itself, our own world somehow gone hideously astray. What is to be emphasized is that this is how Greene really sees the modern world, and how, if we attend to him, he can at least for a moment make us see it. Greene's landscapes, a brilliant French critic (Thomas Narcejac) once remarked, "have a hallucinating truthfulness," and the opening pages of *The Power and the Glory* "show us the world as it is and as we should be obliged to feel it if we consented, for just one moment, to break with our intellectual comfort."

Such a vision, hellish and apocalyptic and making heavy inroads upon our intellectual comfort, has informed a good deal of the most consequential American fiction in recent years: one need think only of writers such as Ralph Ellison and John Barth, Joseph Heller and Thomas Pynchon. Those writers, to be sure, have usually engaged in apocalyptic *satire*, as though throwing up their hands in comical despair over the enormity of what is happening to our society and our culture and ourselves. *The Power and the Glory* eschews both satire and despair and clings to the faint persistent possibility of hope, rooted in the faith that gleams in the priest's bloodshot eyes, that is audible in his inane little giggle, that is palpable amid the reeking atmosphere of fate. And that is just the point.

Greene shares many of the darkest apprehensions of those American novelists who, today, speak most urgently to our condition. His view of things is more closely bound than that of the Americans to the ancient forms of Christian ritual dramas, discovering in Tabasco and Liberia, London and Haiti, the outlines of the old morality plays that his "simplified" characters repeatedly re-enact. But paradoxically, this only brings Greene and *The Power and the Glory* closer to our situation. It is a matter of ultimate commitment against overwhelming odds, whatever the circumstances and whatever the particular shape of the spiritual challenge. We live in a time when anyone of us is likely to find himself, like the whisky priest, an outlaw, to find himself torn between the longing to escape the country and the commitment to stay and struggle and perhaps be destroyed. Greene in *The Power and the Glory* and in his own terms suggests what an individual can do in a situation like that. He can, in a commonplace phrase of immense import, keep the faith—whatever that faith happens to be: in peace, in justice, in decency, in truthfulness, or, as in Greene's case, in the "appalling mystery of the mercy of God." But one must, like the priest, keep the faith with compassion and humor and in utter humility; above all, without a trace of self-righteousness.

CHRONOLOGY

1904: Graham Greene born October 2 in Berkhamsted, England, the fourth of six children. Greene's elementary education was at Berkhamsted School, of which his father was headmaster. Contributed early prose and verse to *Saturday Westminster*.

1922-
1925: Attended Balliol College, Oxford. Edited *Oxford Outlook* and won an exhibition in modern history. Published verse in *Oxford Poetry*.

1925: Publication of *Babbling April*, book of poetry.

1926: Employed by Nottingham *Journal*. Entered Catholic Church.

1926-
1930: Subeditor for the London *Times*, in the Letters department.

1927: Marriage to Vivien Dayrell-Browning. (The Greenes have one son and one daughter.)

1929: Publication of *The Man Within*, a novel.

1930: Publication of *The Name of Action*, a novel.

1931: Publication of *Rumour at Nightfall*, a novel.

1932: Publication of *Stamboul Train*, an entertainment, entitled *Orient Express* in United States.

1934: Publication of *It's a Battlefield*, a novel.

1935: Publication of *England Made Me*, a novel, entitled *The Shipwrecked* in United States. Publication of *The Bear Fell Free* and *The Basement Room*, books of short stories.

1935-
1939: Film critic for the *Spectator*.

1936: Publication of *A Gun for Sale*, an entertainment, entitled *This Gun for Hire* in United States. Trip to Liberia, followed by an account of his travels in *Journey without Maps*.

1937: Part-editor of *Night and Day*. Collaboration with Walter Meade on screenplay for film version of Galsworthy's *The First and the Last*.

1938: Publication of *Brighton Rock*, a novel. Contribution to periodical *Footnotes to the Film*. Trip to Mexico, observations of Tabasco and Chiapas.

1939: Account of the Mexican trip in *The Lawless Roads*, entitled *Another Mexico* in United States. Publication of *The Confidential Agent*, an entertainment.

1940: Publication of *The Power and the Glory*, a novel, entitled *The Labyrinthine Ways* in United States.

1940-
1941: Employed at Ministry of Information.

1941: Literary editor and drama critic for the *Spectator*.

1941- Employed by Foreign Office. Duty in Africa—Lagos for
1946: three months. Freetown until February 1943—and then England.

1941-
1948: Director of Eyre and Spottiswoode, publishers.

1942: Publication of *British Dramatists*, a book of essays.

1943: Publication of *The Ministry of Fear*, an entertainment.

1945: Reviewer for the *Evening Standard*.

1947: Publication of *Nineteen Stories*.

1948: Publication of *Why Do I Write?* (with Elizabeth Bowen and V. S. Pritchett) and *The Heart of The Matter*, a novel.

1950: Publication of *The Third Man* and *The Fallen Idol*, both entertainments.

1951: Publication of *The End of the Affair*, a novel. Trip to Malaya and Indochina. Publication of *The Lost Childhood and Other Essays*.

1952: Publication in America of *Three by Graham Greene*, an omnibus. Second trip to Indochina.

1953: Publication of *The Living Room*, his first play.

1954: Publication of *Twenty-One Stories*.

1954- Third trip to Indochina, as correspondent for Sunday *Times*
1955: and *Figaro*. Greene interviews Ho Chi Minh for Sunday *Times*.

1955: Publication of *The Quiet American,* a novel, and *Loser Takes All,* an entertainment.

1956: Visit to Poland as correspondent for Sunday *Times*. Visit to Cuba.

1958: Publication of *The Potting Shed,* a play, and *Our Man In Havana,* an entertainment.

1959: Publication of *The Complaisant Lover,* a play. Trip to Belgian Congo.

1961: Publication of *A Burnt-Out Case,* a novel, and *In Search of a Character,* a record of his African travels.

1963: Publication of *A Sense of Reality,* a book of short stories. Visit to Haiti.

1966: Publication of *The Comedians,* a novel.

1967: Publication of *May We Borrow Your Husband?,* a book of short stories. Trip to Sierra Leone.

1969: Publication of *Collected Essays.*

1970: Publication of *Travels with My Aunt,* a novel.

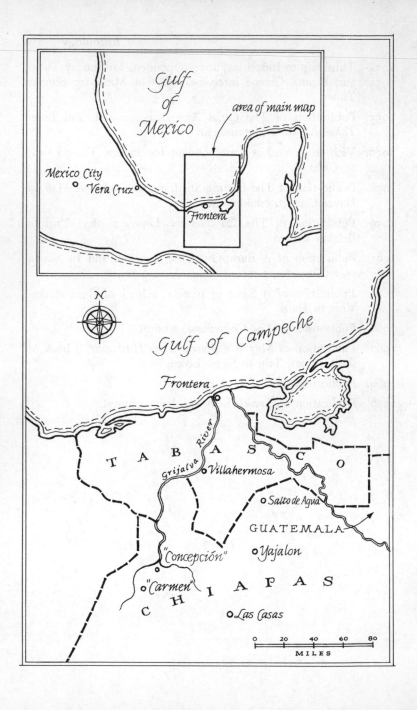

Gulf
of
Mexico

area of main map

Mexico City
Vera Cruz

Frontera

N

Gulf of Campeche

Frontera

T A B A S C O

Grijalva River

Villahermosa

Salto de Agua

GUATEMALA

"Concepción"

Yajalon

"Carmen"

C H I A P A S

Las Casas

0   20   40   60   80
MILES

The priest's journey across the provinces of Tabasco and Chiapas is remarkably similar to Greene's own journey undertaken in 1938 and described in his book *Another Mexico (The Lawless Roads),* which offers much source material for *The Power and the Glory.* Both began their journeys under the blazing sun on a day early in March at Frontera (unnamed in *The Power and the Glory,* like all but one of the other stopping-places in the priest's journey). The priest finds shelter first with the family of the boy Luis in Villahermosa (where he will return twice again, once to be jailed, unrecognized, and finally to be executed), and then at the Fellowses' banana plantation on the banks of the Grijalva. He travels south by mule to Salto, where seven years earlier he had fathered Maria's child Brigida, and then continues southward to Yajalon (called La Candelaria in the novel, the only one of the priest's stopping-places that is named), where he meets the mestizo for the first time. He returns to Villahermosa in search of wine for Mass, is jailed and released, and returns to the now abandoned plantation. He helps an Indian woman and child over the mountains into Chiapas and encounters, as Greene did, the *finca* of Mr. Lehr (Herr R. in *Another Mexico*) and his sister. As he prepares to escape to Las Casas he meets the mestizo for the last time and is persuaded to return to Tabasco to help a dying American gangster. He is greeted by the police lieutenant, who accompanies him on his final journey back to Villahermosa, where he is jailed and executed.

From the holograph manuscript of *The Power and the Glory*, by courtesy of the University of Texas Library.

The Power
and the Glory

The Text

INTRODUCTION

The Power and the Glory was born of a journey to Mexico in the winter of 1937–1938 undertaken for quite other motives than a novel. It was not a very happy journey, clouded politically because England was about to break off diplomatic relations with Mexico and personally because a rather odd libel action had been brought against me by Miss Shirley Temple, the child film star. When I returned from the south to Mexico City with an attack of dysentery, I found a letter from my publisher offering to send me money if I thought it expedient to stay awhile longer in Mexico; the Lord Chief Justice had taken a severe view of the case and there was some danger that I might be arrested on my return. But by the time I had received my mail I had taken such a distaste to Mexico that even an English prison promised relief.

As the purpose of my journey was to write a study of the religious persecution which had by then reached its final stage, most of my time was spent in Tabasco and Chiapas, far from the tourist resorts. I travelled across the Gulf of Mexico from Vera Cruz in a little Mexican boat, where all the passengers, men and women, slept on wooden shelves in one cabin and where the single lavatory had not been cleaned for several voyages, to Frontera and then up the river to Villahermosa. A life insurance was given gratis with the ticket.

At Frontera, where my story was to open, I met the first character in my novel, the dentist Mr. Tench. In fact he was American and not English. He was married to a Mexican woman, who was some relation to the state governor; and he came on board to flee from his wife and children. He took refuge in my hotel in Villahermosa—I don't think there was another—but after a few days his family ambushed him in the corridor. I remember him always in an old yachting cap, even at meals, which he would interrupt if a bone or a piece of gristle stuck in his throat by vomiting promptly and skillfully upon the floor. He would take swigs out of a bottle of olive oil for the sake of his health.

Garrido Canabal, the puritan dictator of Tabasco, had fled to Puerto Rico before I arrived, but Villahermosa had not greatly changed; whatever alterations to the antireligious laws might have been decreed in Mexico City, they had no application here. Tabasco was prohibitionist as well, and the only relief for thirst in the hot and humid town was a *gaseosa*—I must have drunk a dozen of them a day. Garrido had left no churches standing, and the site of the cathedral had become a children's playground, though no children played there (as they would once have played in the cathedral), for the iron swings were too hot to handle.

It was in Villahermosa that I came on traces of my principal character, though I did not recognize him at the time. Nothing was further from my thoughts than a novel. An inhabitant told me of the last priest in the state who had baptized his son, giving him a girl's name by accident, for he was so drunk he could hardly stand for the ceremony, let alone remember a name. Afterward he had disappeared into the mountains on the borders of Chiapas— perhaps he was killed by the Red Shirts, perhaps he had escaped to easier conditions.

I rode through those mountains for three days on a mule, not knowing I was following the footsteps of the priest in his escape from the lieutenant, and came finally to the city of Las Casas, spread out under the mountains at the end of the mule-track, where the churches were still standing, and even open, though no priest was allowed to enter them. (During Holy Week strange services were celebrated by the Indians from the hills who tried to remember what they had been taught.) Perhaps I was even less happy in this city than I had been in Villahermosa, for the place was full of swaggering *pistoleros*—any of whom might have been a model for my Commissioner of Police— and it was impossible to sit in the plaza at evening without being insulted, or to buy a drink in a cantina, for by this time diplomatic relations with England had been broken. As for the idealism of my lieutenant, it was sadly lacking among these shabby revolutionaries.

So it is that the material of a novel accumulates, not always easily, not always without fatigue or pain or even fear.

I think *The Power and the Glory* is the only novel I have written to a thesis; in *The Heart of the Matter*

Wilson sat on a balcony in Freetown watching Scobie pass by in the street long before I was aware of Scobie's problem—his corruption by pity. But I had always, even when I was a schoolboy, listened with impatience to the scandalous stories of tourists concerning the priests they had encountered in remote Latin villages (this priest had a mistress, another was constantly drunk), for I had been adequately taught in my Protestant history books what Catholics believed; I could distinguish even then between the man and his office. Now, many years later, as a Catholic in Mexico, I read and listened to stories of corruption which were said to have justified the persecution of the Church under Presidents Calles and Cárdenas, but I had also observed for myself how courage and the sense of responsibility had revived with persecution—I had seen the devotion of peasants praying in the priestless churches and I had attended Masses in upper rooms where the Sanctus bell could not sound for fear of the police. I had not found the integrity of the lieutenant among the police and *pistoleros* I had encountered. I had to invent him as a counter to the failed priest: the idealistic police officer who stifled life from the best possible motives, the drunken priest who continued to pass life on.

The book gives me more satisfaction than any other I have written. This is not saying much, but it is a saddening thought all the same when I realize it was written more than 22 years ago. It waited nearly 10 years for success. In England the first edition was one of 3,500 copies and it crept out a month or so before Hitler invaded the Low Countries. In the United States it was published under the difficult and misleading title of *The Labyrinthine*

Ways because my title had already been used. (It sold, I think, 2,000 copies.) After the war was over its success in France, due to M. François Mauriac's generous introduction, brought danger from two fronts, Hollywood and the Vatican. A pious film was made by Mr. John Ford who gave the integrity to the priest and the corruption to the lieutenant, while the success of the novel in French Catholic circles caused a reaction, so that it was twice denounced to Rome by French bishops.

An incident which flattered my vanity occurred early in 1948. I happened by chance to be in Prague during the week of the Communist revolution. A message was conveyed to me that a Catholic deputy in hiding wanted a meeting. By a devious route through the confusing streets of Old Prague I was brought to a presbytery where the deputy waited for me. I assumed he wanted some help in his escape, and as I had various sums of foreign currency on me, I offered them to him. Or perhaps it was a message he would like conveyed? No, he said, his escape route was planned, he had no need of my assistance, but he thought it might be of some amusement to me to see a situation which resembled a little what I had described in *The Power and the Glory*. We drank together for half an hour while the priest kept watch. I was glad to hear later that he had escaped over the border.

That incident came to my mind some seven years later when the Archbishop of Westminster read me a letter from the Holy Office condemning my novel because it was "paradoxical" and "dealt with extraordinary circumstances." The price of liberty, even within a Church, is eternal vigilance, but I wonder whether any of the totalitarian states, whether of the right or of the left, with which the Church of Rome is often compared, would have treated me as gently when I refused to revise the book on the casuistical ground that the copyright was in the hands of my publishers. There was no public condemnation, and the affair was allowed to drop into that peaceful oblivion which the Church wisely reserves for unimportant issues.

CHAPTER ONE

MR. TENCH went out to look for his ether cylinder: out into the blazing Mexican sun and the bleaching dust. A few buzzards looked down from the roof with shabby indifference: he wasn't carrion yet. A faint feeling of rebellion stirred in Mr. Tench's heart, and he wrenched up a piece of the road with splintering finger-nails and tossed it feebly up at them. One of them rose and flapped across the town: over the tiny plaza, over the bust of an ex-president, ex-general, ex-human being, over the two stalls which sold mineral water, towards the river and the sea. It wouldn't find anything there: the sharks looked after the carrion on that side. Mr. Tench went on across the plaza.

He said *"Buenos días"* to a man with a gun who sat in a small patch of shade against a wall. But it wasn't like England: the man said nothing at all, just stared malevolently up at Mr. Tench, as if he had never had any dealings with the foreigner, as if Mr. Tench were not responsible for his two gold bicuspid teeth. Mr. Tench went sweating by, past the Treasury which had once been a church, towards the quay. Half-way across he suddenly forgot what he had come out for—a glass of mineral water? That was all there was to drink in this prohibition state— except beer, but that was a government monopoly and too expensive except on special occasions. An awful feeling of nausea gripped Mr. Tench in the stomach—it couldn't have been mineral water he wanted. Of course, his ether cylinder . . . the boat was in. He had heard its exultant piping while he lay on his bed after lunch. He passed the barbers' and two dentists' and came out between a warehouse and the customs onto the river bank.

The river went heavily by towards the sea between the banana plantations: the *General Obregon* was tied up to the bank, and beer was being unloaded—a hundred cases were already stacked upon the quay. Mr. Tench stood in the shade of the customs house and thought: What am I here for? Memory drained out of him in the heat. He gathered his bile together and spat forlornly into the sun. Then he sat down on a case and waited. Nothing to do. Nobody would come to see him before five.

The *General Obregon* was about thirty yards long. A few feet of damaged rail, one lifeboat, a bell hanging on a rotten cord, an oil-lamp in the bow, she looked as if she might weather two or three more Atlantic years—if she didn't strike a norther in the gulf. That, of course, would be the end of her. It didn't really matter: everybody was insured when he bought a ticket—automatically. Half a dozen passengers leant on the rail, among the hobbled turkeys, and stared at the port: the warehouse, the empty baked street with the dentists' and the barbers'.

Mr. Tench heard a revolver-holster creak just behind him and turned his head. A customs officer was watching

him angrily. He said something which Mr. Tench could
not catch. "Pardon me," Mr. Tench said.

"My teeth," the customs man said indistinctly.

"Oh," Mr. Tench said, "yes, your teeth." The man had
none: that was why he couldn't talk clearly: Mr. Tench
had removed them all. He was shaken with nausea—something was wrong—worms, dysentery. . . . He said: "The
set is nearly finished. Tonight," he promised wildly. It
was, of course, quite impossible; but that was how one
lived, putting off everything. The man was satisfied: he
might forget, and in any case what could he *do?* He had
paid in advance. That was the whole world to Mr. Tench:
the heat and the forgetting, the putting off till tomorrow,
if possible cash down—for what? He stared out over the
slow river: the fin of a shark moved like a periscope at the
mouth. In the course of years several ships had stranded
and they now helped to prop up the riverside, the smoke-
stacks leaning over like guns pointing at some distant objective across the banana-trees and the swamps.

Mr. Tench thought: Ether cylinder: I nearly forgot.
His mouth fell open and he began moodily to count the
bottles of Cerveza Moctezuma. A hundred and forty cases.
Twelve times a hundred and forty: the heavy phlegm
gathered in his mouth: twelve fours are forty-eight. He
said aloud in English: "My God, a pretty one": twelve
hundred, sixteen hundred and eighty: he spat, staring
with vague interest at a girl in the bows of the *General
Obregon*—a fine thin figure, they were generally so thick,
brown eyes, of course, and the inevitable gleam of the gold
tooth, but something fresh and young. . . . Sixteen hundred and eighty bottles at a peso a bottle.

Somebody asked in English: "What did you say?"

Mr. Tench swivelled round. "You English?" he said in astonishment, but at the sight of the round and hollow face charred with a three days' beard, he altered his question: "You speak English?"

Yes, the man said, he spoke English. He stood stiffly in the shade, a small man dressed in a shabby dark city suit, carrying a small attaché case. He had a novel under his arm: bits of an amorous scene stuck out, crudely coloured. He said: "Excuse me. I thought just now you were talking to me." He had protuberant eyes: he gave an impression of unstable hilarity, as if perhaps he had been celebrating a birthday . . . alone.

Mr. Tench cleared his mouth of phlegm. "What did I say?" He couldn't remember a thing.

"You said: 'My God, a pretty one.' "

"Now what could I have meant by that?" He stared up at the merciless sky. A buzzard stood there like an observer. "What? Oh, just the girl, I suppose. You don't often see a pretty piece round here. Just one or two a year worth looking at."

"She is very young."

"Oh, I don't have intentions," Mr. Tench said wearily. "A man may look. I've lived alone for fifteen years."

"Here?"

"Hereabouts."

They fell silent and time passed, the shadow of the customs house shifted a few inches farther towards the river: the buzzard moved a little, like the black hand of a clock.

"You came in *her?*" Mr. Tench said.

"No."

"Going in her?"

The little man seemed to evade the question, but then as if some explanation were required, "I was just looking," he said. "I suppose she'll be sailing quite soon?"

"To Vera Cruz," Mr. Tench said. "In a few hours."

"Without calling anywhere?"

"Where could she call?" He asked: "How did you get here?"

The stranger said vaguely: "A canoe."

"Got a plantation, eh?"

"No."

"It's good hearing English spoken," Mr. Tench said. "Now you learnt yours in the States?"

The man agreed. He wasn't very garrulous.

"Ah, what wouldn't I give," Mr. Tench said, "to be there now." He said in a low anxious voice: "You don't happen, do you, to have a drink in that case of yours? Some of you people back there—I've known one or two— a little for medical purposes."

"Only medicine," the man said.

"You a doctor?"

The bloodshot eyes looked slyly out of their corners at Mr. Tench. "You would call me perhaps a—quack?"

"Patent medicines? Live and let live," Mr. Tench said.

"Are *you* sailing?"

"No, I came down here for—for . . . oh, well, it doesn't matter anyway." He put his hand on his stomach and said: "You haven't got any medicine, have you, for—oh, hell. I don't know what. It's just this bloody land. You can't cure me of that. No one can."

"You want to go home?"

"Home," Mr. Tench said; "my home's here. Did you see what the peso stands at in Mexico City? Four to the dollar. Four. Oh, God. *Ora pro nobis.*"

"Are you a Catholic?"

"No, no. Just an expression. I don't believe in anything like that." He said irrelevantly: "It's too hot anyway."

"I think I must find somewhere to sit."

"Come up to my place," Mr. Tench said. "I've got a spare hammock. The boat won't leave for hours—if you want to watch it go."

The stranger said: "I was expecting to see someone. The name was Lopez."

"Oh, they shot him weeks ago," Mr. Tench said.

"Dead?"

"You know how it is round here. Friend of yours?"

"No, no," the man protested hurriedly. "Just a friend of a friend."

"Well, that's how it is," Mr. Tench said. He brought up his bile again and shot it out into the hard sunlight. "They say he used to help . . . oh, undesirables . . . well, to get out. His girl's living with the Chief of Police now."

"His girl? Do you mean his daughter?"

"He wasn't married. I mean the girl he lived with." Mr. Tench was momentarily surprised by an expression on the stranger's face. He said again: "You know how it is." He looked across at the *General Obregon*. "She's a pretty bit. Of course, in two years she'll be like all the rest. Fat and stupid. Oh, God, I'd like a drink. *Ora pro nobis.*"

"I have a little brandy," the stranger said.

Mr. Tench regarded him sharply. "Where?"

The hollow man put his hand to his hip—he might have been indicating the source of his odd nervous hilarity. Mr. Tench seized his wrist. "Careful," he said. "Not here." He looked down the carpet of shadow: a sentry sat on an empty crate asleep beside his rifle. "Come to my place," Mr. Tench said.

"I meant," the little man said reluctantly, "just to see her go."

"Oh, it will be hours yet," Mr. Tench assured him again.

"Hours? Are you certain? It's very hot in the sun."

"You'd better come home."

Home: it was a phrase one used to mean four walls behind which one slept. There had never been a home. They moved across the little burnt plaza where the dead general grew green in the damp and the gaseosa stalls stood under the palms. It lay like a picture postcard on a pile of other postcards: shuffle the pack and you had Nottingham, a Metroland birthplace, an interlude in Southend. Mr. Tench's father had been a dentist too—his first memory was finding a discarded cast in a waste-paper basket —the rough toothless gaping mouth of clay, like something dug up in Dorset—Neanderthal or Pithecanthropus. It had been his favourite toy: they tried to tempt him with Meccano: but fate had struck. There is always one moment in childhood when the door opens and lets the future in. The hot wet river-port and the vultures lay in the waste-paper basket, and he picked them out. We should be thankful we cannot see the horrors and degradations lying around our childhood, in cupboards and bookshelves, everywhere.

There was no paving: during the rains the village (it was really no more) slipped into the mud. Now the ground was hard under the feet like stone. The two men walked in silence past barbers' shops and dentists': the buzzards on the roofs looked contented, like domestic fowls: they searched under wide crude dusty wings for parasites. Mr. Tench said: "Excuse me," stopping at a little wooden hut, one story high, with a veranda where a hammock swung. The hut was a little larger than the others in the narrow street, which petered out two hundred yards away in swamp. He said, nervously: "Would you like to take a look around? I don't want to boast, but I'm the best dentist here. It's not a bad place. As places go." Pride wavered in his voice like a plant with shallow roots.

He led the way inside, locking the door behind him, through a dining-room where two rocking-chairs stood on either side of a bare table: an oil-lamp, some copies of old American papers, a cupboard. He said: "I'll get the glasses out, but first I'd like to show you—you're an educated man . . ." The dentist's operating-room looked out on a yard where a few turkeys moved with shabby nervous pomp: a drill which worked with a pedal, a dentist's chair gaudy in bright red plush, a glass cupboard in which instruments were dustily jumbled. A forceps stood in a cup, a broken spirit-lamp was pushed into a corner, and gags of cotton-wool lay on all the shelves.

"Very fine," the stranger said.

"It's not so bad, is it," Mr. Tench said, "for this town? You can't imagine the difficulties. That drill," he said bitterly, "is made in Japan. I've only had it a month and it's wearing out already. But I can't afford American drills."

"The window," the stranger said, "is very beautiful."

One pane of stained glass had been let in: a Madonna gazed out through the mosquito wire at the turkeys in the yard. "I got it," Mr. Tench said, "when they sacked the church. It didn't feel right—a dentist's room without some stained glass. Not civilized. At home—I mean in England —it was generally the laughing Cavalier—I don't know why—or else a Tudor rose. But one can't pick and choose."

He opened another door and said: "My workroom." The first thing you saw was a bed under a mosquito tent. Mr. Tench said: "You understand—I'm pressed for room." A ewer and basin stood at one end of a carpenter's bench, and a soap-dish: at the other a blow-pipe, a tray of sand, pliers, a little furnace. "I cast in sand," Mr. Tench said. "What else can I do in this place?" He picked up the cast of a lower jaw. "You can't always get them accurate," he said. "Of course, they complain." He laid it down again, and nodded at another object on the bench—something stringy and intestinal in appearance, with two little bladders of rubber. "Congenital fissure," he said. "It's the first time I've tried. The Kingsley case. I doubt if I can do it. But a man must try to keep abreast of things." His mouth fell open: the look of vacancy returned: the heat in the small room was overpowering. He stood there like a man lost in a cavern among the fossils and instruments of an age of which he knows very little. The stranger said: "If we could sit down . . ."

Mr. Tench stared at him—blankly.

"We could open the brandy."

"Oh, yes, the brandy."

Mr. Tench got two glasses out of a cupboard under the bench, and wiped off traces of sand. Then they went and sat in rocking-chairs in the front room. Mr. Tench poured out.

"Water?" the stranger said.

"You can't trust the water," Mr. Tench said. "It's got me here." He put his hand on his stomach and took a long draught. "You don't look too well yourself," he said. He took a longer look. "Your teeth." One canine had gone, and the front teeth were yellow with tartar and carious. He said: "You want to pay attention to them."

"What is the good?" the stranger said. He held a small spot of brandy in his glass warily—as if it were an animal to which he gave shelter, but not trust. He had the air in his hollowness and neglect of somebody of no account who had been beaten up incidentally, by ill-health or restlessness. He sat on the very edge of the rocking-chair, with his small attaché case balanced on his knee and the brandy staved off with guilty affection.

"Drink up," Mr. Tench encouraged him (it wasn't his brandy); "it will do you good." The man's dark suit and sloping shoulders reminded him uncomfortably of a coffin: and death was in his carious mouth already. Mr. Tench poured himself out another glass. He said: "It gets lonely here. It's good to talk English, even to a foreigner. I wonder if you'd like to see a picture of my kids." He drew a yellow snapshot out of his notecase and handed it over. Two small children struggled over the handle of a watering-can in a back garden. "Of course," he said, "that was sixteen years ago."

"They are young men now."

"One died."

"Oh, well," the other said gently, "in a Christian country." He took a gulp of his brandy and smiled at Mr. Tench rather foolishly.

"Yes, I suppose so," Mr. Tench said with surprise. He got rid of his phlegm and said: "It doesn't seem to me, of course, to matter much." He fell silent, his thoughts ambling away; his mouth fell open, he looked grey and vacant, until he was recalled by a pain in the stomach and helped himself to some more brandy. "Let me see. What was it we were talking about? The kids . . . oh, yes, the kids. It's funny what a man remembers. You know, I can remember that watering-can better than I can remember the kids. It cost three and elevenpence three farthings, green; I could lead you to the shop where I bought it. But as for the kids"—he brooded over his glass into the past— "I can't remember much else but them crying."

"Do you get news?"

"Oh, I gave up writing before I came here. What was the use? I couldn't send any money. It wouldn't surprise me if the wife had married again. Her mother would like it—the old sour bitch: she never cared for me."

The stranger said in a low voice: "It is awful."

Mr. Tench examined his companion again with surprise. He sat there like a black question mark, ready to go, ready to stay, poised on his chair. He looked disreputable in his grey three days' beard, and weak: somebody you could command to do anything. He said: "I mean the world. The way things happen."

"You drink up your brandy."

He sipped at it. It was like an indulgence. He said:

"You remember this place before—before the Red Shirts came?"

"I suppose I do."

"How happy it was then."

"Was it? I didn't notice."

"They had at any rate—God."

"There's no difference in the teeth," Mr. Tench said. He gave himself some more of the stranger's brandy. "It was always an awful place. Lonely. My God. People at home would have said romance. I thought: five years here, and then I'll go. There was plenty of work. Gold teeth. But then the peso dropped. And now I can't get out. One day I will." He said: "I'll retire. Go home. Live as a gentleman ought to live. This"—he gestured at the bare base room—"I'll forget all this. Oh, it won't be long now. I'm an optimist," Mr. Tench said.

The stranger said suddenly: "How long will she take to Vera Cruz?"

"Who?"

"The boat."

Mr. Tench said gloomily: "Forty hours from now and we'd be there. The Diligencia. A good hotel. Dance places too. A gay town."

"It makes it seem close," the stranger said. "And a ticket, how much would that be?"

"You'd have to ask Lopez," Mr. Tench said. "He's the agent."

"But Lopez . . ."

"Oh, yes, I forgot. They shot him."

Somebody knocked on the door. The stranger slipped the attaché case under his chair, and Mr. Tench went cautiously up towards the window. "Can't be too careful," he said. "Any dentist who's worth the name has enemies."

A faint voice implored them: "A friend," and Mr. Tench opened up. Immediately the sun came in like a white-hot bar.

A child stood in the doorway asking for a doctor. He wore a big hat and had stupid brown eyes. Beyond him two mules stamped and whistled on the hot beaten road. Mr. Tench said he was not a doctor: he was a dentist. Looking round he saw the stranger crouched in the rocking-chair, gazing with an effect of prayer, entreaty. . . . The child said there was a new doctor in town: the old one had fever and wouldn't stir. It was his mother who was sick.

A vague memory stirred in Mr. Tench's brain. He said with an air of discovery: "Why, you're a doctor, aren't you?"

"No, no. I've got to catch that boat."

"I thought you said . . ."

"I've changed my mind."

"Oh, well, it won't leave for hours yet," Mr. Tench said. "They're never on time." He asked the child how far. The child said it was six leagues away.

"Too far," Mr. Tench said. "Go away. Find someone else." He said to the stranger: "How things get around. Everyone must know you are in town."

"I could do no good," the stranger said anxiously: he seemed to be asking Mr. Tench's opinion, humbly.

"Go away," Mr. Tench said. The child did not stir. He stood in the hard sunlight looking in with infinite patience. He said his mother was dying. The brown eyes expressed

no emotion: it was a fact. You were born, your parents
died, you grew old, you died yourself.

"If she's dying," Mr. Tench said, "there's no point in a
doctor seeing her."

But the stranger had got up: unwillingly he had been
summoned to an occasion he couldn't pass by. He said
sadly: "It always seems to happen. Like this."

"You'll have a job not to miss the boat."

"I shall miss it," he said. "I am meant to miss it." He
was shaken by a tiny rage. "Give me my brandy." He
took a long pull at it, with his eyes on the impassive child,
the baked street, the buzzards moving in the sky like indigestion spots.

"But if she's dying . . ." Mr. Tench said.

"I know these people. She will be no more dying than I
am."

"You can do no good."

The child watched them as if he didn't care. The argument in a foreign language going on in there was something abstract: he wasn't concerned. He would just wait
here till the doctor came.

"You know nothing," the stranger said fiercely. "That
is what everyone all the time says—you do no good." The
brandy had affected him. He said with monstrous bitterness: "I can hear them saying it all over the world."

"Anyway," Mr. Tench said, "there'll be another boat.
In a fortnight. Or three weeks. You are lucky. You can
get out. You haven't got your capital here." He thought
of his capital: the Japanese drill, the dentist's chair, the
spirit-lamp and the pliers and the little oven for the gold
fillings: a stake in the country.

"Vamos," the man said to the child. He turned back to Mr. Tench and told him that he was grateful for the rest out of the sun. He had the kind of dwarfed dignity Mr. Tench was accustomed to—the dignity of people afraid of a little pain and yet sitting down with some firmness in his chair. Perhaps he didn't care for mule travel. He said with an effect of old-fashioned ways: "I will pray for you."

"You were welcome," Mr. Tench said. The man got up onto the mule, and the child led the way, very slowly under the bright glare, towards the swamp, the interior. It was from there the man had emerged this morning to take a look at the *General Obregon:* now he was going back. He swayed very slightly in his saddle from the effect of the brandy. He became a minute disappointed figure at the end of the street.

It had been good to talk to a stranger, Mr. Tench thought, going back into his room, locking the door behind him (one never knew). Loneliness faced him there, vacancy. But he was as accustomed to both as to his own face in the glass. He sat down in the rocking-chair and moved up and down, creating a faint breeze in the heavy air. A narrow column of ants moved across the room to the little patch on the floor where the stranger had spilt some brandy: they milled in it, then moved on in an orderly line to the opposite wall and disappeared. Down in the river the *General Obregon* whistled twice, he didn't know why.

The stranger had left his book behind. It lay under his rocking-chair: a woman in Edwardian dress crouched sobbing upon a rug embracing a man's brown polished pointed shoes. He stood above her disdainfully with a little waxed moustache. The book was called *La Eterna Mártir*. After a time Mr. Tench picked it up. When he opened it he was taken aback—what was printed inside didn't seem to belong; it was Latin. Mr. Tench grew thoughtful: he picked the book up and carried it into his workroom. You couldn't burn a book, but it might be as well to hide it if you were not sure—sure, that is, of what it was all about. He put it inside the little oven for gold alloy. Then he stood by the carpenter's bench, his mouth hanging open: he had remembered what had taken him to the quay—the ether cylinder which should have come down-river in the *General Obregon*. Again the whistle blew from the river, and Mr. Tench ran without his hat into the sun. He had said the boat would not go before morning, but you could never trust those people *not* to keep to time-table, and sure enough, when he came out onto the bank between the customs and the warehouse, the *General Obregon* was already ten feet off in the sluggish river, making for the sea. He bellowed after it, but it wasn't any good: there was no sign of a cylinder anywhere on the quay. He shouted once again, and then didn't trouble any more. It didn't matter so much after all: a little additional pain was hardly noticeable in the huge abandonment.

On the *General Obregon* a faint breeze began to blow: banana plantations on either side, a few wireless aerials on a point, the port slipped behind. When you looked back you could not have told that it had ever existed at all. The wide Atlantic opened up: the great grey cylindrical waves lifted the bows, and the hobbled turkeys shifted on the deck. The captain stood in the tiny deck-house with a toothpick in his hair. The land went backward at a slow even roll, and the dark came quite suddenly, with a sky of low and brilliant stars. One oil-lamp was lit in the bows, and the girl whom Mr. Tench had spotted from the bank began to sing gently—a melancholy, sentimental, and contented song about a rose which had been stained with true love's blood. There was an enormous sense of freedom and air upon the gulf, with the low tropical shore-line buried in darkness as deeply as any mummy in a tomb. I am happy, the young girl said to herself without considering why, I am happy.

Far back inside the darkness the mules plodded on. The effect of the brandy had long ago worn off, and the man bore in his brain along the marshy tract—which, when the rains came, would be quite impassable—the sound of the *General Obregon's* siren. He knew what it meant: the ship had kept to time-table: he was abandoned. He felt an unwilling hatred of the child ahead of him and the sick woman—he was unworthy of what he carried. A smell of damp came up all round him; it was as if this part of the world had never been dried in the flame when the world was sent spinning off into space: it had absorbed only the mist and cloud of those awful spaces. He began to pray, bouncing up and down to the lurching, slithering mule's stride, with his brandied tongue: "Let me be caught soon. . . . Let me be caught." He had tried to escape, but he was like the King of a West African tribe, the slave of his people, who may not even lie down in case the winds should fail.

CHAPTER TWO

THE squad of police made their way back to the station: they walked raggedly with rifles slung anyhow: ends of cotton where buttons should have been: a puttee slipping down over the ankle: small men with black secret Indian eyes. The small plaza on the hill-top was lighted with globes strung together in threes and joined by trailing overhead wires. The Treasury, the Presidencia, a dentist's, the prison—a low white colonnaded building which dated back three hundred years, and then the steep street down— the back wall of a ruined church: whichever way you went you came ultimately to water and to river. Pink classical façades peeled off and showed the mud beneath, and the mud slowly reverted to mud. Round the plaza the evening parade went on: women in one direction, men in the other: young men in red shirts milled boisterously round the gaseosa stalls.

The lieutenant walked in front of his men with an air of bitter distaste. He might have been chained to them unwillingly: perhaps the scar on his jaw was the relic of an escape. His gaiters were polished, and his pistol-holster: his buttons were all sewn on. He had a sharp crooked nose jutting out of a lean dancer's face: his neatness gave an effect of inordinate ambition in the shabby city. A sour smell came up to the plaza from the river and the vultures were bedded on the roofs, under the tent of their rough black wings. Sometimes a little moron head peered out and down and a claw shifted. At nine-thirty exactly, all the lights in the plaza went out.

A policeman clumsily presented arms and the squad marched into barracks; they waited for no order, hanging up their rifles by the officers' room, lurching on into the courtyard, to their hammocks, or the excusado. Some of them kicked off their boots and lay down. Plaster was peeling off the mud walls: a generation of policemen had scrawled messages on the whitewash. A few peasants waited on a bench, hands between their knees. Nobody paid them any attention. Two men were fighting in the lavatory.

"Where is the jefe?" the lieutenant asked. No one knew: they thought he was playing billiards somewhere in the town. The lieutenant sat down with dapper irritation at the chief's table: behind his head two hearts were entwined in pencil on the whitewash. "All right," he said, "what are you waiting for? Bring in the prisoners." They came in bowing, hat in hand, one behind the other. "So-and-so. Drunk and disorderly." "Fined five pesos." "But I can't pay, your Excellency." "Let him clean out the lavatory and the cells then." "So-and-so. Defaced an election poster." "Fined five pesos." "So-and-so. Found wearing a holy medal under his shirt." "Fined five pesos." The duty drew to a close: there was nothing of importance. Through the open door the mosquitoes came whirring in.

Outside, the sentry could be heard presenting arms: it

was the Chief of Police. He came breezily in, a stout man with a pink fat face, dressed in white flannels with a wide-awake hat and a cartridge-belt and a big pistol clapping his thigh. He held a handkerchief to his mouth: he was in distress. "Toothache again," he said, "toothache."

"Nothing to report," the lieutenant said with contempt.

"The Governor was at me again today," the chief complained.

"Liquor?"

"No, a priest."

"The last was shot weeks ago."

"He doesn't think so."

"The devil of it is," the lieutenant said, "we haven't photographs." He glanced along the wall to the picture of James Calver, wanted in the United States for bank robbery and homicide: a tough uneven face taken at two angles: description circulated to every station in Central America: the low forehead and the fanatic bent-on-one-thing eyes. He looked at it with regret: there was so little chance that he would ever get south: he would be picked up in some dive at the border—in Juarez or Piedras Negras or Nogales.

"He says we have," the chief complained. "My tooth, oh, my tooth!" He tried to find something in his hip-pocket, but the holster got in the way. The lieutenant tapped his polished boot impatiently. "There," the chief said. A large number of people sat round a table: young girls in white muslin: older women with untidy hair and harassed expressions: a few men peered shyly and solicitously out of the background. All the faces were made up of small dots: it was a newspaper photograph of a first communion party taken years ago: a youngish man in a Roman collar sat among the women. You could imagine him petted with small delicacies, preserved for their use in the stifling atmosphere of intimacy and respect. He sat there, plump, with protuberant eyes, bubbling with harmless feminine jokes. "It was taken years ago."

"He looks like all the rest," the lieutenant said. It was obscure, but you could read into the smudgy photograph a well-shaved, well-powdered jowl much too developed for his age. The good things of life had come to him too early —the respect of his contemporaries, a safe livelihood. The trite religious word upon the tongue, the joke to ease the way, the ready acceptance of other people's homage . . . a happy man. A natural hatred as between dog and dog stirred in the lieutenant's bowels. "We've shot him half a dozen times," he said.

"The Governor has had a report . . . he tried to get away last week to Vera Cruz."

"What are the Red Shirts doing that he comes to *us?*"

"Oh, they missed him, of course. It was just luck that he didn't catch the boat."

"What happened to him?"

"They found his mule. The Governor says he must have him this month. Before the rains come."

"Where was his parish?"

"Concepción and the villages round. But he left there years ago."

"Is anything known?"

"He can pass as a gringo. He spent six years at some

American seminary. I don't know what else. He was born in Carmen—the son of a storekeeper. Not that that helps."

"They all look alike to me," the lieutenant said. Something you could almost have called horror moved him when he looked at the white muslin dresses—he remembered the smell of incense in the churches of his boyhood, the candles and the laciness and the self-esteem, the immense demands made from the altar steps by men who didn't know the meaning of sacrifice. The old peasants knelt there before the holy images with their arms held out in the attitude of the cross: tired by the long day's labour in the plantations, they squeezed out a further mortification. And the priest came round with the collecting-bag taking their centavos, abusing them for their small comforting sins, and sacrificing nothing at all in return—except a little sexual indulgence. And that was easy, the lieutenant thought. He himself felt no need of women. He said: "We will catch him. It is only a question of time."

"My tooth," the chief wailed again. He said: "It poisons the whole of life. Today my biggest break was twenty-five."

"You will have to change your dentist."

"They are all the same."

The lieutenant took the photograph and pinned it on the wall. James Calver, bank robber and homicide, stared in harsh profile towards the first communion party. "He is a man at any rate," the lieutenant said, with approval.

"Who?"

"The gringo."

The chief said: "You heard what he did in Houston.

Got away with ten thousand dollars. Two C-men were shot."

"G-men."

"It's an honour—in a way—to deal with such people." He slapped furiously out at a mosquito.

"A man like that," the lieutenant said, "does no real harm. A few men dead. We all have to die. The money— somebody has to spend it. We do more good when we catch one of these." He had the dignity of an idea, standing in the little whitewashed room in his polished boots and his venom. There was something disinterested in his ambition: a kind of virtue in his desire to catch the sleek respected guest of the first communion party.

The chief said mournfully: "He must be devilishly cunning if he's been going on for years."

"Anybody could do it," the lieutenant said. "We haven't really troubled about them—unless they put themselves in our hands. Why, I could guarantee to fetch this man in, inside a month if . . ."

"If what?"

"If I had the power."

"It's easy to talk," the chief said. "What would you do?"

"This is a small state. Mountains on the north, the sea on the south. I'd beat it as you beat a street, house by house."

"Oh, it sounds easy," the chief wailed indistinctly with his handkerchief against his mouth.

The lieutenant said suddenly: "I will tell you what I'd do. I would take a man from every village in the state as a hostage. If the villagers didn't report the man when he came, the hostages would be shot—and then we'd take more."

"A lot of them would die, of course."

"Wouldn't it be worth it?" the lieutenant said with a kind of exultation. "To be rid of those people for ever."

"You know," the chief said, "you've got something there."

The lieutenant walked home through the shuttered town. All his life had lain here: the Syndicate of Workers and Peasants had once been a school. He had helped to wipe out that unhappy memory. The whole town was changed: the cement playground up the hill near the cemetery where iron swings stood like gallows in the moony darkness was the site of the cathedral. The new children would have new memories: nothing would ever be as it was. There was something of a priest in his intent observant walk—a theologian going back over the errors of the past to destroy them again.

He reached his own lodging. The houses were all one-storied, whitewashed, built round small patios, with a well and a few flowers. The windows on the street were barred. Inside the lieutenant's room there was a bed made of old packing-cases with a straw mat laid on top, a cushion and a sheet. There was a picture of the President on the wall, a calendar, and on the tiled floor a table and a rocking-chair. In the light of a candle it looked as comfortless as a prison or a monastic cell.

The lieutenant sat down upon his bed and began to take off his boots. It was the hour of prayer. Black beetles exploded against the walls like crackers. More than a dozen crawled over the tiles with injured wings. It infuriated him to think that there were still people in the state who believed in a loving and merciful God. There are mystics who are said to have experienced God directly. He was a mystic, too, and what he had experienced was vacancy—a complete certainty in the existence of a dying, cooling world, of human beings who had evolved from animals for no purpose at all. He knew.

He lay down in his shirt and breeches on the bed and blew out the candle. Heat stood in the room like an enemy. But he believed against the evidence of his senses in the cold empty ether spaces. A radio was playing somewhere: music from Mexico City, or perhaps even from London or New York, filtered into this obscure neglected state. It seemed to him like a weakness: this was his own land, and he would have walled it in with steel if he could, until he had eradicated from it everything which reminded him of how it had once appeared to a miserable child. He wanted to destroy everything: to be alone without any memories at all. Life began five years ago.

The lieutenant lay on his back with his eyes open while the beetles detonated on the ceiling. He remembered the priest the Red Shirts had shot against the wall of the cemetery up the hill, another little fat man with popping eyes. He was a monsignor, and he thought that would protect him: he had a sort of contempt for the lower clergy, and right up to the last he was explaining his rank. Only at the very end had he remembered his prayers. He knelt down and they had given him time for a short act of contrition. The lieutenant had watched: he wasn't directly concerned. Altogether they had shot about five priests—

two or three had escaped, the bishop was safely in Mexico City, and one man had conformed to the Governor's law that all priests must marry. He lived now near the river with his house-keeper. That, of course, was the best solution of all, to leave the living witness to the weakness of their faith. It showed the deception they had practised all these years. For if they really believed in heaven or hell, they wouldn't mind a little pain now, in return for what immensities. . . . The lieutenant, lying on his hard bed, in the damp hot dark, felt no sympathy at all with the weakness of the flesh.

In the back room of the Academia Comercial a woman was reading to her family. Two small girls of six and ten sat on the edge of their bed, and a boy of fourteen leant against the wall with an expression of intense weariness.

" 'Young Juan,' " the mother read, " 'from his earliest years was noted for his humility and piety. Other boys might be rough and revengeful; young Juan followed the precept of Our Lord and turned the other cheek. One day his father thought that he had told a lie and beat him: later he learnt that his son had told the truth, and he apologized to Juan. But Juan said to him: "Dear father, just as Our Father in heaven has the right to chastise when he pleases . . ." ' "

The boy rubbed his face impatiently against the white-wash and the mild voice droned on. The two little girls sat with beady intense eyes, drinking in the sweet piety.

" 'We must not think that young Juan did not laugh and play like other children, though there were times when he would creep away with a holy picture-book to his father's cow-house from the circle of his merry play-mates.' "

The boy squashed a beetle with his bare foot and thought gloomily that after all everything had an end—some day they would reach the last chapter and young Juan would die against a wall, shouting: *"Viva el Cristo Rey."* But then, he supposed, there would be another book: they were smuggled in every month from Mexico City: if only the customs men had known where to look.

" 'No, young Juan was a true young Mexican boy, and if he was more thoughtful than his fellows, he was also always the first when any play-acting was afoot. One year his class acted a little play before the bishop, based on the persecution of the Early Christians, and no one was more amused than Juan when he was chosen to play the part of Nero. And what comic spirit he put into his acting—this child, whose young manhood was to be cut short by a ruler far worse than Nero. His class-mate, who later became Father Miguel Cerra, S.J., writes: "None of us who were there will ever forget that day . . ." ' "

One of the little girls licked her lips secretively. This was life.

" 'The curtain rose on Juan wearing his mother's best bath-robe, a charcoal moustache, and a crown made from a tin biscuit-box. Even the good old bishop smiled when Juan strode to the front of the little home-made stage and began to declaim . . .' "

The boy strangled a yawn against the whitewashed wall. He said wearily: "Is he really a saint?"

"He will be, one day soon, when the Holy Father pleases."

"And are they all like that?"

"Who?"

"The martyrs."

"Yes. All."

"Even Padre José?"

"Don't mention him," the mother said. "How dare you? That despicable man. A traitor to God."

"He told me he was more of a martyr than the rest."

"I've told you many times not to speak to him. My dear child, oh, my dear child . . ."

"And the other one—the one who came to see us?"

"No, he is not—exactly—like Juan."

"Is he despicable?"

"No, no. Not despicable."

The smallest girl said suddenly: "He smelt funny."

The mother went on reading: " 'Did any premonition touch young Juan that night that he, too, in a few short years, would be numbered among the martyrs? We cannot say, but Father Miguel Cerra tells how that evening Juan spent longer than usual upon his knees, and when his class-mates teased him a little, as boys will . . .' "

The voice went on and on, mild and deliberate, inflexibly gentle: the small girls listened intently, framing in their minds little pious sentences with which to surprise their parents, and the boy yawned against the whitewash. Everything has an end.

Presently the mother went in to her husband. She said: "I am so worried about the boy."

"Why not about the girls? There is worry everywhere."

"They are two little saints already. But the boy—he

asks such questions—about that whisky priest. I wish we had never had him in the house."

"They would have caught him if we hadn't, and then he would have been one of your martyrs. They would write a book about him and you would read it to the children."

"That man—never."

"Well, after all," her husband said, "he carries on. I don't believe all that they write in these books. We are all human."

"You know what I heard today? About a poor woman who took him her son to be baptized. She wanted him called Pedro—but he was so drunk that he took no notice at all and baptized the boy Carlota. Carlota."

"Well, it's a good saint's name."

"There are times," the mother said, "when I lose all patience with you. And now the boy has been talking to Padre José."

"This is a small town," her husband said. "And there is no use pretending. We have been abandoned here. We must get along as best we can. As for the Church—the Church is Padre José and the whisky priest—I don't know of any other. If we don't like the Church, well, we must leave it."

He watched her with patience. He had more education than his wife: he could use a typewriter and knew the elements of book-keeping: once he had been to Mexico City: he could read a map. He knew the extent of their abandonment—the ten hours down-river to the port, the forty-two hours in the Gulf of Vera Cruz—that was one way out. To the north the swamps and rivers petering out against the mountains which divided them from the next state. And on the other side no roads—only mule-tracks and an occasional unreliable plane: Indian villages and the huts of herds: two hundred miles away the Pacific.

She said: "I would rather die."

"Oh," he said, "of course. That goes without saying. But we have to go on living."

The old man sat on a packing-case in the little dry patio. He was very fat and short of breath: he panted a little as if after great exertion in the heat. Once he had been something of an astronomer and now he tried to pick out the constellations, staring up into the night sky. He wore only a shirt and trousers: his feet were bare, but there remained something unmistakably clerical in his manner. Forty years of the priesthood had branded him. There was complete silence over the town: everybody was asleep.

The glittering worlds lay there in space like a promise —the world was not the universe. Somewhere Christ might not have died. He could not believe that to a watcher there *this* world could shine with such brilliance: it would roll heavily in space under its fog like a burning and abandoned ship. The whole globe was blanketed with his own sin.

A woman called from the only room he possessed: 'José, José." He crouched like a galley-slave at the sound: his eyes left the sky, and the constellations fled upwards: the beetles crawled over the patio. "José, José." He thought with envy of the men who had died: it was over so soon. They were taken up there to the cemetery and shot against the wall: in two minutes life was extinct. And they called

that martyrdom. Here life went on and on: he was only
sixty-two. He might live to ninety. Twenty-eight years—
that immeasurable period between his birth and his first
parish: all childhood and youth and the seminary lay
there.

"José. Come to bed." He shivered: he knew that he
was a buffoon. An old man who married was grotesque
enough, but an old priest. . . . He stood outside himself
and wondered whether he was even fit for hell. He was just
a fat old impotent man mocked and taunted between the
sheets. But then he remembered the gift he had been given
which nobody could take away. That was what made him
worthy of damnation—the power he still had of turning
the wafer into the flesh and blood of God. He was a sacrilege. Wherever he went, whatever he did, he defiled God.
Some mad renegade Catholic, puffed up with the Governor's politics, had once broken into a church (in the days
when there were still churches) and seized the Host. He
had spat on it, trampled it, and then the people had got
him and hanged him as they did the stuffed Judas on Holy
Thursday from the belfry. He wasn't so bad a man, Padre
José thought—he would be forgiven, he was just a politician, but he himself, he was worse than that—he was like
an obscene picture hung here every day to corrupt children with.

He belched on his packing-case shaken by wind. "José,
what are you doing? You come to bed." There was never
anything to do at all—no daily Office, no Masses, no confessions, and it was no good praying any longer at all: a
prayer demanded an act and he had no intention of acting. He had lived for two years now in a continuous state

of mortal sin with no one to hear his confession: nothing to do at all but sit and eat—eat far too much: she fed him and fattened him and preserved him like a prize boar. "José." He began to hiccup with nerves at the thought of facing for the seven hundred and thirty-eighth time his harsh house-keeper—his wife. There she would be, lying in the big shameless bed that filled up half the room, a bony shadow within the mosquito tent, a lanky jaw and a short grey pigtail and an absurd bonnet. She thought she had a position to keep up: a government pensioner: the wife of the only married priest. She was proud of it. "José." "I'm—hic—coming, my love," he said, and lifted himself from the crate. Somebody somewhere laughed.

He lifted little pink eyes like those of a pig conscious of the slaughter-room. A high child's voice said: "José." He stared in a bewildered way around the patio. At a barred window opposite, three children watched him with deep gravity. He turned his back and took a step or two to-wards his door, moving very slowly because of his bulk. "José," somebody squeaked again, "José." He looked back over his shoulder and caught the faces out in expressions of wild glee: his little pink eyes showed no anger—he had no right to be angry: he moved his mouth into a ragged and baffled, disintegrated smile, and as if that sign of weakness gave them all the licence they needed, they squealed back at him without disguise: "José, José. Come to bed, José." Their little shameless voices filled the patio, and he smiled humbly and sketched small gestures for si-lence, and there was no respect anywhere left for him in his home, in the town, in the whole abandoned star.

CHAPTER THREE

CAPTAIN FELLOWS sang loudly to himself, while the little motor chugged in the bows of the canoe. His big sunburned face was like the map of a mountain region—patches of varying brown with two small blue lakes that were his eyes. He composed his songs as he went, and his voice was quite tuneless. "Going home, going home, the food will be good for m-e-e. I don't like the food in the bloody citee." He turned out of the main stream into a tributary: a few alligators lay on the sandy margin. "I don't like your snouts, O trouts. I don't like your snouts, O trouts." He was a happy man.

The banana plantations came down on either bank: his voice boomed under the hard sun: that and the churr of the motor were the only sounds anywhere—he was completely alone. He was borne up on a big tide of boyish joy—doing a man's job, the heart of the wild: he felt no responsibility for anyone. In only one other country had he felt more happy, and that was in war-time France, in the ravaged landscape of trenches. The tributary corkscrewed farther into the marshy overgrown state, and a buzzard lay spread out in the sky. Captain Fellows opened a tin

box and ate a sandwich—food never tasted so good as out
of doors. A monkey made a sudden chatter at him as he
went by, and Captain Fellows felt happily at one with
nature—a wide shallow kinship with all the world moved
with the blood-stream through the veins: he was at home
anywhere. The artful little devil, he thought, the artful
little devil. He began to sing again—somebody else's
words a little jumbled in his friendly unretentive memory.
"Give to me the life I love, bread I dip in the river, under
the wide and starry sky, the hunter's home from the sea."
The plantations petered out, and far behind the mountains
came into view, heavy black lines drawn low-down across
the sky. A few bungalows rose out of the mud. He was
home. A very slight cloud marred his happiness.

He thought: After all, a man likes to be welcomed.

He walked up to his bungalow: it was distinguished
from the others which lay along the bank by a tiled roof,
a flagpost without a flag, a plate on the door with the title,
"Central American Banana Company." Two hammocks
were strung up on the veranda, but there was nobody
about. Captain Fellows knew where to find his wife—it
was not she he had expected. He burst boisterously
through a door and shouted: "Daddy's home." A scared
thin face peeked at him through a mosquito-net; his boots
ground peace into the floor; Mrs. Fellows flinched away
into the white muslin tent. He said: "Pleased to see me,
Trix?" and she drew rapidly on her face the outline of
her frightened welcome. It was like a trick you do with a
blackboard. Draw a dog in one line without lifting the
chalk—and the answer, of course, is a sausage.

"I'm glad to be home," Captain Fellows said, and he be-

lieved it. It was his one firm conviction—that he really felt
the correct emotions of love and joy and grief and hate.
He had always been a good man at zero hour.

"All well at the office?"

"Fine," Fellows said, "fine."

"I had a bit of fever yesterday."

"Ah, you need looking after. You'll be all right now,"
he said vaguely, "that I'm home." He shied merrily away
from the subject of fever—clapping his hands, a big
laugh, while she trembled in her tent. "Where's Coral?"

"She's with the policeman," Mrs. Fellows said.

"I hoped she'd meet me," he said, roaming aimlessly
about the little, inferior room, full of boot-trees, while his
brain caught up with her. "Policeman? What policeman?"

"He came last night and Coral let him sleep on the veranda. He's looking for somebody, she says."

"What an extraordinary thing! *Here?*"

"He's not an ordinary policeman. He's an officer. He
left his men in the village—Coral says."

"I do think you ought to be up," he said. "I mean—
these fellows, you can't trust them." He felt no conviction when he added: "She's just a kid."

"I tell you I had fever," Mrs. Fellows wailed. "I felt so
terribly ill."

"You'll be all right. Just a touch of the sun. You'll see
—now *I'm* home."

"I had such a headache. I couldn't read or sew. And
then this man . . ."

Terror was always just behind her shoulder: she was
wasted by the effort of not turning round. She dressed up
her fear, so that she could look at it—in the form of fever,

rats, unemployment. The real thing was taboo—death coming nearer every year in the strange place: everybody packing up and leaving, while she stayed in a cemetery no one visited, in a big above-ground tomb.

He said: "I suppose I ought to go and see the man."

He sat down on the bed and put his hand upon her arm. They had something in common—a kind of diffidence. He said absent-mindedly: "That dago secretary of the boss has gone."

"Where?"

"West." He could feel her arm go stiff: she strained away from him towards the wall. He had touched the taboo —he shared it, the bond was broken, he couldn't tell why. "Headache, darling?"

"Hadn't you better see the man?"

"Oh, yes, yes. I'll be off." But he didn't stir: it was the child who came to him.

She stood in the doorway watching them with a look of immense responsibility. Before her serious gaze they became a boy you couldn't trust and a ghost you could almost puff away: a piece of frightened air. She was very young—about thirteen—and at that age you are not afraid of many things, age and death, all the things which may turn up, snake-bite and fever and rats and a bad smell. Life hadn't got at her yet: she had a false air of impregnability. But she had been reduced already, as it were, to the smallest terms—everything was there but on the thinnest lines. That was what the sun did to a child, reduced it to a framework. The gold bangle on the bony wrist was like a padlock on a canvas door a fist could break. She said: "I told the policeman you were home."

"Oh, yes, yes," Captain Fellows said. "Got a kiss for your old father?"

She came solemnly across the room and kissed him formally upon the forehead—he could feel the lack of meaning. She had other things to think about. She said: "I told cook that mother would not be getting up for dinner."

"I think you ought to make the effort, dear," Captain Fellows said.

"Why?" Coral said.

"Oh, well . . ."

Coral said: "I want to talk to you alone." Mrs. Fellows shifted inside her tent—just so she could be certain Coral would arrange the final evacuation. Common sense was a horrifying quality she had never possessed: it was common sense which said: "The dead can't hear" or "She can't know now" or "Tin flowers are more practical."

"I don't understand," Captain Fellows said uneasily, "why your mother shouldn't hear."

"She wouldn't want to. It would only scare her."

Coral—he was accustomed to it by now—had an answer to everything. She never spoke without deliberation: she was prepared—but sometimes the answers she had prepared seemed to him of a wildness. . . . They were based on the only life she could remember—this. The swamp and vultures and no children anywhere, except a few in the village, with bellies swollen by worms, who ate dirt from the bank, inhumanly. A child is said to draw parents together, and certainly he felt an immense unwillingness to entrust himself to this child. Her answers might carry him anywhere. He felt through the net for his wife's hand—

secretively: they were adults together. This was the
stranger in their house. He said boisterously: "You're
frightening us."

"I don't think," the child said, with care, "that *you'll*
be frightened."

He said weakly, pressing his wife's hand: "Well, my
dear, our daughter seems to have decided . . ."

"First you must see the policeman. I want him to go.
I don't like him."

"Then he must go, of course," Captain Fellows said,
with a hollow unconfident laugh.

"I told him that. I said we couldn't refuse him a hammock for the night, when he arrived so late. But now he
must go."

"And he disobeyed you?"

"He said he wanted to speak to you."

"He little knew," Captain Fellows said, "he little knew."
Irony was his only defence, but it was not understood:
nothing was understood which was not clear—like an al-
phabet or a simple sum or a date in history. He relin-
quished his wife's hand and allowed himself to be led unwillingly into the afternoon sun. The police officer stood in
front of the veranda: a motionless olive figure: he wouldn't
stir a foot to meet Captain Fellows.

"Well, lieutenant?" Captain Fellows said breezily. It
occurred to him that Coral had more in common with the
policeman than with himself.

"I am looking for a man," the lieutenant said. "He has
been reported in this district."

"He can't be here."

"Your daughter tells me the same."

"She knows."

"He is wanted on a very serious charge."

"Murder?"

"No. Treason."

"Oh, treason," Captain Fellows said, all his interest dropping: there was so much treason everywhere—it was like petty larceny in a barracks.

"He is a priest. I trust you will report at once if he is seen." The lieutenant paused. "You are a foreigner living under the protection of our laws. We expect you to make a proper return for our hospitality. You are not a Catholic?"

"No."

"Then I can trust you to report?" the lieutenant said.

"I suppose so."

The lieutenant stood there like a little dark menacing question mark in the sun: his attitude seemed to indicate that he wouldn't even accept the benefit of shade from a foreigner. But he had used a hammock: that, Captain Fellows supposed, he must have regarded as a requisition. "Have a glass of gaseosa?"

"No. No, thank you."

"Well," Captain Fellows said, "I can't offer you anything else, can I? It's treason to drink spirits."

The lieutenant suddenly turned on his heel as if he could no longer bear the sight of them and strode away along the path which led to the village: his gaiters and his pistol-holster winked in the sunlight. When he had gone some way they could see him pause and spit: he had not been discourteous, he had waited till he supposed that they no longer watched him before he got rid of his hatred and contempt for a different way of life, for ease, safety, toleration, and complacency.

"I wouldn't want to be up against him," Captain Fellows said.

"Of course he doesn't trust us."

"They don't trust anyone."

"I think," Coral said, "he smelt a rat."

"They smell them everywhere."

"You see, I wouldn't let him search the place."

"Why ever not?" Captain Fellows said—and then his vague mind went off at a tangent. "How did you stop him?"

"I said I'd loose the dogs on him—and complain to the Minister. He hadn't any right . . ."

"Oh, right," Captain Fellows said. "They carry their right on their hips. It wouldn't have done any harm to let him look."

"I gave him my word." She was as inflexible as the lieutenant: small and black and out of place among the banana groves. Her candour made allowances for nobody: the future, full of compromises, anxieties, and shame, lay outside: the gate was closed which would one day let it in. But at any moment now a word, a gesture, the most trivial act might be her sesame—to what? Captain Fellows was touched with fear: he was aware of an inordinate love: it robbed him of authority. You cannot control what you love—you watch it driving recklessly towards the broken bridge, the torn-up track, the horror of seventy years ahead. He closed his eyes—he was a happy man—and hummed a tune.

Coral said: "I shouldn't have liked a man like that to catch me out—lying, I mean."

"Lying? Good God," Captain Fellows said, "you don't mean he's here?"

"Of course he's here," Coral said.

"Where?"

"In the big barn," she explained gently. "We couldn't let them catch him."

"Does your mother know about this?"

She said with devastating honesty: "Oh, no. I couldn't trust *her*." She was independent of both of them: they belonged together in the past. In forty years' time they would be dead as last year's dog. He said: "You'd better show me."

He walked slowly: happiness drained out of him more quickly and completely than out of an unhappy man: an unhappy man is always prepared. As she walked in front of him, her two meagre tails of hair bleaching in the sunlight, it occurred to him for the first time that she was of an age when Mexican girls were ready for their first man. What was to happen? He flinched away from problems which he had never dared to confront. As they passed the window of his bedroom he caught sight of a thin shape lying bunched and bony and alone in a mosquito tent. He remembered with self-pity and nostalgia his happiness on the river, doing a man's job without thinking of other people. If I had never married. . . . He wailed like a child at the merciless immature back: "We've no business interfering in their politics."

"This isn't politics," she said gently. "I know about politics. Mother and I are doing the Reform Bill." She took a key out of her pocket and unlocked the big barn in which they stored bananas before sending them down the river to the port. It was very dark inside after the glare: there was a scuffle in a corner. Captain Fellows picked up an electric torch and shone it on somebody in a torn, dark suit—a small man who blinked and needed a shave.

"*Quién es usted?*" Captain Fellows said.

"I speak English." He clutched a small attaché case to his side, as if he were waiting to catch a train he must on no account miss.

"You've no business here."

"No," the man said, "no."

"It's nothing to do with us," Captain Fellows said. "We are foreigners."

The man said: "Of course. I will go." He stood with his head a little bent like a man in an orderly-room listening to an officer's decision. Captain Fellows relented a little. He said: "You'd better wait till dark. You don't want to be caught."

"No."

"Hungry?"

"A little. It does not matter." He said with a rather repulsive humility: "If you would do me a favour . . ."

"What?"

"A little brandy."

"I'm breaking the law enough for you as it is," Captain Fellows said. He strode out of the barn, feeling twice the size, leaving the small bowed figure in the darkness among the bananas. Coral locked the door and followed him. "What a religion!" Captain Fellows said. "Begging for brandy. Shameless."

"But you drink it sometimes."

"My dear," Captain Fellows said, "when you are older you'll understand the difference between drinking a little brandy after dinner and—well, needing it."

"Can I take him some beer?"

"*You* won't take him anything."

"The servants wouldn't be safe."

He was powerless and furious; he said: "You see what a hole you've put us in." He stumped back into the house and into his bedroom, roaming restlessly among the boot-trees. Mrs. Fellows slept uneasily, dreaming of weddings. Once she said aloud: "My train. Be careful of my train."

"What's that?" he said petulantly. "What's that?"

Dark fell like a curtain: one moment the sun was there, the next it had gone. Mrs. Fellows woke to another night. "Did you speak, dear?"

"It was you who spoke," he said. "Something about trains."

"I must have been dreaming."

"It will be a long time before they have trains here," he said, with gloomy satisfaction. He came and sat on the bed, keeping away from the window: out of sight, out of mind. The crickets were beginning to chatter and beyond the mosquito wire fireflies moved like globes. He put his heavy, cheery, needing-to-be-reassured hand on the shape under the sheet and said: "It's not such a bad life, Trixy. Is it now? Not a bad life?" But he could feel her stiffen: the word "life" was taboo: it reminded you of death. She turned her face away from him towards the wall and then hopelessly back again—the phrase "turn to the wall" was taboo too. She lay panic-stricken, while the boundaries of her

fear widened and widened to include every relationship
and the whole world of inanimate things: it was like an infection. You could look at nothing for long without becoming aware that it, too, carried the germ . . . the word
"sheet" even. She threw the sheet off her and said: "It's so
hot, it's so hot." The usually happy and the always unhappy one watched the night thicken from the bed with
distrust. They were companions cut off from all the world:
there was no meaning anywhere outside their own hearts:
they were carried like children in a coach through the
huge spaces without any knowledge of their destination.
He began to hum with desperate cheerfulness a song of the
war years: he wouldn't listen to the footfall in the yard
outside, going in the direction of the barn.

Coral put down the chicken legs and tortillas on the
ground and unlocked the door. She carried a bottle of
Cerveza Moctezuma under her arm. There was the same
scuffle in the dark: the noise of a frightened man. She said:
"It's me," to quieten him, but she didn't turn on the
torch. She said: "There's a bottle of beer here, and some
food."

"Thank you. Thank you."

"The police have gone from the village—south. You
had better go north."

He said nothing.

She asked, with the cold curiosity of a child: "What
would they do to you if they found you?"

"Shoot me."

"You must be very frightened," she said with interest.

He felt his way across the barn towards the door and

the pale starlight. He said: "I *am* frightened," and stumbled on a bunch of bananas.

"Can't you escape from here?"

"I tried. A month ago. The boat was leaving and then— I was summoned."

"Somebody needed you?"

"She didn't need me," he said bitterly. Coral could just see his face now, as the world swung among the stars: what her father would call an untrustworthy face. He said: "You see how unworthy I am. Talking like this."

"Unworthy of what?"

He clasped his little attaché case closely and said: "Could you tell me what month it is? Is it still February?"

"No. It's the seventh of March."

"I don't often meet people who know. That means another month—six weeks—before the rains." He went on: "When the rains come I am nearly safe. You see, the police can't get about."

"The rains are best for you?" she asked: she had a keen desire to learn. The Reform Bill and Senlac and a little French lay like treasure-trove in her brain. She expected answers to every question, and she absorbed them hungrily.

"Oh, no, no. They mean another six months living like this." He tore at a chicken leg. She could smell his breath: it was disagreeable, like something which has lain about too long in the heat. He said: "I'd rather be caught."

"But can't you," she said logically, "just give yourself up?"

He had answers as plain and understandable as her questions. He said: "There's the pain. To choose pain like that—it's not possible. And it's my duty not to be caught. You see, my bishop is no longer here." Curious pedantries moved him. "This is my parish." He found a tortilla and began to eat ravenously.

She said solemnly: "It's a problem." She could hear a gurgle as he drank out of the bottle. He said: "I try to remember how happy I was once." A firefly lit his face like a torch and then went out—a tramp's face: what could ever have made it happy? He said: "In Mexico City now they are saying Benediction. The bishop's there. . . . Do you imagine he ever thinks . . . ? They don't even know I'm alive."

She said: "Of course you could—renounce."

"I don't understand."

"Renounce your faith," she said, using the words of her European History.

He said: "It's impossible. There's no way. I'm a priest. It's out of my power."

The child listened intently. She said: "Like a birth-mark." She could hear him sucking desperately at the bottle. She said: "I think I could find my father's brandy."

"Oh, no, you mustn't steal." He drained the beer: a long glassy whistle in the darkness: the last drop must have gone. He said: "I must go. At once."

"You can always come back here."

"Your father would not like it."

"He needn't know," she said. "I could look after you. My room is just opposite this door. You would just tap at my window. Perhaps," she went seriously on, "it would be better to have a code. You see, somebody else might tap."

He said in a horrified voice: "Not a man?"

"Yes. You never know. Another fugitive from justice."

"Surely," he asked in bewilderment, "that is not likely?"

She said airily: "These things do happen."

"Before today?"

"No, but I expect they will again. I want to be prepared. You must tap three times. Two long taps and a short one."

He giggled suddenly like a child. "How do you tap a long tap?"

"Like this."

"Oh, you mean a loud one?"

"I call them long taps—because of Morse." He was hopelessly out of his depth. He said: "You are very good. Will you pray for me?"

"Oh," she said, "I don't believe in that."

"Not in praying?"

"You see, I don't believe in God. I lost my faith when I was ten."

"Dear, dear," he said. "Then I will pray for you."

"You can," she said patronizingly, "if you like. If you come again I shall teach you the Morse code. It would be useful to you."

"How?"

"If you were hiding in the plantation I could flash to you with my mirror news of the enemy's movements."

He listened seriously. "But wouldn't they see you?"

"Oh," she said, "I would invent an explanation." She moved logically forward a step at a time, eliminating all objections.

"Good-bye, my child," he said.

He lingered by the door. "Perhaps—you do not care

for prayers. Perhaps you would like . . . I know a good conjuring trick."

"I like tricks."

"You do it with cards. Have you any cards?"

"No."

He sighed. "Then that's no good," and giggled—she could smell the beer on his breath—"I shall just have to pray for you."

She said: "You don't sound afraid."

"A little drink," he said, "will work wonders in a cowardly man. With a little brandy, why, I'd defy—the devil." He stumbled in the doorway.

"Good-bye," she said. "I hope you'll escape." A faint sigh came out of the darkness: she said gently: "If they kill you I shan't forgive them—ever." She was ready to accept any responsibility, even that of vengeance, without a second thought. It was her life.

Half a dozen huts of mud and wattle stood in a clearing; two were in ruins. A few pigs rooted round, and an old woman carried a burning ember from hut to hut, lighting a little fire on the centre of each floor to fill the hut with smoke and keep mosquitoes away. Women lived in two of the huts, the pigs in another, in the last unruined hut, where maize was stored, an old man and a boy and a tribe of rats. The old man stood in the clearing watching the fire being carried round: it flickered through the darkness like a ritual repeated at the same hour for a lifetime. White hair, a white stubbly beard, and hands brown and fragile as last year's leaves, he gave an effect of immense permanence. Nothing much could ever change him, living on the edge of subsistence. He had been old for years.

The stranger came into the clearing. He wore what used to be town shoes, black and pointed: only the uppers were left, so that he walked to all intents barefoot. The shoes were symbolic, like the cobwebbed flags in churches. He wore a shirt and a pair of black torn trousers and he carried his attaché case—as if he were a season-ticket holder. He had nearly reached the state of permanency too, but he carried about with him still the scars of time—the damaged shoes implied a different past, the lines on his face suggested hopes and fears of the future. The old woman with the ember stopped between two huts and watched him. He came on into the clearing with his eyes on the ground and his shoulders hunched, as if he felt exposed. The old man advanced to meet him: he took the stranger's hand and kissed it.

"Can you let me have a hammock for the night?"

"Ah, father, for a hammock you must go to a town. Here you must take only the luck of the road."

"Never mind. Anywhere to lie down. Can you give me —a little spirit?"

"Coffee, father. We have nothing else."

"Some food."

"We have no food."

"Never mind."

The boy came out of the hut and watched them: everybody watched: it was like a bull-fight: the animal was tired and they awaited the next move. They were not hardhearted: they were watching the rare spectacle of something worse off than themselves. He limped on towards the hut. Inside it was dark from the knees upwards: there was no flame on the floor, just a slow burning away. The place was half-filled by a stack of maize: rats rustled among the dry outer leaves. There was a bed made of earth with a straw mat on it, and two packing-cases made a table. The stranger lay down, and the old man closed the door on them both.

"Is it safe?"

"The boy will watch. He knows."

"Were you expecting me?"

"No, father. But it is five years since we have seen a priest . . . it was bound to happen one day."

The priest fell uneasily asleep, and the old man crouched on the floor, fanning the fire with his breath. Somebody tapped on the door and the priest jerked upright. "It is all right," the old man said. "Just your coffee, father." He brought it to him—grey maize coffee smoking in a tin mug, but the priest was too tired to drink. He lay on his side perfectly still: a rat watched him from the maize.

"The soldiers were here yesterday," the old man said. He blew on the fire: the smoke poured up and filled the hut. The priest began to cough, and the rat moved quickly like the shadow of a hand into the stack.

"The boy, father, has not been baptized. The last priest who was here wanted two pesos. I had only one peso. Now I have only fifty centavos."

"Tomorrow," the priest said wearily.

"Will you say Mass, father, in the morning?"

"Yes, yes."

"And Confession, father, will you hear our confessions?"

"Yes, but let me sleep first." He turned on his back and closed his eyes to keep out the smoke.

"We have no money, father, to give you. The other priest, Padre José . . ."

"Give me some clothes instead," he said impatiently.

"But we have only what we wear."

"Take mine in exchange."

The old man hummed dubiously to himself, glancing sideways at what the fire showed of the black torn cloth. "If I must, father," he said. He blew quietly at the fire for a few minutes. The priest's eyes closed again.

"After five years there is so much to confess."

The priest sat up quickly. "What was that?" he said.

"You were dreaming, father. The boy will warn us if the soldiers come. I was only saying——"

"Can't you let me sleep for five minutes?" He lay down again: somewhere, in one of the women's huts, someone was singing—"I went down to my field and there I found a rose."

The old man said softly: "It would be a pity if the soldiers came before we had time . . . such a burden on poor souls, father . . ." The priest shouldered himself upright against the wall and said furiously: "Very well. Begin. I will hear your confession." The rats scuffled in the maize. "Go on then," he said. "Don't waste time. Hurry. When did you last . . ." The old man knelt beside the fire, and across the clearing the woman sang: "I went down to my field and the rose was withered."

"Five years ago." He paused and blew at the fire. "It's hard to remember, father."

"Have you sinned against purity?"

The priest leant against the wall with his legs drawn up beneath him, and the rats accustomed to the voices moved again in the maize. The old man picked out his sins with difficulty, blowing at the fire. "Make a good act of contrition," the priest said, "and say—say—have you a rosary? —then say the Joyful Mysteries." His eyes closed, his lips and tongue stumbled over the Absolution, failed to finish . . . he sprang awake again.

"Can I bring the women?" the old man was saying. "It is five years . . ."

"Oh, let them come. Let them all come!" the priest cried angrily. "I am your servant." He put his hand over his eyes and began to weep. The old man opened the door: it was not completely dark outside under the enormous arc of starry ill-lit sky. He went across to the women's huts and knocked. "Come," he said. "You must say your confessions. It is only polite to the father." They wailed at him that they were tired . . . the morning would do. "Would you insult him?" he said. "What do you think he has come here for? He is a very holy father. There he is in my hut now weeping for our sins." He hustled them out: one by one they picked their way across the clearing towards the hut: and the old man set off down the path towards the river to take the place of the boy who watched the ford for soldiers.

CHAPTER FOUR

IT WAS years since Mr. Tench had written a letter. He sat before the work-table sucking at a steel nib—an old impulse had come to him to project this stray letter towards the last address he had—in Southend. Who knew who was alive still? He tried to begin: it was like breaking the ice at a party where you knew nobody. He began to write the envelope—Mrs. Henry Tench, care of Mrs. Marsdyke, 3, The Avenue, Westcliffe. It was her mother's house: the dominating, interfering creature who had induced him to set up his plate in Southend for a fatal while. "Please forward," he wrote. She wouldn't do it if she knew, but she had probably forgotten—by this time—his handwriting.

He sucked the inky nib—how to go on? It would have been easier if there had been some purpose behind it other than the vague desire to put on record—to somebody— that he was still alive. It might prove awkward, if she had married again, but in that case she wouldn't hesitate to tear the letter up. He wrote: "Dear Sylvia," in a big clear immature script, listening to the furnace purring on the bench. He was making a gold alloy—there were no depots here where he could buy his material ready-made. Besides, the depots didn't favour 14-carat gold for dental work, and he couldn't afford finer material.

The trouble was—nothing ever happened here. His life was as sober, respectable, regular as even Mrs. Marsdyke could require.

He took a look at the crucible: the gold was on the point of fusion with the alloy, so he flung in a spoonful of vegetable charcoal to protect the mixture from the air, took up his pen again and sat mooning over the paper. He couldn't remember his wife clearly—only the hats she wore. How surprised she would be at hearing from him after this long while: there had been one letter written by each of them since the little boy died. The years really meant nothing to him—they drifted fairly rapidly by without changing a habit. He had meant to leave six years ago, but the peso dropped with a revolution, and so he had come south. Now he had more money saved, but a month ago the peso had dropped again—another revolution somewhere. There was nothing to do but wait ... the nib went back between his teeth and memory melted in the little hot room. Why write at all? He couldn't remember now what had given him the odd idea. Somebody knocked on the outer door and he left the letter on the bench—"Dear Sylvia," staring up, big and bold and hopeless. A boat's bell rang by the riverside: it was the *General Obregon* back from Vera Cruz. A memory stirred: it was as if something alive and in pain moved in the little front room among the rocking-chairs—"an interesting afternoon: what happened to him, I wonder, when"—then died, or got away: Mr. Tench was used to pain, it was his profession. He waited cautiously till a hand beat on the door again and a voice said: *"Con amistad"*—there was no trust anywhere—before he drew the bolts and opened up, to admit a patient.

Padre José went in, under the big classical gateway marked in black letters *"Silencio,"* to what people used to call the Garden of God. It was like a building estate where nobody had paid attention to the architecture of the next house. The big stone tombs of above-ground burial were any height and any shape: sometimes an angel stood on the roof with lichenous wings: sometimes through a glass window you could see some rusting metal flowers upon a shelf—it was like looking into the kitchen of a house whose owners have moved on, forgetting to clean out the vases. There was a sense of intimacy—you could go anywhere and see anything. Life here had withdrawn altogether.

He walked very slowly among the tombs because of his bulk: he could be alone here, there were no children about, and he could waken a faint sense of homesickness which was better than no feeling at all. He had buried some of these people. His small inflamed eyes turned here and there. Coming round the huge grey bulk of the Lopez tomb—a merchant family which fifty years ago had owned the only hotel in the capital—he found he was not alone. A grave was being dug at the edge of the cemetery next the wall: two men were working rapidly: a woman stood by and an old man. A child's coffin lay at their feet—it took no time at all in the spongy soil to get down far enough: a little water collected; that was why those who could afford it lay above ground.

They all paused a moment and looked at Padre José,

and he sidled back towards the Lopez tomb as if he were an intruder. There was no sign of grief anywhere in the bright hot day: a buzzard sat on a roof outside the cemetery. Somebody said: "Father."

Padre José put up his hand deprecatingly as if he were trying to indicate that he was not there, that he was gone, away, out of sight.

The old man said: "Padre José." They all watched him hungrily: they had been quite resigned until he had appeared, but now they were anxious, eager. . . . He ducked and dodged away from them. "Padre José," the old man repeated. "A prayer?" They smiled at him, waiting. They were quite accustomed to people dying, but an unforeseen hope of happiness had bobbed up among the tombs: they could boast after this that one at least of their family had gone into the ground with an official prayer.

"It's impossible," Padre José said.

"Yesterday was her saint's day," the woman said, as if that made a difference. "She was five." She was one of those garrulous women who show to strangers the photographs of their children: but all she had to show was a coffin.

"I am sorry."

The old man pushed the coffin aside with his foot the better to approach Padre José: it was small and light and might have contained nothing but bones. "Not a whole service, you understand—just a prayer. She was—innocent," he said. The word sounded odd and archaic and local in the little stony town, outdated like the Lopez tomb, belonging only here.

"It is against the law."

"Her name," the woman went on, "was Anita. I was sick when I had her," she explained, as if to excuse the child's delicacy which had led to all this inconvenience.

"The law . . ."

The old man put his finger to his nose. "You can trust us. It is just the case of a short prayer. I am her grandfather. This is her mother, her father, her uncle. You can trust us."

But that was the trouble—he could trust no one. As soon as they got back home one or other of them would certainly begin to boast. He walked backwards all the time, weaving his plump fingers, shaking his head, nearly bumping into the Lopez tomb. He was scared, and yet a curious pride bubbled in his throat, because he was being treated as a priest again, with respect. "If I could," he said, "my children . . ."

Suddenly and unexpectedly there was agony in the cemetery. They had been used to losing children, but they hadn't been used to what the rest of the world knows best of all—the hope which peters out. The woman began to cry—dryly, without tears, the trapped noise of something wanting to be released; the old man fell on his knees with his hands held out. "Padre José," he said, "there is no one else. . . ." He looked as if he were asking for a miracle. An enormous temptation came to Padre José to take the risk and say a prayer over the grave: he felt the wild attraction of doing one's duty and stretched a sign of the cross in the air; then fear came back, like a drug. Contempt and safety waited for him down by the quay: he wanted to get away. He sank hopelessly down on his knees and entreated them: "Leave me alone." He said: "I am unworthy. Can't you see? I am a coward." The two old men faced each other on their knees among the tombs, the small coffin shoved aside like a pretext—an absurd spectacle. He knew it was absurd: a lifetime of self-analysis enabled him to see himself as he was, fat and ugly and old and humiliated. It was as if a whole seducing choir of angels had silently withdrawn and left the voices of the children in the patio—"Come to bed, José, come to bed," sharp and shrill and worse than they had ever been. He knew he was in the grip of the unforgivable sin, despair.

" 'At last the blessed day arrived,' " the mother read aloud, " 'when the days of Juan's novitiate were over. Oh, what a joyful day was that for his mother and sister! And a little sad too, for the flesh cannot always be strong and how could they help mourning awhile in their hearts for the loss of a small son and an elder brother? Ah, if they had known that they were gaining that day a saint in heaven to pray for them.' "

The younger girl on the bed said: "Have *we* got a saint?"

"Of course."

"Why did they want another saint?"

The mother went on reading: " 'Next day the whole family received communion from the hands of a son and brother. Then they said a fond good-bye—they little knew that it was the last—to the new soldier of Christ and returned to their home in Morelos. Already clouds were darkening the heavens, and President Calles was discussing the anti-Catholic laws in the Palace at Chapultepec. The devil was ready to assail poor Mexico.' "

"Is the shooting going to begin soon?" the boy asked, moving restlessly against the wall. His mother went relentlessly on: " 'Juan, unknown to all but his Confessor, was preparing himself for the evil days ahead with the most rigorous mortifications. His companions suspected nothing, for he was always the heart and soul of every merry conversation, and on the feast-day of the founder of the Order it was he . . .' "

"I know, I know," the boy said. "He acted a play."

The little girls opened astounded eyes.

"And why not, Luis?" the mother said, pausing with her finger on the prohibited book. He stared sullenly back at her. "And why not, Luis?" she repeated. She waited awhile, and then read on: the little girls watched their brother with horror and admiration. " 'It was he,' " she said, " 'who obtained permission to perform a little one-act play founded on . . .' "

"I know, I know," the boy said. "The catacombs."

The mother, compressing her lips, continued: " '. . . the persecution of the Early Christians. Perhaps he remembered that occasion in his boyhood when he acted Nero before the good old Bishop, but this time he insisted on taking the comic part of a Roman fishmonger . . .' "

"I don't believe a word of it," the boy said, with sullen fury, "not a word of it."

"How dare you!"

"Nobody could be such a fool."

The little girls sat motionless, their eyes large and brown and pious, enjoying themselves like Hell.

"Go to your father."

"Anything to get away from this—this—" the boy said.

"Tell him what you've told me."

"This . . ."

"Leave the room."

He slammed the door behind him: his father stood at the barred window of the sala, looking out: the beetles detonated against the oil-lamp and crawled with broken wings across the stone floor. The boy said: "My mother told me to tell you that I told her that I didn't believe that the book she's reading . . ."

"What book?"

"The Holy Book."

He said sadly: "Oh, that." Nobody passed in the street, nothing happened: it was after nine-thirty and all the lights were out. He said: "You must make allowances. For us, you know, everything seems over. That book—it is like our own childhood."

"It sounds so silly."

"You don't remember the time when the Church was here. I was a bad Catholic, but it meant—well, music, lights, a place where you could sit out of this heat—and for your mother, well, there was always something for her to do. If we had a theatre, anything at all instead, we shouldn't feel so—left."

"But this Juan," the boy said. "He sounds so silly."

"He was killed, wasn't he?"

"Oh, so were Villa, Obregon, Madero . . ."

"Who tells you about them?"

"We all of us play them. Yesterday I was Madero. They shot me in the plaza—the law of flight." Somewhere

in the heavy night a drum beat: the sour river smell filled
the room: it was familiar, like the taste of soot in cities.
"We tossed up. I was Madero: Pedro had to be Huerta.
He fled to Vera Cruz down by the river. Manuel chased
him—he was Carranza." His father struck a beetle off his
shirt, staring into the street: the sound of marching feet
came nearer. He said: "I suppose your mother's angry."

"You aren't," the boy said.

"What's the good? It's not your fault. We have been
deserted."

The soldiers went by, returning to barracks, up the hill
near what had once been the cathedral: they marched out
of step in spite of the drum beat, they looked undernour-
ished, they hadn't yet made much of war. They passed
lethargically by in the dark street and the boy watched
them out of sight with excited and hopeful eyes.

Mrs. Fellows rocked backwards and forwards, backwards and forwards. " 'And so Lord Palmerston said if
the Greek Government didn't do right to Don Pacifico
. . .' " She said: "My darling, I've got such a headache I
think we must stop today."

"Of course. I have a little one too."

"I expect yours will be better soon. Would you mind
putting the books away?" The little shabby books had
come by post from a firm in Paternoster Row called Private Tutorials, Ltd.—a whole education which began with
"Reading without Tears" and went methodically on to the
Reform Bill and Lord Palmerston and the poems of Victor
Hugo. Once every six months an examination paper was
delivered, and Mrs. Fellows laboriously worked through

the answers and awarded marks. These she sent back to
Paternoster Row, and there, weeks later, they were filed:
once she had forgotten her duty when there was shooting
in Zapata, and had received a printed slip beginning:
"Dear Parent, I regret to see . . ." The trouble was, they
were years ahead of schedule by now—there were so few
other books to read—and so the examination papers were
years behind. Sometimes the firm sent embossed certificates
for framing, announcing that Miss Coral Fellows had
passed third with honours into the second grade, signed
with a rubber stamp Henry Beckley, B.A., Director of
Private Tutorials, Ltd., and sometimes there would be
little personal letters typewritten, with the same blue
smudgy signature, saying: "Dear Pupil, I think you
should pay more attention this week to . . ." The letters
were always six weeks out of date.

"My darling," Mrs. Fellows said, "will you see the cook
and order lunch? Just yourself. I can't eat a thing, and
your father's out on the plantation."

"Mother," the child said, "do you believe there's a
God?"

The question scared Mrs. Fellows. She rocked furiously
up and down and said: "Of course."

"I mean the Virgin Birth—and everything."

"My dear, what a thing to ask. Whom have you been
talking to?"

"Oh," she said, "I've been thinking, that's all." She
didn't wait for any further answer: she knew quite well
there would be none—it was always her job to make decisions. Henry Beckley, B.A., had put it all into an early
lesson—it hadn't been any more difficult to accept then

than the giant at the top of the beanstalk, and at the age
of ten she had discarded both relentlessly. By that time
she was starting algebra.

"Surely your father hasn't . . ."

"Oh, no."

She put on her sun-helmet and went out into the blazing
ten o'clock heat to find the cook—she looked more fragile
than ever and more indomitable. When she had given her
orders she went to the warehouse to inspect the alligator
skins tacked out on a wall, then to the stables to see that
the mules were in good shape. She carried her responsibilities carefully like crockery across the hot yard: there
was no question she wasn't prepared to answer: the vultures rose languidly at her approach.

She returned to the house and her mother. She said:
"It's Thursday."

"Is it, dear?"

"Hasn't father got the bananas down to the quay?"

"I'm sure I don't know, dear."

She went briskly back into the yard and rang a bell:
an Indian came: no, the bananas were still in the store;
no orders had been given. "Get them down," she said, "at
once, quickly. The boat will be here soon." She fetched her
father's ledger and counted the bunches as they were carried out—a hundred bananas or more to a bunch, which
was worth a few pence: it took more than two hours to
empty the store: somebody had got to do the work, and
once before her father had forgotten the day. After half
an hour she began to feel tired—she wasn't used to weariness so early in the day: she leant against the wall and it
scorched her shoulder-blades. She felt no resentment at all

at being there, looking after things: the word "play" had
no meaning there at all—the whole of life was adult. In
one of Henry Beckley's early reading-books there had
been a picture of a doll's tea-party: it was incomprehensible, like a ceremony she hadn't learned: she couldn't see
the point of pretending. Four hundred and fifty-six. Four
hundred and fifty-seven. The sweat poured down the
peons' bodies steadily like a shower-bath. An awful pain
took her suddenly in the stomach—she missed a load and
tried to catch up in her calculations: the sense of responsibility for the first time felt like a load borne for too many
years. Five hundred and twenty-five. It was a new pain
(not worms this time), but it didn't scare her: it was as if
her body had expected it, had grown up to it, as the mind
grows up to the loss of tenderness. You couldn't call it
childhood draining out of her: childhood was something
she had never really been conscious of.

"Is that the last?" she said.

"Yes, Señorita."

"Are you sure?"

"Yes, Señorita."

But she had to see for herself. Never before had it occurred to her to do a job unwillingly—if she didn't do a
thing, nobody would—but today she wanted to lie down,
to sleep: if all the bananas didn't get away it was her
father's fault. She wondered whether she had fever: her feet
felt so cold on the hot ground. Oh, well, she thought, and
went patiently into the barn, found the torch, and switched
it on. Yes, the place seemed empty enough, but she never
left a job half done. She advanced towards the back wall,
holding the torch in front of her. An empty bottle rolled

away—she dropped the light on it: Cerveza Moctezuma.
Then the torch lit the back wall: low down near the ground
somebody had scrawled in chalk—she came closer—a lot
of little crosses lay in the circle of light. He must have
lain down among the bananas and tried—mechanically—
to relieve his fear by writing something, and this was all
he could think of. The child stood in pain and looked at
them: a horrible novelty enclosed her whole morning: it
was as if today everything was memorable.

The Chief of Police was in the cantina playing billiards
when the lieutenant found him. The jefe had a handkerchief tied all round his face with some idea that it relieved
the toothache. He was chalking his cue for a difficult shot
when the lieutenant pushed through the swing door. On
the shelves behind were nothing but gaseosa bottles and a
yellow liquid called sidral—warranted non-alcoholic. The
lieutenant stood protestingly in the doorway: the situation
was ignoble; he wanted to eliminate anything in the state
at which a foreigner might have cause to sneer. He said:
"Can I speak to you?" The jefe winced at a sudden jab of
pain and came with unusual alacrity towards the door: the
lieutenant glanced at the score, marked in rings strung
on a cord across the room—the jefe was losing. "Back—
moment," the jefe said, and explained to the lieutenant:
"Don't want open mouth." As they pushed the door somebody raised a cue and surreptitiously pushed back one of
the jefe's rings.

They walked up the street side by side: the fat one and
the lean. It was a Sunday and all the shops closed at noon
—that was the only relic of the old time. No bells rang

anywhere. The lieutenant said: "Have you seen the Governor?"

"You can do anything," the jefe said, "anything."

"He leaves it to us?"

"On conditions," he winced.

"What are they?"

"He'll hold you—responsible—if—not caught before—rains."

"As long as I'm not responsible for anything else . . ." the lieutenant said moodily.

"You asked for it. You got it."

"I'm glad." It seemed to the lieutenant that all the world he cared about now lay at his feet. They passed the new hall built for the Syndicate of Workers and Peasants: through the window they could see the big, bold, clever murals—of one priest caressing a woman in the confessional, another tippling on the sacramental wine. The lieutenant said: "We will soon make these unnecessary." He looked at the pictures with the eye of a foreigner: they seemed to him barbarous.

"Why? They are—fun."

"One day they'll forget there ever was a Church here."

The jefe said nothing. The lieutenant knew he was thinking: What a fuss about nothing. He said sharply: "Well, what are my orders?"

"Orders?"

"You are my chief."

The jefe was silent: he studied the lieutenant unobtrusively with little astute eyes. Then he said: "You know I trust you. Do what you think best."

"Will you put that in writing?"

"Oh—not necessary. We know each other."

All the way up the road they fenced warily for positions.

"Didn't the Governor give you anything in writing?" the lieutenant asked.

"No. He said we knew each other."

It was the lieutenant who gave way because it was he who really cared. He was indifferent to his personal future. He said: "I shall take hostages from every village."

"Then he won't stay in the villages."

"Do you imagine," the lieutenant said bitterly, "that they don't know where he is? He has to keep some touch— or what good is he?"

"Just as you like," the jefe said.

"And I shall shoot as often as it's necessary."

The jefe said with factitious brightness: "A little blood never hurt anyone. Where will you start?"

"His parish, I think, Concepción, and then—perhaps —his home."

"Why there?"

"He may think he's safe there." He brooded past the shuttered shops. "It's worth a few deaths, but will *he*, do you think, support me if they make a fuss in Mexico?"

"It isn't likely, is it?" the jefe said. "But it's what—" He was stopped by a stab of pain.

"It's what I wanted," the lieutenant said for him.

He made his way on alone towards the police station: and the chief went back to billiards. There were few people about; it was too hot. If only, he thought, we had a proper photograph—he wanted to know the features of his enemy. A swarm of children had the plaza to themselves.

They were playing some obscure and intricate game from bench to bench: an empty gaseosa bottle sailed through the air and smashed at the lieutenant's feet. His hand went to his holster and he turned: he caught a look of consternation on a boy's face.

"Did you throw that bottle?"

The heavy brown eyes stared sullenly back at him.

"What were you doing?"

"It was a bomb."

"Were you throwing it at me?"

"No."

"What then?"

"A gringo."

The lieutenant smiled—an awkward movement of the lips: "That's right, but you must aim better." He kicked the broken bottle into the road and tried to think of words which would show these children that they were on the same side. He said: "I suppose the gringo was one of those rich Yankees who think . . ." and surprised an expression of devotion in the boy's face; it called for something in return, and the lieutenant became aware in his own heart of a sad and unsatisfiable love. He said: "Come here." The child approached, while his companions stood in a scared semi-circle and watched from a safe distance. "What is your name?"

"Luis."

"Well," the lieutenant said, at a loss for words, "you must learn to aim properly."

The boy said passionately: "I wish I could." He had his eye on the holster.

"Would you like to see my gun?" the lieutenant said.

He drew his heavy automatic from the holster and held it out: the children drew cautiously in. He said: "This is the safety-catch. Lift it. So. Now it's ready to fire."

"Is it loaded?" Luis asked.

"It's always loaded."

The tip of the boy's tongue appeared: he swallowed. Saliva came from the glands as if he smelt food. They all stood close in now. A daring child put out his hand and touched the holster. They ringed the lieutenant round: he was surrounded by an insecure happiness as he fitted the gun back on his hip.

"What is it called?" Luis asked.

"A Colt No. 5."

"How many bullets?"

"Six."

"Have you killed somebody with it?"

"Not yet," the lieutenant said.

They were breathless with interest. He stood with his hand on his holster and watched the brown intent patient eyes: it was for these he was fighting. He would eliminate from their childhood everything which had made him miserable, all that was poor, superstitious, and corrupt. They deserved nothing less than the truth—a vacant universe and a cooling world, the right to be happy in any way they chose. He was quite prepared to make a massacre for their sakes—first the Church and then the foreigner and then the politician—even his own chief would one day have to go. He wanted to begin the world again with them, in a desert.

"Oh," Luis said, "I wish . . . I wish . . ." as if his ambition were too vast for definition. The lieutenant put out his hand in a gesture of affection—a touch, he didn't know what to do with it. He pinched the boy's ear and saw him flinch away with the pain: they scattered from him like birds and he went on alone across the plaza to the police station, a little dapper figure of hate carrying his secret of love. On the wall of the office the gangster still stared stubbornly in profile towards the first communion party: somebody had inked the priest's head round to detach him from the girls' and the women's faces: the unbearable grin peeked out of a halo. The lieutenant called furiously out into the patio: "Is there nobody here?" Then he sat down at the desk while the gun-butts scraped the floor.

CHAPTER ONE

THE mule suddenly sat down under the priest: it was not an unnatural thing to do, for they had been travelling through the forest for nearly twelve hours. They had been going west, but news of soldiers met them there and they had turned east: the Red Shirts were active in that direction, so they had tacked north, wading through the swamps, diving into the mahogany darkness. Now they were both tired out and the mule simply sat down. The priest scrambled off and began to laugh. He was feeling happy. It is one of the strange discoveries a man makes that life, however you lead it, contains moments of exhilaration: there are always comparisons which can be made with worse times: even in danger and misery the pendulum swings.

He came cautiously out of the belt of trees into a marshy clearing: the whole state was like that, river and swamp and forest: he knelt down in the late sunlight and bathed his face in a brown pool which reflected back at him like a piece of glazed pottery the round, stubbly, and hollow features; they were so unexpected that he grinned at them—with the shy evasive untrustworthy smile of a

man caught out. In the old days he often practised a gesture a long while in front of a glass so that he had come to
know his own face as well as an actor does. It was a form
of humility—his own natural face hadn't seemed the right
one. It was a buffoon's face, good enough for mild jokes to
women, but unsuitable at the altar rail. He had tried to
change it—and indeed, he thought, indeed I have succeeded, they'll never recognize me now, and the cause of
his happiness came back to him like the taste of brandy,
promising temporary relief from fear, loneliness, a lot of
things. He was being driven by the presence of the soldiers
to the very place where he most wanted to be. He had
avoided it for six years, but now it wasn't his fault—it was
his duty to go there—it couldn't count as sin. He went
back to his mule and kicked it gently: "Up, mule, up"—a
small gaunt man in torn peasant's clothes going for the
first time in many years, like any ordinary man, to his
home.

In any case, even if he could have gone south and
avoided the village, it was only one more surrender: the
years behind him were littered with similar surrenders—
feast-days and fast-days and days of abstinence had been
the first to go: then he had ceased to trouble more than
occasionally about his breviary—and finally he had left it
behind altogether at the port in one of his periodic attempts at escape. Then the altar stone went—too dangerous to carry with him. He had no business to say Mass
without it: he was probably liable to suspension, but pen-
alties of the ecclesiastical kind began to seem unreal in a
state where the only penalty was the civil one of death.
The routine of his life like a dam was cracked and forget-

fulness came dribbling in, wiping out this and that. Five years ago he had given way to despair—the unforgivable sin—and he was going back now to the scene of his despair with a curious lightening of the heart. For he had got over despair too. He was a bad priest, he knew it: they had a word for his kind—a whisky priest—but every failure dropped out of sight and out of mind: somewhere they accumulated in secret—the rubble of his failures. One day they would choke up, he supposed, altogether the source of grace. Until then he carried on, with spells of fear, weariness, with a shamefaced lightness of heart.

The mule splashed across the clearing and they entered the forest again. Now that he no longer despaired it didn't mean, of course, that he wasn't damned—it was simply that after a time the mystery became too great, a damned man putting God into the mouths of men: an odd sort of servant, that, for the devil. His mind was full of a simplified mythology: Michael dressed in armour slew a dragon, and the angels fell through space like comets with beautiful streaming hair because they were jealous, so one of the fathers had said, of what God intended for men—the enormous privilege of life—this life.

There were signs of cultivation: stumps of trees and the ashes of fires where the ground was being cleared for a crop. He stopped beating the mule on: he felt a curious shyness. . . . A woman came out of a hut and watched him lagging up the path on the tired mule. The tiny village, not more than two dozen huts round a dusty plaza, was made to pattern: but it was a pattern which lay close to his heart; he felt secure—he was confident of a welcome— that in this place there would be at least one person he could trust not to betray him to the police. When he was quite close the mule sat down again—this time he had to roll on the ground to escape. He picked himself up and the woman watched him as if he were an enemy. "Ah, Maria," he said, "and how are you?"

"Well," she exclaimed, "it is you, father?"

He didn't look directly at her: his eyes were sly and cautious. He said: "You didn't recognize me?"

"You've changed." She looked him up and down with a kind of contempt. She said: "When did you get those clothes, father?"

"A week ago."

"What did you do with yours?"

"I gave them in exchange."

"Why? They were good clothes."

"They were very ragged—and conspicuous."

"I'd have mended them and hidden them away. It's a waste. You look like a common man."

He smiled, looking at the ground, while she chided him like a house-keeper: it was just as in the old days when there was a presbytery and meetings of the Children of Mary and all the guilds and gossip of a parish, except of course that . . . He said gently, not looking at her, with the same embarrassed smile: "How's Brigida?" His heart jumped at the name: a sin may have enormous consequences: it was six years since he had been—home.

"She's as well as the rest of us. What did you expect?"

He had his satisfaction: it was connected with his crime: he had no business to feel pleasure at anything attached to that past. He said mechanically: "That's good," while his heart beat with its secret and appalling love. He said:

"I'm very tired. The police were about near Zapata . . ."

"Why didn't you make for Montecristo?"

He looked quickly up with anxiety. It wasn't the welcome that he had expected: a small knot of people had gathered between the huts and watched him from a safe distance—there was a little decaying bandstand and a single stall for gaseosas—people had brought their chairs out for the evening. Nobody came forward to kiss his hand and ask his blessing. It was as if he had descended by means of his sin into the human struggle to learn other things besides despair and love, that a man can be unwelcome even in his own home. He said: "The Red Shirts were there."

"Well, father," the woman said, "we can't turn you away. You'd better come along." He followed her meekly, tripping once in the long peon trousers, with the happiness wiped off his face and the smile somehow left behind like the survivor of a wreck. There were seven or eight men, two women, half a dozen children: he came among them like a beggar. He couldn't help remembering the last time . . . the excitement, the gourds of spirit brought out of holes in the ground . . . his guilt had still been fresh, yet how he had been welcomed. It was as if he had returned to them in their vicious prison as one of themselves—an émigré who comes back to his native place enriched.

"This is the father," the woman said. Perhaps it was only that they hadn't recognized him, he thought, and waited for their greetings. They came forward one by one and kissed his hand and then stood back and watched him. He said: "I am glad to see you . . ." He was going to say "my children," but then it seemed to him that only the

childless man has the right to call strangers his children.
The real children were coming up now to kiss his hand,
one by one, under the pressure of their parents. They were
too young to remember the old days when the priests
dressed in black and wore Roman collars and had soft
superior patronizing hands: he could see they were mysti-
fied at the show of respect to a peasant like their parents.
He didn't look at them directly, but he was watching them
closely all the same. Two were girls: a thin washed-out
child—of five, six, seven? he couldn't tell—and one who
had been sharpened by hunger into an appearance of
devilry and malice beyond her age. A young woman stared
out of the child's eyes. He watched them disperse again,
saying nothing: they were strangers.

One of the men said: "Will you be here long, father?"

He said: "I thought, perhaps . . . I could rest . . . a
few days."

One of the other men said: "Couldn't you go a bit farther north, father, to Pueblita?"

"We've been travelling for twelve hours, the mule and
I."

The woman suddenly spoke for him, angrily: "Of course
he'll stay here tonight. It's the least we can do."

He said: "I'll say Mass for you in the morning," as if
he were offering them a bribe, but it might almost have
been stolen money from their expressions of shyness and
unwillingness.

Somebody said: "If you don't mind, father, very early
. . . in the night perhaps . . ."

"What is the matter with you all?" he said. "Why
should you be afraid?"

"Haven't you heard . . . ?"

"Heard?"

"They are taking hostages now—from all the villages where they think you've been. And if people don't tell . . . somebody is shot . . . and then they take another hostage. It happened in Concepción."

"Concepción?" One of his lids began to twitch, up and down, up and down: in such trivial ways the body expresses anxiety, horror, or despair. He said: "Who?" They looked at him stupidly. He said furiously: "Whom did they murder?"

"Pedro Montez."

He gave a little yapping cry like a dog's—the absurd shorthand of grief. The old-young child laughed. He said: "Why don't they catch me? The fools. Why don't they catch *me?*" The little girl laughed again: he stared at her sightlessly, as if he could hear the sound, but couldn't see the face. Happiness was dead again before it had had time to breathe; he was like a woman with a stillborn child —bury it quickly and forget and begin again. Perhaps the next would live.

"You see, father," one of the men said, "why . . ."

He felt as a guilty man does before his judges. He said: "Would you rather that I was like . . . like Padre José in the capital . . . you have heard of him . . . ?"

They said unconvincingly: "Of course not, father."

He said: "What am I saying now? It's not what you want or what I want." He said sharply, with authority: "I will sleep now. . . . You can wake me an hour before dawn . . . half an hour to hear your confessions . . . then Mass, and I will be gone."

But where? There wouldn't be a village in the state to which he wouldn't be an unwelcome danger now.

The woman said: "This way, father."

He followed her into a small room where all the furniture had been made out of packing-cases—a chair, a bed of boards tacked together and covered with a straw mat, a crate on which a cloth had been laid, and on the cloth an oil-lamp. He said: "I don't want to turn anybody out of here."

"It's mine."

He looked at her doubtfully: "Where will you sleep?" He was afraid of claims. He watched her covertly: was this all there was in marriage, this evasion and suspicion and lack of ease? When people confessed to him in terms of passion, was this all they meant—the hard bed and the busy woman and the not talking about the past . . . ?

"When you are gone."

The light flattened out behind the forest and the long shadows of the trees pointed towards the door. He lay down upon the bed, and the woman busied herself somewhere out of sight: he could hear her scratching at the earth floor. He couldn't sleep. Had it become his duty then to run away? He had tried to escape several times, but he had always been prevented . . . now they wanted him to go. Nobody would stop him, saying a woman was ill or a man dying. He was a sickness now.

"Maria," he said. "Maria, what are you doing?"

"I have saved a little brandy for you."

He thought: If I go, I shall meet other priests: I shall go to confession: I shall feel contrition and be forgiven: eternal life will begin for me all over again. The Church taught that it was every man's first duty to save his own soul. The simple ideas of hell and heaven moved in his brain: life without books, without contact with educated men, had peeled away from his memory everything but the simplest outline of the mystery.

"There," the woman said. She carried a small medicine bottle filled with spirit.

If he left them, they would be safe: and they would be free from his example: he was the only priest the children could remember. It was from him they would take their ideas of the faith. But it was from him too they took God— in their mouths. When he was gone it would be as if God in all this space between the sea and the mountains ceased to exist. Wasn't it his duty to stay, even if they despised him, even if they were murdered for his sake, even if they were corrupted by his example? He was shaken with the enormity of the problem: he lay with his hands over his eyes: nowhere, in all the wide flat marshy land, was there a single person he could consult. He raised the brandy bottle to his mouth.

He said shyly: "And Brigida . . . is she . . . well?"

"You saw her just now."

"No." He couldn't believe that he hadn't recognized her. It was making light of his mortal sin: you couldn't do a thing like that and then not even recognize . . .

"Yes, she was there." Maria went to the door and called: "Brigida, Brigida," and the priest turned on his side and watched her come in out of the outside landscape of terror and lust—that small malicious child who had laughed at him.

"Go and speak to the father," Maria said. "Go on."

He made an attempt to hide the brandy bottle, but there was nowhere . . . he tried to minimize it in his hands, watching her, feeling the shock of human love.

"She knows her catechism," Maria said, "but she won't say it. . . ."

The child stood there, watching him with acuteness and contempt. They had spent no love in her conception: just fear and despair and half a bottle of brandy and the sense of loneliness had driven him to an act which horrified him —and this scared shamefaced overpowering love was the result. He said: "Why not? Why won't you say it?" taking quick secret glances, never meeting her gaze, feeling his heart pound in his breast unevenly, like an old donkey engine, with the balked desire to save her from—everything.

"Why should I?"

"God wishes it."

"How do you know?"

He was aware of an immense load of responsibility: it was indistinguishable from love. This, he thought, must be what all parents feel: ordinary men go through life like this crossing their fingers, praying against pain, afraid. . . . This is what we escape at no cost at all, sacrificing an unimportant motion of the body. For years, of course, he had been responsible for souls, but that was different . . . a lighter thing. You could trust God to make allowances, but you couldn't trust smallpox, starvation, men. . . . He said: "My dear," tightening his grip upon the brandy bottle . . . he had baptized her at his last visit: she had been like a rag doll with a wrinkled, aged face—it seemed unlikely that she would live long. . . . He had felt nothing but a regret; it was difficult even to feel shame where no one blamed him. He was the only priest most of them had ever known—they took their standard of the priesthood from him. Even the women.

"Are you the gringo?"

"What gringo?"

The woman said: "The silly little creature. It's because the police have been looking for a man." It seemed odd to hear of any other man they wanted but himself.

"What has he done?"

"He's a Yankee. He murdered some people in the north."

"Why should he be here?"

"They think he's making for Quintana Roo—the chicle plantations." It was where many criminals in Mexico ended up: you could work on a plantation and earn good money and nobody interfered.

"Are you the gringo?" the child repeated.

"Do I look like a murderer?"

"I don't know."

If he left the state, he would be leaving her too, abandoned. He said humbly to the woman: "Couldn't I stay a few days here?"

"It's too dangerous, father."

He caught a look in the child's eyes which frightened him—it was again as if a grown woman was there before her time, making her plans, aware of far too much. It was like seeing his own mortal sin look back at him, without contrition. He tried to find some contact with the child and not the woman; he said: "My dear, tell me what games you play. . . ." The child sniggered. He turned his face quickly away and stared up at the roof, where a spider moved. He remembered a proverb—it came out of the recesses of his own childhood: his father had used it—"The best smell is bread, the best savour salt, the best love that of children." It had been a happy childhood, except that he had been afraid of too many things, and had hated poverty, like a crime: he had believed that when he was a priest he would be rich and proud—that was called having a vocation. He thought of the immeasurable distance a man travels—from the first whipping-top to this bed, on which he lay clasping the brandy. And to God it was only a moment. The child's snigger and the first mortal sin lay together more closely than two blinks of the eye. He put out his hand as if he could drag her back by force from—something; but he was powerless; the man or the woman waiting to complete her corruption might not yet have been born: how could he guard her against the non-existent?

She started out of his reach and put her tongue out at him. The woman said: "You little devil, you," and raised her hand.

"No," the priest said. "No." He scrambled into a sitting position. "Don't you dare . . ."

"I'm her mother."

"We haven't any right." He said to the child: "If only I had some cards I could show you a trick or two. You could teach your friends . . ." He had never known how to talk to children except from the pulpit. She stared back at him with insolence. He said: "Do you know how to send messages with taps—long, short, long? . . ."

"What on earth, father!" the woman exclaimed.

"It's a game children play. I know." He said to the child: "Have you any friends?"

The child suddenly laughed again knowingly. The seven-year-old body was like a dwarf's: it disguised an ugly maturity.

"Get out of here," the woman said. "Get out before I teach you . . ."

She made a last impudent and malicious gesture and was gone—perhaps for ever as far as he was concerned. To those you love you do not always say good-bye beside a deathbed, in an atmosphere of leisure and incense. He said: "I wonder what *we* can teach . . ." He thought of his own death and her life going on: it might be his hell to watch her rejoining him gradually through the debasing years, sharing his weakness like tuberculosis. . . . He lay back on the bed and turned his head away from the draining light: he appeared to be sleeping, but he was wide awake. The woman busied herself with small jobs, and as the sun went down the mosquitoes came out, flashing through the air to their mark unerringly, like sailors' knives.

"Shall I put up a net, father?"

"No. It doesn't matter." He had had more fevers in the last ten years than he could count: he had ceased to bother: they came and went and made no difference—they were part of his environment.

Presently she left the hut and he could hear her voice gossiping outside. He was astonished and a bit relieved by her resilience: once for five minutes seven years ago they had been lovers—if you could give that name to a relationship in which she had never used his baptismal name: to

her it was just an incident, a scratch which heals completely in the healthy flesh: she was even proud of having
been the priest's woman. He alone carried a wound, as if
a whole world had ended.

It was dark outside: no sign yet of the dawn. Perhaps
two dozen people sat on the earth floor of the largest hut
while he preached to them. He couldn't see them with any
distinctness: the candles on the packing-case smoked
steadily upwards—the door was shut and there was no
current of air. He was talking about heaven, standing between them and the candles in the ragged peon trousers
and the torn shirt. They grunted and moved restlessly: he
knew they were longing for the Mass to be over: they had
awakened him very early, because there were rumours of
police. . . .

He said: "One of the fathers has told us that joy always
depends on pain. Pain is part of joy. We are hungry and
then think how we enjoy our food at last. We are
thirsty . . ." He stopped suddenly, with his eyes glancing
away into the shadows, expecting the cruel laugh that
never came. He said: "We deny ourselves so that we can
enjoy. You have heard of rich men in the north who eat
salted foods, so that they can be thirsty—for what they
call the cocktail. Before the marriage, too, there is the
long betrothal. . . ." Again he stopped. He felt his own
unworthiness like a weight at the back of the tongue.
There was a smell of hot wax from where a candle drooped
in the immense nocturnal heat: people shifted on the hard
floor in the shadows. The smell of unwashed human beings
warred with the wax. He cried out stubbornly in a voice

of authority: "That is why I tell you that heaven is here: this is a part of heaven just as pain is a part of pleasure." He said: "Pray that you will suffer more and more and more. Never get tired of suffering. The police watching you, the soldiers gathering taxes, the beating you always get from the jefe because you are too poor to pay, small-pox and fever, hunger . . . that is all part of heaven—the preparation. Perhaps without them—who can tell?—you wouldn't enjoy heaven so much. Heaven would not be complete. And heaven. What is heaven?" Literary phrases from what seemed now to be another life altogether—the strict quiet life of the seminary—became confused on his tongue: the names of precious stones: Jerusalem the golden. But these people had never seen gold.

He went rather stumblingly on: "Heaven is where there is no jefe, no unjust laws, no taxes, no soldiers, and no hunger. Your children do not die in heaven." The door of the hut opened and a man slipped in. There was whisper-ing out of range of the candlelight. "You will never be afraid there—or unsafe. There are no Red Shirts. No-body grows old. The crops never fail. Oh, it is easy to say all the things that there will *not* be in heaven: what is there is God. That is more difficult. Our words are made to de-scribe what we know with our senses. We say 'light,' but we are thinking only of the sun, 'love' . . ." It was not easy to concentrate: the police were not far away. That man had probably brought news. "That means perhaps a child . . ." The door opened again: he could see another day drawn across like a grey slate outside. A voice whis-pered urgently to him: "Father."

"Yes?"

"The police are on the way: they are only a mile off, coming through the forest."

This was what he was used to: the words not striking home, the hurried close, the expectation of pain coming between him and his faith. He said stubbornly: "Above all remember this—heaven is here." Were they on horseback or on foot? If they were on foot, he had twenty minutes left to finish Mass and hide. "Here now, at this minute, your fear and my fear are part of heaven, where there will be no fear any more for ever." He turned his back on them and began very quickly to recite the Credo. There was a time when he had approached the Canon of the Mass with actual physical dread—the first time he had consumed the body and blood of God in a state of mortal sin: but then life bred its excuses—it hadn't after a while seemed to matter very much, whether he was damned or not, so long as these others . . .

He kissed the top of the packing-case and turned to bless . . . in the inadequate light he could just see two men kneeling with their arms stretched out in the shape of a cross—they would keep that position until the consecration was over, one more mortification squeezed out of their harsh and painful lives. He felt humbled by the pain ordinary men bore voluntarily; his pain was forced on him. "O Lord, I have loved the beauty of Thy house . . ." The candles smoked and the people shifted on their knees—an absurd happiness bobbed up in him again before anxiety returned: it was as if he had been permitted to look in from the outside at the population of heaven. Heaven must contain just such scared and dutiful and hunger-lined faces. For a matter of seconds he felt an immense

satisfaction that he could talk of suffering to them now
without hypocrisy—it is hard for the sleek and well-fed
priest to praise poverty. He began the prayer for the living: the long list of the Apostles and Martyrs fell like
footsteps—Cornelii, Cypriani, Laurentii, Chrysologi—
soon the police would reach the clearing where his mule
had sat down under him and he had washed in the pool.
The Latin words ran into each other on his hasty tongue:
he could feel impatience all round him. He began the Consecration of the Host (he had finished the wafers long ago
—it was a piece of bread from Maria's oven); impatience
abruptly died away: everything in time became a routine
but this—"Who the day before He suffered took Bread
into His holy and venerable hands . . ." Whoever moved
outside on the forest path, there was no movement here—
"*Hoc est enim Corpus Meum.*" He could hear the sigh of
breaths released: God was here in the body for the first
time in six years. When he raised the Host he could imagine the faces lifted like famished dogs'. He began the
Consecration of the Wine—in a chipped cup. That was
one more surrender—for two years he had carried a chalice round with him: once it would have cost him his life—
if the police officer who opened his case had not been a
Catholic. It may very well have cost the officer his life, if
anybody had discovered the evasion—he didn't know: you
went round making God knew what martyrs—in Concepción or elsewhere—when you yourself were without grace
enough to die.

The Consecration was in silence: no bell rang. He knelt
by the packing-case exhausted, without a prayer. Somebody opened the door: a voice whispered urgently:

"They're here." They couldn't have come on foot then, he thought vaguely. Somewhere in the absolute stillness of the dawn—it couldn't have been more than a quarter of a mile away—a horse whinnied.

He got on his feet—Maria stood at his elbow; she said: "The cloth, father, give me the cloth." He put the Host hurriedly into his mouth and drank the wine: one had to avoid profanation: the cloth was whipped away from the packing-case. She nipped the candles, so that the wick should not leave a smell . . . the room was already cleared, only the owner hung by the entrance waiting to kiss his hand: through the door the world was faintly visible, and a cock in the village crowed.

Maria said: "Come to the hut quickly."

"I'd better go." He was without a plan. "Not be found here."

"They are all round the village."

Was this the end at last? he wondered. Somewhere fear waited to spring at him, he knew, but he wasn't afraid yet. He followed the woman, scurrying across the village to her hut, repeating an act of contrition mechanically as he went. He wondered when the fear would start: he had been afraid when the policeman opened his case—but that was years ago. He had been afraid hiding in the shed among the bananas, hearing the child argue with the police officer —that was only a few weeks away. Fear would undoubtedly begin again soon. There was no sign of the police— only the grey morning, and the chickens and turkeys stirring, flopping down from the trees in which they had roosted during the night. Again the cock crew. If they were so careful, they must know beyond the shadow of doubt that he was here. It *was* the end.

Maria plucked at him. "Get in. Quick. Onto the bed." Presumably she had an idea—women were appallingly practical: they built new plans at once out of the ruins of the old. But what was the good? She said: "Let me smell your breath. Oh, God, anyone can tell . . . wine . . . what would we be doing with wine?" She was gone again, inside, making a lot of bother in the peace and quiet of the dawn. Suddenly, out of the forest, a hundred yards away, an officer rode. In the absolute stillness you could hear the creaking of his revolver-holster as he turned and waved.

All round the little clearing the police appeared—they must have marched very quickly, for only the officer had a horse. Rifles at the trail, they approached the small group of huts—an exaggerated and rather absurd show of force. One man had a puttee trailing behind him—it had probably caught on something in the forest. He tripped on it and fell with a great clatter of cartridge-belt on gunstock: the lieutenant on the horse looked round and then turned his bitter and angry face upon the silent huts.

The woman was pulling at him from inside the hut. She said: "Bite this. Quick. There's no time . . ." He turned his back on the advancing police and came into the dusk of the room. She had a small raw onion in her hand. "Bite it," she said. He bit it and began to weep. "Is that better?" she said. He could hear the pad, pad of the cautious horse hoofs advancing between the huts.

"It's horrible," he said with a giggle.

"Give it to me." She made it disappear somewhere into

her clothes: it was a trick all women seemed to know. He said: "Where's my case?"

"Never mind your case. Get onto the bed."

But before he could move, a horse blocked the doorway: they could see a leg in riding-boots piped with scarlet: brass fittings gleamed: a hand in a glove rested on the high pommel. Maria put a hand upon his arm—it was as near as she had ever come to a movement of affection: affection was taboo between them. A voice cried: "Come on out, all of you." The horse stamped and a little pillar of dust went up. "Come on out, I said"—somewhere a shot was fired. The priest left the hut.

The dawn had really broken: light feathers of colour were blown up the sky: a man still held his gun pointed upwards: a little balloon of grey smoke hung at the muzzle. Was this how the agony was to start?

Out of all the huts the villagers were reluctantly emerging—the children first: they were curious and not frightened. The men and women had the air already of people condemned by authority—authority was never wrong. None of them looked at the priest. They stared at the ground and waited: only the children watched the horse as if it was the most important thing there.

The lieutenant said: "Search the huts." Time passed very slowly: even the smoke of the shot seemed to remain in the air for an unnatural period. Some pigs came grunting out of a hut, and a turkey-cock paced with evil dignity into the centre of the circle, puffing out its dusty feathers and tossing the long pink membrane from its beak. A soldier came up to the lieutenant and saluted sketchily. He said: "They're all here."

"You've found nothing suspicious?"

"No."

"Then look again."

Once more time stopped like a broken clock. The lieutenant drew out a cigarette-case, hesitated and put it back again. Again the policeman approached and reported: "Nothing."

The lieutenant barked out: "Attention. All of you. Listen to me." The outer ring of police closed in, pushing the villagers together into a small group in front of the lieutenant: only the children were left free. The priest saw his own child standing close to the lieutenant's horse: she could just reach above his boot: she put up her hand and touched the leather. The lieutenant said: "I am looking for two men—one is a gringo, a Yankee, a murderer. I can see very well he is not here. There is a reward of five hundred pesos for his capture. Keep your eyes open." He paused and ran his eye over them: the priest felt his gaze come to rest; he looked down like the others at the ground.

"The other," the lieutenant said, "is a priest." He raised his voice: "You know what this means—traitor to the republic. Anyone who shelters him is a traitor too." Their immobility seemed to anger him. He said: "You're fools if you still believe what the priests tell you. All they want is your money. What has God ever done for you? Have you got enough to eat? Have your children got enough to eat? Instead of food they talk to you about heaven. Oh, everything will be fine after you are dead, they say. I tell you—everything will be fine when *they* are dead, and you must help." The child had her hand on his boot. He looked down at her with dark affection. He said with conviction: "This child is worth more than the Pope in Rome." The police leant on their guns: one of them yawned—the turkey-cock went hissing back towards the huts. The lieutenant said: "If you've seen this priest, speak up. There's a reward of seven hundred pesos. . . ."

Nobody spoke.

The lieutenant yanked his horse's head round towards them; he said: "We know he's in this district. Perhaps you don't know what happened to a man in Concepción." One of the women began to weep. He said: "Come up—one after the other—and let me have your names. No, not the women, the men."

They filed sullenly up and he questioned them: "What's your name? What do you do? Married? Which is your wife? Have you heard of this priest?" Only one man now stood between the priest and the horse's head. He recited an act of contrition silently with only half a mind— ". . . my sins, because they have crucified my loving Saviour . . . but above all because they have offended . . ." He was alone in front of the lieutenant—"I hereby resolve never more to offend Thee . . ." It was a formal act, because a man had to be prepared: it was like making your will—and might be as valueless.

"Your name?"

The name of the man in Concepción came back to him. He said: "Montez."

"Have you ever seen the priest?"

"No."

"What do you do?"

"I have a little land."

"Are you married?"

"Yes."

"Which is your wife?"

Maria suddenly broke out: "It's me. Why do you want to ask so many questions. Do you think *he* looks like a priest?"

The lieutenant was examining something on the pommel of his saddle: it seemed to be an old photograph. "Let me see your hands," he said.

The priest held them up: they were as hard as a labourer's. Suddenly the lieutenant leant down from the saddle and sniffed at his breath. There was complete silence among the villagers—a dangerous silence, because it seemed to convey to the lieutenant a fear. . . . He stared back at the hollow stubbled face, looked back at the photograph. "All right," he said, "next," and then as the priest stepped aside: "Wait." He put his hand down to Brigida's head and gently tugged at her black stiff hair. He said: "Look up. You know everyone in this village, don't you?"

"Yes," she said.

"Who's that man, then? What's his name?"

"I don't know," the child said. The lieutenant caught his breath. "You don't know his name?" he said. "Is he a stranger?"

Maria cried: "Why, the child doesn't know her own name! Ask her who her father is."

"Who's your father?"

The child stared up at the lieutenant and then turned her knowing eyes upon the priest. . . . "Sorry and beg pardon for all my sins," he was repeating to himself with his fingers crossed for luck. The child said: "That's him. There."

"All right," the lieutenant said. "Next." The interrogations went on—name? work? married?—while the sun came up above the forest. The priest stood with his hands clasped in front of him: again death had been postponed: he felt an enormous temptation to throw himself in front of the lieutenant and declare himself—"I am the one you want." Would they shoot him out of hand? A delusive promise of peace tempted him. Far up in the sky a buzzard watched: they must appear from that height as two groups of carnivorous animals who might at any time break into conflict, and it waited there, a tiny black spot, for carrion. Death was not the end of pain—to believe in peace was a kind of heresy.

The last man gave his evidence.

The lieutenant said: "Is no one willing to help?"

They stood silent beside the decayed bandstand. He said: "You heard what happened at Concepción. I took a hostage there . . . and when I found that this priest had been in the neighbourhood I put the man against the nearest tree. I found out because there's always someone who changes his mind—perhaps because somebody at Concepción loved the man's wife and wanted him out of the way. It's not my business to look into reasons. I only know we found wine later in Concepción. . . . Perhaps there's somebody in this village who wants your piece of land—or your cow. It's much safer to speak now. Because I'm going to take a hostage from here too." He paused. Then he said: "There's no need even to speak, if he's here among you. Just look at him. No one will know then that it was you who gave him away. He won't know himself if you're afraid of his curses. Now . . . this is your last chance."

The priest looked at the ground—he wasn't going to make it difficult for the man who gave him away.

"Right," the lieutenant said, "then I shall choose my man. You've brought it on yourselves."

He sat on his horse watching them—one of the policemen had leant his gun against the bandstand and was doing up a puttee. The villagers still stared at the ground: everyone was afraid to catch his eye. He broke out suddenly: "Why won't you trust me? I don't want any of you to die. In my eyes—can't you understand?—you are worth far more than he is. I want to give you"—he made a gesture with his hands which was valueless, because no one saw him—"everything." He said in a dull voice: "You. You there. I'll take you."

A woman screamed: "That's my boy. That's Miguel. You can't take my boy."

He said dully: "Every man here is somebody's husband or somebody's son. I know that."

The priest stood silently with his hands clasped: his knuckles whitened as he gripped . . . he could feel all round him the beginning of hate. Because he was no one's husband or son. He said: "Lieutenant . . ."

"What do you want?"

"I'm getting too old to be much good in the fields. Take me."

A rout of pigs came rushing round the corner of a hut, taking no notice of anybody. The soldier finished his puttee and stood up. The sunlight coming up above the forest winked on the bottles of the gaseosa stall.

The lieutenant said: "I'm choosing a hostage, not offering free board and lodging to the lazy. If you are no good in the fields, you are no good as a hostage." He gave an order. "Tie the man's hands and bring him along."

It took no time at all for the police to be gone—they took with them two or three chickens, a turkey, and the man called Miguel. The priest said aloud: "I did my best." He went on: "It's *your* job—to give me up. What do you expect me to do? It's my job not to be caught."

One of the men said: "That's all right, father. Only will you be careful . . . to see that you don't leave any wine behind . . . like you did at Concepción?"

Another said: "It's no good staying, father. They'll get you in the end. They won't forget your face again. Better go north, to the mountains. Over the border."

"It's a fine state over the border," a woman said. "They've still got churches there. Nobody can go in them, of course—but they are there. Why, I've heard that there are priests too in the towns. A cousin of mine went over the mountains to Las Casas once and heard Mass—in a house, with a proper altar, and the priest all dressed up like in the old days. You'd be happy there, father."

The priest followed Maria to the hut. The bottle of brandy lay on the table: he touched it with his fingers—there wasn't much left. He said: "My case, Maria? Where's my case?"

"It's too dangerous to carry that around any more," Maria said.

"How else can I take the wine?"

"There isn't any wine."

"What do you mean?"

She said: "I'm not going to bring trouble on you and

everyone else. I've broken the bottle. Even if it brings a curse . . ."

He said gently and sadly: "You musn't be superstitious. That was simply—wine. There's nothing sacred in wine. Only it's hard to get hold of here. That's why I kept a store of it in Concepción. But they've found that."

"Now perhaps you'll go—go away altogether. You're no good any more to anyone," she said fiercely. "Don't you understand, father? We don't want you any more."

"Oh, yes," he said. "I understand. But it's not what you want—or I want . . ."

She said savagely: "I know about things. I went to school. I'm not like these others—ignorant. I know you're a bad priest. That time we were together—I bet that wasn't all you've done. I've heard things, I can tell you. Do you think God wants you to stay and die—a whisky priest like you?" He stood patiently in front of her, as he had stood in front of the lieutenant, listening. He hadn't known she was capable of all this thought. She said: "Suppose you die. You'll be a martyr, won't you? What kind of a martyr do you think you'll make? It's enough to make people mock."

That had never occurred to him—that anybody would consider him a martyr. He said: "It's difficult. Very difficult. I'll think about it. I wouldn't want the Church to be mocked. . . ."

"Think about it over the border then . . ."

"Well . . ."

She said: "When you-know-what happened, I was proud. I thought the good days would come back. It's not everyone who's a priest's woman. And the child . . . I thought you could do a lot for her. But you might as well be a thief for all the good . . ."

He said vaguely: "There've been a lot of good thieves."

"For God's sake take this brandy and go."

"There was one thing," he said. "In my case . . . there was something . . ."

"Go and find it yourself on the rubbish-tip then. I won't touch it again."

"And the child," he said, "you're a good woman, Maria. I mean—you'll try and bring her up well . . . as a Christian."

"She'll never be good for anything, you can see that."

"She can't be very bad—at her age," he implored her.

"She'll go on the way she's begun."

He said: "The next Mass I say will be for her."

She wasn't even listening. She said: "She's bad through and through." He was aware of faith dying out between the bed and the door—the Mass would soon mean no more to anyone than a black cat crossing the path. He was risking all their lives for the sake of spilt salt, or a crossed finger. He began: "My mule . . ."

"They are giving it maize now."

She added: "You'd better go north. There's no chance to the south any more."

"I thought perhaps Carmen . . ."

"They'll be watching there."

"Oh, well . . ." He said sadly: "Perhaps one day . . . when things are better . . ." He sketched a cross and blessed her, but she stood impatiently before him, willing him to be gone for ever.

"Well, good-bye, Maria."

"Good-bye."

He walked across the plaza with his shoulders hunched: he felt that there wasn't a soul in the place who wasn't watching him with satisfaction—the trouble-maker whom for obscure and superstitious reasons they preferred not to betray to the police; he felt envious of the unknown gringo whom they wouldn't hesitate to trap—he at any rate had no burden of gratitude to carry round with him.

Down a slope churned up with the hoofs of mules and ragged with tree-roots there was the river—not more than two feet deep, littered with empty cans and broken bottles. Under a notice which hung on a tree reading: "It is forbidden to deposit rubbish . . ." all the refuse of the village was collected and slid gradually down into the river. When the rains came it would be washed away. He put his foot among the old tins and the rotting vegetables and reached for his case. He sighed: it had been quite a good case: one more relic of the quiet past. . . . Soon it would be difficult to remember that life had ever been any different. The lock had been torn off: he felt inside the silk lining. . . .

The papers were there: reluctantly he let the case fall —a whole important and respected youth dropped among the cans—he had been given it by his parishioners in Concepción on the fifth anniversary of his ordination. . . . Somebody moved behind a tree. He lifted his feet out of the rubbish—flies buzzed round his ankles. With the papers hidden in his fist he came round the trunk to see who was spying. . . . The child sat on a root, kicking her heels against the bark. Her eyes were shut tight fast. He said: "My dear, what is the matter with you . . . ?" They came quickly open—red-rimmed and angry, with an expression of absurd pride.

She said: "You . . . you . . ."

"Me?"

"You are the matter."

He moved towards her with infinite caution, as if she were an animal who distrusted him. He felt weak with longing. He said: "My dear, why me . . . ?"

She said furiously: "They laugh at me."

"Because of me?"

She said: "Everyone else has a father . . . who works."

"I work too."

"You're a priest, aren't you?"

"Yes."

"Pedro says you aren't a man. You aren't any good for women." She said: "I don't know what he means."

"I don't suppose he knows himself."

"Oh, yes, he does," she said. "He's ten. And I want to know. You're going away, aren't you?"

"Yes."

He was appalled again by her maturity, as she whipped up a smile from a large and varied stock. She said: "Tell me—" enticingly. She sat there on the trunk of the tree by the rubbish-tip with an effect of abandonment. The world was in her heart already, like the small spot of decay in a fruit. She was without protection—she had no grace, no charm to plead for her; his heart was shaken by the conviction of loss. He said: "My dear, be careful . . ."

"What of? Why are you going away?"

He came a little nearer: he thought—a man may kiss his own daughter: but she started away from him. "Don't you touch me," she screeched at him in her ancient voice, and giggled. Every child was born with some kind of knowledge of love, he thought; they took it with the milk at the breast: but on parents and friends depended the kind of love they knew—the saving or the damning kind. Lust too was a kind of love. He saw her fixed in her life like a fly in amber—Maria's hand raised to strike: Pedro talking prematurely in the dusk: and the police beating the forest—violence everywhere. He prayed silently: "O God, give me any kind of death—without contrition, in a state of sin—only save this child."

He was a man who was supposed to save souls: it had seemed quite simple once, preaching at Benediction, organizing the guilds, having coffee with elderly ladies behind barred windows, blessing new houses with a little incense, wearing black gloves . . . it was as easy as saving money: now it was a mystery. He was aware of his own desperate inadequacy.

He went down on his knees and pulled her to him, while she giggled and struggled to be free. He said: "I love you. I am your father and I love you. Try to understand that." He held her tightly by the wrist and suddenly she stayed still, looking up at him. He said: "I would give my life, that's nothing, my soul . . . my dear, my dear, try to understand that you are—so important." That was the difference, he had always known, between his faith and theirs, the political leaders of the people who cared only for things like the state, the republic: this child was more important than a whole continent. He said: "You must take care of yourself because you are so—necessary. The President up in the capital goes guarded by men with guns—

but, my child, you have all the angels of heaven—" She stared back at him out of dark and unconscious eyes: he had a sense that he had come too late. He said: "Good-bye, my dear," and clumsily kissed her—a silly infatuated age-ing man, who as soon as he released her and started pad-ding back to the plaza could feel behind his hunched shoul-ders the whole vile world coming round the child to ruin her. His mule was there, saddled, by the gaseosa stall. A man said: "Better go north, father," and stood waving his hand. One mustn't have human affections—or rather one must love every soul as if it were one's own child. The pas-sion to protect must extend itself over a world—but he felt it tethered and aching like a hobbled animal to the tree trunk. He turned his mule south.

He was travelling in the actual track of the police: so long as he went slowly and didn't overtake any stragglers it seemed a fairly safe route. What he needed now was wine—and it had to be made with grapes: without it he was useless; he might as well escape north into the moun-tains and the safe state beyond, where the worst that could happen to him was a fine and a few days in prison because he couldn't pay. But he wasn't ready yet for the final sur-render—every small surrender had to be paid for in a further endurance, and now he felt the need of somehow ransoming his child. He would stay another month, an-other year . . . jogging up and down on the mule he tried to bribe God with promises of firmness. . . . The mule sud-denly dug in its hoofs and stopped dead: a tiny green snake raised itself like an affronted woman on the path and then hissed away into the grass like a match-flame. The mule went on.

When he came near a village he would stop the mule and advance as close as he could on foot—the police might have stopped there—then he would ride quickly through, speaking to nobody beyond a *buenos días*, and again on the forest path he would pick up the track of the lieutenant's horse. He had no clear idea now about anything: he only wanted to put as great a distance as possible between him and the village where he had spent the night. In one hand he still carried the scrumpled ball of paper. Somebody had tied a bunch of about fifty bananas to his saddle, beside the machete and the small bag which contained his store of candles, and every now and then he ate one—ripe, brown, and sodden, tasting of soap. It left a smear like a moustache over his mouth.

After six hours' travelling he came to La Candelaria, which lay, a long mean tin-roofed village, beside one of the tributaries of the Grijalva River. He came cautiously out into the dusty street—it was early afternoon: the buzzards sat on the roofs with their small heads hidden from the sun, and a few men lay in hammocks in the narrow shade the houses cast. The mule plodded forward very slowly through the heavy day. The priest leant forward on his pommel.

The mule came to a stop of its own accord beside a hammock: a man lay in it, bunched diagonally, with one leg trailing to keep the hammock moving, up and down, up and down, making a tiny current of air. The priest said: *"Buenas tardes."* The man opened his eyes and watched him.

"How far is it to Carmen?"

"Three leagues."

"Can I get a canoe across the river?"

"Yes."

"Where?"

The man waved a languid hand—as much as to say anywhere but here. He had only two teeth left—canines which stuck yellowly out at either end of his mouth like the teeth of long-extinct animals which you find enclosed in clay.

"What were the police doing here?" the priest asked, and a cloud of flies came down, settling on the mule's neck: he poked at them with a stick and they rose heavily, leaving a small trickle of blood, and dropped again on the tough grey skin. The mule seemed to feel nothing, standing in the sun with its head drooping.

"Looking for someone," the man said.

"I've heard," the priest said, "that there's a reward out —for a gringo."

The man swung his hammock back and forth. He said: "It's better to be alive and poor than rich and dead."

"Can I overtake them if I go towards Carmen?"

"They aren't going to Carmen."

"No?"

"They are making for the city."

The priest rode on: twenty yards farther he stopped again beside a gaseosa stall and asked the boy in charge: "Can I get a boat across the river?"

"There isn't a boat."

"No boat?"

"Somebody stole it."

"Give me a sidral." He drank down the yellow, bubbly chemical liquid: it left him thirstier than before. He said: "How do I get across?"

"Why do you want to get across?"

"I'm making for Carmen. How did the police get over?"

"They swam."

"*Mula. Mula,*" the priest said, urging the mule on, past the inevitable bandstand and a statue in florid taste of a woman in a toga waving a wreath: part of the pedestal had been broken off and lay in the middle of the road—the mule went round it. The priest looked back: far down the street the mestizo was sitting upright in the hammock watching him. The mule turned off down a steep path to the river, and again the priest looked back—the half-caste was still in the hammock, but he had both feet upon the ground. An habitual uneasiness made the priest beat at the mule—"*Mula. Mula*"—but the mule took its time, sliding down the bank towards the river.

By the riverside it refused to enter the water: the priest split the end of his stick with his teeth and jabbed a sharp point into the mule's flank. It waded reluctantly in, and the water rose—to the stirrups and then to the knees: the mule began to swim, splayed out flat with only the eyes and nostrils visible, like an alligator. Somebody shouted from the bank.

The priest looked round: at the river's edge the mestizo stood and called, not very loudly: his voice didn't carry. It was as if he had a secret purpose which nobody but the priest must hear. He waved his arm, summoning the priest back, but the mule lurched out of the water and up the bank beyond and the priest paid no attention—uneasiness was lodged in his brain. He urged the mule forward through the green half-light of a banana grove, not looking behind. All these years there had been two places to which he could always return and rest safely in hiding— one had been Concepción, his old parish, and that was closed to him now: the other was Carmen, where he had been born and where his parents were buried. He had imagined there might be a third, but he would never go back now. . . . He turned the mule's head towards Carmen, and the forest took them again. At this rate they would arrive in the dark, which was what he wanted. The mule, unbeaten, went with extreme languor, head drooping, smelling a little of blood. The priest, leaning forward on the high pommel, fell asleep. He dreamed that a small girl in stiff white muslin was reciting her Catechism—somewhere in the background there was a bishop and a group of Children of Mary, elderly women with grey hard pious faces wearing pale blue ribbons. The bishop said: "Excellent . . . excellent," and clapped his hands, plop, plop. A man in a morning coat said: "There's a deficit of five hundred pesos on the new organ. We propose to hold a special musical performance, when it is hoped . . ." He remembered with appalling suddenness that he oughtn't to be there at all . . . he was in the wrong parish . . . he should be holding a retreat at Concepción. The man Montez appeared behind the child in white muslin, gesticulating, reminding him. . . . Something had happened to Montez, he had a dry wound on his forehead. He felt with dreadful certainty a threat to the child. He said: "My dear, my dear," and woke to the slow rolling stride of the mule and the sound of footsteps.

He turned: it was the mestizo, padding behind him, dripping water: he must have swum the river. His two teeth stuck out over his lower lip, and he grinned ingratiatingly.

"What do you want?" the priest said sharply.

"You didn't tell me you were going to Carmen."

"Why should I?"

"You see, I want to go to Carmen, too. It's better to travel in company." He was wearing a shirt, a pair of white trousers, and gym shoes through which one big toe showed—plump and yellow like something which lives underground. He scratched himself under the armpits and came chummily up to the priest's stirrup. He said: "You are not offended, Señor?"

"Why do you call me Señor?"

"Anyone can tell you're a man of education."

"The forest is free to all," the priest said.

"Do you know Carmen well?" the man said.

"Not well. I have a few friends."

"You're going on business, I suppose?"

The priest said nothing. He could feel the man's hand on his foot, a light and deprecating touch. The man said: "There's a *finca* off the road two leagues from here. It would be as well to stay the night."

"I am in a hurry," the priest said.

"But what good would it be reaching Carmen at one, two in the morning? We could sleep at the *finca* and be there before the sun was high."

"I do what suits me."

"Of course, Señor, of course." The man was silent for a little while, and then said: "It isn't wise travelling at night if the Señor hasn't got a gun. It's different for a man like me . . ."

"I am a poor man," the priest said. "You can see for yourself. I am not worth robbing."

"And then there's the gringo—they say he's a wild kind of a man, a real *pistolero*. He comes up to you and says in his own language—Stop: what is the way to—well, some place, and you do not understand what he is saying and perhaps you make a movement and he shoots you dead. But perhaps you know Americano, Señor?"

"Of course I don't. How should I? I am a poor man. But I don't listen to every fairy-tale."

"Do you come from far?"

The priest thought a moment: "Concepción." He could do no more harm there.

The man for the time being seemed satisfied. He walked along by the mule, a hand on the stirrup: every now and then he spat: when the priest looked down he could see the big toe moving like a grub along the ground—he was probably harmless. It was the general condition of life that made for suspicion. The dusk fell and then almost at once the dark. The mule moved yet more slowly. Noise broke out all round them: it was like a theatre when the curtain falls and behind in the wings and passages hubbub begins. Things you couldn't put a name to—jaguars perhaps—cried in the undergrowth, monkeys moved in the upper boughs, and the mosquitoes hummed all round like sewing machines. "It's thirsty walking," the man said. "Have you by any chance, Señor, got a little drink . . . ?"

"No."

"If you want to reach Carmen before three, you will have to beat the mule. Shall I take the stick . . . ?"

"No, no, let the poor brute take its time. It doesn't matter to me . . ." he said drowsily.

"You talk like a priest."

He came quickly awake, but under the tall dark trees he could see nothing. He said: "What nonsense you talk."

"I am a very good Christian," the man said, stroking the priest's foot.

"I dare say. I wish I were."

"Ah, you ought to be able to tell the people you can trust." He spat in a comradely way.

"I have nothing to trust anyone with," the priest said. "Except these trousers—they are very torn. And this mule—it isn't a good mule; you can see for yourself."

There was silence for a while, and then as if he had been considering the last statement the half-caste went on: "It wouldn't be a bad mule if you treated it right. Nobody can teach me anything about mules. I can see for myself it's tired out."

The priest looked down at the grey swinging stupid head. "Do you think so?"

"How far did you travel yesterday?"

"Perhaps twelve leagues."

"Even a mule needs rest."

The priest took his bare feet out of the deep leather stirrups and scrambled to the ground. The mule for less than a minute took a longer stride and then dropped to a yet slower pace. The twigs and roots of the forest path cut the priest's feet—after five minutes he was bleeding.

He tried in vain not to limp. The half-caste exclaimed:
"How delicate your feet are! You should wear shoes."

Stubbornly he reasserted: "I am a poor man."

"You will never get to Carmen at this rate. Be sensible,
man. If you don't want to go as far off the road as the
finca, I know a little hut less than half a league from here.
We can sleep a few hours and still reach Carmen at day-
break." There was a rustle in the grass beside the path—
the priest thought of snakes and his unprotected feet. The
mosquitoes jabbed at his wrists: they were like little surgi-
cal syringes filled with poison and aimed at the blood-
stream. Sometimes a firefly held its lighted globe close to
the half-caste's face, turning it on and off like a torch. He
said accusingly: "You don't trust me. Just because I am
a man who likes to do a good turn to strangers, because I
try to be a Christian, you don't trust me." He seemed to
be working himself into a little artificial rage. He said: "If
I had wanted to rob you, couldn't I have done it already?
You're an old man."

"Not so very old," the priest said mildly. His conscience
began automatically to work: it was like a slot machine
into which any coin could be fitted, even a cheater's blank
disk. The words proud, lustful, envious, cowardly, un-
grateful—they all worked the right springs—he was all
these things. The half-caste said: "Here I have spent
many hours guiding you to Carmen—I don't want any
reward because I am a good Christian: I have probably
lost money by it at home—never mind that . . ."

"I thought you said you had business in Carmen?" the
priest said gently.

"When did I say that?" It was true—he couldn't re-

member . . . perhaps he was unjust too. . . . "Why should
I say a thing which isn't true? No, I give up a whole day
to helping you, and you pay no attention when your guide
is tired. . . ."

"I didn't need a guide," he protested mildly.

"You say that when the road is plain, but if it wasn't
for me, you'd have taken the wrong path a long time ago.
You said yourself you didn't know Carmen well. That was
why I came."

"But of course," the priest said, "if you are tired, we
will rest." He felt guilty at his own lack of trust, but all
the same, it remained like a growth only a knife could rid
him of.

After half an hour they came to the hut: made of mud
and twigs, it had been set up in a minute clearing by a
small farmer the forest must have driven out, edging in
on him, an unstayable natural force which he couldn't defeat with his machete and his small fires. There were still
signs in the blackened ground of an attempt to clear the
brushwood for some meagre, limited, and inadequate crop.
The man said: "I will see to the mule. You go in and lie
down and rest."

"But it is you who are tired."

"Me tired?" the half-caste said. "What makes you say
that? I am never tired."

With a heavy heart the priest took off his saddle-bag,
pushed at the door and went in—to complete darkness:
he struck a light—there was no furniture: only a raised
dais of hard earth and a straw mat too torn to have been
worth removing. He lit a candle and stuck it in its own
wax on the dais: then sat down and waited: the man was a

long time. In one fist he still carried the ball of paper sal-
vaged from his case—a man must retain some sentimental
relics if he is to live at all. The argument of danger applies
only to those who live in safety. He wondered whether
the mestizo had stolen his mule, and reproached himself
for the necessary suspicion. Then the door opened and the
man came in—the two yellow canine teeth, the finger-nails
scratching in the armpit. He sat down on the earth, with
his back against the door, and said: "Go to sleep. You are
tired. I'll wake you when we need to start."

"I'm not very sleepy."

"Blow out the candle. You'll sleep better."

"I don't like darkness," the priest said. He was afraid.

"Won't you say a prayer, father, before we sleep?"

"Why do you call me that?" he said sharply, peering
across the shadowy floor to where the half-caste sat against
the door.

"Oh, I guessed, of course. But you needn't be afraid of
me. I'm a good Christian."

"You're wrong."

"I could easily find out, couldn't I?" the half-caste said.
"I'd just have to say—father, hear my confession. You
couldn't refuse a man in mortal sin."

The priest said nothing, waiting for the demand to
come: the hand which held the papers trembled. "Oh, you
needn't fear me," the mestizo went carefully on. "I
wouldn't betray you. I'm a Christian. I just thought a
prayer . . . would be good . . ."

"You don't need to be a priest to know a prayer." He
began: "*Pater noster qui es in coelis . . .*" while the mosquitoes came droning towards the candle-flame. He was

determined not to sleep—the man had some plan: even his conscience ceased to accuse him of uncharity. He knew. He was in the presence of Judas.

He leant his head back against the wall and half closed his eyes—he remembered Holy Week in the old days when a stuffed Judas was hanged from the belfry and boys made a clatter with tins and rattles as he swung out over the door. Old staid members of the congregation had sometimes raised objections: it was blasphemous, they said, to make this guy out of Our Lord's betrayer; but he had said nothing and let the practice continue—it seemed to him a good thing that the world's traitor should be made a figure of fun. It was too easy otherwise to idealize him as a man who fought with God—a Prometheus, a noble victim in a hopeless war.

"Are you awake?" a voice whispered from the door. The priest suddenly giggled—as if this man, too, were absurd with stuffed straw legs and a painted face and an old straw hat who would presently be burnt in the plaza while people made political speeches and the fireworks went off.

"Can't you sleep?"

"I was dreaming," the priest whispered. He opened his eyes and saw the man by the door was shivering—the two sharp teeth jumped up and down on the lower lip. "Are you ill?"

"A little fever," the man said. "Have you any medicine?"

"No."

The door creaked as the man's back shook. He said: "It was getting wet in the river . . ." He slid farther down upon the floor and closed his eyes—mosquitoes with singed wings crawled over the earth bed. The priest thought: I mustn't sleep, it's dangerous, I must watch him. He opened his fist and smoothed out the paper. There were faint pencil lines visible—single words, the beginnings and ends of sentences, figures. Now that his case was gone, it was the only evidence left that life had ever been different: he carried it with him as a charm—because if life had been like that once, it might be so again. The candle-flame in the hot marshy lowland air burned to a smoky point, vibrating. . . . The priest held the paper close to it and read the words Altar Society, Guild of the Blessed Sacrament, Children of Mary, and then looked up again and across the dark hut, saw the yellow malarial eyes of the mestizo watching him. Christ would not have found Judas sleeping in the garden: Judas could watch more than one hour.

"What's that paper . . . father?" he said enticingly, shivering against the door.

"Don't call me father. It is a list of seeds I have to buy in Carmen."

"Can you write?"

"I can read."

He looked at the paper again and a little mild impious joke stared up at him in faded pencil—something about "of one substance." He had been referring to his corpulency and the good dinner he had just eaten: the parishioners had not much relished his humour.

It had been a dinner given at Concepción in honour of the tenth anniversary of his ordination. He sat in the middle of the table with—who was it on his right hand? There

were twelve dishes—he had said something about the
Apostles, too, which was not thought to be in the best of
taste. He was quite young and he had been moved by a
gentle devilry, surrounded by all the pious and middle-
aged and respectable people of Concepción, wearing their
guild ribbons and badges. He had drunk just a little too
much: in those days he wasn't used to liquor. It came back
to him now suddenly who was on his right hand—it was
Montez, the father of the man they had shot.

Montez had talked at some length. He had reported the
progress of the Altar Society in the last year—they had a
balance in hand of twenty-two pesos. He had noted it
down for comment—there it was, A.S. 22. Montez had
been very anxious to start a branch of the Society of St.
Vincent de Paul—and some woman had complained that
bad books were being sold in Concepción, fetched from
the capital by mule: her child had got hold of one called *A
Husband for a Night*. In his speech he said he would write
to the Governor on the subject.

The moment he had said that the local photographer
had set off his flare, and so he could remember himself at
that instant, just as if he had been a stranger looking in
from the outside—attracted by the noise—on some happy
and festal and strange occasion: noticing with envy, and
perhaps a little amusement, the fat youngish priest who
stood with one plump hand splayed authoritatively out
while the tongue played pleasantly with the word "Governor." Mouths were open all round—fishily, and the faces
glowed magnesium-white, with all the lines and individuality wiped out.

That moment of authority had jerked him back to seriousness—he had ceased to unbend and everybody was happier. He said: "The balance of twenty-two pesos in the accounts of the Altar Society—though quite revolutionary for Concepción—is not the only cause for congratulation in the last year. The Children of Mary have increased their membership by nine—and the Guild of the Blessed Sacrament last autumn made our annual retreat more than usually successful. But we mustn't rest on our laurels—and I confess I have got plans you may find a little startling. You already think me a man, I know, of inordinate ambitions—well, I want Concepción to have a better school—and that means a better presbytery too, of course. We are a big parish and the priest has a position to keep up. I'm not thinking of myself but of the Church. And we shall not stop there—though it will take a good many years, I'm afraid, even in a place the size of Concepción, to raise the money for that." As he talked a whole serene life lay ahead—he *had* ambition: he saw no reason why one day he might not find himself in the state capital, attached to the cathedral, leaving another man to pay off the debts in Concepción. An energetic priest was always known by his debts. He went on, waving a plump and eloquent hand: "Of course, many dangers here in Mexico threaten our dear Church. In this state we are unusually lucky—men have lost their lives in the north and we must be prepared"—he refreshed his dry mouth with a draught of wine—"for the worst. Watch and pray," he went vaguely on, "watch and pray. The devil like a raging lion—" The Children of Mary stared up at him with their mouths a little open, the pale blue ribbons slanting across their dark best blouses.

He talked for a long while, enjoying the sound of his own voice: he had discouraged Montez on the subject of the St. Vincent de Paul Society—because you had to be careful not to encourage a layman too far, and he had told a charming story about a child's deathbed—she was dying of consumption, very firm in her faith at the age of eleven. She asked who it was standing at the end of her bed, and they had said: "That's Father So-and-so," and she had said: "No, no. I know Father So-and-so. I mean the one with the golden crown." One of the Guild of the Blessed Sacrament had wept. Everybody was very happy. It was a true story too, though he couldn't quite remember where he had heard it. Perhaps he had read it in a book once. Somebody refilled his glass. He took a long breath and said: "My children . . ."

. . . and as the mestizo stirred and grunted by the door he opened his eyes and the old life peeled away like a label: he was lying in torn peon trousers in a dark unventilated hut with a price upon his head. The whole world had changed—no Church anywhere: no brother priest, except Padre José, the outcast, in the capital. He lay listening to the heavy breathing of the half-caste and wondered why he had not gone the same road as Padre José and conformed to the laws. I was too ambitious, he thought, that was it. Perhaps Padre José was the better man—he was so humble that he was ready to accept any amount of mockery: at the best of times he had never considered himself worthy of the priesthood. There had been a conference once of the parochial clergy in the capital—in the happy days of the old Governor, and he could remember Padre

José slinking in at the tail of every meeting, curled up half out of sight in a back row, never opening his mouth. It was not, like some more intellectual priests, that he was over-scrupulous: he had been simply filled with an overwhelming sense of God. At the Elevation of the Host you could see his hands trembling—he was not like St. Thomas, who needed to put his hands into the wounds in order to believe: the wounds bled anew for him over every altar. Once Padre José had said to him in a burst of confidence: "Every time . . . I have such fear." His father had been a peon.

But it was different in his case—he had ambition. He was no more an intellectual than Padre José, but his father was a storekeeper, and he knew the value of a balance of twenty-two pesos and how to manage mortgages. He wasn't content to remain all his life the priest of a not very large parish. His ambitions came back to him now as something faintly comic, and he gave a little gulp of astonished laughter in the candlelight. The half-caste opened his eyes and said: "Are you still not asleep?"

"Sleep yourself," the priest said, wiping a little sweat off his face with his sleeve.

"I am so cold."

"Just a fever. Would you like this shirt? It isn't much, but it might help."

"No, no. I don't want anything of yours. You don't trust me."

No, if he had been humble like Padre José, he might be living in the capital now with Maria on a pension. This was pride, devilish pride, lying here offering his shirt to the man who wanted to betray him. Even his attempts at escape had been half-hearted because of his pride—the sin by which the angels fell. When he was the only priest left in the state his pride had been all the greater; he thought himself the devil of a fellow carrying God around at the risk of his life; one day there would be a reward. . . . He prayed in the half-light: "O God, forgive me—I am a proud, lustful, greedy man. I have loved authority too much. These people are martyrs—protecting me with their own lives. They deserve a martyr to care for them— not a fool like me, who loves all the wrong things. Perhaps I had better escape—if I tell people how it is over here, perhaps they will send a good man with a fire of love . . ." As usual his self-confession dwindled away into the practical problem—what am I to do?

Over by the door the mestizo was uneasily asleep.

How little his pride had to feed on—he had celebrated only four Masses this year, and he had heard perhaps a hundred confessions. It seemed to him that the dunce of any seminary could have done as well . . . or better. He raised himself very carefully and began to move on his naked toes across the floor. He must get to Carmen and away again quickly before this man . . . the mouth was open, showing the pale hard toothless gums: in his sleep he was grunting and struggling; then he collapsed upon the floor and lay still.

There was a sense of abandonment, as if he had given up every struggle from now on and lay there a victim of some power. . . . The priest had only to step over his legs and push the door—it opened outwards.

He put one leg over the body and a hand gripped his
ankle. The mestizo stared up at him. "Where are you
going?"

"I want to relieve myself," the priest said.

The hand still held his ankle. "Why can't you do it
here?" the man whined at him. "What's preventing you,
father? You are a father, aren't you?"

"I have a child," the priest said, "if that's what you
mean."

"You know what I mean. You understand about God,
don't you?" The hot hand clung. "Perhaps you've got
him there—in a pocket. You carry him around, don't you,
in case there's anybody sick. . . . Well, I'm sick. Why don't
you give him to me? Or do you think he wouldn't have anything to do with me . . . if he knew?"

"You're feverish."

But the man wouldn't stop. The priest was reminded of
an oil-gusher which some prospectors had once struck near
Concepción—it wasn't a good enough field apparently to
justify further operations, but there it had stood for
forty-eight hours against the sky, a black fountain spout-
ing out of the marshy useless soil and flowing away to
waste—fifty thousand gallons an hour. It was like the religious sense in man, cracking suddenly upwards, a black
pillar of fumes and impurity, running to waste. "Shall I
tell you what I've done—it's your business to listen. I've
taken money from women to do you know what, and I've
given money to boys . . ."

"I don't want to hear."

"It's your business."

"You're mistaken."

"Oh, no, I'm not. You can't take me in. Listen. I've given money to boys—you know what I mean. And I've eaten meat on Fridays." The awful jumble of the gross, the trivial, and the grotesque shot up between the two yellow fangs, and the hand on the priest's ankle shook and shook with the fever. "I've told lies, I haven't fasted in Lent for I don't know how many years. Once I had two women—I'll tell you what I did . . ." He had an immense self-importance: he was unable to picture a world of which he was only a typical part—a world of treachery, violence, and lust in which his shame was altogether insignificant. How often the priest had heard the same confession—Man was so limited: he hadn't even the ingenuity to invent a new vice: the animals knew as much. It was for this world that Christ had died: the more evil you saw and heard about you, the greater glory lay around the death; it was too easy to die for what was good or beautiful, for home or children or a civilization—it needed a God to die for the half-hearted and the corrupt. He said: "Why do you tell me all this?"

The man lay exhausted, saying nothing: he was beginning to sweat, his hand loosed its hold on the priest's ankle. He pushed the door open and went outside—the darkness was complete. How to find the mule? He stood listening—something howled not very far away. He was frightened. Back in the hut the candle burned—there was an odd bubbling sound: the man was weeping. Again he was reminded of oil land, the little black pools and the bubbles blowing slowly up and breaking and beginning again.

The priest struck a match and walked straight forward —one, two, three paces into a tree. A match in that im-

mense darkness was of no more value than a firefly. He
whispered: *"Mula, mula,"* afraid to call out in case the
half-caste heard him; besides, it was unlikely that the stupid beast would make any reply. He hated it—the lurching mandarin head, the munching greedy mouth, the
smell of blood and ordure. He struck another match and
set off again, and again after a few paces he met a tree.
Inside the hut the gaseous sound of grief went on. He had
got to get to Carmen and away before that man found a
means of communicating with the police. He began again,
quartering the clearing—one, two, three, four—and then
a tree. Something moved under his foot, and he thought
of scorpions. One, two, three—and suddenly the grotesque
cry of the mule came out of the dark; it was hungry, or
perhaps it smelt some animal.

It was tethered a few yards behind the hut—the candle-
flame swerved out of sight. His matches were running low,
but after two more attempts he found the mule. The half-
caste had stripped it and hidden the saddle: he couldn't
waste time looking any more. He mounted, and only then
realized how impossible it was to make it move without
even a piece of rope round the neck—he tried twisting at
its ears, but they had no more sensitivity than door-
handles: it stood planted there like an equestrian statue.
He struck a match and held the flame against its side—it
struck up suddenly with its back hoofs and he dropped the
match: then it was still again, with drooping sullen head
and great antediluvian haunches. A voice said accusingly:
"You are leaving me here—to die."

"Nonsense," the priest said. "I am in a hurry. You will
be all right in the morning, but I can't wait."

There was a scuffle in the darkness and then a hand gripped his naked foot. "Don't leave me alone," the voice said. "I appeal to you—as a Christian."

"You won't come to any harm here."

"How do you know, with the gringo somewhere about?"

"I don't know anything about the gringo. I've met nobody who has seen him. Besides, he's only a man—like one of us."

"I won't be left alone. I have an instinct . . ."

"Very well," the priest said wearily, "find the saddle."

When they had saddled the mule they set off again, the mestizo holding the stirrup. They were silent—sometimes the half-caste stumbled, and the grey false dawn began; a small coal of cruel satisfaction glowed at the back of the priest's mind—this was Judas sick and unsteady and scared in the dark. He had only to beat the mule on to leave him stranded in the forest—once he dug in the point of his stick and forced it forward at a weary trot, and he could feel the pull, pull of the half-caste's arm on the stirrup, holding him back. There was a groan—it sounded like "Mother of God," and he let the mule slacken its pace. He prayed silently: "God forgive me": Christ had died for this man too: how could he pretend with his pride and lust and cowardice to be any more worthy of that death than this half-caste? This man intended to betray him for money which he needed, and he had betrayed God not even for real lust. He said: "Are you sick?" and there was no reply. He dismounted and said: "Get up. I'll walk for a while."

"I'm all right," the man said in a tone of hatred.

"Better get up."

"You think you're very fine," the man said. "Helping your enemies. That's Christian, isn't it?"

"Are you my enemy?"

"That's what you think. You think I want seven hundred pesos—that's the reward. You think a poor man like me can't afford not to tell the police. . . ."

"You're feverish."

The man said in a sick voice of cunning: "You're right, of course."

"Better mount." The man nearly fell: he had to shoulder him up. He leant hopelessly down from the mule with his mouth almost on a level with the priest's, breathing bad air into the other's face. He said: "A poor man has no choice, father. Now if I was a rich man—only a little rich —I should be good."

The priest suddenly—for no reason—thought of the Children of Mary eating pastries. He giggled and said: "I doubt it—" If that were goodness . . .

"What was that you said, father? You don't trust me," he went ambling on, "because I'm poor, and because you don't trust me—" He collapsed over the pommel of the saddle, breathing heavily and shivering. The priest held him on with one hand and they proceeded slowly towards Carmen. It was no good: he couldn't stay there now: it would be unwise even to enter the village; for if it became known, somebody would lose his life—they would take a hostage. Somewhere a long way off a cock crew: the mist came up knee-high out of the spongy ground, and he thought of the flashlight going off in the bare church hall among the trestle tables. What hour did the cocks crow? One of the oddest things about the world these days was that there were no clocks—you could go a year without hearing one strike. They went with the churches, and you were left with the grey slow dawns and the precipitate nights as the only measurements of time.

Slowly, slumped over the pommel, the half-caste became visible, the yellow canines jutting out of the open mouth; really, the priest thought, he deserved his reward—seven hundred pesos wasn't so much, but he could probably live on it—in that dusty hopeless village—for a whole year. He giggled again: he could never take the complications of destiny quite seriously; and it was quite possible, he thought, that a year without anxiety might save this man's soul. You only had to turn up the underside of any situation and out came scuttling these small absurd contradictory situations. He had given way to despair—and out of that had emerged a human soul and love—not the best love, but love all the same. The mestizo said suddenly: "It's fate. I was told once by a fortune-teller . . . a reward . . ."

He held the half-caste firmly in the saddle and walked on—his feet were bleeding, but they would soon harden. An odd stillness dropped over the forest, and welled up in mist from the ground. The night had been noisy, but now all was quiet. It was like an armistice with the guns silent on either side: you could imagine the whole world listening to what they had never heard before—peace.

A voice said: "You *are* the priest, aren't you?"

"Yes." It was as if they had climbed out of their opposing trenches and met in No Man's Land among the wire to fraternize. He remembered stories of the European war —how during the last years men had sometimes met—on

an impulse—between the lines. "Are *you* a German?" they
might have said, with incredulity at the similar face, or:
"Are you English?"

"Yes," he said again, and the mule plodded on. Sometimes, instructing children in the old days, he had been
asked by some black lozenge-eyed Indian child: "What is
God like?" and he would answer facilely with references to
the father and the mother, or perhaps more ambitiously
he would include brother and sister and try to give some
idea of all loves and relationships combined in an immense
and yet personal passion. . . . But at the centre of his own
faith there always stood the convincing mystery—that we
were made in God's image—God was the parent, but He
was also the policeman, the criminal, the priest, the maniac, and the judge. Something resembling God dangled
from the gibbet or went into odd attitudes before the bullets in a prison yard or contorted itself like a camel in the
attitude of sex. He would sit in the confessional and hear
the complicated dirty ingenuities which God's image had
thought out: and God's image shook now, up and down
on the mule's back, with the yellow teeth sticking out over
the lower lip; and God's image did its despairing act of
rebellion with Maria in the hut among the rats. It must
sometimes be a comfort to a soldier that the atrocities on
either side were equal: nobody was ever alone. He said:
"Do you feel better now? Not so cold, eh? Or so hot?" and
pressed his hand with a kind of driven tenderness upon
the shoulders of God's image.

The man didn't answer, as the mule's backbone slid him
first to one side, then the other.

"It isn't more than two leagues now," the priest said

encouragingly—he had to make up his mind. He carried around with him a clearer picture of Carmen than of any other village or town in the state; the long slope of grass which led up from the river to the cemetery on a tiny hill of perhaps twenty feet where his parents were buried. The wall of the burial-ground had fallen in: one or two crosses had been smashed by enthusiasts: an angel had lost one of its stone wings, and what grave-stones were left undamaged leant at an acute angle in the long marshy grass. One image of the Mother of God had lost ears and arms and stood like a pagan Venus over the grave of some rich, forgotten timber merchant. It was odd—this fury to deface, because, of course, you could never deface enough. If God had been like a toad, you could have rid the globe of toads, but when God was like yourself, it was no good being content with stone figures—you had to kill yourself among the graves.

He said: "Are you strong enough now to hold on?" He took away his hand. The path divided—one way led to Carmen, the other west. He pushed the mule on, down the Carmen path, flogging at its haunches. He said: "You'll be there in two hours," and stood watching the mule go on towards his home with the informer humped over the pommel.

The half-caste tried to sit upright. "Where are you going?"

"You'll be my witness," the priest said. "I haven't been in Carmen. But if you mention me—they'll give you food."

"Why . . . why . . . ?" The half-caste tried to wrench round the mule's head, but he hadn't enough strength: it

just went on. The priest called out: "Remember. I haven't
been in Carmen." But where else now could he go? The
conviction came to him that there was only one place in
the whole state where there was no danger of an innocent
man's being taken as a hostage—but he couldn't go there in
these clothes. . . . The half-caste held hard onto the pommel and swivelled his yellow eyes beseechingly: "You
wouldn't leave me here—alone." But it was more than the
half-caste he was leaving behind on the forest track: the
mule stood sideways like a barrier, nodding a stupid head,
between him and the place where he had been born. He
felt like a man without a passport who is turned away
from every harbour.

The half-caste was calling after him: "Call yourself a
Christian." He had somehow managed to get himself upright. He began to shout abuse—a meaningless series of
indecent words which petered out in the forest like the
weak blows of a hammer. He whispered: "If I see you
again, you can't blame *me*. . . ." Of course, he had every
reason to be angry: he had lost seven hundred pesos. He
shrieked hopelessly: "I don't forget a face."

CHAPTER TWO

THE young men and women walked round and round the plaza in the hot electric night: the men one way, the girls another, never speaking to each other. In the northern sky the lightning flapped. It was like a religious ceremony which had lost all meaning, but at which they still wore their best clothes. Sometimes a group of older women would join in the procession—with a little more excitement and laughter, as if they retained some memory of how things used to go before all the books were lost. A man with a gun on his hip watched from the Treasury steps, and a small withered soldier sat by the prison door with a gun between his knees, and the shadows of the palms pointed at him like a zariba of sabres. Lights were burning in a dentist's window, shining on the swivel chair and the red plush cushions and the glass for rinsing on its little stand and the child's chest-of-drawers full of fittings. Behind the wire-netted windows of the private houses grandmothers swung back and forth in rocking-chairs, among the family photographs—nothing to do, nothing to say, with too many clothes on, sweating a little. This was the capital city of a state.

The man in the shabby drill suit watched it all from a bench. A squad of armed police went by to their quarters, walking out of step, carrying their rifles anyhow. The plaza was lit at each corner by clusters of three globes joined by ugly trailing overhead wires, and a beggar worked his way from seat to seat without success.

He sat down next the man in drill and started a long explanation. There was something confidential, and at the same time threatening in his manner. On every side the streets ran down towards the river and the port and the marshy plain. He said that he had a wife and so many children and that during the last few weeks they had eaten so little—he broke off and fingered the cloth of the other's drill suit. "And how much," he said, "did this cost?"

"You'd be surprised how little."

Suddenly as a clock struck nine-thirty all the lights went out. The beggar said: "It's enough to make a man desperate." He looked this way and that as the parade drifted away down-hill. The man in drill got up, and the other got up too, tagging after him towards the edge of the plaza: his flat bare feet went slap, slap on the pavement. He said: "A few pesos wouldn't make any difference to you. . . ."

"Ah, if you knew what a difference they would make."

The beggar was put out. He said: "A man like me sometimes feels that he would do anything for a few pesos." Now that the lights were out all over town, they stood intimately in the shadow. He said: "Can you blame me?"

"No, no. It would be the last thing I would do."

Everything he said seemed to feed the beggar's irritation. "Sometimes," the beggar said, "I feel as if I could kill . . ."

"That, of course, would be very wrong."

"Would it be wrong if I got a man by the throat . . . ?"

"Well, a starving man has got the right to save himself, certainly."

The beggar watched with rage, while the other talked on as if he were considering a point of academic interest. "In my case, of course, it would hardly be worth the risk. I possess exactly fifteen pesos seventy-five centavos in the world. I haven't eaten myself for forty-eight hours."

"Mother of God," the beggar said, "you're as hard as a stone. Haven't you a heart?"

The man in the drill suit suddenly giggled. The other said: "You're lying. Why haven't you eaten—if you've got fifteen pesos?"

"You see, I want to spend them on drink."

"What sort of drink?"

"The kind of drink a stranger doesn't know how to get in a place like this."

"You mean spirits?"

"Yes—and wine."

The beggar came very close: his leg touched the leg of the other man: he put a hand upon the other's sleeve. They might have been great friends or even brothers standing intimately together in the dark: even the lights in the houses were going out now, and the taxis which during the day waited half-way down the hill for fares who never seemed to come were already dispersing—a tail-lamp winked and went out past the police barracks. The beggar said: "Man, this is your lucky day. How much would you pay me . . . ?"

"For some drink?"

"For an introduction to someone who could let you have a little brandy—real fine Vera Cruz brandy?"

"With a throat like mine," the man in drill explained, "it's wine I really want."

"Pulque or maguey—he's got everything."

"Wine?"

"Quince wine?"

"I'd give everything I've got," the other swore solemnly and exactly, "—except the centavos, that's to say—for some real genuine grape wine." Somewhere down the hill by the river a drum was beating: one, two, one, two: and the sound of marching feet kept a rough time—the soldiers—or the police—were going home to bed.

"How much?" the beggar repeated impatiently.

"Well, I would give you the fifteen pesos and you would get the wine for what you cared to spend."

"You come with me."

They began to go down the hill: at the corner where one street ran up past the chemist's shop towards the barracks and another ran down to the hotel, the quay, the warehouse of the United Banana Company, the man in drill stopped. The police were marching up, rifles slung at ease. "Wait a moment." Among them walked a half-caste with two fang-like teeth jutting out over his lip. The man in drill standing in the shadow watched him go by: once the mestizo turned his head and their eyes met. Then the police went by, up into the plaza. "Let's go. Quickly."

The beggar said: "They won't interfere with us. They're after bigger game."

"What was that man doing with them, do you think?"

"Who knows? A hostage perhaps."

"If he had been a hostage, they would have tied his hands, wouldn't they?"

"How do I know?" He had the grudging independence you find in countries where it is the right of a poor man to beg. He said: "Do you want the spirits or don't you?"

"I want wine."

"I can't say he'll have this or that. You must take what comes."

He led the way down towards the river. He said: "I don't even know if he's in town." The beetles were flocking out and covering the pavements: they popped under the feet like puff-balls, and a sour green smell came up from the river. The white bust of a general glimmered in a tiny public garden, all hot paving and dust, and an electric dynamo throbbed on the ground-floor of the only hotel. Wide wooden stairs crawling with beetles ran up to the first floor. "I've done my best," the beggar said; "a man can't do more."

On the first floor a man dressed in formal dark trousers and a white skin-tight vest came out of a bedroom with a towel over his shoulder. He had a little grey aristocratic beard and he wore braces as well as a belt. Somewhere in the distance a pipe gurgled, and the beetles detonated against a bare globe. The beggar started talking earnestly, and once as he talked the light went off altogether and then flickered unsatisfactorily on again. The head of the stairs was littered with wicker rocking-chairs, and on a big slate were chalked the names of the guests—three only for twenty rooms.

The beggar turned back to his companion. "The gentleman," he said, "is not in. The manager says so. Shall we wait for him?"

"Time to me is of no account."

They went into a big bare bedroom with a tiled floor. The little black iron bedstead was like something somebody has left behind by accident when moving out. They sat down on it side by side and waited, and the beetles came popping in through the gaps in the mosquito wire. "He is a very important man," the beggar said. "He is the cousin of the Governor—he can get anything for you, anything at all. But, of course, you must be introduced by someone he trusts."

"And he trusts you?"

"I worked for him once." He added frankly: "He has to trust me."

"Does the Governor know?"

"Of course not. The Governor is a hard man."

Every now and then the water-pipes swallowed noisily.

"And why should he trust me?"

"Oh, anyone can tell a drinker. You'll want to come back for more. It's good stuff he sells. Better give me the fifteen pesos." He counted them carefully twice. He said: "I'll get you a bottle of the best Vera Cruz brandy. You see if I don't." The light went off, and they sat on in the dark: the bed creaked as one of them shifted.

"I don't want brandy," a voice said. "At least—not very much."

"What do you want then?"

"I told you—wine."

"Wine's expensive."

"Never mind that. Wine or nothing."

"Quince wine?"

"No, no. French wine."

"Sometimes he has California wine."

"That would do."

"Of course himself—he gets it for nothing. From the customs."

The dynamo began throbbing again below and the light came dimly on. The door opened and the manager beckoned the beggar; a long conversation began. The man in the drill suit leant back on the bed: his chin was cut in several places where he had been shaving too closely: his face was hollow and ill—it gave the impression that he had once been plump and round-faced but had caved in. He had the appearance of a business man who had fallen on hard times.

The beggar came back. He said: "The gentleman's busy, but he'll be back soon. The manager sent a boy to look for him."

"Where is he?"

"He can't be interrupted. He's playing billiards with the Chief of Police." He came back to the bed, squashing two beetles under his naked feet. He said: "This is a fine hotel. Where do you stay? You're a stranger, aren't you?"

"Oh, I'm just passing through."

"This gentleman is very influential. It would be a good thing to offer him a drink. After all, you won't want to take it all away with you. You may as well drink here as anywhere else."

"I should like to keep a little—to take home."

"It's all one. I say that home is where there is a chair and a glass."

"All the same—" Then the light went out again, and on the horizon the lightning bellied out like a curtain. The sound of thunder came through the mosquito-net from very far away like the noise you hear from the other end of a town when the Sunday bull-fight is on.

The beggar said confidentially: "What's your trade?"

"Oh, I pick up what I can—where I can."

They sat in silence together listening to the sound of feet on the wooden stairs. The door opened, but they could see nothing. A voice swore resignedly and asked: "Who's there?" Then a match was struck and showed a large blue jaw and went out. The dynamo churned away and the light went on again. The stranger said wearily: "Oh, it's you."

"It's me."

He was a small man with a too large pasty face and he was dressed in a tight grey suit. A revolver bulged under his waistcoat. He said: "I've got nothing for you. Nothing."

The beggar padded across the room and began to talk earnestly in a very low voice: once he gently squeezed with his bare toes the other's polished shoe. The man sighed and blew out his cheeks and watched the bed closely as if he feared they had designs on it. He said sharply to the one in the drill suit: "So you want some Vera Cruz brandy, do you? It's against the law."

"Not brandy. I don't want brandy."

"Isn't beer good enough for you?"

He came fussily and authoritatively into the middle of

the room, his shoes squeaking on the tiles—the Governor's cousin. "I could have you arrested," he threatened.

The man in the drill suit cringed formally. He said: "Of course, your Excellency . . ."

"Do you think I've got nothing better to do than slake the thirst of every beggar who chooses . . ."

"I would never have troubled you if this man had not . . ."

The Governor's cousin spat on the tiles.

"But if your Excellency would rather that I went away . . ."

He said sharply: "I'm not a hard man. I always try to oblige my fellows . . . when it's in my power and does no harm. I have a position, you understand. These drinks come to me quite legally."

"Of course."

"And I have to charge what they cost me."

"Of course."

"Otherwise I'd be a ruined man." He walked delicately to the bed as if his shoes were cramping him and began to unmake it. "Are you a talker?" he asked over his shoulder.

"I know how to keep a secret."

"I don't mind you telling—the right people." There was a large rent in the mattress: he pulled out a handful of straw and put in his fingers again. The man in drill gazed out with false indifference at the public garden, the dark mud-banks, and the masts of sailing-ships: the lightning flapped behind them, and the thunder came nearer.

"There," said the Governor's cousin, "I can spare you that. It's good stuff."

"It wasn't really brandy I wanted."

"You must take what comes."

"Then I think I'd rather have my fifteen pesos back."

The Governor's cousin exclaimed sharply: "*Fifteen* pesos!" The beggar began rapidly to explain that the gentleman wanted to buy a little wine as well as brandy: they began to argue fiercely by the bed in low voices about prices. The Governor's cousin said: "Wine's very difficult to get. I can let you have two bottles of brandy."

"One of brandy and one of . . ."

"It's the best Vera Cruz brandy."

"But I am a wine drinker . . . you don't know how I long for wine. . . ."

"Wine costs me a great deal of money. How much more can you pay?"

"I have only seventy-five centavos left in the world."

"I could let you have a bottle of tequila."

"No, no."

"Another fifty centavos then. . . . It will be a large bottle." He began to scrabble in the mattress again, pulling out straw. The beggar winked at the man in drill and made the motions of drawing a cork and filling a glass.

"There," the Governor's cousin said, "take it or leave it."

"Oh, I will take it."

The Governor's cousin suddenly lost his surliness. He rubbed his hands and said: "A stuffy night. The rains are going to be early this year, I think."

"Perhaps your Excellency would honour me by taking a glass of brandy to toast our business."

"Well, well . . . perhaps . . ." The beggar opened the door and called briskly for glasses.

"It's a long time," the Governor's cousin said, "since I had a glass of wine. Perhaps it would be more suitable for a toast."

"Of course," the man in drill said, "as your Excellency chooses." He watched the cork drawn with a look of painful anxiety. He said: "If you will excuse me, I think I will have brandy," and smiled raggedly, with an effort, watching the wine level fall.

They toasted each other, all three sitting on the bed—the beggar drank brandy. The Governor's cousin said: "I'm proud of this wine. It's good wine. The best California." The beggar winked and motioned and the man in drill said: "One more glass, your Excellency—or I can recommend this brandy."

"It's good brandy—but I think another glass of wine." They refilled their glasses. The man in drill said: "I'm going to take some of that wine back—to my mother. She loves a glass."

"She couldn't do better," the Governor's cousin said, emptying his own. He said: "So you have a mother?"

"Haven't we all?"

"Ah, you're lucky. Mine's dead." His hand strayed towards the bottle, grasped it. "Sometimes I miss her. I called her 'my little friend.' " He tilted the bottle. "With your permission?"

"Of course, your Excellency," the other said hopelessly, taking a long draught of brandy. The beggar said: "I too have a mother."

"Who cares?" the Governor's cousin said sharply. He leant back and the bed creaked. He said: "I have often thought a mother is a better friend than a father. Her influence is towards peace, goodness, charity. . . . Always on the anniversary of her death I go to her grave—with flowers."

The man in drill caught a hiccup politely. He said: "Ah, if I could too . . ."

"But you said your mother was alive?"

"I thought that you were speaking of your grandmother."

"How could I? I can't remember my grandmother."

"Nor can I."

"I can," the beggar said.

The Governor's cousin said: "You talk too much."

"Perhaps I could send him to have this wine wrapped up. . . . For your Excellency's sake I mustn't be seen . . ."

"Wait, wait. There's no hurry. You are very welcome here. Anything in this room is at your disposal. Have a glass of wine."

"I think brandy . . ."

"Then with your permission . . ." He tilted the bottle: a little of it splashed over onto the sheets. "What were we talking about?"

"Our grandmothers."

"I don't think it can have been that. I can't even remember mine. The earliest thing I can remember . . ."

The door opened. The manager said: "The Chief of Police is coming up the stairs."

"Excellent. Show him in."

"Are you sure?"

"Of course. He's a good fellow." He said to the others: "But at billiards you can't trust him."

A large stout man in a singlet, white trousers, and a revolver-holster appeared in the doorway. The Governor's cousin said: "Come in. Come in. How is your toothache? We were talking about our grandmothers." He said sharply to the beggar: "Make room for the jefe."

The jefe stood in the doorway, watching them with dim embarrassment. He said: "Well, well . . ."

"We're having a little private party. Will you join us? It would be an honour."

The jefe's face suddenly lit up at the sight of the wine: "Of course—a little beer never comes amiss."

"That's right. Give the jefe a glass of beer." The beggar filled his own glass with wine and held it out. The jefe took his place upon the bed and drained the glass: then he took the bottle himself. He said: "It's good beer. Very good beer. Is this the only bottle?" The man in drill watched him with frigid anxiety.

"I'm afraid the only bottle."

"*Salud!*"

"And what," the Governor's cousin asked, "were we talking about?"

"About the first thing you could remember," the beggar said.

"The first thing I can remember," the jefe began, with deliberation, "—but this gentleman is not drinking."

"I will have a little brandy."

"*Salud!*"

"*Salud!*"

"The first thing I can remember with any distinctness

is my first communion. Ah, the thrill of the soul, my parents round me . . ."

"How many parents, then, have you got?"

"Two, of course."

"They could not have been around you—you would have needed at least four—ha, ha."

"*Salud!*"

"*Salud!*"

"No, but as I was saying—life has such irony. It was my painful duty to watch the priest who gave me that communion shot—an old man. I am not ashamed to say that I wept. The comfort is that he is probably a saint and that he prayed for us. It is not everyone who earns a saint's prayers."

"An unusual way . . ."

"But then life is mysterious."

"*Salud!*"

The man in drill said: "A glass of brandy, jefe?"

"There is so little left in this bottle that I may as well . . ."

"I was very anxious to take a little back for my mother."

"Oh, a drop like this. It would be an insult to take it. Just the dregs." He turned it up over his glass and chuckled: "If you can talk of beer having dregs." Then he stopped with the bottle held over the glass and said with astonishment: "Why, man, you're crying." All three watched the man in drill with their mouths a little open. He said: "It always takes me like this—brandy. Forgive me, gentlemen. I get drunk very easily and then I see . . ."

"See what?"

"Oh. I don't know, all the hope of the world draining away."

"Man, you're a poet."

The beggar said: "A poet is the soul of his country."

Lightning filled the windows like a white sheet, and thunder crashed suddenly overhead. The one globe flickered and faded up near the ceiling. "This is bad news for my men," the jefe said, stamping on a beetle which had crawled too near.

"Why bad news?"

"The rains coming so early. You see they are on a hunt."

"The gringo . . . ?"

"He doesn't really matter, but the Governor's found there's still a priest, and you know what he feels about that. If it was me, I'd let the poor devil alone. He'd starve or die of fever or give up. He can't be doing any good— or any harm. Why, nobody even noticed he was about till a few months ago."

"You'll have to hurry."

"Oh, he hasn't any real chance. Unless he gets over the border. We've got a man who knows him. Spoke to him, spent a night with him. Let's talk of something else. Who wants to be a policeman?"

"Where do you think he is?"

"You'd be surprised."

"Why?"

"He's here—in this town, I mean. That's deduction. You see, since we started taking hostages from the villages, there's really nowhere else. . . . They turn him away, they

won't have him. So we've set this man I told you about
loose like a dog—he'll run into him one day or another—
and then . . ."

The man in drill said: "Have you had to shoot many
hostages?"

"Not yet. Three or four perhaps. Well, here goes the
last of the beer. *Salud!*" He put the glass regretfully
down. "Perhaps now I could have just a drop of your—
sidral, shall we call it?"

"Yes. Of course."

"Have I met you before? Your face somehow . . ."

"I don't think I've had the honour."

"That's another mystery," the jefe said, stretching out
a long fat limb and gently pushing the beggar towards
the bed-knobs, "how you think you've seen people—and
places—before. Was it in a dream or in a past life? I once
heard a doctor say it was something to do with the focus-
ing of the eyes. But he was a Yankee. A materialist."

"I remember once . . . " the Governor's cousin said. The
lightning shot down over the harbour and the thunder
beat on the roof: this was the atmosphere of a whole state
—the storm outside and the talk just going on—words
like "mystery" and "soul" and "the source of life" came in
over and over again, as they sat on the bed talking, with
nothing to do and nothing to believe and nowhere better
to go.

The man in drill said: "I think perhaps I had better be
moving on."

"Where to?"

"Oh . . . friends," he said vaguely, sketching widely
with his hands a whole world of fictitious friendships.

"You'd better take your drink with you," the Governor's cousin said. He admitted: "After all you paid for it."

"Thank you, Excellency." He picked up the brandy bottle. Perhaps there were three fingers left. The bottle of wine, of course, was quite empty.

"Hide it, man, hide it," the Governor's cousin said sharply.

"Oh, of course, Excellency, I will be careful."

"You don't have to call him Excellency," the jefe said. He gave a bellow of laughter and thrust the beggar right off the bed onto the floor.

"No, no, that is . . ." He sidled cautiously out, with a smudge of tears under his red sore eyes and from the hall heard the conversation begin again—"mystery," "soul"— going interminably on to no end.

The beetles had disappeared: the rain had apparently washed them away: it came perpendicularly down, with a sort of measured intensity, as if it were driving nails into a coffin lid. But the air was no clearer: sweat and rain hung together on the clothes. The priest stood for a few seconds in the doorway of the hotel, the dynamo thudding behind him, then he darted a few yards into another doorway and hesitated, staring over past the bust of the general to the tethered sailing-boats and one old barge with a tin funnel. He had nowhere to go: rain hadn't entered into his calculations: he had believed that it would be possible just to hang on somehow, sleeping on benches or by the river.

A couple of soldiers arguing furiously came down the

street towards the quay—they just let the rain fall on them, as if it didn't matter, as if things were so bad anyway you couldn't notice. . . . The priest pushed the wooden door against which he stood—a cantina door coming down only to the knees—and went in out of the rain: stacks of gaseosa bottles and a single billiard table with the score strung on rings, three or four men—somebody had laid his holster on the bar. The priest moved too quickly and jolted the elbow of a man who was making a shot. He turned furiously: "Mother of God!": he was a Red Shirt. Was there no safety anywhere, even for a moment?

The priest apologized humbly, edging back towards the door, but again he was too quick—his pocket caught against the wall and the brandy bottle chinked. Three or four faces looked at him with malicious amusement: he was a stranger and they were going to have fun. "What's that you've got in your pocket?" the Red Shirt asked. He was a youth not out of his teens, with gold teeth and a jesting conceited mouth.

"Lemonade," the priest said.

"What do you want to carry lemonade with you for?"

"I take it at night—with my quinine."

The Red Shirt swaggered up and poked the pocket with the butt of his cue. "Lemonade, eh?"

"Yes, lemonade."

"Let's have a look at the lemonade." He turned proudly to the others and said: "I can scent a smuggler at ten paces." He thrust his hand into the priest's pocket and hauled at the brandy bottle: "There," he said. "Didn't I tell you—" The priest flung himself against the swing door and burst out into the rain. A voice shouted: "Catch him." They were having the time of their lives.

He was off up the street towards the plaza, turned left and right again—it was lucky the streets were dark and the moon obscured. As long as he kept away from lighted windows he was almost invisible—he could hear them calling to each other. They were not giving up: it was better than billiards: somewhere a whistle blew—the police were joining in.

This was the town to which it had been his ambition to be promoted, leaving the right kind of debts behind at Concepción: he thought of the cathedral and Montez and a canon he once knew, as he doubled this way and that. Something buried very deep, the will to escape, cast a momentary and appalling humour over the whole situation— he giggled and panted and giggled again. He could hear them hallooing and whistling in the dark, and the rain came down: it drove and jumped upon the cement floor of the useless fronton which had once been the cathedral (it was too hot to play pelota and a few iron swings stood like gallows at its edge). He worked his way down-hill again: he had an idea.

The shouts came nearer, and then up from the river a new lot of men approached: these were pursuing the hunt methodically—he could tell it by their slow pace, the police, the official hunters. He was between the two—the amateurs and the professionals. But he knew the door—he pushed it open, came quickly through into the patio, and closed it behind him.

He stood in the dark and panted, hearing the steps

come nearer up the street, while the rain drove down. Then he realized that somebody was watching him from a window, a small dark withered face, like one of the preserved heads tourists buy. He came up to the grille and said: "Padre José?"

"Over there." A second face appeared behind the other's shoulder, lit uncertainly by a candle-flame, then a third: faces sprouted like vegetables. He could feel them watching him as he splashed back across the patio and banged on a door.

He didn't for a second or two recognize Padre José— in the absurd billowing nightshirt, holding a lamp. The last time he had seen him was at the conference, sitting in the back row, biting his nails, afraid to be noticed. It hadn't been necessary: none of the busy cathedral clergy even knew what he was called. It was odd to think that now he had won a kind of fame superior to theirs. He said "José" gently, winking up at him from the splashing dark.

"Who are you?"

"Don't you remember me? Of course, it's years now . . . don't you remember the conference at the cathedral? . . ."

"Oh, God," Padre José said.

"They are looking for me. I thought perhaps just for tonight you could perhaps . . ."

"Go away," Padre José said, "go away."

"They don't know who I am. They think I'm a smuggler—but up at the police station they'll know."

"Don't talk so loud. My wife . . ."

"Just show me some corner," he whispered. He was beginning to feel fear again. Perhaps the effect of the brandy was wearing off (it was impossible in this hot damp climate to stay drunk for long: alcohol came out again under the armpits: it dripped from the forehead) or perhaps it was only that the desire of life, which moves in cycles, was returning—any sort of life.

In the lamplight Padre José's face wore an expression of hatred. He said: "Why come to me? Why should you think . . . ? I'll call the police if you don't go. You know what sort of a man I am."

He pleaded gently: "You're a good man, José. I've always known that."

"I'll shout if you don't go."

He tried to remember some cause of hatred. There were voices in the street—arguments, a knocking—were they searching the houses? He said: "If I ever offended you, José, forgive me. I was conceited, proud, overbearing—a bad priest. I always knew in my heart you were the better man."

"Go," José screeched at him, "go! I don't want martyrs here. I don't belong any more. Leave me alone. I'm all right as I am." He tried to gather up his venom into spittle and shot it feebly at the other's face: it didn't even reach, fell impotently through the air. He said: "Go and die quickly. That's your job," and slammed the door to. The door of the patio came suddenly open and the police were there. He caught a glimpse of Padre José peering through a window and then an enormous shape in a white nightshirt engulfed him and drew him away—whisked him off, like a guardian spirit, from the disastrous human struggle. A voice said: "That's him." It was the young Red Shirt. He let his fist open and dropped by Padre

José's wall a little ball of paper: it was like the final surrender of a whole past.

He knew it was the beginning of the end—after all these years. He began to say silently an act of contrition, while they picked the brandy bottle out of his pocket, but he couldn't give his mind to it. That was the fallacy of the deathbed repentance—penitence was the fruit of long training and discipline: fear wasn't enough. He tried to think of his child with shame, but he could only think of her with a kind of famished love—what would become of her? And the sin itself was so old that like an ancient picture the deformity had faded and left a kind of grace. The Red Shirt smashed the bottle on the stone paving and the smell of spirit rose all round them—not very strongly: there hadn't really been much left.

Then they took him away: now that they had caught him they treated him in a friendly way, poking fun at his attempt to escape—except the Red Shirt whose shot he had spoiled. He couldn't find any answer to their jokes: self-preservation lay across his brain like a horrifying obsession. When would they discover who he really was? When would he meet the half-caste, or the lieutenant who had interrogated him already? They moved in a bunch slowly up the hill to the plaza. A rifle-butt grounded outside the station as they came in: a small lamp fumed against the dirty whitewashed wall: in the courtyard hammocks swung, bunched around sleeping bodies like the nets in which poultry is tied. "You can sit down," one of the men said, and pushed him in a comradely way towards a bench. Everything now seemed irrevocable: the sentry passed back and forth outside the door, and in the courtyard among the hammocks the ceaseless murmur of sleep went on.

Somebody had spoken to him: he gaped helplessly up. "What?" There seemed to be an argument in progress between the police and the Red Shirt—as to whether somebody should be disturbed. "But it's his duty," the Red Shirt kept on repeating: he had rabbity front teeth. He said: "I'll report it to the Governor."

A policeman said: "You plead guilty, don't you?"

"Yes," the priest said.

"There. What more do you want? It's a fine of five pesos. Why disturb anybody?"

"And who gets the five pesos, eh?"

"That's none of your business."

The priest said suddenly: "No one gets them."

"No one?"

"I have only twenty-five centavos in the world."

The door of an inner room opened and the lieutenant came out. He said: "What in God's name is all the noise . . . ?" The police came raggedly and unwillingly to attention.

"I've caught a man carrying spirits," the Red Shirt said.

The priest sat with his eyes on the ground . . . "because it has crucified . . . crucified . . . crucified . . ." Contrition stuck hopelessly over the formal words. He felt no emotion but fear.

"Well," the lieutenant said. "What is it to do with you? We catch dozens."

"Shall we bring him in?" one of the men asked.

The lieutenant took a look at the bowed servile figure

on the bench. "Get up," he said. The priest rose. Now, he thought, now . . . he raised his eyes. The lieutenant looked away, out of the door where the sentry slouched to and fro. His dark pinched face looked rattled, harassed. . . .

"He has no money," one of the policemen said.

"Mother of God," the lieutenant said, "can I never teach you . . . ?" He took two steps towards the sentry and turned. "Search him. If he has no money, put him in a cell. Give him some work. . . ." He went outside and suddenly raising his open hand he struck the sentry on the ear. He said: "You're asleep. March as if you had some pride . . . pride," he repeated again, while the small acetylene lamp fumed up the whitewashed wall and the smell of urine came up out of the yard and the men lay in their hammocks netted and secured.

"Shall we take his name?" a sergeant said.

"Yes, of course," the lieutenant said, not looking at him, walking briskly and nervously back past the lamp into the courtyard: he stood there unsheltered, looking round while the rain fell on his dapper uniform. He looked like a man with something on his mind: it was as if he were under the influence of some secret passion which had broken up the routine of his life. Back he came. He couldn't keep still.

The sergeant pushed the priest ahead into the inner room: a bright commercial calendar hung on the flaking whitewash—a dark-skinned mestizo girl in a bathing-dress advertised some gaseous water: somebody had pencilled in a neat pedagogic hand a facile and over-confident statement about man having nothing to lose but his chains.

"Name?" the sergeant said. Before the priest could check himself he had replied: "Montez."

"Home?"

He named a random village: he was absorbed in his own portrait. There he sat among the white-starched dresses of the first communicants. Somebody had put a ring round his face—to pick it out. There was another picture on the wall too—the gringo from San Antonio, Texas, wanted for murder and bank robbery.

"I suppose," the sergeant said cautiously, "that you bought the drink from a stranger . . ."

"Yes."

"Whom you can't identify?"

"No."

"That's the way," the sergeant said approvingly: it was obvious he didn't want to start anything. He took the priest quite confidingly by the arm and led him out and across the courtyard: he carried a large key like the ones used in morality plays or fairy-stories as a symbol. A few men moved in the hammocks—a large unshaven jaw hung over the side like something left over on a butcher's counter: a big torn ear: a naked black-haired thigh. He wondered when the mestizo's face would appear, elated with recognition.

The sergeant unlocked a small grated door and let out with his boot at something straddled across the entrance. He said: "They are all good fellows, all good fellows here," kicking his way in. An appalling smell lay on the air and somebody in the absolute darkness wept.

The priest lingered on the threshold trying to see; the lumpy blackness seemed to shift and stir. He said: "I am so dry. Could I have water?" The stench poured up his nostrils and he retched.

"In the morning," the sergeant said, "you've drunk enough now," and laying a large considerate hand upon the priest's back, he pushed him in, then slammed the door to. He trod on a hand, an arm, and pressing his face against the grille, protested in feeble horror: "There's no room. I can't see. Who are these people?" Outside among the hammocks the sergeant began to laugh. "*Hombre,*" he said, "*hombre,* have you never been in jail before?"

CHAPTER THREE

A VOICE near his foot said: "Got a cigarette?" He drew quickly back and trod on an arm. A voice said imperatively: "Water, quick," as if whoever it was thought he could take a stranger unawares, and make him fork out.

"Got a cigarette?"

"No." He said weakly: "I have nothing at all," and imagined he could feel enmity fuming up all round him like smoke. He moved again. Somebody said: "Look out for the bucket." That was where the stench came from. He stood perfectly still and waited for his sight to return. Outside the rain began to stop: it dropped haphazardly and the thunder moved away. You could count forty now between the lightning flash and the roll. Forty miles, superstition said. Half-way to the sea, or half-way to the mountains. He felt around with his foot, trying to find enough space to sit down—but there seemed to be no room at all. When the lightning went on he could see the hammocks at the edge of the courtyard.

"Got something to eat?" a voice said, and when he didn't answer, "Got something to eat?"

"No."

"Got any money?" another voice said.

"No."

Suddenly, from about five feet away, there came a tiny scream—a woman's. A tired voice said: "Can't you be quiet?" Among the furtive movements came again the muffled painless cries. He realized with horror that pleasure was going on even in this crowded darkness. Again he put out his foot and began to edge his way inch by inch away from the grille. Behind the human voices another noise went permanently on: it was like a small machine, an electric belt set at a certain tempo. It filled any silences that there were, louder than human breath. It was the mosquitoes.

He had moved perhaps six feet from the grille, and his eyes began to distinguish heads—perhaps the sky was clearing: they hung around him like gourds. A voice said: "Who are you?" He made no reply, feeling panic edging in: suddenly he found himself against the back wall: the stone was wet against his hand—the cell could not have been more than twelve feet deep. He found he could just sit down if he kept his feet drawn up under him. An old man lay slumped against his shoulder: he told his age from the feather-weight lightness of the bones, the feeble uneven flutter of the breath. He was either somebody close to birth or death—and he could hardly be a child in this place. He said suddenly: "Is that you, Catarina?" and his breath went out in a long patient sigh, as if he had been waiting for a long while and could afford to wait a lot longer.

The priest said: "No. Not Catarina." When he spoke everybody became suddenly silent, listening, as if what he said had importance: then the voices and movements began again. But the sound of his own voice, the sense of communication with a neighbour, calmed him.

"You wouldn't be," the old man said. "I didn't really think you were. She'll never come."

"Is she your wife?"

"What's that you're saying? I haven't got a wife."

"Catarina."

"She's my daughter." Everybody was listening again: except the two invisible people who were concerned only in their hooded and cramped pleasure.

"Perhaps they won't allow her here."

"She'll never try," the old hopeless voice pronounced with absolute conviction. The priest's feet began to ache, drawn up under his haunches. He said: "If she loves you . . ." Somewhere across the huddle of dark shapes the woman cried again—that finished cry of protest and abandonment and pleasure.

"It's the priests who've done it," the old man said.

"The priests?"

"The priests."

"Why the priests?"

"The priests."

A low voice near his knees said: "The old man's crazy. What's the use of asking him questions?"

"Is that you, Catarina?" He added: "I don't really believe it, you know. It's just a question."

"Now *I've* got something to complain about," the voice went on. "A man's got to defend his honour. You'll admit that, won't you?"

"I don't know anything about honour."

"I was in the cantina and the man I'm telling you about came up to me and said: 'Your mother's a whore.' Well, I couldn't do anything about it: he'd got his gun on him. All I could do was wait. He drank too much beer—I knew he would—and when he was staggering I followed him out. I had a bottle and I smashed it against a wall. You see, I hadn't got my gun. His family's got influence with the jefe or I'd never be here."

"It's a terrible thing to kill a man."

"You talk like a priest."

"It was the priests who did it," the old man said. "You're right, there."

"What does he mean?"

"What does it matter what an old man like that means? I'd like to tell you about something else. . . ."

A woman's voice said: "They took the child away from him."

"Why?"

"It was a bastard. They acted quite correctly."

At the word bastard his heart moved painfully: it was as when a man in love hears a stranger name a flower which is also the name of a woman. Bastard: the word filled him with miserable happiness. It brought his own child nearer: he could see her under the tree by the rubbish-dump, unguarded. He repeated "Bastard?" as he might have repeated her name—with tenderness disguised as indifference.

"They said he was no fit father. But, of course, when the priests fled, she had to go to him. Where else could she go?" It was like a happy ending until she said: "Of course she hated him. They'd taught her about things." He could

imagine the small set mouth of an educated woman. What
was she doing here?

"Why is he in prison?"

"He had a crucifix."

The stench from the pail got worse all the time: the
night stood round them like a wall, without ventilation,
and he could hear somebody making water, drumming on
the tin sides. He said: "They had no business . . ."

"They were doing what was right, of course. It was a
mortal sin."

"No right to make her hate him."

"They know what's right."

He said: "They were bad priests to do a thing like that.
The sin was over. It was their duty to teach—well, love."

"You don't know what's right. The priests know."

He said after a moment's hesitation, very distinctly: "I
am a priest."

It was like the end: there was no need to hope any
longer. The ten years' hunt was over at last. There was
silence all round him. This place was very like the world:
overcrowded with lust and crime and unhappy love: it
stank to heaven; but he realized that after all it was possible to find peace there, when you knew for certain that
the time was short.

"A priest?" the woman said at last.

"Yes."

"Do *they* know?"

"Not yet."

He could feel a hand fumbling at his sleeve. A voice
said: "You shouldn't have told us. Father, there are all
sorts here. Murderers . . ."

The voice which had described the crime to him said: "You've no cause to abuse me. Because I kill a man it doesn't mean . . ." Whispering started everywhere. The voice said bitterly: "I'm not an informer just because when a man says: 'Your mother's a whore . . .' "

The priest said: "There's no need for anyone to inform on me. That would be a sin. When it's daylight they'll discover for themselves."

"They'll shoot you, father," the woman's voice said.

"Yes."

"Are you afraid?"

"Yes. Of course."

A new voice spoke, in the corner from which the sounds of pleasure had come. It said roughly and obstinately: "A man isn't afraid of a thing like that."

"No?" the priest said.

"A bit of pain. What do you expect? It has to come."

"All the same," the priest said, "I *am* afraid."

"Toothache is worse."

"We can't all be brave men."

The voice said with contempt: "You believers are all the same. Christianity makes you cowards."

"Yes. Perhaps you are right. You see I am a bad priest and a bad man. To die in a state of mortal sin"—he gave an uneasy chuckle—"it makes you think."

"There. It's as I say. Believing in God makes cowards." The voice was triumphant, as if it had proved something.

"So then?" the priest said.

"Better not to believe—and be a brave man."

"I see—yes. And, of course, if one believed the Governor did not exist or the jefe, if we could pretend that this prison was not a prison at all but a garden, how brave we could be then."

"That's just foolishness."

"But when we found that the prison was a prison, and the Governor up there in the square undoubtedly existed, well, it wouldn't much matter if we'd been brave for an hour or two."

"Nobody could say that this prison was not a prison."

"No? You don't think so? I can see you don't listen to the politicians." His feet were giving him great pain: he had cramp in the soles, but he could bring no pressure on the muscles to relieve them. It was not yet midnight: the hours of darkness stretched ahead interminably.

The woman said suddenly: "Think. We have a martyr here . . ."

The priest giggled: he couldn't stop himself. He said: "I don't think martyrs are like this." He became suddenly serious, remembering Maria's words—it wouldn't be a good thing to bring mockery on the Church. He said: "Martyrs are holy men. It is wrong to think that just because one dies . . . no. I tell you I am in a state of mortal sin. I have done things I couldn't talk to you about: I could only whisper them in the confessional." Everybody, when he spoke, listened attentively to him as if he were addressing them in church: he wondered where the inevitable Judas was sitting now, but he wasn't aware of Judas as he had been in the forest hut. He was moved by an enormous and irrational affection for the inhabitants of this prison. A phrase came to him: "God so loved the world . . ." He said: "My children, you must never think the holy martyrs are like me. You have a name for me. Oh, I've heard you use it before now. I am a whisky priest. I am in here now because they found a bottle of brandy in my pocket." He tried to move his feet from under him: the cramp had passed: now they were lifeless: all feeling gone. Oh, well, let them stay. He wouldn't have to use them often again.

The old man was muttering, and the priest's thoughts went back to Brigida. The knowledge of the world lay in her like the dark explicable spot in an X-ray photograph: he longed—with a breathless feeling in the breast—to save her, but he knew the surgeon's decision—the ill was incurable.

The woman's voice said pleadingly: "A little drink, father . . . it's not so important." He wondered why she was here—probably for having a holy picture in her house. She had the tiresome intent note of a pious woman. They were extraordinarily foolish over pictures. Why not burn them? One didn't need a picture. . . . He said sternly: "Oh, I am not only a drunkard." He had always been worried by the fate of pious women: as much as politicians, they fed on illusion: he was frightened for them. They came to death so often in a state of invincible complacency, full of uncharity. It was one's duty, if one could, to rob them of their sentimental notions of what was good . . . He said in hard accents: "I have a child."

What a worthy woman she was! her voice pleaded in the darkness: he couldn't catch what she said, but it was something about the Good Thief. He said: "My child, the thief repented. I haven't repented." He remembered her coming into the hut, the dark malicious knowing look with the sunlight at her back. He said: "I don't know how to repent." That was true: he had lost the faculty. He couldn't say to himself that he wished his sin had never existed, because the sin seemed to him now so unimportant —and he loved the fruit of it. He needed a confessor to draw his mind slowly down the drab passages which led to horror, grief, and repentance.

The woman was silent now: he wondered whether after all he had been too harsh with her. If it helped her faith to believe that he was a martyr . . . but he rejected the idea: one was pledged to truth. He shifted an inch or two on his hams and said: "What time does it get light?"

"Four . . . five . . ." a man replied. "How can we tell, father? We haven't clocks."

"Have you been here long?"

"Three weeks."

"Are you kept here all day?"

"Oh, no. They let us out to clean the yard."

He thought: That is when I shall be discovered—unless it's earlier: for surely one of these people will betray me first. A long train of thought began, which led him to announce after a while: "They are offering a reward for me. Five hundred, six hundred pesos, I'm not sure." Then he was silent again. He couldn't urge any man to inform against him—that would be tempting him to sin—but at the same time if there was an informer here, there was no reason why the wretched creature should be bilked of his reward. To commit so ugly a sin—it must count as murder—and to have no compensation in this world . . . He thought simply: it wouldn't be fair.

"Nobody here," a voice said, "wants their blood money."

Again he was touched by an extraordinary affection. He was just one criminal among a herd of criminals . . .

he had a sense of companionship which he had never received in the old days when pious people came kissing his
black cotton glove.

The pious woman's voice leapt hysterically out at him:
"It is so stupid to tell them that. You don't know the sort
of wretches who are here, father. Thieves, murderers . . ."

"Well," an angry voice said, "why are you here?"

"I had good books in my house," she announced, with
unbearable pride. He had done nothing to shake her complacency. He said: "They are everywhere. It's no different
here."

"Good books?"

He giggled. "No, no. Thieves, murderers . . . Oh, well,
my child, if you had more experience you would know
there are worse things to be." The old man seemed to be
uneasily asleep: his head lay sideways against the priest's
shoulder, and he muttered angrily. God knows, it had
never been easy to move in this place, but the difficulty
seemed to increase as the night wore on and limbs stiffened. He couldn't twitch his shoulder now without waking the old man to another night of suffering. Well, he
thought, it was my kind who robbed him: it's only fair to
be made a little uncomfortable. . . . He sat silent and rigid
against the damp wall, with his dead feet like leprosy
under his haunches. The mosquitoes droned on: it was no
good defending yourself by striking at the air: they per-
vaded the whole place like an element. Somebody as well
as the old man had somewhere fallen asleep and was snoring, a curious note of satisfaction, as though he had eaten
and drunk well at a good dinner and was now taking a
snooze. . . . The priest tried to calculate the hour: how

much time had passed since he had met the beggar in the plaza? It was probably not long after midnight: there would be hours more of this.

It was, of course, the end, but at the same time you had to be prepared for everything, even escape. If God intended him to escape he could snatch him away from in front of a firing squad. But God was merciful: there was only one reason, surely, which would make Him refuse His peace—if there was any peace—that he could still be of use in saving a soul, his own or another's. But what good could he do now? They had him on the run: he dared not enter a village in case somebody else should pay with his life: perhaps a man who was in mortal sin and unrepentant: it was impossible to say what souls might not be lost simply because he was obstinate and proud and wouldn't admit defeat. He couldn't even say Mass any longer—he had no wine. It had all gone down the dry gullet of the Chief of Police. It was—appallingly—complicated. He was still afraid of death; he would be more afraid of death yet when the morning came, but it was beginning to attract him by its simplicity.

The pious woman was whispering to him: she must have somehow edged her way nearer: she was saying: "Father, will you hear my confession?"

"My dear child, here! It's quite impossible. Where would be the secrecy?"

"It's been so long . . ."

"Say an act of contrition for your sins. You must trust God, my dear, to make allowances . . ."

"I wouldn't mind suffering . . ."

"Well, you are here."

"That's nothing. In the morning my sister will have raised the money for my fine."

Somewhere against the far wall pleasure began again: it was unmistakable: the movements, the breathlessness, and then the cry. The pious woman said aloud with fury: "Why won't they stop it? The brutes, the animals!"

"What's the good of your saying an act of contrition now in this state of mind?"

"But the ugliness . . ."

"Don't believe that. It's dangerous. Because suddenly we discover that our sins have so much beauty."

"Beauty," she said with disgust. "Here. In this cell. With strangers all round."

"Such a lot of beauty. Saints talk about the beauty of suffering. Well, we are not saints, you and I. Suffering to us is just ugly. Stench and crowding and pain. *That* is beautiful in that corner—to them. It needs a lot of learning to see things with a saint's eye: a saint gets a subtle taste for beauty and can look down on poor ignorant palates like theirs. But we can't afford to."

"It's mortal sin."

"We don't know. It may be. But I'm a bad priest, you see. I know—from experience—how much beauty Satan carried down with him when he fell. Nobody ever said the fallen angels were the ugly ones. Oh, no, they were just as quick and light and . . ."

Again the cry came, an expression of intolerable pleasure. The woman said: "Stop them. It's a scandal." He felt fingers on his knee, grasping, digging. He said: "We're all fellow prisoners. I want drink at this moment more than anything, more than God. That's a sin too."

"Now," the woman said, "I can see you're a bad priest. I wouldn't believe it before. I do now. You sympathize with these animals. If your bishop heard you . . ."

"Ah, he's a very long way off."

He thought of the old man now—in the capital: living in one of those ugly comfortable pious houses, full of images and holy pictures, saying Mass on Sundays at one of the cathedral altars.

"When I get out of here, I shall write . . ."

He couldn't help laughing: she had no sense of change at all. He said: "If he gets the letter he'll be interested—to hear I'm alive." But again he became serious. It was more difficult to feel pity for her than for the half-caste who a week ago had tagged him through the forest; but her case might be worse. He had so much excuse—poverty and fever and innumerable humiliations. He said: "Try not to be angry. Pray for me instead."

"The sooner you are dead the better."

He couldn't see her in the darkness, but there were plenty of faces he could remember from the old days which fitted the voice. When you visualized a man or woman carefully, you could always begin to feel pity . . . that was a quality God's image carried with it . . . when you saw the lines at the corners of the eyes, the shape of the mouth, how the hair grew, it was impossible to hate. Hate was just a failure of imagination. He began again to feel an enormous responsibility for this pious woman. "You and Padre José," she said. "It's people like you who make people mock—at real religion." She had, after all, as many excuses as the half-caste. He saw the kind of salon in which she spent her days, with the rocking-chair and

the family photographs, meeting no one. He said gently:
"You are not married, are you?"

"Why do you want to know?"

"And you never had a vocation?"

"They wouldn't believe it," she said bitterly.

He thought: Poor woman, she's had nothing, nothing at
all. If only one could find the right word . . . he leant hopelessly back, moving carefully so as not to wake the old
man. But the right words never came to him. He was more
out of touch with her kind than he had ever been: he
would have known what to say to her in the old days, feeling no pity at all, speaking with half a mind a platitude
or two. Now he felt useless: he was a criminal and ought
only to talk to criminals: he had done wrong again, trying
to break down her complacency. He might just as well
have let her go on thinking him a martyr.

His eyes closed and immediately he began to dream. He
was being pursued: he stood outside a door banging on it,
begging for admission, but nobody answered—there was
a word, a password, which would save him, but he had forgotten it. He tried desperately at random—cheese and
child, California, excellency, milk, Vera Cruz. His feet had
gone to sleep and he knelt outside the door. Then he knew
why he wanted to get in: he wasn't being pursued after
all: that was a mistake. His child lay beside him bleeding to
death and this was a doctor's house. He banged on the
door and shouted: "Even if I can't think of the right
word, haven't you a heart?" The child was dying and
looked up at him with middle-aged complacent wisdom.
She said: "You animal," and he woke again crying. He
couldn't have slept for more than a few seconds because

the woman was still talking about the vocation the nuns had refused to recognize. He said: "That made you suffer, didn't it? To suffer like that—perhaps it was better than being a nun and happy," and immediately after he had spoken he thought: A silly remark, what does it mean? Why can't I find something to say to her which she could remember? He gave up the effort: this place was very like the world elsewhere: people snatched at causes of pleasure and pride in cramped and disagreeable surroundings: there was no time to do anything worth doing, and always one dreamed of escape . . .

He didn't sleep again: he was striking yet another bargain with God. This time, if he escaped from the prison, he would escape altogether. He would go north, over the border. His escape was so improbable that, if it happened, it couldn't be anything else but a sign—an indication that he was doing more harm by his example than good by his occasional confessions. The old man moved against his shoulder and the night just stayed around them. The darkness was always the same and there were no clocks— there was nothing to indicate time passing. The only punctuation of the night was the sound of urination.

Suddenly, he realized that he could see a face, and then another: he had begun to forget that it would ever be another day, just as one forgets that one will ever die. It comes suddenly on one in a screeching brake or a whistle in the air, the knowledge that time moves and comes to an end. All the voices slowly became faces—there were no surprises: the confessional teaches you to recognize the shape of a voice—the loose lip or the weak chin and the false candour of the too straightforward eyes. He saw the pious woman a few feet away—uneasily dreaming with her prim mouth open, showing strong teeth like tombs: the old man: the boaster in the corner, and his woman asleep untidily across his knees. Now that the day was at last here, he was the only one awake, except for a small Indian boy who squatted cross-legged near the door with an expression of interested happiness, as if he had never known such friendly company. Over the courtyard the whitewash became visible upon the opposite wall. He began formally to pay his farewell to the world: he couldn't put any heart into it. His corruption was less evident to his sense than his death. One bullet, he thought, is almost certain to go directly through the heart—a squad must contain one accurate marksman. Life would go out in a "fraction of a second" (that was the phrase), but all night he had been realizing that time depends on clocks and the passage of light. There were no clocks and the light wouldn't change. Nobody really knew how long a second of pain could be. It might last a whole purgatory—or for ever. For some reason he thought of a man he had once shrived who was on the point of death with cancer—his relatives had had to muffle their faces, the smell of the rotting interior was so appalling. He wasn't a saint. Nothing in life was as ugly as death.

A voice in the yard called: "Montez." He sat on upon his dead feet; he thought automatically: "This suit isn't good for much more": it was smeared and fouled by the cell floor and his fellow prisoners: he had obtained it at great risk in a store down by the river, pretending to be a small farmer with ideas above his station. Then he remembered he wouldn't need it much longer—it came with an odd shock, like locking the door of one's house for the last time. The voice repeated impatiently: "Montez."

He remembered that that, for the moment, was his name. He looked up from his ruined suit and saw the sergeant unlocking the cell door. "Here, Montez." He let the old man's head fall gently back against the sweating wall and tried to stand up, but his feet crumpled like pastry. "Do you want to sleep all day?" the sergeant complained testily: something had irritated him: he wasn't as friendly as he had been the night before. He let out a kick at a sleeping man and beat on the cell door: "Come on. Wake up, all of you. Out into the yard." Only the Indian boy obeyed, sliding unobtrusively out, with his look of alien happiness. The sergeant complained: "The dirty hounds. Do they want us to wash them? You, Montez." Life began to return painfully to his feet. He managed to reach the door.

The yard had come sluggishly to life. A queue of men were bathing their faces at a single tap; a man in a vest and pants sat on the ground hugging a rifle. "Get out into the yard and wash," the sergeant yelled at them, but when the priest stepped out he snapped at him: "Not you, Montez."

"Not me."

"We've got other plans for you," the sergeant said.

The priest stood waiting while his fellow prisoners filed out into the yard. One by one they went past him: he looked at their feet and not their faces, standing like a temptation at the door. Nobody said a word: a woman's feet went draggingly by in black worn low-heeled shoes. He whispered without looking up: "Pray for me."

"What's that you said, Montez?"

He couldn't think of a lie: he felt as if ten years had exhausted his whole stock of deceit.

"What's that you said?"

The shoes had stopped moving. The woman's voice said: "He was begging." She added mercilessly: "He ought to have more sense. I've nothing for him." Then she went on, flat-footed, into the yard.

"Did you sleep well, Montez?" the sergeant badgered him.

"Not very well."

"What do you expect?" the sergeant said. "It'll teach you to like brandy too well, won't it?"

"Yes." He wondered how much longer all these preliminaries would take.

"Well, if you spend all your money on brandy, you've got to do a bit of work in return for a night's lodging. Fetch the pails out of the cells and mind you don't spill them—this place stinks enough as it is."

"Where do I take them to?"

The sergeant pointed to the door of the *excusado* beyond the tap. "Report to me when you've finished that," he said, and went bellowing orders back into the yard.

The priest bent down and took the pail: it was full and very heavy: he went bowed with the weight across the yard: sweat got into his eyes. He wiped them free and saw one behind another in the washing queue faces he knew— the hostages. There was Miguel, whom he had seen taken

away: he remembered the mother screaming out and the
lieutenant's tired anger and the sun coming up. They saw
him at the same time: he put down the heavy pail and
looked at them. Not to recognize them would have been
like a hint, a claim, a demand to them to go on suffering
and let him escape. Miguel had been beaten up: there was
a sore under his eye—flies buzzed round it as they buzz
round a mule's raw flank. Then the queue moved on: they
looked at the ground and passed him: strangers took their
place. He prayed silently: O God, send them someone more
worthwhile to suffer for. It seemed to him a damnable
mockery that they should sacrifice themselves for a whisky
priest with a bastard child. The soldier sat in his pants
with his gun between his knees paring his nails and biting
off the loose skin. In an odd way he felt abandoned because they had shown no sign of recognition.

The *excusado* was a cesspool with two planks across it
on which a man could stand. He emptied the pail and went
back across the yard to the row of cells. There were six:
one by one he took the pails: once he had to stop and
retch: splash, splash, to and fro across the yard. He came
to the last cell. It wasn't empty: a man lay back against
the wall: the early sun just reached his feet. Flies buzzed
around a mound of vomit on the floor. The eyes opened
and watched the priest stooping over the pail: two fangs
protruded. . . .

The priest moved quickly and splashed the floor. The
half-caste said in that too-familiar nagging tone: "Wait
a moment. You can't do that in here." He explained
proudly: "I'm not a prisoner. I'm a guest." The priest
made a motion of apology (he was afraid to speak) and

moved again. "Wait a moment," the half-caste commanded him again. "Come here."

The priest stood stubbornly, half-turned away, near the door.

"Come here," the half-caste said. "You're a prisoner, aren't you?—and I'm a guest—of the Governor. Do you want me to shout for a policeman? Then do as you're told: come here."

It seemed as if God were deciding . . . finally. He came, pail in hand, and stood beside the large flat naked foot, and the half-caste looked up at him from the shadow of the wall, asking him sharply and anxiously: "What are you doing here?"

"Cleaning up."

"You know what I mean."

"I was caught with a bottle of brandy," the priest said, trying to roughen his voice.

"I know you," the half-caste said, "I couldn't believe my eyes, but when you speak . . ."

"I don't think . . ."

"That priest's voice," the half-caste said with disgust. He was like a dog of a different breed: he couldn't help his hackles' rising. The big toe moved plumply and inimically. The priest put down the pail. He argued hopelessly: "You're drunk."

"Beer, beer," the half-caste said, "nothing but beer. They promised me the best of everything, but you can't trust them. Don't I know the jefe's got his own brandy locked away?"

"I must empty the pail."

"If you move, I'll shout. I've got so many things to

think about," the half-caste complained bitterly. The priest waited: there was nothing else to do: he was at the man's mercy—a silly phrase, for those malarial eyes had never known what mercy is. He was saved at any rate from the indignity of pleading.

"You see," the mestizo carefully explained, "I'm comfortable here." His yellow toes curled luxuriously beside the vomit. "Good food, beer, company, and this roof doesn't leak. You don't have to tell me what'll happen after—they'll kick me out like a dog, like a dog." He became shrill and indignant. "What have they got you here for? That's what I want to know. It looks crooked to me. It's my job, isn't it, to find you? Who's going to have the reward if they've got you already? The jefe, I shouldn't wonder, or that bastard sergeant." He brooded unhappily: "You can't trust a soul these days."

"And there's a Red Shirt," the priest said.

"A Red Shirt?"

"He really caught me."

"Mother of God," the mestizo said, "and they all have the ear of the Governor." He looked beseechingly up. He said: "You're an educated man. Advise me."

The priest said:

"It would be murder, a mortal sin."

"I don't mean that. I mean about the reward. You see, as long as they don't *know*, well, I'm comfortable here. A man deserves a few weeks' holiday. And you can't escape far, can you? It would be better, wouldn't it, to catch you out of here? In the town somewhere? I mean nobody else could claim . . ." He said furiously: "A poor man has so much to think about."

"I dare say," the priest said, "they'd give you *something* even here."

"Something," the mestizo said, levering himself up against the wall; "why shouldn't I have it all?"

"What's going on in here?" the sergeant said. He stood in the doorway, in the sunlight, looking in.

The priest said slowly: "He wanted me to clear up his vomit. I said you hadn't told me . . ."

"Oh, he's a guest," the sergeant said. "He's got to be treated right. You do as he says."

The mestizo smirked. He said: "And another bottle of beer, sergeant?"

"Not yet," the sergeant said. "You've got to look round the town first."

The priest picked up the pail and went back across the yard, leaving them arguing. He felt as if a gun were levelled at his back: he went into the *excusado* and emptied the pail: then came out again into the sun—the gun was levelled at his breast. The two men stood in the cell door talking. He walked across the yard: they watched him come. The sergeant said to the mestizo: "You say you're bilious and can't see properly this morning. You clean up your own vomit then. If you don't do *your* job . . ." Behind the sergeant's back the mestizo gave him a cunning and unreassuring wink. Now that the immediate fear was over, he felt only regret. God had decided. He had to go on with life, go on making decisions, acting on his own advice, making plans. . . .

It took him another half-hour to finish cleaning the cells, throwing a bucket of water over each floor; he watched the pious woman disappear—as if for ever—

through the archway to where her sister waited with the fine: they were both tied up in black shawls like something bought in the market, something hard and dry and second-hand. Then he reported again to the sergeant, who inspected the cells and criticized his work and ordered him to throw more water down, and then suddenly got tired of the whole business and told him he could go to the jefe for permission to leave. So he waited another hour on the bench outside the jefe's door, watching the sentry move lackadaisically to and fro in the hot sun.

And when at last a policeman led him in, it wasn't the jefe who sat at the desk, but the lieutenant. The priest stood not far from his own portrait on the wall and waited. Once he glanced quickly and nervously up at the old scrumpled newspaper cutting and thought with relief: It's not very like me now. What an unbearable creature he must have been in those days—and yet in those days he had been comparatively innocent. That was another mystery: it sometimes seemed to him that venial sins—impatience, an unimportant lie, pride, a neglected opportunity—cut you off from grace more completely than the worst sins of all. Then, in his innocence, he had felt no love for any-one: now in his corruption he had learnt . . .

"Well," the lieutenant said, "has he cleaned up the cells?"

He didn't take his eyes from his papers. He said: "Tell the sergeant I want two dozen men with properly cleaned rifles—within two minutes." He looked abstractedly up at the priest and said. "Well, what are you waiting for?"

"For permission, Excellency, to go away."

"I am not an excellency. Learn to call things by their

right names." He said sharply: "Have you been here before?"

"Never."

"Your name is Montez. I seem to come across too many people of that name in these days. Relations of yours?" He sat watching him closely, as if memory were beginning to work.

The priest said hurriedly: "My cousin was shot at Concepción."

"That was not my fault."

"I only meant—we were much alike. Our fathers were twins. Not half an hour between them. I thought your Excellency seemed to think . . ."

"As I remember him, he was quite different. A tall thin man . . . narrow shoulders . . ."

The priest said hurriedly: "Perhaps only to the family eye . . ."

"But then I only saw him once." It was almost as if the lieutenant had something on his conscience, as he sat with his dark Indian-blooded hands restless on the pages, brooding. . . . He said: "Where are you going?"

"God knows."

"You are all alike, you people. You never learn the truth—that God knows nothing." Some tiny scrap of life like a grain of smut went racing across the page in front of him: he pressed his finger down on it and said: "You had no money for your fine?" and watched another smut edge out between the leaves, scurrying for refuge: in this heat there was no end to life.

"No."

"How will you live?"

"Some work perhaps . . ."

"You are getting too old for work." He put his hand suddenly in his pocket and pulled out a five-peso piece. "There," he said. "Get out of here, and don't let me see your face again. Mind that."

The priest held the coin in his fist—the price of a Mass. He said with astonishment: "You're a good man."

CHAPTER FOUR

IT WAS still very early in the morning when he crossed the river, and came dripping up the other bank. He wouldn't have expected anybody to be about. The bungalow, the tin-roofed shed, the flag-staff: he had an idea that all Englishmen lowered their flags at sunset and sang "God Save the King." He came carefully round the corner of the shed and the door gave to his pressure. He was inside in the dark where he had been before: how many weeks ago? He had no idea. He only remembered that then the rains were a long way off: now they were beginning to break. In another week only an aeroplane would be able to cross the mountains.

He felt around him with his foot: he was so hungry that even a few bananas would be better than nothing—he had had no food for two days—but there was none here, none at all. He must have arrived on a day when the crop had gone down-river. He stood just inside the door trying to remember what the child had told him—the Morse code, her window: across the dead-white dusty yard the mosquito wire caught the sun. He was reminded suddenly of an empty larder. He began to listen anxiously:

there wasn't a sound anywhere—the day here hadn't yet begun with that first sleepy slap of a shoe on a cement floor, the claws of a dog scratching as it stretched, the knock-knock of a hand on a door. There was just nothing, nothing at all.

What *was* the time? How many hours of light had there been? It was impossible to tell: time was elastic: it stretched to snapping-point. Suppose, after all, it was not very early—it might be six, seven. . . . He realized how much he had counted on this child. She was the only person who could help him without endangering herself. Unless he got over the mountains in the next few days he was trapped—he might as well hand himself over to the police, because how could he live through the rains with nobody daring to give him food or shelter? It would have been better, quicker, if he had been recognized in the police station a week ago: so much less trouble. Then he heard a sound: it was like hope coming tentatively back: a scratching and a whining: this was what one meant by dawn—the noise of life. He waited for it—hungrily—in the doorway.

And it came: a mongrel bitch dragging herself across the yard: an ugly creature with bent ears, trailing a wounded or a broken leg, whimpering. There was something wrong with her back. She came very slowly: he could see her ribs like an exhibit in a natural history museum: it was obvious that she hadn't had food for days: she had been abandoned.

Unlike him, she retained a kind of hope. Hope was an instinct only the reasoning human mind could kill. An animal never knew despair. Watching her wounded progress he had a sense that this had happened daily—perhaps for weeks: he was watching one of the well-rehearsed effects of the new day, like bird-song in happier regions. She dragged herself up to the veranda door and began to scratch with one paw, lying oddly spreadeagled: her nose was down to a crack: she seemed to be breathing in the unused air of empty rooms: then she whined impatiently, and once her tail beat as if she heard something move inside. At last she began to howl.

The priest could bear it no longer: he knew now what it meant: he might as well let his eyes see. He came out into the yard and the animal turned awkwardly—the parody of a watchdog—and began to bark at him. It wasn't anybody she wanted: she wanted what she was used to: she wanted the old world back.

He looked in through a window—perhaps this was the child's room. Everything had been removed from it except the useless or the broken. There was a cardboard box full of torn paper and a small chair which had lost a leg. There was a large nail in the whitewashed wall where a mirror perhaps had been hung—or a picture. There was a broken shoe-horn.

The bitch was dragging itself along the veranda growling: instinct is like a sense of duty—one can confuse it with loyalty very easily. He avoided the animal simply by stepping out into the sun: it couldn't turn quickly enough to follow him: he pushed at the door and it opened—nobody had bothered to lock up. An ancient alligator's skin which had been badly cut and inefficiently dried hung on the wall. There was a snuffle behind him and he turned: the bitch had two paws over the threshold, but now that he was established in the house, she didn't mind him. He was there, in possession, the master, and there were all kinds of smells to occupy her mind. She pushed herself across the floor, making a wet noise.

The priest opened a door on the left—perhaps it had been the bedroom: in a corner lay a pile of old medicine bottles: small fingers of crudely coloured liquid lay in some of them. There were medicines for headaches, stomachaches, medicines to be taken after meals and before meals. Somebody must have been very ill to need so many. There was a hair-slide, broken, and a ball of hair-combings—very fair hair turning dusty white. He thought with relief: It is her mother, only her mother.

He tried another room which faced, through the mosquito wire, the slow and empty river. This had been the living-room, for they had left behind the table—a folding card-table of plywood bought for a few shillings which hadn't been worth taking with them—wherever they'd gone. Had the mother been dying? he wondered. They had cleared the crop perhaps, and gone to the capital, where there was a hospital. He left that room and entered another: this was the one he had seen from the outside—the child's. He turned over the contents of the waste-paper box with sad curiosity. He felt as if he were clearing up after a death, deciding what would be too painful to keep.

He read: "The immediate cause of the American War of Independence was what is called the Boston Tea Party." It seemed to be part of an essay written in large firm letters, carefully. "But the real issue" (the word was spelt wrong, crossed out, and rewritten) "was whether it was right to tax people who were not represented in

Parliament." It must have been a rough copy—there were so many corrections. He picked out another scrap at random—it was about people called Whigs and Tories—the words were incomprehensible to him. Something like a duster flopped down off the roof into the yard: it was a buzzard. He read on: "If five men took three days to mow a meadow of four acres five rods, how much would two men mow in one day?" There was a neat line ruled under the question, and then the calculations began—a hopeless muddle of figures which didn't work out. There was a hint of heat and irritation in the scrumpled paper tossed aside. He could see her very clearly, dispensing with that question decisively: the neat accurately moulded face with the two pinched pigtails. He remembered her readiness to swear eternal enmity against anyone who hurt him—and he remembered his own child enticing him by the rubbish-dump.

He shut the door carefully behind him as if he were preventing an escape. He could hear the bitch—somewhere—growling, and followed her into what had once been the kitchen. She lay in a deathly attitude over a bone with her old teeth bared. An Indian's face hung outside the mosquito wire like something hooked up to dry—dark, withered, and unappetizing. He had his eyes on the bone as if he coveted it. He looked up as the priest came across the kitchen and immediately was gone as if he had never been there, leaving the house just as abandoned. The priest, too, looked at the bone.

There was a lot of meat on it still: a small cloud of flies hung above it a few inches from the bitch's muzzle, and the bitch kept her eye fixed, now that the Indian was gone, on the priest. They were all in competition. The priest advanced a step or two and stamped twice: "Go," he said, "go," flapping his hands, but the mongrel wouldn't move, flattened above the bone, with all the resistance left in the broken body concentrated in the yellow eyes, burring between her teeth. It was like hate on a deathbed. The priest came cautiously forward: he wasn't yet used to the idea that the animal couldn't spring—one associates a dog with action, but this creature, like any crippled human being, could only think. You could see the thoughts—hunger and hope and hatred—stuck on the eyeball.

The priest put out his hand towards the bone and the flies buzzed upwards: the animal became silent, watching. "There, there," the priest said cajolingly; he made little enticing movements in the air and the animal stared back. Then the priest turned and moved away as if he were abandoning the bone: he droned gently to himself a phrase from the Mass, elaborately paying no attention. Then he switched quickly round again: it hadn't worked: the bitch watched him, screwing round her neck to follow his ingenious movements.

For a moment he became furious—that a mongrel bitch with a broken back should steal the only food. He swore at it—popular expressions picked up beside bandstands: he would have been surprised in other circumstances that they came so readily to his tongue. Then suddenly he laughed: this was human dignity disputing with a bitch over a bone. When he laughed the animal's ears went back, twitching at the tips—apprehensive. But he felt no pity— her life had no importance beside that of a human being: he looked round for something to throw, but the room had

been cleared of nearly everything except the bone; perhaps—who knows?—that had been left deliberately for
this mongrel; he could imagine the child remembering that,
before she left with the sick mother and the stupid father:
he had the impression that it was always she who had to
think. He could find for his purpose nothing better than
a broken wire rack which had been used for vegetables.

He advanced again towards the bitch and struck her
lightly on the muzzle. She snapped at the wire with her
old broken teeth and wouldn't move. He beat at her again
more fiercely and she caught the wire—he had to rasp it
away. He struck again and again before he realized that
she couldn't, except with great exertion, move at all: she
was unable to escape his blows or leave the bone. She just
had to endure: her eyes yellow and scared and malevolent
shining back at him between the blows.

So then he changed his method: he used the vegetable
rack as a kind of muzzle, holding back the teeth with it,
while he bent and captured the bone. One paw tugged at
it and gave way; he lowered the wire and jumped back—
the animal tried without success to follow him, then lapsed
upon the floor. The priest had won: he had his bone. The
bitch no longer tried to growl.

The priest tore off some of the raw meat with his teeth
and began to chew: no food had ever tasted so good, and
now that for the moment he was happy he began to feel a
little pity. He thought: I will eat just so much and she can
have the rest. He marked mentally a point upon the bone
and tore off another piece. The nausea he had felt for
hours now began to die away and leave an honest hunger:
he ate on and the bitch watched him. Now that the fight

was over she seemed to bear no malice: her tail began to beat the floor, hopefully, questioningly. The priest reached the point he had marked, but now it seemed to him that his previous hunger had been imaginary: this was hunger, what he felt now: a man's need was greater than a dog's: he would leave that knuckle of meat at the joint. But when the moment came he ate that too—after all, the dog had teeth: she would eat the bone itself. He dropped it under her muzzle and left the kitchen.

He made one more progress through the empty rooms. A broken shoe-horn: medicine bottles: an essay on the American War of Independence—there was nothing to tell him why they had gone away. He came out onto the veranda and saw through a gap in the planks that a book had fallen to the ground and lay between the rough pillars of brick which raised the house out of the track of ants. It was months since he had seen a book. It was almost like a promise, mildewing there under the piles, of better things to come—life going on in private houses with wireless sets and bookshelves and beds made ready for the night and a cloth laid for food. He knelt down on the ground and reached for it. He suddenly realized that when once the long struggle was over and he had crossed the mountains and the state line, life might, after all, be enjoyed again.

It was an English book—but from his years in an American seminary he retained enough English to read it, with a little difficulty. Even if he had been unable to understand a word, it would still have been a book. It was called *Jewels Five Words Long; A Treasury of English Verse*, and on the fly-leaf was pasted a printed certificate —Awarded to . . . and then the name Coral Fellows filled up in ink . . . for proficiency in English Composition, Third Grade. There was an obscure coat-of-arms, which seemed to include a griffin and an oak leaf, a Latin motto: *"Virtus Laudata Crescit,"* and a signature from a rubber stamp, Henry Beckley, B.A., Principal of Private Tutorials, Ltd.

The priest sat down on the veranda steps. There was silence everywhere—no life around the abandoned banana station except the buzzard which hadn't yet given up hope. The Indian might never have existed at all. After a meal, the priest thought with sad amusement, a little reading, and opened the book at random. Coral—so that was the child's name; he thought of the shops in Vera Cruz full of it—the hard brittle jewellery which was thought for some reason so suitable for young girls after their first communion. He read:

> "I come from haunts of coot and hern,
> I make a sudden sally,
> And sparkle out among the fern,
> To bicker down a valley."

It was a very obscure poem, full of words which were like Esperanto. He thought: So this is English poetry: how odd. The little poetry he knew dealt mainly with agony, remorse, and hope. These verses ended on a philosophical note—"For men may come and men may go. But I go on for ever." The triteness and untruth of "for ever" shocked him a little: a poem like this ought not to be in a child's hands. The buzzard came picking its way across the yard, a dusty and desolate figure: every now and then it lifted sluggishly from the earth and flapped down twenty yards on. The priest read:

> " 'Come back! Come back!' he cried in grief
>   Across the stormy water,
>   'And I'll forgive your Highland chief—
>   My daughter, O my daughter.' "

That sounded to him more impressive—though hardly, perhaps, any more than the other—stuff for children. He felt in the foreign words the ring of genuine passion and repeated to himself on his hot and lonely perch the last line—"My daughter, O my daughter." The words seemed to contain all that he felt himself of repentance, longing, and unhappy love.

It was the oddest thing that ever since that hot and crowded night in the cell he had passed into a region of abandonment—almost as if he had died there with the old man's head on his shoulder and now wandered in a kind of limbo, because he wasn't good or bad enough. . . . Life didn't exist any more: it wasn't merely a matter of the banana station. Now as the storm broke and he scurried for shelter he knew quite well what he would find—nothing.

The huts leapt up in the lightning and stood there shaking—then disappeared again in the rumbling darkness. The rain hadn't come yet: it was sweeping up from Campeche Bay in great sheets, covering the whole state in its methodical advance. Between the thunderbreaks he could imagine that he heard it—a gigantic rustle moving across

towards the mountains which were now so close to him—
a matter of twenty miles.

He reached the first hut: the door was open, and as the
lightning quivered he saw, as he expected, nobody at all.
Just a pile of maize and the indistinct grey movement of—
perhaps—a rat. He dashed for the next hut, but it was
the same as ever (the maize and nothing else), just as if all
human life were receding before him, as if Somebody had
determined that from now on he was to be left alone—altogether alone. As he stood there the rain reached the clearing: it came out of the forest like thick white smoke and
moved on. It was as if an enemy were laying a gas-cloud
across a whole territory, carefully, to see that nobody escaped. The rain spread and stayed just long enough, as
though the enemy had his stop-watch out and knew to a
second the limit of the lungs' endurance. The roof held the
rain out for a while and then let it through—the twigs bent
under the weight of water and shot apart: it came through
in half a dozen places, pouring down in black funnels:
then the downpour stopped and the roof dripped and the
rain moved on, with the lightning quivering on its flanks
like a protective barrage. In a few minutes it would reach
the mountains: a few more storms like this and they would
be impassable.

He had been walking all day and he was very tired: he
found a dry spot and sat down. When the lightning struck
he could see the clearing: all around was the gentle noise
of the dripping water. It was nearly like peace, but not
quite. For peace you needed human company—his alone-
ness was like a threat of things to come. Suddenly he remembered—for no apparent reason—a day of rain at the

American seminary, the glass windows of the library steamed over with the central heating, the tall shelves of sedate books, and a young man—a stranger from Tucson —drawing his initials on the pane with his finger—that was peace. He looked at it from the outside: he couldn't believe that he would ever again get in. He had made his own world, and this was it—the empty broken huts, the storm going by, and fear again—fear because he was not alone after all.

Somebody was moving outside, cautiously. The footsteps would come a little way and then stop. He waited apathetically, and the roof dripped behind him. He thought of the half-caste padding around the city, seeking a really cast-iron occasion for his betrayal. A face peered round the hut door at him and quickly withdrew— an old woman's face, but you could never tell with Indians —she mightn't have been more than twenty. He got up and went outside—she scampered back from before him in her heavy sack-like skirt, her black plaits swinging heavily. Apparently his loneliness was only to be broken by these evasive faces—creatures who looked as if they had come out of the Stone Age, who withdrew again quickly.

He was stirred by a sort of sullen anger—this one should not withdraw. He pursued her across the clearing, splashing in the pools, but she had a start and no sense of shame and she got into the forest before him. It was useless looking for her there, and he returned towards the nearest hut. It wasn't the hut which he had been sheltering in before, but it was just as empty. What had happened to these people? He knew well enough that these more or less savage encampments were temporary only: the Indians would cultivate a small patch of ground and when they had exhausted the soil for the time being, they would simply move away—they knew nothing about the rotation of crops, but when they moved they would take their maize with them. This was more like flight—from force or disease. He had heard of such flights in the case of sickness, and the horrible thing, of course, was that they carried the sickness with them wherever they moved: sometimes they became panicky like flies against a pane, but discreetly, letting nobody know, muting their hubbub. He turned moodily again to stare out at the clearing, and there was the Indian woman creeping back—towards the hut where he had sheltered. He called out to her sharply and again she fled, shambling, towards the forest. Her clumsy progress reminded him of a bird feigning a broken wing. . . . He made no movement to follow her, and before she reached the trees she stopped and watched him; he began to move slowly back towards the other hut. Once he turned: she was following him at a distance, keeping her eyes on him. Again he was reminded of something animal or bird-like, full of anxiety. He walked on, aiming directly at the hut—far away beyond it the lightning stabbed down, but you could hardly hear the thunder: the sky was clearing overhead and the moon came out. Suddenly he heard an odd artificial cry, and turning he saw the woman making back towards the forest—then she stumbled, flung up her arms, and fell to the ground—like the bird offering herself.

He felt quite certain now that something valuable was in the hut, perhaps hidden among the maize, and he paid her no attention, going in. Now that the lightning had moved on, he couldn't see—he felt across the floor until he reached the pile of maize. Outside the padding footsteps came nearer. He began to feel all over it—perhaps food was hidden there—and the dry crackle of the leaves was added to the drip of water and the cautious footsteps, like the faint noises of people busy about their private businesses. Then he put his hand on a face.

He couldn't be frightened any more by a thing like that —it was something human he had his fingers on. They moved down the body: it was that of a child who lay completely quiet under his hand. In the doorway the moonlight showed the woman's face indistinctly: she was probably convulsed with anxiety, but you couldn't tell. He thought —I must get this into the open where I can see. . . .

It was a male child—perhaps three years old: a withered bullet head with a mop of black hair: unconscious— but not dead: he could feel the faintest movement in the breast. He thought of disease again until he took out his hand and found that the child was wet with blood, not sweat. Horror and disgust touched him—violence everywhere: was there no end to violence? He said to the woman sharply: "What happened?" It was as if man in all this state had been left to man.

The woman knelt two or three feet away, watching his hands. She knew a little Spanish, because she replied: "*Americano*." The child wore a kind of brown one-piece smock: he lifted it up to the neck: he had been shot in three places. Life was going out of him all the time: there was nothing—really—to be done, but one had to try. . . . He said "Water" to the woman, "Water," but she didn't seem to understand, squatting there, watching him. It was a mistake one easily made, to think that just because the eyes expressed nothing, there was no grief. When he touched the child he could see her move on her haunches— she was ready to attack him with her teeth if the child so much as moaned.

He began to speak slowly and gently (he couldn't tell how much she understood): "We must have water. To wash him. You needn't be afraid of me. I will do him no harm." He took off his shirt and began to tear it into strips—it was hopelessly insanitary, but what else was there to do? except pray, of course, but one didn't pray for life, this life. He repeated again: "Water." The woman seemed to understand—she gazed hopelessly round at where the rain stood in pools—that was all there was. Well, he thought, the earth's as clean as any vessel would have been. He soaked a piece of his shirt and leant over the child: he could hear the woman slide closer along the ground—a menacing approach. He tried to reassure her again: "You needn't be afraid of me. I am a priest."

The word "priest" she understood: she leant forward and grabbed at the hand which held the wet scrap of shirt and kissed it. At that moment, while her lips were on his hand, the child's face wrinkled, the eyes opened and glared at them, the tiny body shook with a kind of fury of pain; they watched the eyeballs roll up and suddenly become fixed, like marbles in a solitaire-board, yellow and ugly with death. The woman let go his hand and scrambled to a pool of water, cupping her fingers for it. The priest said: "We don't need that any more," standing up with his hands full of wet shirt. The woman opened her fingers and let the water fall. She said "Father" imploringly, and he wearily went down on his knees and began to pray.

He could feel no meaning any longer in prayers like these—the Host was different: to lay that between a dying man's lips was to lay God. That was a fact—something you could touch, but this was no more than a pious aspiration. Why should Anyone listen to *his* prayers? Sin was like a constriction which prevented their escape: he could feel his prayers like undigested food heavy in his body, unable to escape.

When he had finished he lifted up the body and carried it back into the hut like a piece of furniture—it seemed a waste of time to have taken it out, like a chair you carry out into the garden and back again because the grass is wet. The woman followed him meekly—she didn't seem to want to touch the body, just watched him put it back in the dark upon the maize. He sat down on the ground and said slowly: "It will have to be buried."

She understood that, nodding.

He said: "Where is your husband? Will he help you?"

She began to talk rapidly: it might have been Camacho she was speaking: he couldn't understand more than an occasional Spanish word here and there. The word "Americano" occurred again—and he remembered the wanted man whose portrait had shared the wall with his. He asked her: "Did *he* do this?" She shook her head. What had happened? he wondered. Had the man taken shelter here and had the soldiers fired into the huts? It was not unlikely. He suddenly had his attention caught: she had said the name of the banana station—but there had been no dying person there: no sign of violence—unless silence and desertion were signs. He had assumed the mother had been taken ill: it might be something worse—and he imagined that stupid Captain Fellows taking down his gun, presenting himself clumsily armed to a man whose chief talent it was to draw quickly or to shoot directly from the pocket. That poor child . . . what responsibilities she had perhaps been forced to undertake.

He shook the thought away and said: "Have you a spade?" She didn't understand that, and he had to go through the motions of digging. Another roll of thunder came between them: a second storm was coming up, as if the enemy had discovered that the first barrage after all had left a few survivors—this would flatten them. Again he could hear the enormous breathing of the rain miles away: he realized the woman had spoken the one word "church." Her Spanish consisted of isolated words. He wondered what she meant by that. Then the rain reached them. It came down like a wall between him and escape, fell altogether in a heap and built itself up around them. All the light went out except when the lightning flashed.

The roof couldn't keep out *this* rain: it came dripping through everywhere: the dry maize leaves where the dead child lay crackled like burning wood. He shivered with cold: he was probably on the edge of fever—he must get away before he was incapable of moving at all. The woman (he couldn't see her now) said *"Iglesia"* again imploringly. It occurred to him that she wanted her child buried near a church or perhaps only taken to an altar, so that he might be touched by the feet of a Christ. It was a fantastic notion.

He took advantage of a long quivering stroke of blue light to describe with his hands his sense of the impossibility. "The soldiers," he said, and she replied immediately: "*Americano.*" That word always came up, like one with many meanings which depends on the accent whether it is to be taken as an explanation, a warning, or a threat. Perhaps she meant that the soldiers were all occupied in the chase—but even so, this rain was ruining everything. It was still twenty miles to the border, and the mountain paths after the storm were probably impassable—and a church—he hadn't the faintest idea of where there would be a church. He hadn't so much as seen such a thing for years now: it was difficult to believe that they still existed only a few days' journey off. When the lightning went on again he saw the woman watching him with stony patience.

For the last thirty hours they had had only sugar to eat —large brown lumps of it the size of a baby's skull: they had seen no one, and they had exchanged no words at all. What was the use when almost the only words they had in common were "*iglesia*" and "*Americano*"? The woman followed at his heels with the dead child strapped on her back: she seemed never to tire. A day and a night brought them out of the marshes to the foot-hills: they slept fifty feet up above the slow green river, under a projecting piece of rock where the soil was dry—everywhere else was deep mud. The woman sat with her knees drawn up, and her head down—she showed no emotion, but she put the child's body behind her as if it needed protection from marauders like other lifeless possessions. They had travelled by the sun until the black wooded bar of mountain

told them where to go. They might have been the only survivors of a world which was dying out—they carried the
visible marks of the dying with them.

Sometimes he wondered whether he was safe, but when
there are no visible boundaries between one state and another—no passport examination or customs house—danger just seems to go on, travelling with you, lifting its
heavy feet in the same way as you do. There seemed to be
so little progress: the path would rise steeply, perhaps five
hundred feet, and fall again, clogged with mud. Once it
took an enormous hairpin bend, so that after three hours
they had returned to a point opposite their starting-place,
less than a hundred yards away.

At sunset on the second day they came out onto a wide
plateau covered with short grass: an odd grove of crosses
stood up blackly against the sky, leaning at different
angles—some as high as twenty feet, some not much more
than eight. They were like trees that had been left to seed.
The priest stopped and stared at them: they were the first
Christian symbols he had seen for more than five years
publicly exposed—if you could call this empty plateau in
the mountains a public place. No priest could have been
concerned in the strange rough group; it was the work of
Indians and had nothing in common with the tidy vestments of the Mass and the elaborately worked out symbols of the liturgy. It was like a short cut to the dark and
magical heart of the faith—to the night when the graves
opened and the dead walked. There was a movement behind him and he turned.

The woman had gone down on her knees and was shuf-
fling slowly across the cruel ground towards the group of

crosses: the dead baby rocked on her back. When she reached the tallest cross she unhooked the child and held the face against the wood and afterwards the loins: then she crossed herself, not as ordinary Catholics do, but in a curious and complicated pattern which included the nose and ears. Did she expect a miracle? And if she did, why should it not be granted her? the priest wondered. Faith, one was told, could move mountains, and here was faith—faith in the spittle that healed the blind man and the voice that raised the dead. The evening star was out: it hung low down over the edge of the plateau: it looked as if it was within reach: and a small hot wind stirred. The priest found himself watching the child for some movement. When none came, it was as if God had missed an opportunity. The woman sat down, and taking a lump of sugar from her bundle, began to eat, and the child lay quiet at the foot of the cross. Why, after all, should we expect God to punish the innocent with more life?

"*Vamos*," the priest said, but the woman scraped the sugar with her sharp front teeth, paying no attention. He looked up at the sky and saw the evening star blotted out by black clouds. "*Vamos*." There was no shelter anywhere on this plateau.

The woman never stirred: the broken snub-nosed face between the black plaits was completely passive: it was as if she had fulfilled her duty and could now take up her everlasting rest. The priest suddenly shivered: the ache which had pressed like a stiff hat-rim across his forehead all day dug deeper in. He thought: I have to get to shelter —a man's first duty is to himself—even the Church taught that, in a way. The whole sky was blackening: the crosses stuck up like dry and ugly cacti: he made off to the edge of the plateau. Once, before the path led down, he looked back—the woman was still biting at the lump of sugar, and he remembered that it was all the food they had.

The way was very steep—so steep he had to turn and go down backwards: on either side trees grew perpendicularly out of the grey rock, and five hundred feet below the path climbed up again. He began to sweat, and he had an appalling thirst: when the rain came it was at first a kind of relief. He stayed where he was, hunched back against a boulder—there was no shelter before he reached the bottom of the barranca, and it hardly seemed worth while to make that effort. He was shivering now more or less continuously, and the ache seemed no longer inside his head—it was something outside, almost anything, a noise, a thought, a smell. The senses were jumbled up together. At one moment the ache was like a tiresome voice explaining to him that he had taken the wrong path: he remembered a map he had once seen of the two adjoining states. The state from which he was escaping was peppered with villages—in the hot marshy land people bred as readily as mosquitoes, but in the next state—in the north-west corner —there was hardly anything but blank white paper. You're on the blank paper now, the ache told him. But there's a path, he argued wearily. Oh, a path, the ache said, a path may take you fifty miles before it reaches anywhere at all: you know you won't last that distance. There's just white paper all around.

At another time the ache was a face. He became convinced that the American was watching him—he had a skin all over spots like a newspaper photograph. Appar-

ently he had followed them all the way because he wanted
to kill the mother as well as the child: he was sentimental
that way. It was necessary to do something: the rain was
like a curtain behind which almost anything might happen. He thought: I shouldn't have left her alone like that,
God forgive me. I have no responsibility; what can you expect of a whisky priest? And he struggled to his feet and
began to climb back towards the plateau. He was tormented by ideas: it wasn't only the woman: he was responsible for the American as well: the two faces—his own
and the gunman's—were hanging together on the police-
station wall, as if they were brothers in a family portrait
gallery. You didn't put temptation in a brother's way.

Shivering and sweating and soaked with rain he came
up over the edge of the plateau. There was nobody there—
a dead child was not somebody, just a useless object abandoned at the foot of one of the crosses: the mother had
gone home. She had done what she wanted to do. The surprise lifted him, as it were, out of his fever before it
dropped him back again. A small lump of sugar—all that
was left—lay by the child's mouth—in case a miracle
should still happen or for the spirit to eat? The priest
bent down with an obscure sense of shame and took it: the
dead child couldn't growl back at him like a broken dog:
but who was he to disbelieve in miracles? He hesitated,
while the rain poured down: then he put the sugar in his
mouth. If God chose to give back life, couldn't He give
food as well?

Immediately he began to eat, the fever returned: the
sugar stuck in his throat: he felt an appalling thirst.
Crouching down he tried to lick some water from the un-

even ground: he even sucked at his soaked trousers. The child lay under the streaming rain like a dark heap of cattle dung. The priest moved away again, back to the edge of the plateau and down the barranca side: it was loneliness he felt now—even the face had gone; he was moving alone across that blank white sheet, going deeper every moment into the abandoned land.

Somewhere, in some direction, there were towns, of course: go far enough and you reached the coast, the Pacific, the railway track to Guatemala: there were roads there and motor-cars. He hadn't seen a railway train for ten years. He could imagine the black line following the coast along the map, and he could see the fifty, hundred miles of unknown country. That was where he was: he had escaped too completely from men. Nature would kill him now.

All the same, he went on: there was no point in going back towards the deserted village, the banana station with its dying mongrel and its shoe-horn. There was nothing you could do except put one foot forward and then the other: scrambling down and then scrambling up: from the top of the barranca, when the rain passed on, there was nothing to see except a huge scrumpled land, forest and mountain, with the grey wet veil moving over. He looked once and never looked again. It was too like watching despair.

It must have been hours later that he ceased to climb: it was evening and forest: monkeys crashed invisibly among the trees with an effect of clumsiness and recklessness, and what were probably snakes hissed away like match-flames through the grass. He wasn't afraid of them:

they were a form of life, and he could feel life retreating from him all the time. It wasn't only people who were going: even the animals and the reptiles moved away: presently he would be left alone with nothing but his own breath. He began to recite to himself: "O God, I have loved the beauty of Thy house," and the smell of soaked and rotting leaves and the hot night and the darkness made him believe that he was in a mine shaft, going down into the earth to bury himself. Presently he would find his grave.

When a man came towards him carrying a gun he did nothing at all. The man approached cautiously: you didn't expect to find another person underground. He said: "Who are you?" with his gun ready.

The priest gave his name to a stranger for the first time in ten years: Father So-and-so, because he was tired and there seemed no object in going on living.

"A priest?" the man asked, with astonishment. "Where have you come from?"

The fever lifted again: a little reality seeped back: he said: "It is all right. I will not bring you any trouble. I am going on." He screwed up all his remaining energy and walked on: a puzzled face penetrated his fever and receded: there were going to be no more hostages, he assured himself aloud. Footsteps followed him, he was like a dangerous man you see safely off an estate before you go home. He repeated aloud: "It is all right. I am not staying here. I want nothing."

"Father . . ." the voice said, humbly and anxiously.

"I will go right away." He tried to run and came suddenly out of the forest onto a long slope of grass. There

were lights and huts, below, and up here at the edge of the
forest a big whitewashed building—a barracks? were there
soldiers? He said: "If I have been seen I will give myself
up. I assure you no one shall get into trouble because of
me."

"Father . . ." He was racked with his headache; he
stumbled and put his hand against the wall for support.
He felt immeasurably tired. He asked: "The barracks?"

"Father," the voice said, puzzled and worried, "it is our
church."

"A church?" The priest ran his hands incredulously
over the wall like a blind man trying to recognize a particular house, but he was too tired to feel anything at all. He
heard the man with the gun babbling out of sight: "Such
an honour, father. The bell must be rung . . ." and he sat
down suddenly on the rain-drenched grass, and leaning his
head against the white wall, he fell asleep, with home behind his shoulder-blades.

His dream was full of a jangle of cheerful noise.

CHAPTER ONE

THE middle-aged woman sat on the veranda darning socks: she wore pince-nez and she had kicked off her shoes for comfort. Mr. Lehr, her brother, read a New York magazine—it was three weeks old, but that didn't really matter: the whole scene was like peace.

"Just help yourself to water," Miss Lehr said, "when you want it."

A huge earthenware jar stood in a cool corner with a ladle and a tumbler. "Don't you have to boil the water?" the priest asked.

"Oh, no, *our* water's fresh and clean," Miss Lehr said primly, as if she couldn't answer for anybody else's.

"Best water in the state," her brother said. The shiny magazine leaves crackled as they turned, covered with photographs of big clean-shaven mastiff jowls—Senators and Congressmen. Pasture stretched away beyond the garden fence, undulating gently towards the next mountain range, and a tulipan tree blossomed and faded daily at the gate.

"You certainly are looking better, father," Miss Lehr said. They both spoke rather guttural English with slight

American accents—Mr. Lehr had left Germany when he was a boy to escape military service: he had a shrewd lined idealistic face. You needed to be shrewd in this country if you were going to retain any ideals at all: he was cunning in the defence of the good life.

"Oh," Mr. Lehr said. "He only needed to rest up a few days." He was quite incurious about this man whom his foreman had brought in on a mule in a state of collapse three days before. All he knew the priest had told him: that was another thing this country taught you—never to ask questions or to look ahead.

"Soon I can go on," the priest said.

"You don't have to hurry," Miss Lehr said, turning over her brother's sock, looking for holes.

"It's so quiet here."

"Oh," Mr. Lehr said, "we've had our troubles." He turned a page and said: "That Senator Huey Long—they ought to control him. It doesn't do any good insulting other countries."

"Haven't they tried to take your land away?"

The idealistic face turned his way: it wore a look of innocent craft. "Oh, I gave them as much as they asked for—five hundred acres of barren land. I saved a lot on taxes. I never could get anything to grow there." He nodded towards the veranda posts. "That was the last *real* trouble. See the bullet-holes. Villa's men."

The priest got up again and drank more water: he wasn't very thirsty: he was satisfying a sense of luxury. He asked: "How long will it take me to get to Las Casas?"

"You could do it in four days," Mr. Lehr said.

"Not in *his* condition," Miss Lehr said. "Six."

"It will seem so strange," the priest said. "A city with churches, a university . . ."

"Of course," Mr. Lehr said, "my sister and I are Lutherans. We don't hold with your church, father. Too much luxury, it seems to me, while the people starve."

Miss Lehr said: "Now, dear, it isn't the father's fault."

"Luxury?" the priest said: he stood by the earthenware jar, glass in hand, trying to collect his thoughts, staring out over the long and peaceful grassy slopes. "You mean . . . ?" Perhaps Mr. Lehr was right: he had lived very easily once, and here he was, already settling down to idleness again.

"All the gold leaf in the churches."

"It's often just paint, you know," the priest murmured conciliatingly. He thought: Yes, three days and I've done nothing. Nothing, and he looked down at his feet elegantly shod in a pair of Mr. Lehr's shoes, his legs in Mr. Lehr's spare trousers. Mr. Lehr said: "He won't mind my speaking my mind. We're all Christians here."

"Of course. I like to hear . . ."

"It seems to me you people make a lot of fuss about inessentials."

"Yes? You mean . . ."

"Fasting . . . fish on Friday . . ."

Yes, he remembered like something in his childhood that there had been a time when he had observed these rules. He said: "After all, Mr. Lehr, you're a German. A great military nation."

"I was never a soldier. I disapprove . . ."

"Yes, of course, but still you understand—discipline is necessary. Drills may be no good in battle, but they form

the character. Otherwise you get—well, people like me."
He looked down with sudden hatred at the shoes—they
were like the badge of a deserter. "People like me," he repeated with fury.

There was a good deal of embarrassment: Miss Lehr began to say something: "Why, father . . ." but Mr. Lehr
forestalled her, laying down the magazine and its load of
well-shaved politicians. He said in his German-American
voice, with its guttural precision: "Well, I guess it's time
for a bath now. Will you be coming, father?" and the
priest obediently followed him into their common bedroom.
He took off Mr. Lehr's clothes and put on Mr. Lehr's
mackintosh and followed Mr. Lehr barefoot across the
veranda and the field beyond. The day before he had asked
apprehensively: "Are there no snakes?" and Mr. Lehr had
grunted contemptuously that if there were any snakes
they'd pretty soon get out of the way. Mr. Lehr and his
sister had combined to drive out savagery by simply ignor-
ing anything that conflicted with an ordinary German-
American homestead. It was, in its way, an admirable way
of life.

At the bottom of the field there was a little shallow
stream running over brown pebbles. Mr. Lehr took off his
dressing-gown and lay down flat on his back: there was
something upright and idealistic even in the thin elderly
legs with their scrawny muscles. Tiny fishes played over
his chest and made little tugs at his nipples undisturbed:
this was the skeleton of the youth who had disapproved of
militarism to the point of flight: presently he sat up and
began carefully to soap his lean thighs. The priest afterwards took the soap and followed suit. He felt it was ex-

pected of him, though he couldn't help thinking it was a waste of time. Sweat cleaned you as effectively as water. But this was the race which had invented the proverb that cleanliness was next to godliness—cleanliness, not purity.

All the same, one did feel an enormous luxury lying there in the little cold stream while the sun flattened. . . . He thought of the prison cell with the old man and the pious woman, the half-caste lying across the hut door, the dead child and the abandoned station. He thought with shame of his daughter left to her knowledge and her ignorance by the rubbish-dump. He had no right to such luxury.

Mr. Lehr said: "Would you mind—the soap?"

He had heaved over on his face, and now he set to work on his back.

The priest said: "I think perhaps I should tell you—tomorrow I am saying Mass in the village. Would you prefer me to leave your house? I do not wish to make trouble for you."

Mr. Lehr splashed seriously, cleaning himself. He said: "Oh, they won't bother me. But you had better be careful. You know, of course, that it's against the law."

"Yes," the priest said. "I know that."

"A priest I knew was fined four hundred pesos. He couldn't pay and they sent him to prison for a week. What are you smiling at?"

"Only because it seems so—peaceful—here. Prison for a week."

"Well, I've always heard you people get your own back when it comes to collections. Would you like the soap?"

"No, thank you. I have finished."

"We'd better be drying ourselves then. Miss Lehr likes to have her bath before sunset."

As they came back to the bungalow in single file they met Miss Lehr, very bulky under her dressing-gown. She asked mechanically, like a clock with a very gentle chime: "Is the water nice today?" and her brother answered, as he must have answered a thousand times: "Pleasantly cool, dear," and she slopped down across the grass in bedroom slippers, stooping slightly with short sight.

"If you wouldn't mind," Mr. Lehr said, shutting the bedroom door, "staying in here till Miss Lehr comes back. One can see the stream—you understand—from the front of the house." He began to dress, tall and bony and a little stiff. Two brass bedsteads, a single chair and a wardrobe, the room was monastic, except that there was no cross— no "inessentials" as Mr. Lehr would have put it. But there was a Bible. It lay on the floor beside one of the beds in a black oilskin cover. When the priest had finished dressing he opened it.

On the fly-leaf there was a label which stated that the book was furnished by the Gideons. It went on: "A Bible in Every Hotel Guest Room. Winning Commercial Men for Christ. Good News." There was then a list of texts. The priest read with some astonishment:

If you are in trouble	read	Psalm 34.
If trade is poor		Psalm 37.
If very prosperous		I Corinthians, x, xii.
If overcome and back-sliding		James i. Hosea xiv:4–9.
If tired of sin		Psalm 51. Luke xviii:9–14.

If you desire peace, power, and plenty	John xiv.
If you are lonesome and discouraged	Psalms 23 and 27.
If you are losing confidence in men	I Corinthians, xiii.
If you desire peaceful slumbers	Psalm 121.

He couldn't help wondering how it had got here—with its ugly type and its over-simple explanations—into a hacienda in Southern Mexico. Mr. Lehr turned away from his mirror with a big coarse hairbrush in his hand and explained carefully: "My sister ran a hotel once. For drummers. She sold it to join me when my wife died, and she brought one of those from the hotel. You wouldn't understand that, father. You don't like people to read the Bible." He was on the defensive all the time about his faith, as if he was perpetually conscious of some friction, like that of an ill-fitting shoe.

The priest said: "Is your wife buried here?"

"In the paddock," Mr. Lehr said bluntly. He stood listening, brush in hand, to the gentle footsteps outside. "That's Miss Lehr," he said, "come up from her bath. We can go out now."

The priest got off Mr. Lehr's old horse when he reached the church and threw the rein over a bush. This was his first visit to the village since the night he collapsed beside the wall. The village ran down below him in the dusk: tin-roofed bungalows and mud huts faced each other over a single wide grass-grown street. A few lamps had been lit and fire was being carried round among the poorest huts. He walked slowly, conscious of peace and safety. The first man he saw took off his hat and knelt and kissed the priest's hand.

"What is your name?" the priest asked.

"Pedro, father."

"Good night, Pedro."

"Is there to be Mass in the morning, father?"

"Yes. There is to be Mass."

He passed the rural school. The schoolmaster sat on the step: a plump young man with dark brown eyes and horn-rimmed glasses. When he saw the priest coming he looked ostentatiously away. He was the law-abiding element: he wouldn't recognize criminals. He began to talk pedantically and priggishly to someone behind him—something about the infant class. A woman kissed the priest's hand: it was odd to be wanted again: not to feel himself the carrier of death. She said: "Father, will you hear our confessions?"

He said: "Yes. Yes. In Señor Lehr's barn. Before the Mass. I will be there at five. As soon as it is light."

"There are so many of us, father . . ."

"Well, tonight too then. . . . At eight."

"And, father, there are many children to be baptized. There has not been a priest for three years."

"I am going to be here for two more days."

"What will you charge, father?"

"Well—two pesos is the usual charge." He thought: I must hire two mules and a guide. It will cost me fifty pesos to reach Las Casas. Five pesos for the Mass—that left forty-five.

"We are very poor here, father," she haggled gently. "I have four children myself. Eight pesos is a lot of money."

"Four children are a lot of children—if the priest was here only three years ago."

He could hear authority, the old parish intonation coming back into his voice—as if the last years had been a dream and he had never really been away from the guilds, the Children of Mary, and the daily Mass. He said sharply: "How many children are there here—unbaptized?"

"Perhaps a hundred, father."

He made calculations: there was no need to arrive in Las Casas then as a beggar: he could buy a decent suit of clothes, find a respectable lodging, settle down. . . . He said: "You must pay one peso fifty a head."

"One peso, father. We are very poor."

"One peso fifty." A voice from years back said firmly into his ear: they don't value what they don't pay for. It was the old priest he had succeeded at Concepción. He had explained to him: they will always tell you they are poor, starving, but they will always have a little store of money buried somewhere, in a pot. The priest said: "You must bring the money—and the children—to Señor Lehr's barn tomorrow, at two in the afternoon."

She said: "Yes, father." She seemed quite satisfied: she had brought him down by fifty centavos a head. The priest went on. Say a hundred children, he was thinking, that means a hundred and sixty pesos with tomorrow's Mass.

Perhaps I can get the mules and the guide for forty pesos. Señor Lehr will give me food for six days. I shall have a hundred and twenty pesos left. After all these years, it was like wealth. He felt respect all the way up the street: men took off their hats as he passed: it was as if he had got back to the days before the persecution. He could feel the old life hardening round him like a habit, a stony case which held his head high and dictated the way he walked, and even formed his words. A voice from the cantina said: "Father."

The man was very fat, with three commercial chins: he wore a waistcoat in spite of the great heat, and a watch-chain. "Yes?" the priest said. Behind the man's head stood bottles of mineral water, beer, spirits. . . . The priest came in out of the dusty street to the heat of the lamp. He said: "What is it?" with his new-old manner of authority and impatience.

"I thought, father, you might be in need of a little sacramental wine."

"Perhaps . . . but you will have to give me credit."

"A priest's credit, father, is always good enough for me. I am a religious man myself. This is a religious place. No doubt you will be holding a baptism." He leant avidly forward with a respectful and impertinent manner, as if they were two people with the same ideas, educated men.

"Perhaps . . ."

He smiled understandingly. Between people like ourselves, he seemed to indicate, there is no need of anything explicit: we understand each other's thoughts. He said: "In the old days, when the church was open, I was treasurer to the Guild of the Blessed Sacrament. Oh, I am a

good Catholic, father. The people, of course, are very ignorant." He said: "Would you perhaps honour me by taking a glass of brandy?" He was in his way quite sincere.

The priest said doubtfully: "It is kind . . ." The two
glasses were already filled: he remembered the last drink
he had had, sitting on the bed in the dark, listening to the
Chief of Police, and seeing, as the light went on, the last
wine drain away. . . . The memory was like a hand, pulling away the case, exposing him. The smell of brandy
dried his mouth. He thought: What a play-actor I am. I
have no business here, among good people. He turned the
glass in his hand, and all the other glasses turned too: he
remembered the dentist talking of his children, and Maria
unearthing the bottle of spirits she had kept for him—
the whisky priest.

He took a reluctant drink. "It's good brandy, father,"
the man said.

"Yes. Good brandy."

"I could let you have a dozen bottles for sixty pesos."

"Where would I find sixty pesos?" He thought: in some
ways it was better over there, across the border. Fear and
death were not the worst things. It was sometimes a mistake for life to go on.

"I wouldn't make a profit out of you, father. Fifty
pesos."

"Fifty, sixty. It's all the same to me."

"Go on. Have another glass, father. It's good brandy."
The man leant engagingly forward across the counter
and said: "Why not half a dozen, father, for twenty-four
pesos?" He said slyly: "After all, father—there are the
baptisms."

It was appalling how easily one forgot and went back:
he could still hear his own voice speaking in the street with
the Concepción accent—unchanged by mortal sin and un-
repentance and desertion. The brandy was musty on the
tongue with his own corruption. God might forgive cowardice and passion, but was it possible to forgive the habit
of piety? He remembered the woman in the prison and
how impossible it had been to shake her complacency: it
seemed to him that he was another of the same kind. He
drank the brandy down like damnation: men like the half-
caste could be saved: salvation could strike like lightning
at the evil heart, but the habit of piety excluded everything but the evening prayer and the Guild meeting and
the feel of humble lips on your gloved hand.

"Las Casas is a fine town, father. They say you can
hear Mass every day."

This was another pious person. There were a lot of
them about in the world. He was pouring a little more
brandy, but going carefully—not too much. He said:
"When you get there, father, look up a compadre of mine
in Guadalupe Street. He has the cantina nearest the
church—a good man. Treasurer of the Guild of the
Blessed Sacrament—just like I was in this place in the
good days. He'll see you get what you want cheap. Now,
what about some bottles for the journey?"

The priest drank. There was no point in not drinking.
He had the habit now—like piety and the parish voice. He
said: "Three bottles. For eleven pesos. Keep them for me
here." He finished what was left and went back into the
street: the lamps were lit in windows and the wide street

stretched like a prairie in between. He stumbled in a hole
and felt a hand upon his sleeve. "Ah, Pedro. That was the
name, wasn't it? Thank you, Pedro."

"At your service, father."

The church stood in the darkness like a block of ice: it
was melting away in the heat. The roof had fallen in in
one place, a coign above the doorway had crumbled. The
priest took a quick sideways look at Pedro, holding his
breath in case it smelt of brandy, but he could see only the
outlines of the face. He said—with a feeling of cunning
as though he were cheating a greedy prompter inside his
own heart: "Tell the people, Pedro, that I only want one
peso for the baptisms. . . ." There would still be enough
for the brandy then, even if he arrived in Las Casas like
a beggar. There was silence for as long as two seconds and
then the wily village voice began to answer him: "We are
poor, father. One peso is a lot of money. I—for example—I have three children. Say seventy-five centavos,
father."

Miss Lehr stretched out her feet in their easy slippers
and the beetles came up over the veranda from the dark
outside. She said: "In Pittsburgh once . . ." Her brother
was asleep with an ancient newspaper across his knee: the
mail had come in. The priest gave a little sympathetic
giggle as in the old days; it was a try-out which didn't
come off. Miss Lehr stopped and sniffed. "Funny. I
thought I smelt—spirits."

The priest held his breath, leaning back in the rocking-
chair. He thought: How quiet it is, how safe. He remem-

bered townspeople who couldn't sleep in country places because of the silence: silence can be like noise, dinning against the ear-drums.

"What was I saying, father?"

"In Pittsburgh once . . ."

"Of course. In Pittsburgh . . . I was waiting for the train. You see I had nothing to read: books are so expensive. So I thought I'd buy a paper—any paper: the news is just the same. But when I opened it—it was called something like *Police News*. I never knew such dreadful things were printed. Of course, I didn't read more than a few lines. I think it was the most dreadful thing that's ever happened to me. It . . . well, it opened my eyes."

"Yes."

"I've never told Mr. Lehr. He wouldn't think the same of me, I do believe, if he knew."

"But there was nothing wrong . . ."

"It's knowing, isn't it . . . ?"

Somewhere a long way off a bird of some kind called: the lamp on the table began to smoke, and Miss Lehr leant over and turned down the wick: it was as if the only light for miles around was lowered. The brandy returned on his palate: it was like the smell of ether that reminds a man of a recent operation before he's used to life: it tied him to another state of being. He didn't yet belong to this deep tranquillity: he told himself—in time it will be all right, I shall pull up, I only ordered three bottles this time. They will be the last I'll ever drink, I won't need drink there—he knew he lied. Mr. Lehr woke suddenly and said: "As I was saying . . ."

"You were saying nothing, dear. You were asleep."

"Oh, no, we were talking about that scoundrel Hoover."

"I don't think so, dear. Not for a long while."

"Well," Mr. Lehr said, "it's been a long day. The father will be tired too . . . after all that confessing," he added with slight distaste.

There had been a continuous stream of penitents from eight to ten—two hours of the worst evil a small place like this could produce after three years. It hadn't amounted to very much—a city would have made a better show—or would it? There isn't much a man can do. Drunkenness, adultery, uncleanness: he sat there tasting the brandy all the while, sitting on a rocking-chair in a horse-box, not looking at the face of the one who knelt at his side. The others had waited, kneeling in an empty stall —Mr. Lehr's stable had been depopulated these last few years. He had only one old horse left, which blew windily in the dark as the sins came whispering out.

"How many times?"

"Twelve, father. Perhaps more," and the horse blew.

It is astonishing the sense of innocence that goes with sin—only the hard and careful man and the saint are free of it. These people went out of the stable clean: he was the only one left who hadn't repented, confessed, and been absolved. He wanted to say to this man: "Love is not wrong, but love should be happy and open—it is only wrong when it is secret, unhappy . . . it can be more unhappy than anything but the loss of God. It *is* the loss of God. You don't need a penance, my child, you have suffered quite enough," and to this other: "Lust is not the worst thing. It is because any day, any time, lust may turn into love that we have to avoid it. And when we love our sin then we are damned indeed." But the habit of the confessional reasserted itself: it was as if he was back in the little stuffy wooden boxlike coffin in which men bury their uncleanness with their priest. He said: "Mortal sin . . . danger . . . self-control," as if those words meant anything at all. He said: "Say three Our Fathers and three Hail Marys."

He said wearily: "Drink is only the beginning . . ." He found he had no lesson he could draw against even that common vice except himself smelling of brandy in the stable. He gave out the penance quickly, harshly, mechanically. The man would go away, saying: "A bad priest," feeling no encouragement, no interest. . . .

He said: "Those laws were made for man. The Church doesn't expect . . . if you can't fast, you must eat, that's all." The old woman prattled on and on, while the penitents stirred restlessly in the next stall and the horse whinnied, prattled of abstinence days broken, of evening prayers curtailed. Suddenly, without warning, with an odd sense of homesickness, he thought of the hostages in the prison yard, waiting at the water-tap, not looking at him —the suffering and the endurance which went on everywhere the other side of the mountains. He interrupted the woman savagely: "Why don't you confess properly to me? I'm not interested in your fish supply or in how sleepy you are at night . . . remember your real sins."

"But I'm a good woman, father," she squeaked at him with astonishment.

"Then what are you doing here, keeping away the bad people?" He said: "Have you any love for anyone but yourself?"

"I love God, father," she said haughtily. He took a quick look at her in the light of the candle burning on the floor—the hard old raisin eyes under the black shawl—another of the pious—like himself.

"How do you know? Loving God isn't any different from loving a man—or a child. It's wanting to be with Him, to be near Him." He made a hopeless gesture with his hands. "It's wanting to protect Him from yourself."

When the last penitent had gone away he walked back across the yard to the bungalow: he could see the lamp burning, and Miss Lehr knitting, and he could smell the grass in the paddock, wet with the first rains. It ought to be possible for a man to be happy here, if he were not so tied to fear and suffering—unhappiness too can become a habit like piety. Perhaps it was his duty to break it, his duty to discover peace. He felt an immense envy of all those people who had confessed to him and been absolved. In six days, he told himself, in Las Casas, I too . . . but he couldn't believe that anyone anywhere would rid him of his heavy heart. Even when he drank he felt bound to his sin by love. It was easier to get rid of hate.

Miss Lehr said: "Sit down, father. You must be tired. I've never held, of course, with confession. Nor has Mr. Lehr."

"No?"

"I don't know how you can stand sitting there, listening to all the horrible things. . . . I remember in Pittsburgh once . . ."

The two mules had been brought in overnight, so that he could start early immediately after Mass—the second that he had said in Mr. Lehr's barn. His guide was sleeping somewhere, probably with the mules, a thin nervous creature, who had never been to Las Casas: he simply knew the route by hearsay. Miss Lehr had insisted the night before that she must call him, although he woke of his own accord before it was light. He lay in bed and heard the alarm go off in another room—dinning like a telephone; and presently he heard the slop-slop of Miss Lehr's bedroom slippers in the passage outside and a knock-knock on the door. Mr. Lehr slept on undisturbed upon his back with the thin rectitude of a bishop upon a tomb.

The priest had lain down in his clothes and he opened the door before Miss Lehr had time to get away: she gave a small squeal of dismay, a bunchy figure in a hairnet.

"Excuse me."

"Oh, it's quite all right. How long will Mass take, father?"

"There will be a great many communicants. Perhaps three-quarters of an hour."

"I will have some coffee ready for you—and sandwiches."

"You must not bother."

"Oh, we can't send you away hungry."

She followed him to the door, standing a little behind him, so as not to be seen by anything or anybody in the wide empty early world. The grey light uncurled across the pastures: at the gate the tulipan tree bloomed for yet another day: very far off, beyond the little stream where he had bathed, the people were walking up from the vil-

lage on the way to Mr. Lehr's barn; they were too small
at that distance to be human. He had a sense of expectant
happiness all round him, waiting for him to take part,
like an audience of children at a cinema or a rodeo: he was
aware of how happy he might have been if he had left
nothing behind him across the range except a few bad
memories. A man should always prefer peace to violence,
and he was going towards peace.

"You have been very good to me, Miss Lehr."

How odd it had seemed at first to be treated as a guest,
not as a criminal or a bad priest. These were heretics—it
never occurred to them that he was not a good man: they
hadn't the prying insight of fellow Catholics.

"We've enjoyed having you, father. But you'll be glad
to be away. Las Casas is a fine city. A very moral place, as
Mr. Lehr always says. If you meet Father Quintana you
must remember us to him—he was here three years ago."

A bell began to ring: they had brought the church bell
down from the tower and hung it outside Mr. Lehr's barn:
it sounded like any Sunday anywhere.

"I've sometimes wished," Miss Lehr said, "that I could
go to church."

"Why not?"

"Mr. Lehr wouldn't like it. He's very strict. But it happens so seldom nowadays—I don't suppose there'll be another service now for another three years."

"I will come back before then."

"Oh, no," Miss Lehr said. "You won't do that. It's a
hard journey and Las Casas is a fine city. They have electric light in the streets: there are two hotels. Father Quin-

tana promised to come back—but there are Christians
everywhere, aren't there? Why should he come back here?
It isn't even as if we were really badly off."

A little group of Indians passed the gate: gnarled tiny
creatures of the Stone Age: the men in short smocks
walked with long poles, and the women with black plaits
and knocked-about faces carried their babies on their
backs. "The Indians have heard you are here," Miss Lehr
said. "They've walked fifty miles—I shouldn't be surprised."

They stopped at the gate and watched him: when
he looked at them they went down on their knees and
crossed themselves—the strange elaborate mosaic touching the nose and ears and chin. "My brother gets so
angry," Miss Lehr said, "if he sees somebody go on his
knees to a priest—but I don't see that it does any harm."

Round the corner of the house the mules were stamping
—the guide must have brought them out to give them
their maize: they were slow feeders, you had to give them a
long start. It was time to begin Mass and be gone. He
could smell the early morning—the world was still fresh
and green, and in the village below the pastures a few dogs
barked. The alarm clock tick-tocked in Miss Lehr's hand.
He said: "I must be going now." He felt an odd reluctance
to leave Miss Lehr and the house and the brother sleeping
in the inside room. He was aware of a mixture of tenderness and dependence. When a man wakes after a dangerous operation he puts a special value upon the first face
he sees as the anæsthetic wears away.

He had no vestments, but the Masses in this village
were nearer to the old parish days than any he had known

in the last eight years—there was no fear of interruption:
no hurried taking of the sacraments as the police approached. There was even an altar stone brought from the
locked church. But because it was so peaceful he was all
the more aware of his own sin as he prepared to take the
Elements—"Let not the participation of Thy Body, O
Lord Jesus Christ, which I, though unworthy, presume to
receive, turn to my judgment and condemnation." A virtuous man can almost cease to believe in Hell: but he carried Hell about with him. Sometimes at night he dreamed
of it. *Domine, non sum dignus . . . domine, non sum dignus.*
. . . Evil ran like malaria in his veins. He remembered a
dream he had had of a big grassy arena lined with the
statues of the saints—but the saints were alive, they
turned their eyes this way and that, waiting for something.
He waited, too, with an awful expectancy: bearded Peters
and Pauls, with Bibles pressed to their breasts, watched
some entrance behind his back he couldn't see—it had the
menace of a beast. Then a marimba began to play, tinkly
and repetitive, a firework exploded, and Christ danced into
the arena—danced and postured with a bleeding painted
face, up and down, up and down, grimacing like a prostitute, smiling and suggestive. He woke with the sense of
complete despair that a man might feel finding the only
money he possessed was counterfeit.

". . . and we saw His glory, the glory as of the only-
begotten of the Father, full of grace and truth." Mass was
over.

In three days, he told himself, I shall be in Las Casas:
I shall have confessed and been absolved—and the thought
of the child on the rubbish-heap came automatically back

to him with painful love. What was the good of confession when you loved the result of your crime?

The people knelt as he made his way down the barn: he saw the little group of Indians: women whose children he had baptized: Pedro: the man from the cantina was there too, kneeling with his face buried in his plump hands, a chain of beads falling between the fingers. He looked a good man: perhaps he was a good man: perhaps, the priest thought, I have lost the faculty of judging—perhaps that woman in prison was the best person there. A horse cried in the early morning, tethered to a tree, and all the freshness of the morning came in through the open door.

Two men waited beside the mules: the guide was adjusting a stirrup and beside him, scratching under the armpit, awaiting his coming with a doubtful and defensive smile, stood the half-caste. He was like the small pain that reminds a man of his sickness, or perhaps like the unexpected memory which proves that love after all isn't dead. "Well," the priest said, "I didn't expect you here."

"No, father, of course not." He scratched and smiled.

"Have you brought the soldiers with you?"

"What things you do say, father," he protested with a callow giggle. Behind him, across the yard and through an open door, the priest could see Miss Lehr putting up his sandwiches: she had dressed, but she still wore her hairnet. She was wrapping the sandwiches carefully in greaseproof paper, and her sedate movements had a curious effect of unreality. It was the half-caste who was real. He said: "What trick are you playing now?" Had he perhaps bribed his guide to lead him back across the border? He could believe almost anything of that man.

"You shouldn't say things like that, father."

Miss Lehr passed out of sight, with the soundlessness of a dream.

"No?"

"I'm here, father," the man seemed to take a long breath for his surprising stilted statement, "on an errand of mercy."

The guide finished with one mule and began on the next, shortening the already short Mexican stirrup; the priest giggled nervously. "An errand of mercy?"

"Well, father, you're the only priest this side of Las Casas, and the man's dying . . ."

"What man?"

"The Yankee."

"What are you talking about?"

"The one the police wanted. He robbed a bank. You know the one I mean."

"He wouldn't need me," the priest said impatiently, remembering the photograph on the peeling wall, watching the first communion party.

"Oh, he's a good Catholic, father." Scratching under his armpit, he didn't look at the priest. "He's dying, and you and I wouldn't like to have on our conscience what that man . . ."

"We shall be lucky if we haven't worse."

"What do you mean, father?"

The priest said: "He's only killed and robbed. He hasn't betrayed his friends."

"Holy Mother of God. I've never . . ."

"We both have," the priest said. He turned to the guide. "Are the mules ready?"

"Yes, father."

"We'll start then." He had forgotten Miss Lehr completely: the other world had stretched a hand across the border, and he was again in the atmosphere of flight.

"Where are you going?" the half-caste said.

"To Las Casas." He climbed stiffly onto his mule. The half-caste held onto his stirrup-leather, and he was reminded of their first meeting: there was the same mixture of complaint, appeal, abuse. "You're a fine priest," he wailed up at him. "Your bishop ought to hear of this. A man's dying, wants to confess, and just because you want to get to the city . . ."

"Why do you think me such a fool?" the priest said. "I know why you've come. You're the only one they've got who can recognize me, and they can't follow me into this state. Now if I ask you where this American is, you'll tell me—I know—you don't have to speak—that he's just the other side."

"Oh, no, father, you're wrong there. He's just this side."

"A mile or two makes no difference. Nobody here's likely to bring an action . . ."

"It's an awful thing, father," the half-caste said, "never to be believed. Just because once—well, I admit it——"

The priest kicked his mule into motion: they passed out of Mr. Lehr's yard and turned south: the half-caste trotted at his stirrup.

"I remember," the priest said, "that you said you'd never forget my face."

"And I haven't," the man put in triumphantly, "or I wouldn't be here, would I? Listen, father, I'll admit a lot.

You don't know how a reward will tempt a poor man like me. And when you wouldn't trust me, I thought, well, if that's how he feels—I'll show him. But I'm a good Catholic, father, and when a dying man wants a priest . . ."

They climbed the long slope of Mr. Lehr's pastures which led to the next range of hills. The air was still fresh, at six in the morning, at three thousand feet; up there tonight it would be very cold—they had another six thousand feet to climb. The priest said uneasily: "Why should I put my head into *your* noose?" It was too absurd.

"Look, father." The half-caste was holding up a scrap of paper: the familiar writing caught the priest's attention—the large deliberate handwriting of a child. The paper had been used to wrap up food: it was smeared and greasy: he read: "The Prince of Denmark is wondering whether he should kill himself or not, whether it is better to go on suffering all the doubts about his father, or by one blow . . ."

"Not that, father, on the other side. That's nothing."

The priest turned the paper and read a single phrase written in English in blunt pencil: "For Christ's sake, father . . ." The mule, unbeaten, lapsed into a slow heavy walk: the priest made no attempt to urge it on: this piece of paper left no doubt whatever: he felt the trap close again, irrevocably.

He asked: "How did this come to you?"

"It was this way, father. I was with the police when they shot him. It was in a village the other side. He picked up a child to act as a screen, but, of course, the soldiers didn't pay any attention. It was only an Indian. They were both shot, but he escaped."

"Then how . . . ?"

"It was this way, father." He positively prattled. It appeared that he was afraid of the lieutenant—who resented the fact that the priest had escaped, and so he planned to slip across the border, out of reach. He got his chance at night, and on the way—it was probably on this side of the state line, but who knew where one state began or another ended?—he came on the American. He had been shot in the stomach. . . .

"How could he have escaped then?"

"Oh, father, he is a man of superhuman strength." He was dying, he wanted a priest . . .

"How did he tell you that?"

"It only needed two words, father." Then, to prove the story, the man had found enough strength to write this note, and so . . . the story had as many holes in it as a sieve. But what remained was this note, like a memorial stone you couldn't overlook.

The half-caste bridled angrily again. "You don't trust me, father."

"Oh, no," the priest said. "I don't trust you."

"You think I'm lying."

"Most of it is lies."

He pulled the mule up and sat thinking, facing south. He was quite certain that this was a trap—probably the half-caste had suggested it: he was after the reward. But it was a fact that the American was there, dying. He thought of the deserted banana station where something had happened and the Indian child lay dead on the maize: there was no question at all that he was needed. A man with all that on his soul . . . The oddest thing of all was that he felt quite cheerful: he had never really believed in this peace. He had dreamed of it so often on the other side that now it meant no more to him than a dream. He began to whistle a tune—something he had heard somewhere once. "I found a rose in my field": it was time he woke up. It wouldn't really have been a good dream—that confession in Las Casas when he had to admit, as well as everything else, that he had refused confession to a man dying in mortal sin.

He said: "Will the man still be alive?"

"I think so, father," the half-caste caught him eagerly up.

"How far is it?"

"Four—five hours, father."

"You can take it in turns to ride the other mule."

The priest turned his mule back and called out to the guide. The man dismounted and stood inertly there, while he explained. The only remark he made was to the half-caste, motioning him into the saddle: "Be careful of that saddle-bag. The father's brandy's there."

They rode slowly back: Miss Lehr was at her gate. She said: "You forgot the sandwiches, father."

"Oh, yes. Thank you." He stole a quick look round—it didn't mean a thing to him. He said: "Is Mr. Lehr still asleep?"

"Shall I wake him?"

"No, no. But you will thank him for his hospitality?"

"Yes. And perhaps, father, in a few years we shall see you again? As you said." She looked curiously at the half-caste, and he stared back through his yellow insulting eyes.

The priest said: "It's possible," glancing away with a sly secretive smile.

"Well, good-bye, father. You'd better be off, hadn't you? The sun's getting high."

"Good-bye, my dear Miss Lehr." The mestizo slashed impatiently at his mule and stirred it into action.

"Not that way, my man," Miss Lehr called.

"I have to pay a visit first," the priest explained, and breaking into an uncomfortable trot he bobbed down behind the mestizo's mule towards the village. They passed the whitewashed church—that too belonged to a dream. Life didn't contain churches. The long untidy village street opened ahead of them. The schoolmaster was at his door and waved an ironic greeting, malicious and horn-rimmed. "Well, father, off with your spoils?"

The priest stopped his mule. He said to the half-caste: "Really . . . I had forgotten . . ."

"You did well out of the baptisms," the schoolmaster said. "It pays to wait a few years, doesn't it?"

"Come on, father," the half-caste said. "Don't listen to him." He spat. "He's a bad man."

The priest said: "You know the people here better than anyone. If I leave a gift, will you spend it on things that do no harm—I mean food, blankets—not books?"

"They need food more than books."

"I have forty-five pesos here . . ."

The mestizo wailed: "Father, what are you doing . . . ?"

"Conscience money?" the schoolmaster said.

"Yes."

"All the same, of course, I thank you. It's good to see a priest with a conscience. It's a stage in evolution," he said, his glasses flashing in the sunlight, a plump embittered figure in front of his tin-roofed shack, an exile.

They passed the last houses, the cemetery, and began to climb. "Why, father, why?" the half-caste protested.

"He's not a bad man, he does his best, and I shan't need money again, shall I?" the priest asked, and for quite a while they rode without speaking, while the sun came blindingly out, and the mules' shoulders strained on the steep rocky paths, and the priest began to whistle again— "I have a rose"—the only tune he knew. Once the half-caste started a complaint about something: "The trouble with you, father, is . . ." but it petered out before it was defined, because there wasn't really anything to complain about as they rode steadily north towards the border.

"Hungry?" the priest asked at last.

The half-caste muttered something that sounded angry or derisive.

"Take a sandwich," the priest said, opening Miss Lehr's packet.

"THERE," the half-caste said, with a sort of whinny of triumph, as though he had lain innocently all these seven hours under the suspicion of lying. He pointed across the barranca to a group of Indian huts on a peninsula of rock jutting out across the chasm. They were perhaps two hundred yards away, but it would take another hour at least to reach them, winding down a thousand feet and up another thousand.

The priest sat on his mule watching intently: he could see no movement anywhere. Even the look-out, the little platform of twigs built on a mound above the huts, was empty. He said: "There doesn't seem to be anybody about." He was back in the atmosphere of desertion.

"Well," the half-caste said, "you didn't expect anybody, did you? Except him. He's there. You'll soon find that."

"Where are the Indians?"

"There you go again," the man complained. "Suspicion. Always suspicion. How should I know where the Indians are? I told you he was quite alone, didn't I?"

The priest dismounted. "What are you doing now?" the half-caste cried despairingly.

"We shan't need the mules any more. They can be taken back."

"Not need them? How are you going to get away from here?"

"Oh," the priest said. "I won't have to think about that, will I?" He counted out forty pesos and said to the muleteer: "I hired you for Las Casas. Well, this is your good luck. Six days' pay."

"You don't want me any more, father?"

"No, I think you'd better get away from here quickly. Leave you-know-what behind."

The half-caste said excitedly: "We can't walk all that way, father. Why, the man's dying."

"We can go just as quickly on our own hoofs. Now, friend, be off." The mestizo watched the mules pick their way along the narrow stony path with a look of wistful greed: they disappeared round a shoulder of rock—crack, crack, crack, the sound of their hoofs contracted into silence.

"Now," the priest said briskly, "we won't delay any more," and he started down the path, with a small sack slung over his shoulder. He could hear the half-caste panting after him: his wind was bad: they had probably let him have far too much beer in the capital, and the priest thought, with an odd touch of contemptuous affection, of how much had happened to them both since that first encounter in a village of which he didn't even know the name: the half-caste lying there in the hot noonday rocking his hammock with one naked yellow toe. If he had been asleep at that moment, this wouldn't have happened. It was really shocking bad luck for the poor devil that he was to be bur-

dened with a sin of such magnitude. The priest took a
quick look back and saw the big toes protruding like slugs
out of the dirty gym shoes: the man picked his way down,
muttering all the time—his perpetual grievance didn't
help his wind. Poor man, the priest thought, he isn't really
bad enough . . .

And he wasn't strong enough either for *this* journey.
By the time the priest had reached the bottom of the barranca he was fifty yards behind. The priest sat down on a
boulder and mopped his forehead, and the half-caste began to complain long before he was down to his level:
"There isn't so much hurry as all that." It was almost as
though the nearer he got to his treachery the greater the
grievance against his victim became.

"Didn't you say he was dying?" the priest asked.

"Oh, yes, dying, of course. But that can take a long
time."

"The longer the better for all of us," the priest said.
"Perhaps you are right. I'll take a rest here."

But now, like a contrary child, the half-caste wanted to
start again. He said: "You do nothing in moderation.
Either you run or you sit."

"Can I do nothing right?" the priest teased him, and
then he put in sharply and shrewdly: "They will let me see
him, I suppose?"

"Of course," the half-caste said and immediately caught
himself up. "They, they. Who are you talking about now?
First you complain that the place is empty, and then you
talk of *they*." He said with tears in his voice: "You may be
a good man. You may be a saint for all I know, but why

won't you talk plainly, so that a man can understand you?
It's enough to make a man a bad Catholic."

The priest said: "You see this sack here. We don't want
to carry that any farther. It's heavy. I think a little drink
will do us both good. We both need courage, don't we?"

"Drink, father?" the half-caste said with excitement,
and watched the priest unpack a bottle. He never took his
eyes away while the priest drank. His two fangs stuck
greedily out, quivering slightly on the lower lip. Then he
too fastened on the mouth. "It's illegal, I suppose," the
priest said with a giggle, "on this side of the border—if
we are this side." He had another draw himself and handed
it back: it was soon exhausted—he took the bottle and
threw it at a rock and it exploded like shrapnel. The half-
caste started. He said: "Be careful. People might think
you'd got a gun."

"As for the rest," the priest said, "we won't need that."

"You mean there's more of it?"

"Two more bottles—but we can't drink any more in
this heat. We'd better leave it here."

"Why didn't you say it was heavy, father? I'll carry it
for you. You've only to ask me to do a thing. I'm willing.
Only you just won't ask."

They set off again, up-hill, the bottles clinking gently:
the sun shone vertically down on the pair of them. It took
them the best part of an hour to reach the top of the barranca. Then the watch tower gaped over their path like
an upper jaw and the tops of the huts appeared over the
rocks above them. Indians do not build their settlements
on a mule path: they prefer to stand aside and see who

comes. The priest wondered how soon the police would appear: they were keeping very carefully hidden.

"This way, father." The half-caste took the lead, scrambling away from the path up the rocks to the little plateau. He looked anxious, almost as if he had expected something to happen before this. There were about a dozen huts: they stood quiet, like tombs against the heavy sky. A storm was coming up.

The priest felt a nervous impatience: he had walked into this trap, the least they could do was to close it quickly, finish everything off. He wondered whether they would suddenly shoot him down from one of the huts. He had come to the very edge of time: soon there would be no to-morrow and no yesterday, just existence going on for ever; he began to wish he had taken a little more brandy. His voice broke uncertainly when he said: "Well, we are here. Where is this Yankee?"

"Oh, yes, the Yankee," the half-caste said, jumping a little. It was as if for a moment he had forgotten the pretext. He stood there, gaping at the huts, wondering too. He said: "He was over there when I left him."

"Well, he couldn't have moved, could he?"

If it hadn't been for that letter he would have doubted the very existence of the American—and if he hadn't seen the dead child too, of course. He began to walk across the little silent clearing towards the hut: would they shoot him before he got to the entrance? It was like walking a plank blindfold: you didn't know at what point you would step off into space for ever. He hiccuped once and knotted his hands behind his back to stop their trembling. He had been glad in a way to turn away from Miss Lehr's gate—

he had never really believed that he would ever get back to parish work and the daily Mass and the careful appearances of piety; but all the same you needed to be a little drunk to die. He got to the door—not a sound anywhere; then a voice said: "Father."

He looked round. The mestizo stood in the clearing with his face contorted: the two fangs jumped and jumped: he looked frightened.

"Yes, what is it?"

"Nothing, father."

"Why did you call me?"

"I said nothing," he lied.

The priest turned and went in.

The American was there all right. Whether he was alive was another matter. He lay on a straw mat with his eyes closed and his mouth open and his hands on his belly, like a child with stomachache. Pain alters a face—or else successful crime has its own falsity like politics or piety. He was hardly recognizable from the news picture on the police-station wall: that was tougher, arrogant, a man who had made good. This was just a tramp's face. Pain had exposed the nerves and given the face a kind of spurious intelligence.

The priest knelt down and put his face near the man's mouth, trying to hear the breathing. A heavy smell came up to him—a mixture of vomit and cigar smoke and stale drink: it would take more than a few lilies to hide this corruption. A very faint voice close to his ear said in English: "Beat it, father." Outside the door, in the heavy stormy sunlight, the mestizo stood, staring towards the hut, a little loose about the knees.

"So you're alive, are you?" the priest said briskly. "Better hurry. You haven't got long."

"Beat it, father."

"You wanted me, didn't you? You're a Catholic?"

"Beat it," the voice whispered again, as if those were the only words it could remember of a lesson it had learnt some while ago.

"Come now," the priest said. "How long is it since you went to confession?"

The eyelids rolled up and astonished eyes looked up at him. The man said in a puzzled voice: "Ten years, I guess. What are you doing here anyway?"

"You asked for a priest. Come now. Ten years is a long time."

"You got to beat it, father," the man said. He was remembering the lesson now—lying there flat on the mat with his hands folded on his stomach, any vitality that was left accumulated in the brain: he was like a reptile crushed at one end. He said in a strange voice: "That bastard . . ." The priest said furiously: "What sort of a confession is this? I make a five hours' journey . . . and all I get out of you is evil words." It seemed to him horribly unfair that his uselessness should return with his danger—he couldn't do anything for a man like this.

"Listen, father . . ." the man said.

"I am listening."

"You beat it out of here quick. I didn't know . . ."

"I haven't come all this way to talk about myself," the priest said. "The sooner your confession's done, the sooner I will be gone."

"You don't need to trouble about me. I'm through."

"You mean damned?" the priest said angrily.

"Sure. Damned," the man said, licking blood away from his lips.

"You listen to me," the priest said, leaning closer to the stale and nauseating smell, "I have come here to listen to your confession. Do you want to confess?"

"No."

"Did you when you wrote that note . . . ?"

"Maybe."

"I know what you want to tell me. I know it, do you understand? Let that be. Remember you are dying. Don't depend too much on God's mercy. He has given you this chance: He may not give you another. What sort of a life have you led all these years? Does it seem so grand now? You've killed a lot of people—that's about all. Anybody can do that for a while, and then he is killed too. Just as you are killed. Nothing left except pain."

"Father."

"Yes?" The priest gave an impatient sigh, leaning closer. He hoped for a moment that at last he had got the man started on some meagre train of sorrow.

"You take my gun, father. See what I mean? Under my arm."

"I haven't any use for a gun."

"Oh, yes, you have." The man detached one hand from his stomach and began to move it slowly up his body. So much effort: it was unbearable to watch. The priest said sharply: "Lie still. It's not there." He could see the holster empty under the armpit: it was the first definite indication that they and the half-caste were not alone.

"Bastards," the man said, and his hand lay wearily

where it had got to, over his heart; he imitated the prudish attitude of a female statue: one hand over the breast and one upon the stomach. It was very hot in the hut: the heavy light of the storm lay over them.

"Listen, father . . ." The priest sat hopelessly at the man's side: nothing now would shift that violent brain towards peace: once, hours ago perhaps, when he wrote the message—but the chance had come and gone. He was whispering now something about a knife. There was a legend believed by many criminals that dead eyes held the picture of what they had last seen—a Christian could believe that the soul did the same, held absolution and peace at the final moment, after a lifetime of the most hideous crime: or sometimes pious men died suddenly in brothels unabsolved and what had seemed a good life went out with the permanent stamp on it of impurity. He had heard men talk of the unfairness of a deathbed repentance—as if it was an easy thing to break the habit of a life whether to do good or evil. One suspected the good of the life that ended badly—or the viciousness that ended well. He made another desperate attempt. He said: "You believed once. Try and understand—this is your chance. At the last moment. Like the thief. You have murdered men—children perhaps," he added, remembering the little black heap under the cross. "But that need not be so important. It only belongs to this life, a few years—it's over already. You can drop it all here, in this hut, and go on for ever . . ." He felt sadness and longing at the vaguest idea of a life he couldn't lead himself . . . words like peace, glory, love.

"Father," the voice said urgently, "you let me be. You

look after yourself. You take my knife . . ." The hand began its weary march again—this time towards the hip.
The knees crooked up in an attempt to roll over, and then
the whole body gave up the effort, the ghost, everything.

The priest hurriedly whispered the words of conditional
absolution, in case, for one second before it crossed the
border, the spirit had repented—but it was more likely
that it had gone over still seeking its knife, bent on vicari-
ous violence. He prayed: "O merciful God, after all he was
thinking of me, it was for my sake . . ." but he prayed
without conviction. At the best, it was only one criminal
trying to aid the escape of another—whichever way you
looked, there wasn't much merit in either of them.

CHAPTER THREE

A VOICE said: "Well, have you finished now?"

The priest got up and made a small scared gesture of assent. He recognized the police officer who had given him money at the prison, a dark smart figure in the doorway with the stormlight glinting on his leggings. He had one hand on his revolver and he frowned sourly in at the dead gunman. "You didn't expect to see me," he said.

"Oh, but I did," the priest said. "I must thank you——"

"Thank me, what for?"

"For letting me stay alone with him."

"I am not a barbarian," the officer said. "Will you come out now, please? It's no use at all your trying to escape. You can see that," he added, as the priest emerged and looked round at the dozen armed men who surrounded the hut.

"I've had enough of escaping," he said. The half-caste was no longer in sight: the heavy clouds were piling up the sky: they made the real mountains look like little bright toys below them. He sighed and giggled nervously. "What a lot of trouble I had getting across those mountains, and now . . . here I am . . ."

"I never believed you would return."

"Oh, well, lieutenant, you know how it is. Even a coward has a sense of duty." The cool fresh wind which sometimes blows across before a storm breaks touched his skin. He said with badly affected ease: "Are you going to shoot me now?"

The lieutenant said again sharply: "I am not a barbarian. You will be tried . . . properly."

"What for?"

"For treason."

"I have to go all the way back there?"

"Yes. Unless you try to escape." He kept his hand on his gun as if he didn't trust the priest a yard. He said: "I could swear that somewhere . . ."

"Oh, yes," the priest said. "You have seen me twice. When you took a hostage from my village . . . you asked my child: 'Who is he?' She said: 'My father,' and you let me go." Suddenly the mountains ceased to exist: it was as if somebody had dashed a handful of water into their faces.

"Quick," the lieutenant said, "into that hut." He called out to one of the men. "Bring us some boxes so that we can sit."

The two of them joined the dead man in the hut as the storm came up all round them. A soldier dripping with rain carried in two packing-cases. "A candle," the lieutenant said. He sat down on one of the cases and took out his revolver. He said: "Sit down, there, away from the door, where I can see you." The soldier lit a candle and stuck it in its own wax on the hard earth floor, and the priest sat down, close to the American: huddled up in his

attempt to get at his knife he gave an effect of wanting
to reach his companion, to have a word or two in private.
. . . They looked two of a kind, dirty and unshaved: the
lieutenant seemed to belong to a different class altogether.
He said with contempt: "So you have a child?"

"Yes," the priest said.

"You—a priest."

"You mustn't think they are all like me." He watched
the candlelight blink on the bright buttons. He said:
"There are good priests and bad priests. It is just that I
am a bad priest."

"Then perhaps we will be doing your Church a service . . ."

"Yes."

The lieutenant looked sharply up as if he thought he
was being mocked. He said: "You told me twice. That I
had seen you twice."

"Yes, I was in prison. And you gave me money."

"I remember." He said furiously: "What an appalling
mockery! To have had you and then to let you go. Why,
we lost two men looking for you. They'd be alive today. . . ." The candle sizzled as the drops of rain came
through the roof. "This American wasn't worth two lives.
He did no real harm."

The rain poured ceaselessly down. They sat in silence.
Suddenly the lieutenant said: "Keep your hand away from
your pocket."

"I was only feeling for a pack of cards. I thought perhaps it would help to pass the time . . ."

"I don't play cards," the lieutenant said harshly.

"No, no. Not a game. Just a few tricks I can show you. May I?"

"All right. If you wish to."

Mr. Lehr had given him an old pack of cards. The priest said: "Here, you see, are three cards. The ace, the king, and the jack. Now"—he spread them fanwise out on the floor—"tell me which is the ace."

"This, of course," the lieutenant said grudgingly, showing no interest.

"But you are wrong," the priest said, turning it up. "That is the jack."

The lieutenant said contemptuously: "A game for gamblers—or children."

"There is another trick," the priest said, "called Fly-Away Jack. I cut the pack into three—so. And I take this jack of hearts and I put it into the centre pack—so. Now I tap the three packs"—his face lit up as he spoke: it was such a long time since he had handled cards: he forgot the storm, the dead man, and the stubborn unfriendly face opposite him—"I say: 'Fly away, Jack' "—he cut the left-hand pack in half and disclosed the jack—"and there he is."

"Of course there are two jacks."

"See for yourself." Unwillingly the lieutenant leant forward and inspected the centre pack. He said: "I suppose you tell the Indians that that is a miracle of God."

"Oh, no," the priest giggled. "I learnt it from an Indian. He was the richest man in his village. Do you wonder, with such a hand? No, I used to show the tricks at any entertainments we had in the parish—for the guilds, you know."

A look of physical disgust crossed the lieutenant's face. He said: "I remember those guilds."

"When you were a boy?"

"I was old enough to know . . ."

"Yes?"

"The trickery." He broke out furiously with one hand on his gun, as though it had crossed his mind that it would be better to eliminate this beast, now, at this instant, for ever. "What an excuse it all was, what a fake. Sell all and give to the poor—that was the lesson, wasn't it?—and Señora So-and-so, the druggist's wife, would say the family wasn't really deserving of charity, and Señor This, That, and the Other would say that if they starved, what else did they deserve, they were Socialists anyway, and the priest—you—would notice who had done his Easter duty and paid his Easter offering." His voice rose—a policeman looked into the hut anxiously—and withdrew again through the lashing rain. "The Church was poor, the priest was poor, therefore everyone should sell all and give to the Church."

The priest said: "You are so right." He added quickly: "Wrong, too, of course."

"How do you mean?" the lieutenant asked savagely. "Right? Won't you even defend . . . ?"

"I felt at once that you were a good man when you gave me money at the prison."

The lieutenant said: "I only listen to you because you have no hope. No hope at all. Nothing you say will make any difference."

"No."

He had no intention of angering the police officer, but he had had very little practice the last eight years in talking to any but a few peasants and Indians. Now something in his tone infuriated the lieutenant. He said: "You're a danger. That's why we kill you. I have nothing against you, you understand, as a man."

"Of course not. It's God you're against. I'm the sort of man you shut up every day—and give money to."

"No, I don't fight against a fiction."

"But I'm not worth fighting, am I? You've said so. A liar, a drunkard. That man's worth a bullet more than I am."

"It's your ideas." The lieutenant sweated a little in the hot steamy air. He said: "You are so cunning, you people. But tell me this—what have you ever done in Mexico for *us?* Have you ever told a landlord he shouldn't beat his peon—oh, yes, I know, in the confessional perhaps, and it's your duty, isn't it, to forget it at once? You come out and have dinner with him and it's your duty not to know that he has murdered a peasant. That's all finished. He's left it behind in your box."

"Go on," the priest said. He sat on the packing-case with his hands on his knees and his head bent: he couldn't, though he tried, keep all his mind on what the lieutenant was saying. He was thinking—forty-eight hours to the capital. Today is Sunday. Perhaps on Wednesday I shall be dead. He felt it as a treachery that he was more afraid of the pain of the bullets than of what came after.

"Well, we have ideas too," the lieutenant was saying. "No more money for saying prayers, no more money for building places to say prayers in. We'll give people food instead, teach them to read, give them books. We'll see they don't suffer."

"But if they want to suffer . . ."

"A man may want to rape a woman. Are we to allow it because he wants to? Suffering is wrong."

"And you suffer all the time," the priest commented, watching the sour Indian face behind the candle-flame. He said: "It sounds fine, doesn't it? Does the jefe feel like that too?"

"Oh, we have our bad men."

"And what happens afterwards? I mean after everybody has got enough to eat and can read the right books —the books you let them read?"

"Nothing. Death's a fact. We don't try to alter facts."

"We agree about a lot of things," the priest said, idly dealing out his cards. "We have facts, too, we don't try to alter—that the world's unhappy whether you are rich or poor—unless you are a saint, and there aren't many of those. It's not worth bothering too much about a little pain here. There's one belief we both of us have—that it will all be much the same in a hundred years." He fumbled, trying to shuffle, and bent the cards: his hands were not steady.

"All the same, you're worried now about a little pain," the lieutenant said maliciously, watching his fingers.

"But I'm not a saint," the priest said. "I'm not even a brave man." He looked apprehensively up: light was coming back: the candle was no longer necessary. It would soon be clear enough to start the long journey back. He felt a desire to go on talking, to delay even by a few minutes the decision to start. He said: "That's another differ-

ence between us. It's no good your working for your end
unless you're a good man yourself. And there won't always
be good men in your party. Then you'll have all the old
starvation, beating, get-rich-anyhow. But it doesn't matter so much my being a coward—and all the rest. I can put
God into a man's mouth just the same—and I can give him
God's pardon. It wouldn't make any difference to that if
every priest in the Church was like me."

"That's another thing I don't understand," the lieutenant said, "why you—of all people—should have stayed
when the others ran."

"They didn't all run," the priest said.

"But why did you stay?"

"Once," the priest said, "I asked myself that. The fact
is, a man isn't presented suddenly with two courses to follow. One good and one bad. He gets caught up. The first
year—well, I didn't believe there was really any cause to
run. Churches have been burnt before now. You know how
often. It doesn't mean much. I thought I'd stay till next
month, say, and see if things were better. Then—oh, you
don't know how time can slip by." It was quite light again
now: the afternoon rain was over: life had to go on. A
policeman passed the entrance of the hut and looked in
curiously at the pair of them. "Do you know I suddenly
realized that I was the only priest left for miles around?
The law which made priests marry finished them. They
went: they were quite right to go. There was one priest in
particular—who had always disapproved of me. I have a
tongue, you know, and it used to wag. He said—quite
rightly—that I wasn't a firm character. He escaped. It
felt—you'll laugh at this—just as it did at school when a

bully I had been afraid of—for years—got too old for any
more teaching and was turned out. You see, I didn't have
to think about anybody's opinion any more. The people—
they didn't worry me. They liked me." He gave a weak
smile, sideways, towards the humped Yankee.

"Go on," the lieutenant said moodily.

"You'll know all there is to know about me, at this
rate," the priest said, with a nervous giggle, "by the time
I get to, well, prison."

"It's just as well. To know an enemy, I mean."

"That other priest was right. It was when he left I began to go to pieces. One thing went after another. I got
careless about my duties. I began to drink. It would have
been much better, I think, if I had gone too. Because pride
was at work all the time. Not love of God." He sat bowed
on the packing-case, a small plump man in Mr. Lehr's
cast-off clothes. He said: "Pride was what made the angels
fall. Pride's the worst thing of all. I thought I was a fine
fellow to have stayed when the others had gone. And then
I thought I was so grand I could make my own rules. I
gave up fasting, daily Mass. I neglected my prayers—and
one day because I was drunk and lonely—well, you know
how it was, I got a child. It was all pride. Just pride because I'd stayed. I wasn't any use, but I stayed. At least,
not much use. I'd got so that I didn't have a hundred communicants a month. If I'd gone I'd have given God to
twelve times that number. It's a mistake one makes—to
think just because a thing is difficult or dangerous . . ."
He made a flapping motion with his hands.

The lieutenant said in a tone of fury: "Well, you're
going to be a martyr—you've got that satisfaction."

"Oh, no. Martyrs are not like me. They don't think all the time—if I had drunk more brandy I shouldn't be so afraid."

The lieutenant said sharply to a man in the entrance: "Well, what is it? What are you hanging round for?"

"The storm's over, lieutenant. We wondered when we were to start."

"We start immediately."

He got up and put back the pistol in his holster. He said: "Get a horse ready for the prisoner. And have some men dig a grave quickly for the Yankee."

The priest put the cards in his pocket and stood up. He said:

"You have listened very patiently . . ."

"I am not afraid," the lieutenant said, "of other people's ideas."

Outside the ground was steaming after the rain: the mist rose nearly to their knees: the horses stood ready. The priest mounted, but before they had time to move a voice made the priest turn—the same sullen whine he had heard so often. "Father." It was the half-caste.

"Well, well," the priest said. "You again."

"Oh, I know what you're thinking," the half-caste said. "There's not much charity in you, father. You thought all along I was going to betray you."

"Go," the lieutenant said sharply. "You've done your job."

"May I have one word, lieutenant?" the priest asked.

"You're a good man, father," the mestizo cut quickly in, "but you think the worst of people. I just want your blessing, that's all."

"What is the good? You can't sell a blessing," the priest said.

"It's just because we won't see each other again. And I didn't want you to go off there thinking ill things . . ."

"You are so superstitious," the priest said. "You think my blessing will be like a blinker over God's eyes. I can't stop Him knowing all about it. Much better go home and pray. Then if He gives you grace to feel sorry, give away the money. . . ."

"What money, father?" The half-caste shook his stirrup angrily. "What money? There you go again . . ."

The priest sighed. He felt empty with the ordeal. Fear can be more tiring than a long monotonous ride. He said: "I'll pray for you," and beat his horse into position beside the lieutenant's.

"And I'll pray for you, father," the half-caste announced complacently. Once the priest looked back as his horse poised for the steep descent between the rocks. The half-caste stood alone among the huts, his mouth a little open, showing the two long fangs. He might have been snapped in the act of shouting some complaint or some claim—that he was a good Catholic perhaps: one hand scratched under the armpit. The priest waved his hand: he bore no grudge because he expected nothing else of anything human and he had one cause at least of satisfaction—that yellow and unreliable face would be absent "at the death."

"You're a man of education," the lieutenant said. He lay across the entrance of the hut with his head on his rolled cape and his revolver by his side. It was night, but neither man could sleep. The priest, when he shifted, groaned a little with stiffness and cramp: the lieutenant was in a hurry to get home, and they had ridden till midnight. They were down off the hills and in the marshy plain. Soon the whole state would be subdivided by swamp. The rains had really begun.

"I'm not that. My father was a storekeeper."

"I mean, you've been abroad. You can talk like a Yankee. You've had schooling."

"Yes."

"I've had to think things out for myself. But there are some things which you don't have to learn in a school. That there are rich and poor." He said in a low voice: "I've shot three hostages because of you. Poor men. It made me hate your guts."

"Yes," the priest admitted, and tried to stand to ease the cramp in his right thigh. The lieutenant sat quickly up, gun in hand. "What are you doing?"

"Nothing. Just cramp. That's all." He lay down again with a groan.

The lieutenant said: "Those men I shot. They were my own people. I wanted to give them the whole world."

"Well, who knows? Perhaps that's what you did."

The lieutenant spat suddenly, viciously, as if something unclean had got upon his tongue. He said: "You always have answers, which mean nothing."

"I was never any good at books," the priest said. "I haven't any memory. But there was one thing always puzzled me about men like yourself. You hate the rich and love the poor. Isn't that right?"

"Yes."

"Well, if I hated you, I wouldn't want to bring up my child to be like you. It's not sense."

"That's just twisting . . ."

"Perhaps it is. I've never got your ideas straight. We've always said the poor are blessed and the rich are going to find it hard to get into heaven. Why should we make it hard for the poor man too? Oh, I know we are told to give to the poor, to see they are not hungry—hunger can make a man do evil just as much as money can. But why should we give the poor power? It's better to let him die in dirt and wake in heaven—so long as we don't push his face in the dirt."

"I hate your reasons," the lieutenant said. "I don't want reasons. If you see somebody in pain, people like you reason and reason. You say—perhaps pain's a good thing, perhaps he'll be better for it one day. I want to let my heart speak."

"At the end of a gun."

"Yes. At the end of a gun."

"Oh, well, perhaps when you're my age you'll know the heart's an untrustworthy beast. The mind is too, but it doesn't talk about love. Love. And a girl puts her head under water or a child's strangled, and the heart all the time says love, love."

They lay quiet for a while in the hut. The priest thought the lieutenant was asleep until he spoke again. "You never talk straight. You say one thing to me—but to another man, or a woman, you say: 'God is love.' But you think that stuff won't go down with me, so you say different things. Things you think I'll agree with."

"Oh," the priest said, "that's another thing altogether

—God *is* love. I don't say the heart doesn't feel a taste of it, but what a taste. The smallest glass of love mixed with a pint pot of ditch-water. We wouldn't recognize *that* love. It might even look like hate. It would be enough to scare us—God's love. It set fire to a bush in the desert, didn't it, and smashed open graves and set the dead walking in the dark? Oh, a man like me would run a mile to get away if he felt that love around."

"You don't trust Him much, do you? He doesn't seem a grateful kind of God. If a man served me as well as you've served Him, well, I'd recommend him for promotion, see he got a good pension . . . if he was in pain, with cancer, I'd put a bullet through his head."

"Listen," the priest said earnestly, leaning forward in the dark, pressing on a cramped foot, "I'm not as dishonest as you think I am. Why do you think I tell people out of the pulpit that they're in danger of damnation if death catches them unawares? I'm not telling them fairy-stories I don't believe myself. I don't know a thing about the mercy of God: I don't know how awful the human heart looks to Him. But I do know this—that if there's ever been a single man in this state damned, then I'll be damned too." He said slowly: "I wouldn't want it to be any different. I just want justice, that's all."

"We'll be in before dark," the lieutenant said. Six men rode in front and six behind: sometimes, in the belts of forest between the arms of the river, they had to ride in single file. The lieutenant didn't speak much, and once when two of his men struck up a song about a fat shopkeeper and his woman, he told them savagely to be silent.

It wasn't a very triumphal procession: the priest rode
with a weak grin fixed on his face. It was like a mask he
had stuck on, so that he could think quickly without anyone's noticing. What he thought about mostly was pain.

"I suppose," the lieutenant said, scowling ahead, "you're
hoping for a miracle."

"Excuse me. What did you say?"

"I said I suppose you're hoping for a miracle."

"No."

"You believe in them, don't you?"

"Yes. But not for me. I'm no more good to anyone, so
why should God keep me alive?"

"I can't think how a man like you can believe in those
things. The Indians, yes. Why, the first time they see an
electric light they think it's a miracle."

"And I dare say the first time you saw a man raised
from the dead you might think so too." He giggled unconvincingly behind the smiling mask. "Oh, it's funny,
isn't it? It isn't a case of miracles not happening—it's
just a case of people calling them something else. Can't
you see the doctors round the dead man? He isn't breathing any more, his pulse has stopped, his heart's not beating: he's dead. Then somebody gives him back his life, and
they all—what's the expression?—reserve their opinion.
They won't say it's a miracle, because that's a word they
don't like. Then it happens again and again perhaps—
because God's about on earth—and they say: there aren't
miracles, it is simply that we have enlarged our conception of what life is. Now we know you can be alive without
pulse, breath, heart-beats. And they invent a new word to
describe that state of life, and they say science has again

disproved a miracle." He giggled again. "You can't get round them."

They were out of the forest track onto a hard beaten road, and the lieutenant dug in his spur and the whole cavalcade broke into a canter. They were nearly home now. The lieutenant said grudgingly: "You aren't a bad fellow. If there's anything I can do for you . . ."

"If you would give permission for me to confess . . ."

The first houses came into sight: little hard-baked houses of earth falling into ruin: a few classical pillars just plaster over mud, and a dirty child playing in the rubble.

The lieutenant said: "But there's no priest."

"Padre José."

"Oh, Padre José," the lieutenant said, with contempt, "he's no good to you."

"He's good enough for me. It's not likely I'd find a saint here, is it?"

The lieutenant rode for a little while in silence: they came to the cemetery, full of chipped angels, and passed the great portico with its black letters: *Silencio*. He said: "All right. You can have him." He wouldn't look at the cemetery as they went by—there was the wall where the prisoners were shot. The road went steeply down-hill towards the river: on the right, where the cathedral had been, the iron swings stood empty in the hot afternoon. There was a sense of desolation everywhere, more of it than in the mountains because a lot of life had once existed here. The lieutenant thought: No pulse, no breath, no heart-beat, but it's still life—we've only got to find a name for it. A small boy watched them pass: he called out to the lieutenant: "Lieutenant, have you got him?" and the lieutenant dimly remembered the face—one day in the plaza—a broken bottle, and he tried to smile back, an odd sour grimace, without triumph or hope. One had to begin again with that.

CHAPTER FOUR

THE lieutenant waited till after dark and then he went himself. It would be dangerous to send another man because the news would be around the city in no time that Padre José had been permitted to carry out a religious duty in the prison. It was wiser not to let even the jefe know: one didn't trust one's superiors when one was more successful than they were. He knew the jefe wasn't pleased that he had brought the priest in—an escape would have been better from his point of view.

In the patio he could feel himself watched by a dozen eyes: the children clustered there ready to shout at Padre José if he appeared. He wished he had promised the priest nothing, but he was going to keep his word—because it would be a triumph for that old corrupt God-ridden world if it could show itself superior on any point—whether of courage, truthfulness, justice . . .

Nobody answered his knock: he stood darkly in the patio like a petitioner. Then he knocked again, and a voice called: "A moment. A moment."

Padre José put his face against the bars of his window and said: "Who's there?" He seemed to be fumbling at something near the ground.

"Lieutenant of police."

"Oh," Padre José squeaked. "Excuse me. It is my trousers. In the dark." He seemed to heave at something and there was a sharp crack, as if his belt or braces had given way. Across the patio the children began to squeak: "Padre José. Padre José." When he came to the door he wouldn't look at them, muttering tenderly: "The little devils."

The lieutenant said: "I want you to come up to the police station."

"But I've done nothing. Nothing. I've been so careful."

"Padre José," the children squeaked.

He said imploringly: "If it's anything about a burial, you've been misinformed. I wouldn't even say a prayer."

"Padre José. Padre José."

The lieutenant turned and strode across the patio. He said furiously to the faces at the grille: "Be quiet. Go to bed. At once. Do you hear me?" They dropped out of sight one by one, but immediately the lieutenant's back was turned, they were there again watching.

Padre José said: "Nobody can do anything with those children."

A woman's voice said: "Where are you, José?"

"Here, my dear. It is the police."

A huge woman in a white night-dress came billowing out at them: it wasn't much after seven: perhaps she lived, the lieutenant thought, in that dress—perhaps she lived in bed. He said: "Your husband," dwelling on the term with satisfaction, "your husband is wanted at the station."

"Who says so?"

"I do."

"He's done nothing."

"I was just saying, my dear . . ."

"Be quiet. Leave the talking to me."

"You can both stop jabbering," the lieutenant said. "You're wanted at the station to see a man—a priest. He wants to confess."

"To me?"

"Yes. There's no one else."

"Poor man," Padre José said. His little pink eyes swept the patio. "Poor man." He shifted uneasily, and took a furtive look at the sky where the constellations wheeled.

"You won't go," the woman said.

"It's against the law, isn't it?" Padre José asked.

"You needn't trouble about that."

"Oh, we needn't, eh?" the woman said. "I can see through you. You don't want my husband to be let alone. You want to trick him. I know your work. You get people to ask him to say prayers—he's a kind man. But I'd have you remember this—he's a pensioner of the government."

The lieutenant said slowly: "This priest—he has been working for years secretly—for *your* Church. We've caught him and, of course, he'll be shot tomorrow. He's not a bad man, and I told him he could see you. He seems to think it will do him good."

"I know him," the woman interrupted, "he's a drunkard. That's all he is."

"Poor man," Padre José said. "He tried to hide here once."

"I promise you," the lieutenant said, "nobody shall know."

"Nobody know?" the woman cackled. "Why, it will be all over town. Look at those children there. They never leave José alone." She went on: "There'll be no end to it —everybody will be wanting to confess, and the Governor will hear of it, and the pension will be stopped."

"Perhaps, my dear," José said, "it's my duty . . ."

"You aren't a priest any more," the woman said, "you're my husband." She used a coarse word. "That's your duty now."

The lieutenant listened to them with acid satisfaction. It was like rediscovering an old belief. He said: "I can't wait here while you argue. Are you going to come with me?"

"He can't make you," the woman said.

"My dear, it's only that . . . well . . . I *am* a priest."

"A priest," the woman cackled, "you a priest!" She went off into a peal of laughter, which was taken tentatively up by the children at the window. Padre José put his fingers up to his pink eyes as if they hurt. He said: "My dear . . ." and the laughter went on.

"Are you coming?"

Padre José made a despairing gesture—as much as to say, what does one more failure matter in a life like this? He said: "I don't think it's—possible."

"Very well," the lieutenant said. He turned abruptly —he hadn't any more time to waste on mercy, and heard Padre José's voice speak imploringly: "Tell him I shall pray." The children had gained confidence: one of them called sharply out: "Come to bed, José," and the lieutenant laughed once—a poor unconvincing addition to the general laughter which now surrounded Padre José, ringing up all round to the disciplined constellations he had once known by name.

The lieutenant opened the cell door: it was very dark inside: he shut the door carefully behind him and locked it, keeping his hand on his gun. He said: "He won't come."

A little bunched figure in the darkness was the priest. He crouched on the floor like a child playing. He said: "You mean—not tonight?"

"I mean he won't come at all."

There was silence for some while, if you could talk of silence where there was always the drill-drill of mosquitoes and the little crackling explosion of beetles against the wall. At last the priest said: "He was afraid, I suppose . . ."

"His wife wouldn't let him come."

"Poor man." He tried to giggle, but no sound could have been more miserable than the half-hearted attempt. His head drooped between his knees: he looked as if he had abandoned everything, and been abandoned.

The lieutenant said: "You had better know everything. You've been tried and found guilty."

"Couldn't I have been present at my own trial?"

"It wouldn't have made any difference."

"No." He was silent, preparing an attitude. Then he asked with a kind of false jauntiness: "And when, if I may ask . . . ?"

"Tomorrow." The promptness and brevity of the reply called his bluff. His head went down again and he seemed, as far as it was possible to see in the dark, to be biting his nails.

The lieutenant said: "It's bad being alone on a night like this. If you would like to be transferred to the common cell . . ."

"No, no. I'd rather be alone. I've got plenty to do." His voice failed, as though he had a heavy cold. He wheezed: "So much to think about."

"I should like to do something for you," the lieutenant said. "I've brought you some brandy."

"Against the law?"

"Yes."

"It's very good of you." He took the small flask. "You wouldn't need this, I dare say. But I've always been afraid of pain."

"We have to die some time," the lieutenant said. "It doesn't seem to matter so much when."

"You're a good man. You've got nothing to be afraid of."

"You have such odd ideas," the lieutenant complained. He said: "Sometimes I feel you're just trying to talk me round."

"Round to what?"

"Oh, to letting you escape perhaps—or to believing in the Holy Catholic Church, the communion of saints . . . how does that stuff go?"

"The forgiveness of sins."

"You don't believe much in that, do you?"

"Oh, yes, I believe," the little man said obstinately.

"Then what are you worried about?"

"I'm not ignorant, you see. I've always known what I've been doing. And I can't absolve myself."

"Would Padre José coming here have made all that difference?"

He had to wait a long while for his answer, and then he didn't understand it when it came: "Another man . . . it makes it easier . . ."

"Is there nothing more I can do for you?"

"No. Nothing."

The lieutenant reopened the door, mechanically putting his hand again upon his revolver: he felt moody, as though now that the last priest was under lock and key there was nothing left to think about. The spring of action seemed to be broken. He looked back on the weeks of hunting as a happy time which was over now for ever. He felt without a purpose, as if life had drained out of the world. He said with bitter kindness (he couldn't summon up any hate of the small hollow man): "Try to sleep."

He was closing the door when a scared voice spoke. "Lieutenant."

"Yes."

"You've seen people shot. People like me."

"Yes."

"Does the pain go on—a long time?"

"No, no. A second," he said roughly, and closed the door, and picked his way back across the whitewashed yard. He went into the office: the pictures of the priest and the gunman were still pinned up on the wall: he tore them down—they would never be wanted again. Then he sat at the desk and put his head upon his hands and fell

asleep with utter weariness. He couldn't remember afterwards anything of his dreams except laughter, laughter
all the time, and a long passage in which he could find no
door.

The priest sat on the floor, holding the brandy flask.
Presently he unscrewed the cap and put his mouth to it.
The spirit didn't do a thing to him: it might have been
water. He put it down again and began some kind of
general confession, speaking in a whisper. He said: "I
have committed fornication." The formal phrase meant
nothing at all: it was like a sentence in a newspaper: you
couldn't feel repentance over a thing like that. He started
again: "I have lain with a woman," and tried to imagine
the other priest asking him: "How many times? Was she
married?" "No." Without thinking what he was doing, he
took another drink of brandy.

As the liquid touched his tongue he remembered his
child, coming in out of the glare: the sullen unhappy
knowledgeable face. He said: "O God, help her. Damn
me, I deserve it, but let her live for ever." This was the
love he should have felt for every soul in the world: all
the fear and the wish to save concentrated unjustly on
the one child. He began to weep: it was as if he had to
watch her drown slowly from the shore because he had forgotten how to swim. He thought: This is what I should
feel all the time for everyone, and he tried to turn his
brain away towards the half-caste, the lieutenant, even a
dentist he had once sat with for a few minutes, the child at
the banana station, calling up a long succession of faces,
pushing at his attention as if it were a heavy door which

wouldn't budge. For those were all in danger too. He prayed: "God help them," but in the moment of prayer he switched back to his child beside the rubbish-dump, and he knew it was only for her that he prayed. Another failure.

After a while he began again: "I have been drunk—I don't know how many times; there isn't a duty I haven't neglected; I have been guilty of pride, lack of charity . . ." The words were becoming formal again, meaning nothing. He had no confessor to turn his mind away from the formula to the fact.

He took another drink of brandy, and getting up with pain because of his cramp, he moved to the door and looked through the bars at the hot moony square. He could see the police asleep in their hammocks, and one man who couldn't sleep lazily rocking up and down, up and down. There was an odd silence everywhere, even in the other cells: it was as if the whole world had tactfully turned its back to avoid seeing him die. He felt his way back along the wall to the farthest corner and sat down with the flask between his knees. He thought: If I hadn't been so useless, useless. . . . The eight hard hopeless years seemed to him to be only a caricature of service: a few communions, a few confessions, and an endless bad example. He thought: If I had only one soul to offer, so that I could say: Look what I've done. . . . People had died for him: they had deserved a saint, and a tinge of bitterness spread across his mind for their sake that God hadn't thought fit to send them one. Padre José and me, he thought, Padre José and me, and he took a drink again from the brandy flask. He thought of the cold faces of the saints rejecting him.

This night was slower than the last he spent in prison because he was alone. Only the brandy, which he finished about two in the morning, gave him any sleep at all. He felt sick with fear, his stomach ached, and his mouth was dry with the drink. He began to talk aloud to himself because he couldn't stand the silence any more. He complained miserably: "It's all very well . . . for saints," and later: "How does he know it only lasts a second? How long's a second?": then he began to cry, beating his head gently against the wall. They had given a chance to Padre José, but they had never given him a chance at all. Perhaps they had got it all wrong—just because he had escaped them for such a time. Perhaps they really thought he would refuse the conditions Padre José had accepted, that he would refuse to marry, that he was proud. Perhaps if he suggested it himself, he would escape yet. The hope calmed him for a while, and he fell asleep with his head against the wall.

He had a curious dream. He dreamed he was sitting at a café table in front of the high altar of the cathedral. About six dishes were spread before him, and he was eating hungrily. There was a smell of incense and an odd sense of elation. The dishes—like all food in dreams—did not taste of much, but he had a sense that when he had finished them, he would have the best dish of all. A priest passed to and fro before the altar saying Mass, but he took no notice: the service no longer seemed to concern him. At last the six plates were empty; someone out of sight rang the sanctus bell, and the serving priest knelt before he raised the Host. But *he* sat on, just waiting, paying no attention to the God over the altar, as if that was a God for other people and not for him. Then the glass by his plate began to fill with wine, and looking up he saw that the child from the banana station was serving him. She said: "I got it from my father's room."

"You didn't steal it?"

"Not exactly," she said in her careful and precise voice.

He said: "It is very good of you. I had forgotten the code—what did you call it?"

"Morse."

"That was it. Morse. Three long taps and one short one," and immediately the taps began: the priest by the altar tapped, a whole invisible congregation tapped along the aisles—three long and one short. He said: "What is it?"

"News," the child said, watching him with a stern, responsible, and interested gaze.

When he woke up it was dawn. He woke with a huge feeling of hope which suddenly and completely left him at the first sight of the prison yard. It was the morning of his death. He crouched on the floor with the empty brandy flask in his hand trying to remember an act of contrition. "O God, I am sorry and beg pardon for all my sins . . . crucified . . . worthy of Thy dreadful punishments." He was confused, his mind was on other things: it was not the good death for which one always prayed. He caught sight of his own shadow on the cell wall: it had a look of surprise and grotesque unimportance. What a fool he had been to think that he was strong enough to stay when others fled. What an impossible fellow I am, he thought, and how useless. I have done nothing for anybody. I might just as well have never lived. His parents were dead—soon he wouldn't even be a memory—perhaps after all he wasn't really Hell-worthy. Tears poured down his face: he was not at the moment afraid of damnation— even the fear of pain was in the background. He felt only an immense disappointment because he had to go to God empty-handed, with nothing done at all. It seemed to him at that moment that it would have been quite easy to have been a saint. It would only have needed a little self-restraint and a little courage. He felt like someone who has missed happiness by seconds at an appointed place. He knew now that at the end there was only one thing that counted—to be a saint.

CHAPTER ONE

MRS. FELLOWS lay in bed in the hot hotel room, listening to the siren of a boat on the river. She could see nothing because she had a handkerchief soaked in eau-de-Cologne over her eyes and forehead. She called sharply out: "My dear. My dear," but nobody replied. She felt that she had been prematurely buried in this big brass family tomb, all alone on two pillows, under a canopy. "Dear," she said again sharply, and waited.

"Yes, Trixy." It was Captain Fellows. He said: "I was asleep, dreaming . . ."

"Put some more Cologne on this handkerchief, dear. My head's splitting."

"Yes, Trixy."

He took the handkcherchief away: he looked old and tired and bored—a man without a hobby, and walking over to the dressing-table, he soaked the linen.

"Not too much, dear. It will be days before we can get any more."

He didn't answer, and she said sharply: "You heard what I said, dear, didn't you?"

"Yes."

"You are so silent these days. You don't realize what it is to be ill and alone."

"Well," Captain Fellows said, "you know how it is."

"But we agreed, dear, didn't we, that it was better just to say nothing at all, ever? We mustn't be morbid."

"No."

"We've got our own life to lead."

"Yes."

He came across to the bed and laid the handkerchief over his wife's eyes. Then sitting down on a chair, he slipped his hand under the net and felt for her hand. They gave an odd effect of being children, lost in a strange town, without adult care.

"Have you got the tickets?" she asked.

"Yes, dear."

"I must get up later and pack, but my head hurts so. Did you tell them to collect the boxes?"

"I forgot."

"You really must try to think of things," she said weakly and sullenly. "There's no one else," and they both sat silent at a phrase they should have avoided. He said suddenly: "There's a lot of excitement in town."

"Not a revolution?"

"Oh, no. They've caught a . . . this morning, poor . . . . . a priest and he's being shot it's . . . poor devil. I can't help wondering whether . . . the man Coral—I mean the man we sheltered."

"It's not likely."

"No."

"There are so many priests."

He let go of her hand, and going to the window looked

out. Boats on the river, a small stony public garden with a bust, and buzzards everywhere.

Mrs. Fellows said: "It will be good to be back home. I sometimes thought I should die in this place."

"Of course not, dear."

"Well, people do."

"Yes, they do," he said glumly.

"Now, dear," Mrs. Fellows said sharply, "your promise." She gave a long sigh: "My poor head."

He said: "Would you like some aspirin?"

"I don't know where I've put it. Somehow nothing is ever in its place."

"Shall I go out and get you some more?"

"No, dear, I can't bear being left alone." She went on with dramatic brightness: "I expect I shall be all right when we get home. I'll have a proper doctor then. I sometimes think it's more than a headache. Did I tell you that I'd heard from Norah?"

"No."

"Get me my glasses, dear, and I'll read you—what concerns us."

"They're on your bed."

"So they are." One of the sailing-boats cast off and began to drift down the wide sluggish stream, going towards the sea. She read with satisfaction: " 'Dear Trix: how you have suffered. That scoundrel . . .' " She broke abruptly off: "Oh, yes, and then she goes on: 'Of course, you and Charles must stay with us for a while until you have found somewhere to live. If you don't mind semi-detached . . .' "

Captain Fellows said suddenly and harshly: "I'm not going back."

"The rent is only fifty-six pounds a year, exclusive, and there's a maid's bathroom."

"I'm staying."

"A 'cookanheat.' What on earth are you saying, dear?"

"I'm not going back."

"We've been over that so often, dear. You know it would kill me to stay."

"You needn't stay."

"But I couldn't go alone," Mrs. Fellows said. "What on earth would Norah think? Besides—oh, it's absurd."

"A man here can do a job of work."

"Picking bananas," Mrs. Fellows said. She gave a little cold laugh. "And you weren't much good at that."

He turned furiously towards the bed. "You don't mind," he said, "do you—running away and leaving *her . . . ?*"

"It wasn't my fault. If you'd been at home . . ." She began to cry bunched up under the mosquito-net. She said: "I'll never get home alive."

He came wearily over to the bed and took her hand again. It was no good. They had both been deserted. They had to stick together. "You won't leave me alone, will you, dear?" she asked. The room reeked of eau-de-Cologne.

"No, dear."

"You do realize how absurd it is?"

"Yes."

They sat in silence for a long while, as the morning sun climbed outside and the room got stiflingly hot. Mrs. Fellows said at last: "A penny, dear."

"What?"

"For your thoughts."

"I was just thinking of that priest. A queer fellow. He drank. I wonder if it's him."

"If it is, I expect he deserves all he gets."

"But the odd thing is—the way she went on afterwards—as if he'd told her things."

"Darling," Mrs. Fellows repeated, with harsh weakness from the bed, "your promise."

"Yes, I'm sorry. I was trying, but it seems to come up all the time."

"We've got each other, dear," Mrs. Fellows said, and the letter from Norah rustled as she turned her head, swathed in handkerchief, away from the hard outdoor light.

Mr. Tench bent over the enamel basin washing his hands with pink soap. He said in his bad Spanish: "You don't need to be afraid. You can tell me directly it hurts."

The jefe's room had been fixed up as a kind of temporary dentist's office—at considerable expense, for it had entailed transporting not only Mr. Tench himself, but Mr. Tench's cabinet, chair, and all sorts of mysterious packing-cases which seemed to contain little but straw and which were unlikely to return empty.

"I've had it for months," the jefe said. "You can't imagine the pain . . ."

"It was foolish of you not to call me in sooner. Your mouth's in a very bad state. You are lucky to have escaped pyorrhœa."

He finished washing and suddenly stood, towel in hand, thinking of something. "What's the matter?" the jefe said. Mr. Tench woke with a jump, and coming forward to his cabinet, began to lay out the drill needles in a little metallic row of pain. The jefe watched with apprehension. He said: "Your hand is very jumpy. Are you quite sure you are well enough this morning?"

"It's indigestion," Mr. Tench said. "Sometimes I have so many spots in front of my eyes I might be wearing a veil." He fitted a needle into the drill and bent the arm round. "Now open your mouth very wide." He began to stuff the jefe's mouth with plugs of cotton. He said: "I've never seen a mouth as bad as yours—except once."

The jefe struggled to speak. Only a dentist could have interpreted the muffled and uneasy question.

"He wasn't a patient. I expect someone cured him. You cure a lot of people in this country, don't you, with bullets?"

As he picked and picked at the tooth, he tried to keep up a running fire of conversation: that was how one did things at Southend. He said: "An odd thing happened to me just before I came up the river. I got a letter from my wife. Hadn't so much as heard from her for—oh, twenty years. Then out of the blue she . . ." He leant closer and levered furiously with his pick: the jefe beat the air and grunted. "Wash out your mouth," Mr. Tench said, and began grimly to fix his drill. He said: "What was I talking about? Oh, the wife, wasn't it? Seems she had got religion of some kind. Some sort of a group—Oxford. What would she be doing in Oxford? Wrote to say that she had forgiven me and wanted to make things legal. Divorce, I mean. Forgiven *me*," Mr. Tench said, looking round the little hideous room, lost in thought, with his hand on the drill. He belched and put his other hand against his stom-

ach, pressing, pressing, seeking an obscure pain which was
nearly always there. The jefe leant back exhausted with
his mouth wide open.

"It comes and goes," Mr. Tench said, losing the thread
of his thought completely. "Of course, it's nothing. Just
indigestion. But it gets me locked." He stared moodily
into the jefe's mouth as if a crystal were concealed between
the carious teeth. Then, as if he were exerting an awful
effort of will, he leant forward, brought the arm of the
drill round, and began to pedal. Buzz and grate. Buzz and
grate. The jefe stiffened all over and clutched the arms of
the chair, and Mr. Tench's foot went up and down, up and
down. The jefe made odd sounds and waved his hands.
"Hold hard," Mr. Tench said, "hold hard. There's just
one tiny corner. Nearly finished. There she comes. There."
He stopped and said: "Good God, what's that?"

He left the jefe altogether and went to the window. In
the yard below a squad of police had just grounded their
arms. With his hand on his stomach he protested: "Not
another revolution?"

The jefe levered himself upright and spat out a gag.
"Of course not," he said. "A man's being shot."

"What for?"

"Treason."

"I thought you generally did it," Mr. Tench said, "up
by the cemetery?" A horrid fascination kept him by the
window: this was something he had never seen. He and the
buzzards looked down together on the little whitewashed
courtyard.

"It was better not to this time. There might have been
a demonstration. People are so ignorant."

A small man came out of a side door: he was held up by two policemen, but you could tell that he was doing his best—it was only that his legs were not fully under his control. They paddled him across to the opposite wall: an officer tied a handkerchief round his eyes. Mr. Tench thought: But I know him. Good God, one ought to do something. This was like seeing a neighbour shot.

The jefe said: "What are you waiting for? The air gets into this tooth."

Of course there was nothing to do. Everything went very quickly like a routine. The officer stepped aside, the rifles went up, and the little man suddenly made jerky movements with his arms. He was trying to say something: what was the phrase they were always supposed to use? That was routine too, but perhaps his mouth was too dry, because nothing came out except a word that sounded more like "Excuse." The crash of the rifles shook Mr. Tench: they seemed to vibrate inside his own guts: he felt rather sick and shut his eyes. Then there was a single shot, and opening his eyes again he saw the officer stuffing his gun back into his holster, and the little man was a routine heap beside the wall—something unimportant which had to be cleared away. Two knock-kneed men approached quickly. This was an arena, and there was the bull dead, and there was nothing more to wait for any longer.

"Oh," the jefe moaned from the chair, "the pain, the pain." He implored Mr. Tench: "Hurry," but Mr. Tench was lost in thought beside the window, one hand automatically seeking in his stomach for the hidden uneasiness. He remembered the little man rising bitterly and hopelessly from his chair that blinding afternoon to follow the child out of town; he remembered a green watering-can, the photo of the children, that case he was making out of sand for a split palate.

"The stopping," the jefe pleaded, and Mr. Tench's eyes went to the little mound of gold on the glass dish. Currency—he would insist on foreign currency: this time he was going to clear out, clear out for good. In the yard everything had been tidied away: a man was throwing sand out of a spade, as if he were filling a grave. But there was no grave: there was nobody there: an appalling sense of loneliness came over Mr. Tench, doubling him with indigestion. The little fellow had spoken English and knew about his children. He felt deserted.

" 'And now,' " the woman's voice swelled triumphantly, and the two little girls with beady eyes held their breath, " 'the great testing day had come.' " Even the boy showed interest, standing by the window, looking out into the dark curfew-emptied street—this was the last chapter, and in the last chapter things always happened violently. Perhaps all life was like that—dull and then a heroic flurry at the end.

" 'When the Chief of Police came to Juan's cell he found him on his knees, praying. He had not slept at all, but had spent his last night preparing for martyrdom. He was quite calm and happy, and smiling at the Chief of Police, he asked him if he had come to lead him to the banquet. Even that evil man, who had persecuted so many innocent people, was visibly moved.' "

If only it would get on towards the shooting, the boy thought: the shooting never failed to excite him, and he always waited anxiously for the *coup de grâce*.

" 'They led him out into the prison yard. No need to bind those hands now busy with his beads. In that short walk to the wall of execution, did young Juan look back on those few, those happy years he had so bravely spent? Did he remember days in the seminary, the kindly rebukes of his elders, the moulding discipline: days, too, of frivolity when he acted Nero before the old bishop? Nero was here beside him, and this the Roman amphitheatre.' "

The mother's voice was getting a little hoarse: she fingered the remaining pages rapidly: it wasn't worth while stopping now, and she raced more and more rapidly on.

" 'Reaching the wall, Juan turned and began to pray— not for himself, but for his enemies, for the squad of poor innocent Indian soldiers who faced him and even for the Chief of Police himself. He raised the crucifix at the end of his beads and prayed that God would forgive them, would enlighten their ignorance, and bring them at last— as Saul the persecutor was brought—into his eternal kingdom.' "

"Had they loaded?" the boy said.

"What do you mean—had they loaded?"

"Why didn't they fire and stop him?"

"Because God decided otherwise." She coughed and went on: " 'The officer gave the command to present arms. In that moment a smile of complete adoration and happiness passed over Juan's face. It was as if he could see the arms of God open to receive him. He had always told his mother and sisters that he had a premonition that he would

be in heaven before them. He would say with a whimsical
smile to his mother, the good but over-careful housewife:
"I will have tidied everything up for you." Now the moment had come, the officer gave the order to fire, and—' "
She had been reading too fast because it was past the little
girls' bedtime and now she was thwarted by a fit of hic-
cups. " 'Fire,' " she repeated, " 'and . . .' "

The two little girls sat placidly side by side—they
looked nearly asleep—this was the part of the book they
never cared much about; they endured it for the sake of
the amateur theatricals and the first communion, and of
the sister who became a nun and paid a moving farewell to
her family in the third chapter.

" 'Fire,' " the mother tried again, " 'and Juan, raising
both arms above his head, called out in a strong brave
voice to the soldiers and the levelled rifles: "Hail Christ
the King!" Next moment he fell riddled with a dozen bullets and the officer, stooping over his body, put his revolver
close to Juan's ear and pulled the trigger.' "

A long sigh came from the window.

" 'No need to have fired another shot. The soul of the
young hero had already left its earthly mansion, and the
happy smile on the dead face told even those ignorant men
where they would find Juan now. One of the men there that
day was so moved by his bearing that he secretly soaked
his handkerchief in the martyr's blood, and that handkerchief, cut into a hundred relics, found its way into many
pious homes.' And now," the mother went rapidly on, clapping her hands, "to bed."

"And that one," the boy said slowly, "they shot today.
Was he a hero too?"

"Yes."

"The one who stayed with us that time?"

"Yes. He was one of the martyrs of the Church."

"He had a funny smell," one of the little girls said.

"You must never say that again," the mother said. "He may be one of the saints."

"Shall we pray to him then?"

The mother hesitated. "It would do no harm. Of course, before we *know* he is a saint, there will have to be miracles . . ."

"Did he call *Viva el Cristo Rey?*" the boy asked.

"Yes. He was one of the heroes of the faith."

"And a handkerchief soaked in blood?" the boy went on. "Did anyone do that?"

The mother said ponderously: "I have reason to believe . . . Señora Jiminez told me . . . I think if your father will give me a little money, I shall be able to get a relic."

"Does it cost money?"

"How else could it be managed? Everybody can't have a piece."

"No."

He squatted beside the window, staring out, and behind his back came the muffled sound of small girls going to bed. It brought it home to one—to have had a hero in the house, though it had only been for twenty-four hours. And he was the last. There were no more priests and no more heroes. He listened resentfully to the sound of booted feet coming up the pavement. Ordinary life pressed round him. He got down from the window-seat and picked up his candle—Zapata, Villa, Madero, and the rest, they were all

dead, and it was people like the man out there who killed
them. He felt deceived.

The lieutenant came along the pavement: there was
something brisk and stubborn about his walk, as if he were
saying at every step: "I have done what I have done." He
looked in at the boy holding the candle with a look of in-
decisive recognition. He said to himself: "I would do much
more for him and them, much more, life is never going to
be again for them what it was for me," but the dynamic
love which used to move his trigger-finger felt flat and
dead. Of course, he told himself, it will come back. It was
like love of a woman and went in cycles: he had satisfied
himself that morning, that was all. This was satiety. He
smiled painfully at the child through the window and said:
"*Buenas noches.*" The boy was looking at his revolver-
holster, and he remembered an incident in the plaza when
he had allowed a child to touch his gun—perhaps this boy.
He smiled again and touched it too—to show he remembered, and the boy crinkled up his face and spat through
the window bars, accurately, so that a little blob of spittle
lay on the revolver-butt.

The boy went across the patio to bed. He had a little
dark room with an iron bedstead that he shared with his
father. He lay next the wall and his father would lie on
the outside, so that he could come to bed without waking
his son. He took off his shoes and undressed glumly by
candlelight: he could hear the whispering of prayers in
the other room; he felt cheated and disappointed because
he had missed something. Lying on his back in the heat

he stared up at the ceiling, and it seemed to him that there was nothing in the world but the store, his mother reading, and silly games in the plaza.

But very soon he went to sleep. He dreamed that the priest whom they had shot that morning was back in the house dressed in the clothes his father had lent him and laid out stiffly for burial. The boy sat beside the bed and his mother read out of a very long book all about how the priest had acted in front of the bishop the part of Julius Cæsar: there was a fish basket at her feet, and the fish were bleeding, wrapped in her handkerchief. He was very bored and very tired and somebody was hammering nails into a coffin in the passage. Suddenly the dead priest winked at him—an unmistakable flicker of the eyelid, just like that.

He woke and there was the crack, crack of the knocker on the outer door. His father wasn't in bed and there was complete silence in the other room. Hours must have passed. He lay listening: he was frightened, but after a short interval the knocking began again, and nobody stirred anywhere in the house. Reluctantly, he put his feet on the ground—it might be only his father locked out: he lit the candle and wrapped a blanket round himself and stood listening again. His mother might hear it and go, but he knew very well that it was *his* duty. He was the only man in the house.

Slowly he made his way across the patio towards the outer door. Suppose it was the lieutenant come back to revenge himself for the spittle. . . . He unlocked the heavy iron door and swung it open. A stranger stood in the street: a tall pale thin man with a rather sour mouth, who carried a small suitcase. He named the boy's mother and asked if this was the Señora's house. Yes, the boy said, but she was asleep. He began to shut the door, but a pointed shoe got in the way.

The stranger said: "I have only just landed. I came up the river tonight. I thought perhaps . . . I have an introduction for the Señora from a great friend of hers."

"She is asleep," the boy repeated.

"If you would let me come in," the man said with an odd frightened smile, and suddenly lowering his voice he said to the boy: "I am a priest."

"You?" the boy exclaimed.

"Yes," he said gently. "My name is Father——" But the boy had already swung the door open and put his lips to his hand before the other could give himself a name.

Critical Comments

Footnotes by the Editors are followed by the abbreviation "Ed." Omissions are indicated by ellipses in square brackets.

FRANÇOIS MAURIAC

Recipient of the Nobel Prize for Literature in 1952, François Mauriac was a member of l'Académie Française and the author of some twenty volumes of fiction, drama, and criticism. He is often compared with Graham Greene in studies of modern Catholic writing.

"THE POWER AND THE GLORY"

The work of an English Catholic novelist—of an Englishman converted to Catholicism—like *The Power and the Glory* by Graham Greene, at first always gives me the sensation of homelessness. Of course, I recognize my spiritual homeland there, and Greene introduces me to the heart of a familiar mystery. But it all appears as if I had entered the old domain through a secret door, unknown to me, hidden in the ivy-covered wall; as if I advanced, behind the hero of the novel, through the tangled branches and suddenly recognized the wide path of the park where I had played as a child, and there deciphered, on the trunk of an oak, my initials carved one day on vacation long ago.

A French Catholic comes into the Church only through the main door; he is deeply involved with its official history; he has taken sides in all the debates which have torn at it through the course of centuries and which have especially divided the French church. In all that he writes, one immediately discovers if he is on the side of Port-Royal or the Jesuits, if he has espoused Bossuet's cause against Fénelon, if he is on the side of Lamennais and Lacordaire or if he agrees with Louis Veuillot. The work of Bernanos, of which it is impossible not to think while

---

This essay, translated by Peter J. Conn, appeared in *Renascence*, Vol. I, No. 2 (Spring, 1949). Copyright 1949 by the Catholic Renascence Society.

reading *The Power and the Glory*, is very significant in this regard. All the Catholic controversies of the past four centuries are displayed in his pages. Behind the Abbé Donissan in *Soleil du Satan* appears the Curé of Ars. The saints of Bernanos, like his generous priests, like the pious laity which he describes with such cheerful ferocity, betray his venerations and his hatred.

Graham Greene, on the other hand, has entered like a burglar into the unknown kingdom, the kingdom of nature and of grace. No set purpose troubles his vision. No current of ideas turns him aside from the discovery of that key which he has suddenly found. He has no preconceived opinion of what we call a bad priest; and it could be said that he has no model of sanctity in mind. There is corrupted nature and all-powerful grace; there is the wretched man, who is nothing, even in sin, and the mysterious love which pulls him from the depths of his misery and shame to make a saint and martyr of him.

The power and the glory of the Father shine in this Mexican priest who drinks too much and who has begotten a child on one of his parishioners. Such a common fellow, so mediocre, that his mortal sins elicit only mockery and a shrug of the shoulders, and he knows it. What this extraordinary book shows us, if I may venture to say so, is the use of sin by grace. This priest, defiant and condemned to death by the authorities, with a price on his head (the story takes place in a Mexico given over to a government of atheists and persecutors), who looks to save himself, as have all the other priests including even the most virtuous, who indeed saves himself and crosses the border, but who returns each time a dying person needs him, even when he believes that his help will be in vain, and even when he is aware that he is going into an ambush and that the one who has called him has already betrayed him; this drunken priest, impure, trembling in the face of death, gives his life without losing for one moment the conviction of his vileness and his shame. He would think it a joke if someone called him a saint. He is miraculously saved from pride, from conceit, from self-satisfaction. He dies a martyr, having always in his mind the vision of the sullied and sacrilegious nothingness that is a priest in mortal sin; so that he sacrifices himself in returning to God all the power and glory which had triumphed in the one whom he considered the most wretched of men: himself.

And as he comes closer to his end, we see this mediocre sinner forming himself slowly in Christ until he resembles Him; or more: until he identifies himself with his Lord and God. The Passion begins again around this victim chosen from human waste, who repeats what Christ did, no longer at the altar, where it costs him nothing, offering the blood and body under the species of wine and bread, but in delivering up as if on the Cross his own blood, his own body. In this false bad priest, it is not virtue which appears as the opposite of sin, it is faith—faith in the sign that he received on the day of his ordination, in the treasure that he alone (since all the other priests have been killed or have fled) still carries in his unworthy and yet consecrated hands.

The last priest who remains in the country, he must believe that after him there will be no one left to offer the Sacrifice, or to give absolution, or to distribute the bread which is no longer bread, or to aid the dying on the threshold of eternal life. And yet his faith does not vacillate, even though he is unaware that hardly will he have perished under the bullets than another priest will appear suddenly, furtively.

We feel that this hidden presence of God in an atheistic world, this subterranean circulation of grace, fascinates Graham Greene far more than the majestic façades that the temporal Church still raises up above the people. If there exists a Christian who would not be troubled by the collapse of the visible Church, he is certainly the Graham Greene whom I heard in Brussels, before thousands of astonished Belgian Catholics—and in the presence of a pensive Apostolic nuncio— evoke the last Pope of a totally de-Christianized Europe, taking his place in line at a commissary, dressed in stained gabardine, and holding in his hand (on which the ring of the Fisherman was still gleaming) a cardboard valise.

Which is to say that this book providentially addresses itself to the generation that the absurdity of a mad world has seized by the throat. To the young contemporaries of Camus, and Sartre, desperate prey of a mocking liberty, Greene will perhaps reveal that this absurdity is in truth that of a boundless love.

The message is also directed to believers, to the virtuous, to those who do not doubt their merits and who always have in their minds several models of sanctity, with the appropriate techniques for attaining to the several levels of mystical ascension. It directs itself in particular to Christian priests and laity, and especially to writers who preach the Cross but of whom it is not enough to say that they are not crucified. A great lesson is given to those obsessed by perfection, to those scrupulous people who cut by three-quarters their miserable failings and who forget that on their last day, according to the words of Saint John of the Cross, it is on their love that they will be judged.

Dear Graham Greene, to whom I am attached by so many bonds, and at first by gratitude (since thanks to you my books find in England today the same fervent reception they received in my own country when I was a young and fortunate author), how gratifying it is for me to think that France, where your work is already so well-esteemed, is going to discover, thanks to this great work *The Power and the Glory*, its true meaning! This state which you describe, which tracks down its last priest and murders him, is in fact the same one we see building itself before our eyes. It is the hour of the Prince of this world, but you paint it without hatred: even the hangmen, even your chief of police is marked by you with a sign of mercy: they look for the truth; they believe, like our communists, that they have attained it and serve it, this truth that demands the sacrifice of consecrated creatures. Shadows cover all the earth that you describe to us, but what a shining beam cuts across them! Come what may, we know that we must not fear; you recall for us that the inexplicable will be made clear, that there remains a key to apply to this absurd world. Through you we know the precious limit of the liberty that Sartre concedes to man: we know that creatures who are loved as much as we have no other liberty than refusing that love, as it has been made known to us, and under the appearances in which it has chosen to clothe itself.

✿◇

KARL PATTEN

A professor of English at Bucknell University, Karl Patten specializes in modern poetry and fiction and the poetry of the Renaissance.

THE STRUCTURE OF
THE POWER AND THE GLORY

The nameless whisky priest of Graham Greene's *The Power and the Glory* is that characteristic Greene figure, *l'homme traqué*, and the novel itself has the familiar narrative line of the pursuit, but *The Power and the Glory* contains, by common consent, a wealth of dimension that is not always found in Greene's novels. It is a rich book because it is made of two distinct but interrelated structures. When I speak of structures in a context that would seem to call for the singular, my point is that *The Power and the Glory* is bistructured, as are in fact most modern symbolic novels. As Edwin Muir has said:

But to say that a plot is spatial does not deny a temporal movement to it, any more, indeed, than to say that a plot is temporal means that it has no setting in space. . . . The main object of the one plot is to proceed by widening strokes, and to agree that it does so is to imply space as its dimension. The main object of the other is to trace a development, and a development equally implies time. The construction of both plots will be inevitably determined by their aim. In one we shall find a loosely woven pattern, in the other, the logic of causality.[1]

More than any other novel of Greene's, *The Power and the Glory* is a book of symbolic identifications, and the spatial

---

[1] Edwin Muir, *The Structure of the Novel* (London: The Hogarth Press, 1928), p. 64. Muir uses "plot" as a synonym for "structure."

From *Modern Fiction Studies.* © 1969 by Purdue Research Foundation, Lafayette, Indiana.

pattern of the novel depends entirely on this series of identifications. The priest is, obviously, at the center, and all of the other characters are symbolically related to him, as the spokes of a wheel relate to the hub. I would like to call this a "radial pattern," or, more allusively but in line with "the kingdom and the power and the glory," a "radiant pattern." And we may say further that the book "radiates" more than most of Greene's books, for there is hope and promise at the end—a strong contrast with the total loss that awaits Rose at the end of *Brighton Rock*. "Radiant," then, because that word, while it carries the original notion of the wheel, goes beyond to suggest the religious theme of the book and the central symbolic link between the life of the whisky priest and the life of Christ.

My method will be to take each of the characters who relate to the priest and to show in detail the quality and meaning of these relationships. First, though, we must see that the priest's story is remarkably like the story of Christ. He is betrayed by a Judas, whom he forgives; he enters the death trap wittingly and willingly; he is hung, figuratively, beside a thief; and, of course, he is executed for his faith. However, the priest does not stand for Christ in any simple allegorical equation; he is Christlike in that he has consecrated himself, as any Christian should, to live a life in the pattern of Christ. He is not the Son of God who redeems the sins of mankind, but he can redeem himself and be a witness, albeit flawed, to the Christian way in an unchristian world, an example to mankind.

Of the characters who surround the priest, I will look first at Mr. Tench, the English dentist who is stranded in the port town in which we first see the priest. He is modelled on *The* American dentist Doc Winter, whom Greene describes in *The Lawless Roads*: "Without a memory and without a hope in the immense heat, he loomed during those days as big as a symbol—I am not sure of what, unless the aboriginal calamity, 'having no hope, and without God in the world.' "[2] Mr. Tench,

---

[2] Greene, *The Lawless Roads* (London: Eyre and Spottiswoode, 1950), p. 156. "The aboriginal calamity" is quoted from epigraph to *The*

cut off from the family he can hardly remember, is, like the priest, trapped in the dark land, the land abandoned by God. He, too, dreams of escape. In another way, he is like the priest, for "Mr. Tench was used to pain, it was his profession," and amid the pain he goes on, endures. He symbolizes both a hopeless tenacity in clinging to life and the immense loneliness and desolation of the land. Ironically, it is through his eyes that we see the execution of the priest, for he is filling the teeth of the Chief of Police as the little man is dragged to the bloody wall ("'Oh,' the jefe moaned from the chair, 'the pain, the pain'"). In an unusual moment for him, Mr. Tench feels for another person and swears that he will "clear out for good," but we know that he will not; he is caught.

The police lieutenant who successfully tracks down the priest may at first look like a perfect antithesis to the hunted man; he believes in the social revolution, he has a purely materialistic view of life, and he is fanatically anticlerical, but actually he, too, symbolizes a side of the priest's character, and, fundamentally, the two men are more alike than different. Like the priest, the lieutenant has a vocation to which he has given his life. He thinks of the children of the state:

. . . it was for these he was fighting. He would eliminate from their childhood everything which had made him miserable, all that was poor, superstitious, and corrupt. They deserved nothing less than the truth—a vacant universe and a cooling world, the right to be happy in any way they chose. He was quite prepared to make a massacre for their sakes—first the Church and then the foreigner and then the politician—even his own chief would one day have to go. He wanted to begin the world again with them, in a desert.

Greene makes the likeness between the priest and the lieutenant explicit; the latter's room in a lodging house is "as comfortless as a prison or a monastic cell," and "There was something of a

---

Lawless Roads, which is from Newman's *Apologia pro Vita Sua* (New York: Modern Library, 1950), pp. 240-241. The final quotation is from Ephesians ii, 12. Greene's Mexican travel book provides us with nearly all of the raw material of *The Power and the Glory*.

priest in his intent observant walk—a theologian going back over the errors of the past to destroy them again." He is an ascetic, with a priest's horror of women. His relentless, cruel pursuit of the priest contrasts with the priest's animal-like wandering, but their roles become reversed after he has "succeeded" in catching his quarry, for he is brought to a state of confusion by the priest's quiet assurance in his faith, and on the evening of the day before the execution, "He felt without a purpose, as if life had drained out of the world." However, he is a "good man," as the disguised priest tells him when the lieutenant gives him money; he has an embarrassed incipient charity, shown also in his awkward love for children. If we see how in his devotion to his calling he is like the priest, we must also see the implications of his relationship to the priest as Christ. Victor de Pange has pointed these out. He says: *"Le lieutenant n'est certainement pas au nombre des damnés. En cherchant à nier Dieu il a appris à le mieux connaître. Peut-être, lui aussi, est-il sur un chemin de Damas?"** And we may think of this hard persecutor as the type of Saul of Tarsus, for his unsettled and purposeless state at the end of the book promises some change.

Entrapment and vocation. The third radial point is that of the priest who has renounced his vows and who knows that he is "in the grip of the unforgivable sin, despair." This is Padre José, who has submitted to the tyranny of the state and has married. Once, "he had been simply filled with an overwhelming sense of God. At the Elevation of the Host you could see his hands trembling . . . the wounds bled anew for him over every altar," but now he has no function and is cut off from God. He represents, in his identifying relation to the whisky priest, the ever-present bad temptation to which the fugitive is so frequently drawn.

The whisky priest feels that he is not a martyr, but there is a

---

* "The lieutenant is certainly not among the damned. By seeking to deny God he has learned to know him better. Is he perhaps also on a road to Damascus?"—Ed.

martyr, albeit an ironic one, in the novel. He is the priest Juan, whose pious life is being read aloud by a mother to her three children. Here Greene's love of irony broadens out into parody, and he has written several sanctimonious pages in the style of the adulatory biography. Although Juan is presented as a saint of the future who died for his church, his life is unreal in its inhuman charity and foresight; the authentic martyr, the whisky priest, prowls the dark streets in fear of capture and death, conscious of his weakness and his unworthiness. Greene fixes another spoke in his wheel-like structure.

The mestizo with the two yellow fangs is the Judas of *The Power and the Glory.* The priest himself recognizes him as a betrayer early in the book, and he knows, with the kind of foreknowledge that Christ had, that when the mestizo comes to bring him back from his safety across the border that he is leading him into a trap. He goes, however, not only to be present with the dying murderer, but because he knows that God does not mean him to escape, that it is his fate to remain and to die, if necessary, in Tabasco. And for the betrayer the priest has a feeling of charity. He thinks, as he helps the feverish mestizo, "Christ had died for this man too," and again, with a wry sadness, "Poor man . . . he isn't really bad enough" to be a Judas; it is a shame that he damns himself for so little. But Greene's process of making identifying relations goes on, for the priest is not totally different from the mestizo, either; they are alike in that he too has betrayed. He has given up most of his sacerdotal duties and functions, he has fathered a child, and he rightly considers himself unworthy. He has betrayed certain of his solemn vows, and he is painfully conscious that he has "to go to God empty-handed, with nothing done at all." This self-valuation may be false, or partly so, but it is what he genuinely feels before his death, and he has reason for feeling thus; he is well acquainted with the Judas within himself.

The children of *The Power and the Glory* also have their relationship to the priest. Brigida, the priest's young-old daughter, warped and wizened by the blighted land, and Coral Fellows, daughter of an English banana planter, both retain an odd innocence, something primal, under the fast-growing shell of their early maturity, that corresponds exactly to a hidden and harbored innocence, which is ultimately the source of his salvation, in the weary, world-racked whisky priest.

The last of the characters who radiate from the priest is the American gunman, thief, and murderer. He is, like the priest, a criminal and a fugitive, and his photograph is hung next to the priest's on the wall of the police station: "On the wall of the office the gangster still stared subbornly in profile towards the first communion party: somebody had inked the priest's head round to detach him from the girls' and the women's faces: the unbearable grin peeked out of a halo." The priest feels that they are brothers, and it is clear that Greene has mirrored the situation of the Crucifixion (and the "first communion party" has its significance, too). While the priest tries to make the dying gunman repent his crimes, the gunman urges the priest to take his knife or his gun and fight his way out of the police trap, a passage reminiscent of Luke xxiii, 39 ("And one of the malefactors which were hanged railed on him, saying, 'If thou be Christ, save thyself and us.'"). Once again the pattern reveals itself—those around him are like the priest ("radial") and the priest is like Christ ("radiant"). *The Power and the Glory* finds its deepest source in the Incarnation.

In addition to the wheel-like structure of "radiance" there is the second structure, based on the "logic of causality." This is temporal, rather than spatial, and is based on the pursuit of the priest by the police lieutenant and by God. It is a narrowing, narrative structure that is reminiscent of the film device of "parallel montage,"[3] and it gives the novel its intensity and suspense.

This double pursuit exists on the natural level in the hunt of

---

[3] "Parallel montage" is, according to Eisenstein, "the image of an intricate race between two parallel lines" ("Film Form" in *Essays in Film Theory*, ed. Jay Leyda. [London: Dennis Dobson, 1951], p. 234). Thus, when two events are happening simultaneously, the director, in order to create the illusion of simultaneity and to heighten intensity and suspense, will crosscut back and forth from one to the other.

the lieutenant, who wishes to exterminate the last tiny residue of Catholic superstition in Tabasco, and on the supernatural level by God himself, who harries the sinful priest down the labyrinthine ways to his own salvation. Obviously, the pursuit by God cannot be pictured; we must infer this from the priest's own thoughts and from his reactions to events, which, however, he himself does not always understand, for his tenacity and his willingness to go back over the border are themselves God-given. But the natural pursuit is like that of any of Greene's thrillers. We first see the mysterious figure of the priest at the seaport, but not until the end of the first chapter do we understand that this obviously disguised person is a fugitive. He says, "Let me be caught soon. . . . Let me be caught." And Greene adds, "He had tried to escape, but he was like the King of a West African tribe, the slave of his people, who may not even lie down in case the winds should fail."

Then, in the next chapter, Greene shifts to the pursuer, the vaguely troubled yet seemingly inflexible lieutenant, who learns of the single remaining priest for the first time. The long pursuit begins, and with it the crosscut temporal structure of the book. Over and over again we see the priest ineptly trying to perform his duties, or hiding from the police, or, finally, achieving safety by escaping across the mountains into Chiapas, the neighboring state. And over and over again we see the lieutenant plotting his campaign, taking hostages, always in single-minded pursuit. Several times their paths cross, but never does the lieutenant recognize the priest, and the priest is never apprehended; for in this book the natural pursuit is to fail, and it is the supernatural pursuit, God's hounding of the priest, that is to succeed, for the priest voluntarily chooses capture and death after he is safe; his years in the jungle have made him as cunning as an animal, and he could have escaped the law of the land, but he could not escape the law of his God.

Thus, the method of parallel montage, with its base in Greene's dark, dualistic imagination, provides a narrative structure of high intensity, the rapid line of a flight, or more exactly a fugue—for we can think of this method as contrapuntal in its weaving motion—that reaches its climax when the priest turns his mule back toward Tabasco and is finally caught in the lieutenant's trap, this fugue followed in the closing pages of the book by a large, deep *largo*.

Two structures, then: one, which flows chronologically from the beginning of the book to the end, the other, which must be pictured or diagrammed ideally. But it would be a mistake not to realize that the two constitute a fusion: temporal, drama or melodrama; spatial, symbol. There is nothing unique in Greene's combination; it is the aesthetic method of the modern novel, of all novelists of high style, as Ortega would say. *Moby Dick* is also a symbolic pursuit novel, as are many of Faulkner's novels (*Light in August, The Wild Palms,* or *The Old Man*), and the novels of such different writers as Dostoevski and Henry James, though perhaps not pursuit novels, make the same magic combination of space and time. There are, of course, other symbolic novels which render as little as possible to time, like Virginia Woolf's *The Waves,* which seems to exist in the vacuum of a glass bell, and which we read claustrally, relating one sensitively developed event to another, but a novel like *The Waves* is misguided in intention, for time lends life to fiction.

Aristotle first noted the necessity for an action, a temporal happening, that was significant and probable (that is, conceived and executed with a certain verisimilitude), and which made the play dynamic. Modern poetry, however, has not had as its first interest the description of an action. In content, it has been more interested in states of mind, either of the poet or of his *personae,* and in form it has developed an aesthetic that holds that all of the parts are to be related to the whole. Consequently, it has become a poetry that is allusive and infrarefracting, a poetry that renders and does not state (and modern poets discovered that the best poets of earlier ages wrote similarly), a poetry that does not immediately organize itself on the page, but rather leaves the process of organization, which is essential for comprehension, up to the reader, who must relate for himself, reread, and study.

It is this kind of poetry that the modern novel has taken over for its spatial structure, but it has combined the method of modern poetry with the Aristotelian demand for a significant action. In this combination, however, there may be an important change in one of Aristotle's criteria, for, in the interest of the spatial structure, the symbolic novelist is often willing to relinquish some of the verisimilitude that an earlier novelist would have felt essential. Faulkner and Dostoevski do not hesitate to describe events and characters which are, to say the least, out of the ordinary—Benjy and Prince Myshkin are sufficient examples, and they have been created to make the spatial and symbolic structures of *The Sound and the Fury* and *The Idiot* rather than to contribute primarily to the temporal and probable structures. Mental defectives and epileptics *do* exist, but Aristotle (and Fielding, Jane Austen, or Galsworthy) would not have found them appropriate vehicles for a play or a novel—and not, basically, for reasons of decorum.

Joseph Frank, who first clarified the concept of spatial structure, has pointed out the semblance of the art of primitive peoples to the art of our own century and the likeness of both to periods that "are dominated by a religion that completely rejects the natural world as a realm of evil and imperfection." Now, nothing is clearer than that Greene so regards the world and that original sin is at the very core of his Catholic and personal metaphysics. Frank adds that:

In both cases—the primitive and the transcendental—the will-to-art . . . diverges from naturalism to create aesthetic forms that will satisfy the spiritual needs of their creators; and in both cases these forms are characterized by an emphasis on linear-geometrical patterns, on an elimination of objective, three-dimensional shapes and objective, three dimensional space, on the dominance of the plane in all types of plastic art.[4]

---

[4] Joseph Frank, "Spatial Form in Modern Literature," in *Criticism: The Foundations of Modern Literary Judgment*, ed. Mark Schorer, Josephine Miles, and Gordon McKenzie (New York: Harcourt Brace, 1948), p. 390 (both citations).

And he goes on to show, brilliantly and convincingly, how this generalization is applicable to literature.

Greene's whisky priest, in his namelessness, his frailty, his unsureness of purpose, his backsliding, his desire to be free from his terrible responsibility, his cowardice, and his ultimate underlying strength, is clearly of the type of Everyman, that primitive product of the late medieval imagination. And, more precisely, just as Everyman discovers on his road to the grave that he can take nothing but Good Deeds with him, so the priest must discard all but his essential faith in God.[5] Greene figures this for us by making him, in the course of the novel, literally give up or lose his various holy objects and habits: feast days and fast days, his breviary, the altar stone, a chalice, the papers that sealed him in the priesthood. All go, until he is stripped naked before his fate, a being deprived and alone—except for his God.

Greene has praised *Everyman,* and he has said of Shakespeare:

It must be remembered that we are still within the period of the Morality: they were being acted yet in the country districts: they had been absorbed by Shakespeare, just as much as he absorbed the plays of Marlowe, and the abstraction—the spirit of Revenge (Hamlet), of Jealousy (Othello), of Ambition (Macbeth), of Ingratitude (Lear), of Passion (Anthony and Cleopatra)—still rules the play. And rightly. Here is the watershed between the morality and the play of character: the tension between the two is perfectly kept: there is dialectical perfection.[6]

And what is the difference between the morality and the play of character but the difference between a spatial and a temporal

---

[5] *Everyman,* in its complete emphasis on merit and its striking disregard of faith, is a pre-Reformation work. Greene's attenuated Catholicism (Jansenism?—a favorite charge) bases the issue totally on faith. It is the unwavering essential fidelity of the priest that will save him; his sinful acts and his failure to function adequately as a priest ultimately count for nothing to Greene.

[6] Greene, *British Dramatists,* in *Impressions of English Literature,* ed. W. J. Turner (London: Collins, 1944), p. 114.

structure? The modern novel exists on the thin ridge of that watershed.

Greene has given us in *The Power and the Glory* a study of the character of the whisky priest which is itself temporal, but beyond this he has created a static, symbolic structure which is akin to allegory without ever resolving into a simple series of one-to-one equations between characters and concepts. It is this nearly allegorical structure that makes the wheel-like pattern which can best be conveyed by a diagram ("linear-geometrical patterns"), the radial, radiant, radiating pattern that forces a subtle lack of three-dimensional verisimilitude on the novel.

There is a drive in Greene's imagination here, a drive which makes him create a single priest out of the tiny shards of at least three real priests (as we know from *The Lawless Roads*)[7] and to make his whisky priest a tenacious man of God in a way that goes far beyond the stories of any of the three priests— like Benjy or Myshkin, the priest is beyond what we know or what we expect. And in addition, Greene has, by suggestion, made an analogy, without insisting on a simple correspondence, between his priest and Christ, as Faulkner and Dostoevski have done with their characters.

Why is the priest nameless? And why is his persecutor, the lieutenant, nameless too? Clearly, it is because names individuate and by their very particularity assign small, local associations, while anonymity is suggestive of something larger, and, in this novel, Greene wants to be free of such limiting factors, so that, although he gives both priest and persecutor believable backgrounds, they both have typical backgrounds for what they are. In other novels Greene is apt to make use of signifying names (Anthony Farrant, Conrad Drover, Raven, Harry Lime, Rose), but here his passion inclines him more strongly than ever toward symbolization, so that if the priest is an Everyman who is to be related, by suggestion, to Christ, then the lieutenant is to be understood as a Saul of Tarsus.

---

[7] For information on the three priests, see *The Lawless Roads*, pp. 11-12, 129, and 150.

Further, we see that the people whom the priest meets are all symbolic of some aspect of the human condition: a trapped man (Mr. Tench), a criminal (the American gunman), purposefulness without purpose (the lieutenant), children who cannot be well understood (Brigida and Coral), a lapsed priest (Padre José), Judas (the mestizo), a beggar with inside information (nameless, but like the priest), a pious woman (likewise nameless, but part of his old self), lovers (his temptation) —in short, like Christian in *The Pilgrim's Progress* he travels an unknown way, continually meeting portions of his own character, God-ordained obstructions or revelations which eventually help him to his death and salvation.

Although the pursuit is always present, we realize, through the priest's meetings and confrontations with these characters (who, because of the way in which Greene has presented them, would be "flat" in E. M. Forster's terms), that in back, as it were, of the pursuit there is elaborated another, deeper meaning —the structure of the radiant wheel—and we would not see this if these characters were presented with full verisimilitude.

Paradoxically, however, as we read this novel we feel its roundness, especially as it is rendered in one great scene, and we recognize the all-integrating wholeness of the wheel on which Greene has based his symbolic structure.

In this scene, the priest, disguised, has been jailed, and he is thrust into a crammed, stench-filled cell. In the course of the night he hears (for he cannot see anything) aggressive, importunate people, an old man out of his mind, two people making love, a pious woman, talk of bastard children (especially painful to him), and all the voices of the world—for the cell is the world. He tells his fellow prisoners that he is a priest, and, despite the fact that there is a price on his head, no one reveals him to the police at dawn. The prisoners are sullen, perhaps unhappy, about their loyalty, but we feel that there is a final goodness in their refusal to betray him which is connected with the final greatness (in the terms of Greene's own belief), and that this is related to the final generosity of God in accepting sinners into his kingdom (as we feel that the priest is accepted at the end of the book), but we could not have had this feeling if we had not been prepared for it by the evolving, poetic structure of the whole novel.

Greene has given us, in *The Power and the Glory*, a fusion of the temporal and the spatial, the long, melodramatic pursuit and the slowly developed, carefully related radiant wheel that stands in back of the pursuit, and he has endowed this fusion with the significance that we demand of the modern novel. When we have become fully aware of the wheel and its implications, we have a knowledge of "the thick rotundity of the world."

PETER J. CONN

ACT AND SCENE IN
THE POWER AND THE GLORY

> "I am falling.
> *Santa Maria*, pray for me, I want to stop,
> but I have lost my foothold on the map,
> now falling, falling."
> —ROBERT LOWELL, "Dropping South: Brazil"[1]

Richard Hoggart has perceptively written, "Setting is always important and constitutive in Graham Greene, but in *The Power and the Glory* even more than elsewhere. The theme is indivisibly priest-and-land."[2] Hoggart turns in other directions in his fine essay, but in these notes I would like to follow up his suggestions about the connection between character and place as a way of examining Greene's novel. In *The Power and the Glory* action and setting, or what some critics call act and scene, are mutually dependent and mutually illuminating.

Near the end of Part Two of the novel, as the priest struggles toward freedom, down a mountain path "so steep he had to turn and go down backwards":

. . . he remembered a map he had once seen of the two adjoining states. The state from which he was escaping was peppered with

---

[1] Farrar, Straus & Giroux, Inc.: From "Dropping South: Brazil" from *For the Union Dead* by Robert Lowell. Copyright © 1964 by Robert Lowell. Reprinted with the permission of Farrar, Straus & Giroux, Inc.

[2] Richard Hoggart, "The Force of Caricature: Aspects of the Art of Graham Greene with Particular Reference to *The Power and the Glory*," *Essays in Criticism*, III (October 1953), p. 447. (Most of this essay is reprinted on pp. 341-52).

villages . . . but in the next state—in the north-west corner—there
was hardly anything but blank white paper. You're on the blank
paper now, the ache [inside his head] told him. [. . .] There's just
white paper all around.

Then, within a few hundred lines: "it was loneliness he felt
now." In this passage the priest's isolation is systematically
joined to his alienation from his land. The conjunction is insisted upon by Greene's elaborate figure, which reduces the
adjoining state to something like an abstraction: an empty map,
a vacant piece of paper. As the priest leaves his home, the land
symbolically recedes from him.

The passage cited thus summarizes one of the novel's major
themes, by identifying separation from God and from other
people with separation from one's home. This threefold loneliness is at the heart of the novel's meaning; before it is grasped
as a theme, it has expressed itself in the story's mood, in its
pervasive sense of complete, terrifying, and precisely inhuman
isolation.

In one way or another, all the main characters are, to use the
novel's key and repeated word, abandoned. The priest is an
outlaw, hunted as a criminal in his own land. His government
has abandoned God, largely out of revulsion from the de-
formities in God's human institutions. And the consequences
are personified in the relentless lieutenant, a man whose obsession with "humanity" infects whatever humane instincts he
may have, who loves the idea of man to the exclusion of individual men, and who thus solemnly embraces isolation. The
priest and the lieutenant are the novel's main antagonists, and
they are both outsiders, marked by circumstances or choice
with the mark of Cain.

Finally, the mestizo, who is the chief link between them, is
as much a human symbol as a character: a half-breed and a
wanderer who has neither race nor community nor home to
define him and to relieve him of his burden of alienation. The
mestizo is almost a type for the exile. He alone moves back
and forth between the priest and the lieutenant and finally
brings these larger figures together in an act of treacherous

mediation. When the three men, all alike nameless, are joined in the novel's closing pages, they make up a union that can only be seen as, paradoxically, an antisociety, a community of isolation. This is the first of several crucial paradoxes that define the relation between act and scene.

The priest says of himself shortly before this final, fatal meeting that he "carried Hell about with him." It is a phrase that recalls Milton's Satan: "Which way I fly is Hell; myself am Hell." Greene's priest and Milton's fallen angel are bearing witness to the same fundamental truth, which Greene explores in this novel and in several others: that the "fact" of Hell is not to be found in any inflicted punishment but rather in separation, first from God and then, inevitably, from all other human beings. The Hell-in-life which Greene's people act out is not merely *reflected* in their separateness; their Hell *is* separateness. (There is a cruel and double irony in the fact that the priest's main function is to bring Holy Communion to his people, since the priest insists upon his own unholy isolation.)

The figure through which the priest describes himself late in the book could as well describe many of the characters at many points in the story: he felt "the old life hardening around him like a habit, a stony case which held his head high and dictated the way he walked, and even formed his words." The lieutenant perhaps most obviously, but others too, Padre José, Mrs. Fellows, and the "complacent" Christian woman whom the priest meets in prison, are all isolated in the stony case of the self. Each is in his own way the victim of what Greene has called (in *The Lawless Roads*) "the terrifying egoism of exclusion."

As the people in this novel are cut off, to various degrees, from God and from each other, so are they also alien from their land. On several occasions the land, too, is called "abandoned." Over the land, as over the people, there looms a dark night—of doubt, of unbelief, of hostility. The careful delineation of this novel's world is not merely an attention to the details of landscape for their own sake. Greene and his characters are dramatizing their commitment to *place*: a complicated, often ambivalent, but finally compelling loyalty to one's home. It is an emotion, and a theme, that is not to be explained by inspecting Greene's biographical roots, nor by dissecting the travel book, *The Lawless Roads*, that served as a "source" for the novel.

The commitment is a spiritual reality, and it is given substance in *The Power and the Glory* in two ways. First, it explains an unsystematic but recurring geographical allegory, in which moral or religious values are connected with different parts of the country. An obvious example is the contrast between the two Mexican states that form the novel's setting: as far as the priest is concerned, his chances for salvation decrease radically as he crosses the states' border. Along the same lines, Dominick P. Consolo speaks of "the freedom that lies with the sea and the oppression of the land."[3] In one way or another, the novel's locale is often aligned with its events, and helps to shape its significance. One thinks also of the famous opening paragraph, with its meditation on "the blazing Mexican sun and the bleaching dust," and the buzzards, sharks, and carrion on which that sun blazes.

But the idea of place, as Greene develops it in the novel, is finally more inclusive and more subtle than whatever use it may have as a straightforward system of reference. The novel's attention to place is demanded by the story's major action— the exiled priest's journey in search of his home.

"It's just this bloody land," Mr. Tench complains to the priest in the novel's first scene. "You can't cure me of that. No one can." The priest responds with a question: "You want to go home?" " 'Home,' Mr. Tench said; 'my home's here.' " When, a few moments later he looks over his dental equipment and resigns himself as a man with "a stake in the country," Mr. Tench has offered a summary definition of the priest's motive, together with an implicit standard by which the priest measures his own actions. The land becomes not only the morally resonant arena in which the antagonists confront them-

---

[3] Cf. p. 337.

selves and one another, but also an important *presence* within which the priest must find his salvation.

"O God," the priest recites as he stumbles out of the border forest and completes his escape, "I have loved the beauty of Thy house." The citation is from the Psalms, by way of the Catholic Mass; the rest of the verse, which the priest does not recite, is equally significant: "And [I have loved] the place where Thy glory dwells." The prayer occurs in the novel at a strategic moment. The priest believes that his attempted escape has failed, that "presently he would find his grave." From his point of view, then, it is fitting that he finally redefine this place of "soaked and rotting leaves," of heat and darkness, as the place of God's beauty and glory, as the home for which he has longed.

But in fact, the priest has indeed escaped. From *this* point of view—the novel's—the Psalm is ironic and indicative. As the priest will soon reluctantly realize, his escape cannot lead to a meaningful freedom or to religious and social integration; he will have to return.

Greene underscores all of this by observing, just before the priest recites the prayer, that it "wasn't only people who were going: even the animals and reptiles moved away: presently he would be left alone with nothing but his own breath." The instant of the priest's escape, in other words, is the instant of his most complete alienation. (The map figure cited at the beginning of this essay occurs just two pages before this climactic moment and forms a thoroughly appropriate introduction to it.) If the priest has escaped at all, he has, in his own words, escaped "too completely"; the exile he has known and the terror that has driven him across the border are both of them at last more tolerable than what he is to find in the free state.

Mr. Tench had begun the discussion of "this bloody land," which is also his home, and the priest's. Later in the book another secondary character, Padre José, voices the central emotion that the land evokes. He is walking in a cemetery called the Garden of God, a place which is described as if it, too, were a kind of home: it is like an "estate," a "house." As he walks slowly among the tombs, Padre José feels that "he could waken a faint sense of homesickness. . . ." Now this somewhat contrived longing is obviously not directed toward a place at all but toward a time, the years of peace before the Red Shirts disrupted the padre's comfortable life. The words have no more significance for Padre José, probably, than an expression of emotional self-indulgence. He has been allowed to live, inside the law, but he is forever haunted by his own shame.

But the "sense of homesickness" has a larger point for the novel as a whole: it suggests that the land and its God become intertwined, that a longing for home is finally a longing for a heavenly home with God, and that the path to the Garden of God leads inexorably through death. If for Padre José homesickness is a wish that is father to no deed, for his brother priest the case is quite different. Hearing confession in the barn of the expatriate Lehrs who have given him shelter, fulfilling an essential priestly function in relative security and dignity, "Suddenly, without warning, with an odd sense of homesickness, he thought of the hostages in the prison yard. . . ." For this priest the sudden and painful memory is an impulse, however unwanted, toward the final return.

The remembered images themselves, the hostages and the prison, are important structural choices. Occurring at the novel's last major turning point, the words call the priest back across weeks of time and miles of country to the novel's major episode. The priest's homesickness for the prison and its occupants is clearly not "odd" at all, for it was there, during his long and quite literal dark night, that he learned the meaning of home. During his imprisonment the priest realizes that his flight is actually a search; and although the event is recorded in the middle of the story, it is also in prison that the search comes to a symbolic end.

The scene, to begin with, is introduced in the midst of overt symbols: the priest's picture, isolated in a communion group by an ambiguous halo, and hanging next to the photograph of the gringo murderer who will indirectly cause the priest's death.

The prison episode, however, serves more important ends than foreshadowing future events. It offers a moving definition of the priest's proper "place" and his relation to it. The symbolism through which the scene operates is not fixed but dramatic; there is a spiritual and psychological development that summarizes and comments upon the priest's career.

As he enters the completely darkened cell, the priest "imagined he could feel enmity fuming up all round him like smoke." These opening lines immediately suggest a likeness between the cell and the priest's life: surrounded by an enmity which is, importantly, anonymous; by danger and suspicion which are palpable but invisible. This has been the priest's daily situation as he wandered from village to village across that larger government prison, the state. Having established the tone, as it were, of hostility, the chapter moves on to recount several specific incidents that are related to other parts of the story. The priest hears "a tiny scream—a woman's," and he realizes "with horror that pleasure was going on even in this crowded darkness." This not only suggests the larger Mexican world outside the cell (and indeed, outside the novel) where the poor take solace in sex. It also recalls the priest's sin several years earlier. Similarly, the next incident, an old man calling for his illegitimate daughter, reminds the reader of the fruit of the priests' sin, his own daughter Brigida. And it is this daughter, significantly, whom the priest frequently identifies as the central human link between him and his home. It is therefore fitting that she should enter this cell symbolically. The dark stage is prepared for the priest's meditation.

Suffering from physical discomfort and the interminable blackness, the priest gropes toward the explicit awareness that "This place was very like the world: overcrowded with lust and crime and unhappy love: it stank to heaven. . . ." But this is a generalization grounded in despair, in the priest's hope that "there was no need to hope any longer." These thoughts occupy him just after he has announced to the other prisoners that he is a priest. The announcement is a calculated act of self-betrayal, ordered toward insuring his doom and relieving him of the agony of suspense. He confidently assumes that at least one of the prisoners will want the government's reward badly enough to identify him to the authorities as a priest. The calculation is persuasive, but wrong: an hour's discussion ends with the declaration that "Nobody here . . . wants their blood money." This truth startles the priest into a new awareness, and it evokes what is perhaps the novel's most important statement:

> . . . he was touched by an extraordinary affection. He was just one criminal among a herd of criminals . . . he had a sense of companionship which he had never received in the old days when pious people came kissing his black cotton glove.

An hour before, relishing his own despair, the priest had likened his cell to the world; but it was a likeness only in its sordidness. Further, the priest held himself distant and distinct from that world—he was in it, but not of it. Now at last, in circumstances that "in the old days" he would have judged unintelligible, he exchanges his isolation for the bond of human affection. If God is to be found, he will be found *in* these people: his people, God's people. Completing his recognition a few moments later, the priest embraces the ugliness itself as an instrument of grace. (This is the source of his later transformation of the jungle's "soaked and rotting leaves" into the beauty of God's house.)

It is a moment of epiphany. And the priest is right to say that this night "was like the end." Not because he has escaped into despair, but because he has chosen the bondage of love. It is the novel's climax, too, in the sense that the subsequent events in the priest's story flow inevitably from this moment. In the morning, when none of the prisoners betray him, "In an odd way he felt abandoned because they had shown no sign of recognition." Once again, this feeling is not at all "odd": during his confinement he had overcome alienation and found his home. Now he is again forced outside the circle of human affection. A few days later, when he returns to the Fellows' plantation and finds it strangely empty, he simultaneously finds the appropriate words for his condition. He realizes that "ever since that hot and crowded night in the cell he had passed into a region of abandonment—almost as if he had died there with the old man's head on his shoulder and now wandered in a kind of limbo. . . ."

Only by taking up his chains again can the priest offer freedom to his soul; the journey must end in death. But the priest's search has taken him far. His death is such that Mr. Tench—appropriately Mr. Tench, the "embodiment," as Kenneth Allott points out, of "the decay and corruption of 'the evil land' "[4]—watching the execution in awful fascination from the jefe's room, can speak far more meaningfully than he knows, can indeed speak for the novel and its readers: "This was like seeing a neighbour shot."

With businesslike efficiency the body is carried away and the place is "tidied" up. Mr. Tench feels "an appalling sense of loneliness. . . . He felt deserted." One need not romanticize the priest to see in his death, as Mr. Tench does, a grim triumph for the alienation that afflicts the novel's people. And the land has become "this bloody land" indeed.

[4] Kenneth Allott and Miriam Farris, *The Art of Graham Greene* (New York: Russell & Russell, Inc., 1963), p. 177.

✿◈◇

DOMINICK P. CONSOLO

Dominick P. Consolo is Professor of English at Denison University.
Aside from his studies of Graham Greene, Mr. Consolo has published a critical casebook on D. H. Lawrence.

GRAHAM GREENE:
STYLE AND STYLISTICS IN
THE POWER AND THE GLORY

[. . .] Many of Greene's critics make at least passing reference
to his style, giving it a short glancing blow and careening off
into considerations of theology or metaphysics. Walter Allen
calls it a "swift nervous style,"[1] whatever that means, "and a
technique of montage which he owes to the film." His use of
the camera eye is often mentioned, and Neville Braybrooke
holds that Greene's "technique is simple; it is the adaptation
of the dramatic soliloquy to the confines of the novel," only not
in a Shakespearean way, however, for one "has the impression
not of somebody declaiming his thoughts to the world at large,
but of somebody whispering his inmost doubts and conflicts to
one by telephone."[2] What there is here of critical flatulence has
at least wit to recommend it; whereas Arthur Calder-Marshall
is merely misleading in saying that the "pace" in *The Power*

---

[1] Walter Allen, "Graham Greene," *Writers of Today*, ed. Denys Val
Baker (London, 1946), p. 22.
[2] Neville Braybrooke, "Graham Greene," *Envoy*, III (September 1950),
p. 18.

From *Graham Greene: Some Critical Considerations*, edited by Robert
O. Evans. Copyright © 1963 by the University of Kentucky Press.

and the Glory is that of a "thriller" while "the total effect is dissipated in the confusion of detail. . . ."[3]

It will not do, I think, to give the style a label, trail behind it a series of qualifying phrases, and trust the container to hold only or even as much as was meant to be contained. Since Greene's style is cumulative, the best one can with justice do is to concentrate on those central elements that reveal the method whereby he achieves his effects. Of necessity, then, I must forego an examination of minor elements of his technique—such as the studied detail, the rhythmic device, the rich mesh of image and symbol—giving them but a cursory glance in passing.

First in importance among the essential elements to any novelist is point of view, that is, the theoretical position the novelist takes in respect to his own creation and to the reader. In *Brighton Rock, The Power and the Glory,* and *The Heart of the Matter,* the point of view is omniscient, while in the last two novels, *The End of the Affair* and *The Quiet American,* the narrative unfolds through the eyes of one of its protagonists. The omniscient point of view allows a greater freedom in the handling of scene, characters, time and space simply because the invisible narrator is not committed to a static perspective. He can shift the focus insofar as his skill in handling the perspective is convincing within a particular temporal and spatial context. But the narrator who is himself a part of the action is limited, if he is not to violate probability, by his own intelligence. What the author gains in credibility through the use of an "eye-witness" therefore, must be worth the restriction this point of view imposes. One would expect, then, that the narrative method in Greene's first-person novels would differ sharply from the earlier omniscient ones. And so, apparently, they do. But closer examination reveals this difference to be more *apparent* than *real.*

---

[3] Arthur Calder-Marshall, "The Works of Graham Greene," *Horizon,* I (May 1940), p. 374.

In speaking of Greene's fiction before *The Heart of the Matter*, Calder-Marshall points out that "In the old-fashioned sense, there is no 'comment'; no appeals to the 'dear reader.' The novel appears straight, fast, factual narrative with a concentration on objective details."[4] The verb *appears* is meant to prepare for what he later refers to as Greene's "comment metaphors," although he states emphatically that "the prose [is] carefully free from direct comment. . . ." Examination of the novels will show that this position is hardly tenable. Let it suffice at this point merely to quote Greene on his own view of the matter in his essay on Mauriac.

[Mauriac] is a writer for whom the visible world has not ceased to exist, whose characters have the solidity and importance of men with souls to save or lose, and a writer who claims the traditional and essential right of a novelist, to comment, to express his views. For how tired we have become of the dogmatically "pure" novel [Flaubert, James]. . . . The exclusion of the author can go too far. Even the author, poor devil, has a right to exist. . . .[5]

Greene can be taken at his word, for his own novels are constructed with this insistence on the author's prerogative to express his views—a practice which is not much in favor, for it tends to rupture the illusion and destroy dramatic effect. Greene, however, believes otherwise, that the effect is heightened by an awareness of the author, for he continues:

In such passages one is aware, as in Shakespeare's plays, of a sudden tensing, a hush seems to fall on the spirit—this is something more important than the king, Lear, or the general, Othello, something which is unconfined and unconditioned by the plot. "I" has ceased to speak, I is speaking.

---

4 Arthur Calder-Marshall, "Graham Greene," in *Living Writers*, ed. Gilbert Phelps (London, 1947), p. 41.
5 This and the subsequent quotation are from Graham Greene's "François Mauriac." (The essay is included in Greene's *Collected Essays* [New York: The Viking Press, 1969], pp. 115-21. Excerpts from the essay are reprinted on pp. 493-95.)

This accounts in part for a certain basic similarity among Greene's novels and explains why the change in point of view —from omniscient in the earlier novels to inside narrator in the later ones—is more apparent than real. The author controls the work; he is always in charge and wants you to know it.

This singularity of Greene's technique is attributable also to his recurring images and to the use of a diction alternately plain and rhetorical. Many of his effects are achieved by juxtaposing these two levels of diction. His use of imagery is more complex, for it contributes not only to the atmosphere, but informs character and theme as well; it is a means of communicating the emotion in an attempt to get at the truth. In Greene's words:

By truth I mean accuracy—it is largely a matter of style. It is my duty to society not to write: "I stood above a bottomless gulf" or "going downstairs, I got into a taxi," because these statements are untrue. My characters must not go white in the face or tremble like leaves, not because these phrases are clichés but because they are untrue. This is not only a matter of the artistic conscience but of the social conscience too.[6]

Indeed, few clichés slip into his novels. His images are fresh and arresting, often taking the form of colliding opposites, like the notorious one from *Brighton Rock*: "Virginity straightened in him like sex." This is an example of the baroque quality of Greene's sensibility; one is startled but not quite drawn up short, for in their context, the small units seldom detach themselves from the character or the scene. Appealing strongly to the senses, Greene's images are drawn from various departments of life and nature; he is most fond of those having to do with animals, geography, travel, war, childhood, and the human body. They set the tone of the novels and, more importantly, objectify the emotional responses of the characters.

If Greene's characters tend to run to type, they are not spectral figures, mere shadow-shapes for the author as ventrilo-

---

[6] Graham Greene, "An Exchange of Letters," *Partisan Review*, XV (November 1948), p. 1188.

quist. They are typed by their intensity, their almost hyper-sensitive awareness of a reality beyond this one of the senses. These are the doomed, not necessarily the damned, weighted with consciousness of a morality surmounting human ethics, curiously static because they partake of that quality of ancient heroes whose fatality was shaped by their past. But they are not *predestined* to fall; "between the stirrup and the ground" time remains for the right choice to be made, the supreme choice of man for God. This is the battle Greene usually dramatizes in his novels—a soul at war with its past commitments, struggling by its free will to accept or reject its future.

Or characters are typed by their self-satisfaction and lack of commitment to the higher religious truths that Greene espouses. They are the foils: sensual and pleasure-loving like Ida Arnold, corrupt and insensitive like the racketeer Colleoni and the Mexican jefe, sniveling and cowardly like Wilson, the secret agent; detached like Fowler, or misdirected like the atheistic lieutenant and the Quiet American, Pyle. Each has his role to play in Greene's fictional world; each is tailored to fit that world, and within this microcosm they seem credible.

What captivates the reader and draws him into the illusion whereby the credibility of character is achieved is Greene's story. Morton Dauwen Zabel has pointed out that the ideas come from contemporary newspapers: the Brighton race gang murders, Garrido's persecution of the priests in Tabasco, war-time in the Gold Coast, war-torn London, and finally, the muddle of Indochina.[7] With violence as their common de-nominator and betrayal their theme, a spell is woven about us from the opening pages as we are plunged *in medias res*, the precipitating factors of the conflict having already taken place. The method is classical. Only one causative agent remains to do its work—time. The inevitable is laid, yet anticipation pre-dominates. The chase in its myriad form gets under way, and, disbelief suspended, we journey through a familiar land with

---

[7] Morton Dauwen Zabel, "Graham Greene: the Best and the Worst," reprinted on pp. 353-72.

all of the horror and fascination that attends a nightmare. Superficially, the basic structure can often be reduced to the elements of the so-called "thriller." Suspense, intrigue, mystery, murder, betrayal—these are present in some degree or other in all Greene's fiction. But the salient fact remains that in his novels they subserve a greater design, are made to contribute to the totality of significance which makes up aesthetic value. [. . .] *The Power and the Glory* opens with Mr. Tench, the dentist, coming out into the blazing Mexican sun to claim his ether cylinder from the newly arrived boat. He wrenches up a piece of road and with a "faint feeling of rebellion," throws it at the buzzards squatting on a roof above him.

One of them rose and flapped across the town: over the tiny plaza, over the bust of an ex-president, ex-general, ex-human being, over the two stalls which sold mineral water, towards the river and the sea. It wouldn't find anything there: the sharks looked after the carrion on that side. Mr. Tench went on across the plaza.

A brief and literally a bird's-eye view, sandwiched in quite smoothly with what the dentist takes in on his way to the landing, suggests the wide area for the action. It is significant too at this point that the carrion bird roams freely over it all, a barren exhausted land with little to suggest the presence of anything but what might be called the remnants of human effort. And within the catalogue the designative terms for the bust—ex-president, ex-general, ex-human being—run down climactically to ironic *absurdum*.

For the purpose of contrast—the freedom that lies with the sea and the oppression on the land, shrouded in darkness—the point of focus drops away from the dentist to the ship as the land recedes. We are placed on the ship by the use of the indeterminate pronoun "you" (which Hemingway often employs in the same way): "When you looked back you could not have told that it had ever existed at all." The darkness that covers the land is obviously symbolic of its spiritual loss, and being a natural symbol, the darkness can be repeated unobstrusively for emphasis, by using it as a reference to shift the perspective from the ship—"There was an enormous sense of freedom and air upon the gulf, with the low tropical shore-line buried in darkness"—to the land where the whisky priest is: "Far back inside the darkness the mules plodded on." By the juxtaposition of two different perspectives within two paragraphs, the contrast is underscored dramatically and our interest consequently heightened. We watch the land slip away but only for one necessary moment; then we are plunged into its dark interior with the central figure of the novel, the whisky priest who is the unwilling bearer of light.

Indeed, these two paragraphs which conclude the first chapter, in their spatial and temporal conjoining for effect by contrast, reflect in miniature the pattern that structures the book. Each scene is devoted to a character and a situation; each is separate yet part of the over-all action, functional in itself but dependent for its total meaning on the irony effected through an immediate juxtaposition with another. Consider, for example, the contiguity of these scenes in Part I, Chapter Four: Mr. Tench, the dentist; Padre José, the turncoat priest; the romantic legend of Juan; the education of Coral; the jefe and the lieutenant. The dentist is inured to pain as part of his profession: a memory stirs him briefly, of a hunted priest and an undelivered ether cylinder, and then melts away. The fear of pain and reprisal palsies fat and married Padre José—"If I could," he said, "my children . . ."—and he turns away from the supplications of the funeral party. The easy acceptance of pain in the romantic hagiography of Juan read by the mother instructing her children points up the tortuous trials of the whisky priest in the next scene. The awful way of real martyrdom offers an ironic parallel in the priest's "education" of Coral Fellows, the precocious daughter of the plantation owner. The chapter closes and comes full circle with the symbolic tooth paining the jefe, and with the bitter austerity of that modern Javert, the police lieutenant. Each scene is vivid, alive, and suspenseful, and furthers the action. Infinite strands of complexity are dramatically laid to intersect and interconnect as the novel proceeds to its ultimate, fated close.

If the scenic method frames the book's structure, it is worth-while to examine the making of a single scene by approaching it through point of view. Almost any scene will do, but the one which ends the third chapter is representative of the objective rendering of the priest's plight through setting and dialogue for a telling irony of circumstance. The entire chapter is short, and its purpose is to present the fugitive priest from different angles, to dramatize a character whose traits and peculiarities, if more directly presented, could very well result merely in a caricature. And yet to see him from three different perspectives in a short space may also defeat the purpose by fragmenting the focus. For we look at the priest first through the eyes of self-satisfied Captain Fellows (the owner of the banana plantation where the priest has wandered), then through the eyes of his daughter Coral (who befriends him with food and wine), and finally we see the priest from a new angle amid the squalid surroundings of a tiny village in his former parish. Even though the priest is the connecting link for the scenes, a certain jerkiness, an aesthetic wrenching, would result if the point of view were as diverse as it appears to be. *Appears*, not *is*, for the action in the first two scenes of the chapter, though presented through Fellows and Coral, is controlled by the author: in observations made through images, "You cannot control what you love—you watch it driving recklessly towards the broken bridge, the torn-up track, the horror of seventy years ahead"; by the repetition of rhythmical patterns of expression—phrases, clauses, and sentences balanced in units of three; and above all, by a consistency of tone. Thus Greene can shift from one center of focus to another without a blurring of effect, for if the angle of vision is changed, the controlling center remains constant: it is with the author.

Consequently, in the final scene, although the viewpoint to all intents and purposes seems to become objective, pattern and expression echo the earlier scenes at the plantation where the vision was framed by father and daughter. An old man is tagged as an identifying post of observation, but the setting is described as in a play—meager, suggestive.

Half a dozen huts of mud and wattle stood in a clearing; two were in ruins. A few pigs rooted around, and an old woman carried a burning ember from hut to hut. . . . Women lived in two of the huts, the pigs in another, in the last unruined hut, where maize was stored, an old man and a boy and a tribe of rats. The old man stood in the clearing watching the fire being carried round: it flickered through the darkness like a ritual repeated at the same hour for a lifetime. White hair, a white stubbly beard, and hands brown and fragile as last year's leaves, he gave an effect of immense permanence. Nothing much could ever change, living on the edge of subsistence. He had been old for years.

The stranger came into the clearing.

Since the point of view has been ultimately with the author, there has, in effect, been no shift to a new focus. He has merely changed his vantage point while continuing the accretive process through observations; the main character is still viewed from the outside. His fundamental traits are dramatically rendered through dialogue and action.

The old man said softly: "It would be a pity if the soldiers came before we had time . . . such a burden on poor souls, father. . . ." The priest shouldered himself upright against the wall and said furiously: "Very well. Begin. I will hear your confession." The rats scuffled in the maize.

Hunted, starved, and exhausted, the priest ministers to this abject old man, significantly with his back to the wall and those suggestive rats scuffling in the maize. The scene then ends with the old man ironically entreating the others to confess: " 'Come,' he said. 'You must say your confessions. It is only polite to the father.' " Three brief scenes, three different points of focus with the priest always viewed objectively to reveal a little more, to add something to the growing stature of this mysterious creature chosen against all logic to be God's agent. To this end the scenes function as a dynamic unit since there is no dislocation or change of values. The moral base of each scene, the pity and self-sacrifice that motivate the entire novel, are the standards prevailing throughout. [. . .]

RICHARD HOGGART

Richard Hoggart is Professor of English at Birmingham University in England and Director of the Centre for Contemporary Cultural Studies. He has published *The Uses of Literacy, The Critical Moment,* and several volumes on W. H. Auden. Mr. Hoggart has served as an editor of *Critical Quarterly.*

THE FORCE OF CARICATURE

Aspects of the Art of Graham Greene, with Particular Reference to *The Power and the Glory*

[. . .] Greene's style is nervous, vivid, astringent, the vehicle of a restless and pungent imagination: it picks out the shopkeeper in the Lehrs' village with his "three commercial chins"; the "hooded and cramped pleasure" of the act of sex in prison; the mean-spirited self-righteous sisters leaving jail in the early morning, "they were both tied up in black shawls like things bought in the market, things hard and dry and second-hand"; and the director of Private Tutorials Ltd., "Henry Beckley, B.A."—the name presents him at once . . . a third in English at Oxford; behind the shiny rimless glasses a bright "let me be your father" smile; an incipient predatory hardening of the mouth which would like to be charming. Or one recalls the effect of the word "bastard" on the priest, catching at his heart like the name of someone you love heard in a strange company; or the creation of the atmosphere of collapse in heat and disillusion in the very first paragraph as Mr. Tench, the ruined dentist, goes out hopelessly for the ether cylinder he's bound to miss getting.

From *Essays in Criticism* III (October 1953) by Richard Hoggart, published by Oxford University Press.

These are in themselves important qualities, and need only to be recalled. Yet their total effect over any length is of something overgeneralized and rhetorical. On looking more closely, one finds that the epithets, for instance, are often either unusually arresting or just cliché—"patience" is likely to be either "monstrous patience" or simply "stony patience." The emotions are being pulled out of shape, put into overbold relief: Mr. Tench had been seized by the desire to be a dentist after finding a discarded cast in a wastepaper basket: "fate had struck. . . . We should be thankful we cannot see the horrors and degradations lying around our childhood, in cupboards and bookshelves, everywhere." Coral feels the first pains of menstruation, "The child stood in pain and looked at them: a horrible novelty enclosed her whole morning: it was as if today everything was memorable" (and why should it be only "horrible"?—Greene seems almost to hate the physical aspects of sex). The mother of the priest's child speaks about her, "She said: 'She's bad through and through.' He was aware of faith dying out between the bed and the door." Or one remembers the water pipes which gurgle through Greene's novels. Like the Wurlitzer organ—"the world's wet mouth lamenting over life"—they are among the telltale voices of modern civilization, this time of the individual's loneliness behind all the mechanics. Anthony, the wastrel ex-public schoolboy in *England Made Me,* tries to make yet another anonymous hotel bedroom look friendly: "he stood in the middle of the room wondering what to do next to make the room look like home, listening to the hot-water pipes wailing behind the wall." In *The Power and the Glory* the water pipes play a sad background music to the scene, again in an hotel bedroom, in which the priest's communion wine is drunk for him: "somewhere in the distance a pipe gurgled and the beetles detonated against a bare globe."

Greene uses the selectively typical catalogue as much as Auden, partly because they naturally tend to handle their material similarly, partly because they both began to write in the thirties when reportage made the catalogue very popular. More importantly, or so it seems to me, Greene's use of the catalogue follows from his way of looking at life. If life is seen as a vast pattern, then all the details of life can easily become parts of the pattern; they can be "placed" with a certain sureness and inevitability. At its best the manner is illuminating; at its worst it can suggest a kind of contempt, as though the author is saying, "One knows that people such as these will always dress like this, have this kind of house, this kind of furniture." On the reader the effect may be quietly flattering, though, of course, the author may not intend this. The reader may appear to be invited to collaborate by the suggestion that he, like the author, has seen this kind of thing before; nothing is unexpected to the wide eye of the intelligentsia. This is the detail you will expect to find, it seems to say, if you are one of the cognoscenti; the items are typical of a whole genre—the cheap bookie's house in *Brighton Rock*:

He looked with contempt down the narrow hall—the shell-case converted into an umbrella stand, the moth-eaten stag's head bearing on one horn a bowler hat, a steel helmet used for ferns. . . . He lit the gas fire, turned on a stand lamp in a red silk shade with a bobble fringe. The light glowed on a silver-plated biscuit box, a framed wedding-group.

the garage of the gimcrack villa where Pinkie hides:

a spade, a rusty lawn-mower, and all the junk the owner had no room for in the tiny house: an old rocking horse, a pram which had been converted into a wheelbarrow, a pile of ancient records: "Alexander's Rag Time Band," "Pack Up Your Troubles," "If You Were the Only Girl"; they lay with the trowels, with what was left of the crazy paving, a doll with one glass eye and a dress soiled with mould.

Anthony undressing in *England Made Me*:

the rather torn photograph of Annette which he had stripped from its frame (he leant it against his tooth mug), the ties which he had crammed into his pocket at the lodgings, his new pants, his new vests, his new socks, *The Four Just Men* in a Tauchnitz edition, his dark blue pyjamas, a copy of *Film Fun*. He turned out his pockets: a pencil, a half-crown fountain pen, an empty card-case, a packet of De Reszke cigarettes.

or the Fellows' empty bungalow in *The Power and the Glory*:

He looked in through a window—perhaps this was the child's room. Everything had been removed from it except the useless or the broken. There was a cardboard box full of torn paper and a small chair which had lost a leg. There was a large nail in the whitewashed wall where a mirror perhaps had been hung—or a picture. There was a broken shoe-horn. . . .
The priest opened a door on the left—perhaps it had been the bedroom: in a corner lay a pile of old medicine bottles: small fingers of crudely coloured liquid lay in some of them. There were medicines for headaches, stomachaches, medicines to be taken after meals and before meals. Somebody must have been very ill to need so many. There was a hair-slide, broken, and a ball of hair-combings—very fair hair turning dusty white.

The detail is acutely observed, but is all too typical—we are in the world of *New Statesman* competitions.
Greene's similes are almost always short and sharply juxtapose the concrete, actual, or temporal with the abstract, subjective, or eternal. They can therefore have a genuine and important function in an allegory. But some of them seem to have been written by rote, and there are so many that the cumulative effect is dulling. These are some from *The Power and the Glory* only:

Evil ran like malaria in his veins.

The memory was like a hand, pulling away the past, exposing him.

Heat stood in the room like an enemy.

She carried her responsibilities carefully like crockery across the hot yard [of Coral].

The old life peeled away like a label.

He could feel his prayers weigh him down like undigested food.

Pride wavered in his voice, like a plant with shallow roots.

Sometimes the abstract/concrete relationship is reversed:

It was like hate on a death-bed [of a dog's snarl].

He drank the brandy down like damnation.

The repeated three-steps-down ending gives the effect of a flat "not with a bang but a whimper," hopeless, corner-of-the-mouth tailing-off:

This was what he was used to: the words not striking home, the hurried close, the expectation of pain coming between him and his faith.

You cannot control what you love—you watch it driving recklessly towards the broken bridge, the torn-up track, the horror of seventy years ahead.

Their little shameless voices filled the patio, and he smiled humbly and sketched small gestures for silence, and there was no respect anywhere left for him in his home, in the town, in the whole abandoned star.

The total effect of all these stylistic qualities is of repeated jabs from a hypodermic syringe, of overforcing, of distortion, of style unrealized in anything more than a boldly caricaturish manner.

The narrative of *The Power and the Glory* derives its undoubted force from three main structural features: (1) the extreme simplicity of the over-all pattern, and the skill and complexity with which the themes are interwoven through its three parts; (2) the striking visual quality of the scenes; (3) the speed of transition between those scenes. Henry James used to say that he composed his novels dramatically; one could say that Greene composes his cinematically. The construction here could hardly be simpler; the parts deal respectively with the setting and the arrival of the priest; the pursuit to its apparent end in safety; and the return, the execution, and the arrival of the new priest. Indeed, the pattern is too neat; the new priest comes too pat on his cue, becomes a mechanical metaphor for the assertion that the Faith goes on and the horror is always repeated.

Throughout the eye shifts constantly, without explanatory links. In the first paragraph the solitary figure of Mr. Tench is picked up crossing the hot deserted square: a few vultures look down at him; he tosses something off the road at them and one rises; with it goes the camera and introduces us to the town, the river, the sea. As the paragraph closes we drop to Mr. Tench again, now at the far side of the plaza, and now in his setting. Thereafter the camera moves from the dentist to the police chief, to the pious woman reading, to the Fellows. The process is repeated with variations in the last chapter; the execution is presented as it *affects* the minor characters, and only seen, not through the narrator, but through the eyes of Mr. Tench as he looks from the window of his dingy surgery, whilst the jefe moans with fright in the chair. Greene can assume an audience familiar with unusual camera angles and quick fadings in and out, and uses both with great skill.

The power of the individual scenes comes primarily from Greene's ability to see them in the most striking way, to know how to place them and where to let the light fall—as when the priest and a mangy dog circle a rotten bone, or when the priest turns back. At that point a mule is ready to take him forward to full safety; Miss Lehr stands ready to give a good missionary's "godspeed"; the half-caste has arrived with his story which the priest recognizes as a lie but cannot refute. There is a moment in which he stands between the two, between safety and death; only he knows all that is happening. The moment is held, and then—the mule is wheeled about and the priest sets off to go back.

The predilection for striking juxtaposition which informs Greene's similes is given extended exercise in the composition of scenes. The pious mother reads the silly literary life of a martyr as the hunt starts for one she rejects as a bad priest but who will be martyred; at the close the same situation is picked up again—she is reading yet another literary martyrdom as the real one takes place not far away. The priest, dirty and exhausted in the South American heat, shelters from the savage pursuit in the Fellows' deserted bungalow and reads with difficulty Coral's English literature test paper: "I come from haunts of coot and hern. . . ."

This rapid alternation of stripped narrative and highly-charged scene is, I think, the second main cause of Greene's attraction. He presents everything visually heightened, and with immense deftness. But his manner of composition promotes overexcitement, is not sufficiently complex and qualified. He never bores; he rarely even taxes. This is structure as caricature.

Greene's characters have a kind of intense nervous life which at first almost convinces but is soon seen to be breathed into them by Greene's breath, and always by his breath. They surprise us, as the scenic juxtaposition surprises us, but they surprise so regularly and so neatly that they eventually fail to surprise. They are flat characters given a series of twists; they are revolved rapidly or stood on their heads at intervals; but when one has mastered the direction of the twist and the timing of its recurrence, the pattern is exposed and there is no more surprise. We do not take it any longer for more than set movements with a wooden figure. So the priest, in spite of all the competence that has gone to his making, is no more than an intensely felt idea presented through a puppet. He seems to come to odd life at intervals, but we soon cease to regard it as anything other than one of the puppet's regular reactions. Thus, in tight corners he almost invariably gives a surprised giggle—"a little gulp of astonished laughter"—at some inconsequential memory. The lieutenant's appearance of life comes from the tension between the cold progressive on top and the desire for love underneath, which reveals itself occasionally in unexpected actions, like the giving of a coin to the priest as he dismisses him from prison. But again, the overmanagement kills, as in the lieutenant's unutterable emotion and his gesture with the hands in these extracts; one accepts the first, but the second resembles it so closely that we are irritated into feeling that not only the characters but we, too, are being manipulated. With the boys of the town the lieutenant finds himself moved by feelings he does not understand:

He wanted to begin the world again with them, in a desert. . . . [He] put out his hand in a gesture of affection—a touch, he didn't know what to do with it.

To the villagers he is interrogating soon afterwards he says:

"In my eyes—can't you understand?—you are worth far more than he is. I want to give you"—he made a gesture with his hands which was valueless, because no one saw him—"everything."

Mr. Fellows is beefy, stupid, muddled; his wife a bourgeoise driven neurotic by the strain of exile:

He was powerless and furious; he said: "You see what a hole you've put us in." He stumped back into the house and into his bedroom, roaming restlessly among the boot-trees. Mrs. Fellows slept uneasily, dreaming of weddings. Once she said aloud: "My train. Be careful of my train."

A passage like this is surely cartoon-art; "dreaming of weddings" belongs to the same stylized regions as the huge mothers-in-law of the picture postcards, and "roaming among the boot-trees" is near-Thurberesque fantasy (how many boot-trees were there? were they larger than life? was there a seal behind each of them?).

The characters are being constantly pushed around, put into positions which are more effective for the pattern than probable; for example, the half-caste, finally betraying the priest to the soldiers, simply saying "Father" from the clearing as the priest reaches the door of the hut—it is too obviously the Judas kiss. Or the priest's child sniggering evilly at him from among the refuse-heaps—the cracked vessel of the Truth facing the evidence of original sin; or the prison-companions who do not betray; or the boy who has admired the lieutenant and sensibly rejected the sickly tales of martyrdom, changing without warn-ing when the priest has been executed, spitting at the lieutenant and opening the door for the new priest. Or the frequent, too appropriate dreams. The priest sleeps, with guilt on his soul at the thought of his child:

His eyes closed and immediately he began to dream. He was being pursued: he stood outside a door banging on it, begging for admission, but nobody answered—there was a word, a password, which would save him, but he had forgotten it. He tried desperately at random—cheese and child, California, excellency, milk, Vera Cruz. His feet had gone to sleep and he knelt outside the door. Then he knew why he wanted to get in: he wasn't being pursued after all: that was a mistake. His child lay beside him bleeding to death and this was a doctor's house. He banged on the door and shouted: "Even if I can't think of the right word, haven't you a heart?" The child was dying and looked up at him with middle-aged complacent wisdom. She said: "You animal," and he woke again crying.

The lieutenant should be happy now that he has finally caught the enemy of the new perfectionism, but is only lost and miserable:

He went into the office: the pictures of the priest and the gunman were still pinned up on the wall: he tore them down—they would never be wanted again. Then he sat at the desk and put his head upon his hands and fell asleep with utter weariness. He couldn't remember afterwards anything of his dreams except laughter, laughter all the time, and a long passage in which he could find no door.

The dialogue is occasionally made to fit in the same way, as in the scene—brilliant as what it aims at being—in which the priest's illicit wine and brandy are drunk by the corrupt official and his hangers-on. The dialogue is trimmed to give a despondent, dribbling effect, e.g. the repeated *"salud"* as the precious drink disappears:

"Is this the only bottle?" The man in drill watched him with frigid anxiety.
"I'm afraid the only bottle."

"*Salud!*"

"And what," the Governor's cousin asked, "were we talking about?"

"About the first thing you could remember," the beggar said.

"The first thing I can remember," the jefe began, with deliberation, "—but this gentleman is not drinking."

"I will have a little brandy."

"*Salud!*"

"*Salud!*"

"The first thing I can remember with any distinctness is my first communion. Ah, the thrill of the soul, my parents round me . . ."

"How many parents, then, have you got?"

"Two, of course."

"They could not have been around you—you would have needed at least four—ha, ha."

"*Salud!*"

"*Salud!*"

And so on till all the drink has gone, and the priest is in tears. The scene lives in its dialogue, which has been formalized to the ends of the dramatic situation.

To adduce all this, and especially the smaller instances, as evidence of Greene's faulty characterization may seem carping, but a great number of separate incidents have to be mentioned specifically to make the point. One might accept a few; dissatisfaction becomes acute as one notices the piling-up of detail of just this kind. It all finally confirms the impression of management from outside, of a lack of any submission from within to the intensely difficult and subtle matter of characterization.

"Immense readability," the reviewers say of all this, and they are right; considerable immediate power from skilled overforcing of style, structure, and character, and from a refusal to allow halftones, uncertainties, complexities. I do not mean to imply that Greene deliberately aims at being "readable" in the popular sense, that he aims at commercial success. It seems more likely that both the distortion and the excessive control are results of Greene's view of life. This view is so insistent that it leads him consistently to falsify his fictional life. It has prevented him from producing, up to the present (though in *The*

End of the Affair he was clearly disciplining both his structural and stylistic habits), a novel whose life we can "entertain as a possibility" whilst we are reading. Again, this is exactly where Kafka succeeds as Greene fails; Greene fails because he brings us to the point where we object to the manipulation. But we continue to find his novels interesting simply because of the power of the view of life behind them, that very power which is causing the overmanipulation. We do not find experience convincingly recreated; we know all the time that we are in the presence of an unusually controlled allegory, "a show," to use Gerontion's word. The characters, I suggested, have a kind of life, but that life is always breathed into them by Greene's breath. The novels as a whole have a kind of life, but not the life of, say, *The Possessed*, in which we forget Dostoevski and explore the revolutionary mentality. In Greene's novels we do not "explore experience"; we meet Graham Greene. We enter continual reservations about what is being done to experience, but we find the novels up to a point arresting because they are forceful, melodramatic presentations of an obsessed and imaginative personality.

There may well be a further, and more disturbing, reason for the attraction of Greene's novels, one arising specifically from the fact that they treat of religion. Here I am obliged to move very tentatively, simply to point towards issues whose examination requires another paper and another hand. But the issues do need to be suggested at this point. Greene presents us with a view of the relationship between God and man in which the emphasis is almost entirely on the more dramatic aspects; the "who sweeps a room as for thy sake" element is altogether lacking:

It was like a short cut to the dark and magical heart of the faith . . . to the night when the graves opened and the dead walked.

This is surely only one aspect of religious belief, and to think it all is to have an inadequate view of religion (I am concerned now not with Greene's aims but with what may be the attitudes of those who read him). It may be that exactly here lies an important part of the appeal of these novels. The audience for them is primarily one of unbelievers. To some unbelievers, I think, the more conservative, communal, city-building features of faith are of little interest; if they were to become religious, they wouldn't go in for it halfway; they like their hell-fire neat; they "drink damnation down like brandy," to invert one of Greene's similes. The sort of excitement they derive from these books may therefore be, curiously enough, of the same order as that they find in the more "existentialist" novels. Greene's kind of religion may be found interesting where the less melodramatic poetry of religion would be found dull. Consciously, these readers may think they inhabit a reasonable, ordered universe: but perhaps their taste in fiction betrays a subconscious unease.

MORTON DAUWEN ZABEL

Morton Dauwen Zabel was for many years a professor of English at the University of Chicago, and he also taught at various universities in Europe and South America. He was an influential critic and editor and an authority on the history of American literature. Among his publications are *Craft and Character in Modern Fiction* and *Literary Opinion in America*. He died in 1964.

GRAHAM GREENE: THE BEST AND THE WORST

I

"There was something about a fête which drew Arthur Rowe irresistibly, bound him a helpless victim to the distant blare of a band . . . called him like innocence: it was entangled in childhood, with vicarage gardens, and girls in white summer frocks, and the smell of herbaceous borders, and security." We meet him—in one of those opening pages we have come to recognize as scizing the attention with the immediate spell of the born conjuror—in the blitzed and gutted London of the early 1940s, stumbling on a charity bazaar in a Bloomsbury square: a man alone and a murderer but fcarlcss because he has made a friend of his guilt. When he gave his wife the poison that released her from the suffering he pitied, he had not asked her consent; "he could never tell whether she might not have preferred any sort of life to death." A fortune-teller slips him, mistakenly, the password by which he wins a cake in the raffle. But there are others who want it and the thing concealed in its heart. Visited that night in his shabby room by a cripple, Rowe has barely

From *Craft and Character in Modern Fiction* by Morton Dauwen Zabel. Copyright 1943 by Morton Dauwen Zabel. Reprinted by permission of The Viking Press, Inc.

tasted the hyoscine in his tea when out of a droning sky a bomb drops, explodes the house, and blows him and us into a dream of horrors—manhunt, spies, sabotage, amnesia, murders, and suicide: an "entertainment" by Graham Greene.

Again we enter the familiar spectre of our age—years of fear and mounting premonition in the 1930s, war and its disasters in the forties, its aftermath of treachery and anarchy still around us in the fifties: no matter what the decade, Greene's evocation of it through fourteen novels (of which *The Ministry of Fear* may be taken as typical of those he calls "entertainments") invariably brings with it an effect that he has made classic of its time and that has justly won him the title "the Auden of the modern thriller." Here once more is the haunted England of the twentieth century, the European nightmare of corruption and doom, a *Blick ins Chaos* where

> taut with apprehensive dreads
> The sleepless guests of Europe lay
> Wishing the centuries away,
> And the low mutter of their vows
> Went echoing through her haunted house,
> As on the verge of happening
> There crouched the presence of The Thing.
> All formulas were tried to still
> The scratching on the window-sill,
> All bolts of custom made secure
> Against the pressure on the door,
> But up the staircase of events
> Carrying his special instruments,
> To every bedside all the same
> The dreadful figure swiftly came.[1]

The fustian stage-sets of Oppenheim, Bram Stoker, and Edgar Wallace are gone with their earlier innocent day. We are in a world whose fabulous realities have materialized appallingly out of contemporary legend and prophecy—the porten-

---

[1] W. H. Auden, "New Year Letter" (1940), II. 15-29, in *The Double Man* (New York: Random House, 1941).

tous journalism of Tabouis, Sheean, Thompson, Gunther, and the apotheosis of the foreign correspondent: the films of Lang, Murnau, Renoir, and Hitchcock; the Gothic fables of Ambler, Hammett, and Simenon; the putsches, pogroms, marches, and mobilizations that have mounted to catastrophe in the present moment of our lives. Its synthetic thrills and anarchic savagery are ruses of melodrama no longer. Guilt pervades all life. All of us are trying to discover how we entered the nightmare, by what treachery we were betrayed to the storm of history. "Mother, please listen to me," cries Rowe. "My little boy couldn't kill anyone":

His mother smiled at him in a scared way but let him talk: he was the master of the dream now. He said, "I'm wanted for a murder I didn't do. People want to kill me because I know too much. I'm hiding underground, and up above the Germans are methodically smashing London to bits all round me. You remember St. Clement's—the bells of St. Clement's. They've smashed that— St. James's, Piccadilly, the Burlington Arcade, Garland's Hotel where we stayed for the pantomime, Maples, and John Lewis. It sounds like a thriller, doesn't it?—but the thrillers are like life—more like life than you are, this lawn, your sandwiches, that pine. [. . .] it's what we've all made of the world since you died. I'm your little Arthur who wouldn't hurt a beetle and I'm a murderer too. The world has been remade by William Le Queux."

Every age has its aesthetic of crime and terror, its attempt to give form to its special psychic or neurotic climate. No age has imposed greater handicaps on the effort than ours. Crime has gone beyond Addison's "chink in the chain armour of civilized communities." It has become the symptom of a radical lesion in the stamina of humanity. The hot violence of the Elizabethans is as different from the cold brutality of Hitlerian or Communist Europe, the heroic sin in Aeschylus or Webster from the squalid and endemic degeneracy in Céline or Henry Miller, the universal proportions of Greek or Shakespearean wrong from the gratuitous calculation and *inconséquences* of Gide's aesthetic criminals, as the worth at which the individual life was held in those times from its worthlessness in ours. A criminal takes his dignity from his defiance of the intelligence or merit that surrounds him, from the test his act imposes on the human community. He becomes trivial when that measure is denied him. So the modern thriller is permitted its prodigies of contrivance and hecatombs of death at the cost of becoming a bore. So film audiences fidget restlessly through the newsreel, waiting to be overwhelmed by the "edifying bilge" of Hollywood. The thrill habit, fed by tabloids, drugstore fiction, headlines, and events, has competed successfully with gin, drugs, and aspirin, and doped the moral nerve of a generation.

The hardship this imposes on the artist is obvious. When felony, by becoming political, becomes impersonal, when the *acte gratuit* elicits not only secret but public approval, its dramatist faces the desperate task of restoring to his readers their lost instinct of values, the sense of human worth. It is not enough that the thriller become psychic: Freudian behavior patterns have become as much an open commodity and stock property as spy rings and torture chambers were fifty years ago. It must become moral as well.

The Victorian *frisson* of crime was all the choicer for the rigor of propriety and sentiment that hedged it in. Dickens' terrors are enhanced less by his rhetoric than by his coziness. The reversion to criminality in Dostoevski takes place in a ramifying hierarchy of authority—family life, social caste, political and religious bureaucracy, Tzarist militarism and repression. The horror in *The Turn of the Screw* is framed by the severest decorum, taste, and inhibition. James—like Conrad, Gide, and Thomas Mann—felt the seduction of crime but he also knew its artistic conditions. "Everything you may further do will be grist to my imaginative mill," he once wrote William Roughead of Edinburgh in thanks for a book of the latter's criminal histories: "I'm not sure I enter into such matters best when they are *very* archaic or remote from our familiarities, for then the testimony to manners and morals is rather blurred for me by the *whole* barbarism. . . . The thrilling in the comparatively modern much appeals to me—for there the *special* manners and morals become queerly disclosed. . . . then go back to the dear old human and sociable murders and adulteries and forgeries in which we are so agreeably at home." The admonition might have served as the cue for the talent of Graham Greene.

Greene, dealing in a "whole barbarism" equaling or surpassing anything in history, has undertaken to redeem that dilapidation from the stupefying mechanism and inconsequence to which modern terrorism has reduced it. Arthur Calder-Marshall has rightly said, in an article in *Horizon*, that "few living English novelists derive more material from the daily newspaper than Graham Greene." His *mise-en-scène* includes the Nazi underground and fifth column (*The Confidential Agent, The Ministry of Fear*), Communist politics riddled by schisms and betrayals (*It's a Battlefield*), Kruger and his international swindles (*England Made Me*), Zaharoff and the alliance between munitions-making and *Machtpolitik* (*This Gun for Hire*), the English racetrack gang warfare (*Brighton Rock*), the Mexican church suppression (*The Power and the Glory*), wartime in the Gold Coast (*The Heart of the Matter*), in London (*The End of the Affair*), and in Indochina (*The Quiet American*); while his *Orient Express* is the same train we've traveled on all the way from *Shanghai Express* to *Night Train* and *The Lady Vanishes*. But where once—in James, Conrad, Dostoevski, in Dickens, Defoe, and the Elizabethans —it was society, state, kingdom, world, or the universe itself that supplied the presiding order of law and justice, it is now the isolated, betrayed, but finally indestructible integrity of the individual life that must furnish that measure. Humanity, having contrived a world of mindless and psychotic brutality, reverts for survival to the test of the single man. Marked, hunted, or condemned, he may work for evil or for good, but it is his passion for a moral identity of his own that provides the nexus of values in a world that has reverted to anarchy. His lineage is familiar—Raskolnikov, Stavrogin, Kirilov; Conrad's Jim, Razumov, and Heyst; Mann's Felix Krull and Gide's Lafcadio; Hesse's Steppenwolf and Demian, and, more immediately, Kafka's K. He appears in almost every Greene novel—as hero or victim in Drover, Dr. Czinner, the nameless D., and Major Scobie; as pariah or renegade in Raven, Farrant, Rowe, and the whisky priest of *The Power and the Glory*; as the incarnation of pure malevolence in Pinkie, the boy gangster of *Brighton Rock*.

The plot that involves him is fairly consistent. *Brighton Rock* may be taken as showing it in archetype. Its conflict rests on a basic dualism of forces, saved from the prevalent danger of becoming an inflexible mechanism by Greene's skill in suggestion and insight, yet radical in its antithesis of elements. Pinkie is a believing Catholic. He knows Hell as a reality and accepts his damnation. *Corruptio optimi pessima* is the last faith left him to live or die by. Ida Arnold, the full-blown, life-loving tart whose casual lover the gang has killed, sets out to track him down: "unregenerate, a specimen of the 'natural man,' coarsely amiable, bestially kind, the most dangerous enemy to religion." She pursues him with ruthless and convinced intention, corners him, sees him killed. The boy is sped to his damnation and Ida triumphs ("God doesn't mind a bit of human nature. . . . I know the difference between Right and Wrong.") The hostility is crucial. It figures in all of Greene's mature books—Mather the detective against Raven the assassin in *This Gun for Hire*; the Inspector against Drover in *It's a Battlefield*; the Communist police lieutenant, accompanied by the mestizo who acts as nemesis, against the hunted, shameless, renegade priest in *The Power and the Glory*, trailing his desecrated sanctity through the hovels and jungles of the Mexican state, yet persisting in his office of grace and so embracing the doom that pursues him. It reappears in the hunting down of Major Scobie by the agent Wilson in *The Heart of the Matter*, and it counts in the tragic passion of Bendrix for Sarah Miles in *The End of the Affair*. A critic in *The New Statesman* once put the case concisely: "Mr. Greene is a Catholic, and his novel *Brighton Rock* betrays a misanthropic, almost Jansenist, contempt for the virtues that do not spring from grace."

It is this grace that operates as the principle which makes palpable its necessary enemy, Evil. And it is the evil that

materializes out of vice, crime, nightmare, and moral stupe-
faction in Greene's books that brings him into a notable company. The same evil is made to work behind the dramatic
mystery and psychic confusion in *The Turn of the Screw* and
beneath the squalid violence in Conrad's *The Secret Agent*, that
parent classic in this field of fiction which, appearing in 1907,
established the kind of novel that Greene and his generation
have carried to such exorbitant lengths. To define and objectify
the evil, to extricate it from the relativity of values and abstrac-
tions—arbitrary justice, impersonal humanitarianism and pity,
right and wrong, good and bad—is the ultimate motive of
Greene's work. His pursuit of it has carried him afield among
the totems and obscenities of coastal Africa which he conjured
in *Journey without Maps*, his descent to the heart of darkness:

It isn't a gain to have turned the witch or the masked secret
dancer, the sense of supernatural evil, into the small human viciousness of the thin distinguished military gray head in Kensington
Gardens with the soft lips and the eye which dwelt with dull lustre
on girls and boys of a certain age. . . . They are not, after all, so
far from the central darkness. . . . when one sees to what unhappiness, to what peril of extinction, centuries of celebration have
brought us, one sometimes has a curiosity to discover if one can
from what we have come, to recall at which point we went astray.

An echo clearly sounds here from a passage in T. S. Eliot's
essay on Baudelaire (1930) which has become a classic statement of the problem in recent criticism:

So far as we are human, what we do must be either evil or good;
so far as we do evil or good, we are human; and it is better, in a
paradoxical way, to do evil than to do nothing: at least, we exist.
It is true to say that the glory of man is his capacity for salvation;
it is also true to say that his glory is his capacity for damnation.
The worst that can be said of most of our malefactors, from states-
men to thieves, is that they are not men enough to be damned.

And Greene has pointed to another definition of his subject in
one of the epigraphs he prefixed to his book on Mexico in 1939
—a passage, too long to quote here in full, from Newman:

To consider the world in its length and breadth, its various history, the many races of man, their starts, their fortunes, their mutual alienation, their conflicts . . . the impotent conclusion of long-standing facts, the tokens so faint and broken of a superintending design, the blind evolution of what turn out to be great powers or truth . . . the greatness and littleness of man, his far-reaching aims, his short duration, the curtain hung over his futurity, the disappointments of life, the defeat of good, the success of evil . . . the prevalence and intensity of sin, the pervading idolatries, the corruptions, the dreary hopeless irreligion, that condition of the whole race . . . all this is a vision to dizzy and appall; and inflicts upon the mind the sense of a profound mystery, which is absolutely beyond human solution.

What shall be said to this heart-piercing, reason-bewildering fact? I can only answer, that either there is no Creator, or this living society of men is in a true sense discarded from His presence . . . *if* there be a God, *since* there is a God, the human race is implicated in some terrible aboriginal calamity.

The drama and present issue of that calamity are what make the continuous theme of Greene's fiction in its development over the past quarter-century.

II

Greene's beginnings in the novel were in a vein of romantic Stevensonian adventure in *The Man Within*, but he emphasized even there, in a title taken from Thomas Browne, the dualism of the moral personality ("There's another man within me that's angry with me," a derivation from Paul's "law in my members" in the Epistle to the Romans). He next applied the motif to the situation of moral anarchy in modern politics and society and began to adopt for the purpose the devices of intrigue and mystery as the modern thriller had developed them (*The Name of Action, Rumour at Nightfall, Orient Express*). These tales, at first crude and exaggerated in contrivance (Greene has dropped the first two of the last named from his collected edition), soon advanced into his characteristic kind of expertness, and all of them implied a dissatisfaction with the current tendencies in English fiction. This became explicit in his reviews of the modern novelists. Henry James, possibly Conrad, were the last masters of the English novel to preserve its powers in anything like their full tragic and moral potentialities. "After the death of Henry James," he wrote in an essay on Mauriac, "a disaster overtook the English novel: indeed long before his death one can picture that quiet, impressive, rather complacent figure, like the last survivor on a raft, gazing out over a sea scattered with wreckage."

For [he continued] with the death of James the religious sense was lost to the English novel, and with the religious sense went the sense of the importance of the human act. It was as if the world of fiction had lost a dimension: the characters of such distinguished writers as Mrs. Virginia Woolf and Mr. E. M. Forster wandered like cardboard symbols through a world that was paper-thin. Even in one of the most materialistic of our great novelists—in Trollope—we are aware of another world against which the actions of the characters are thrown into relief. The ungainly clergyman picking his black-booted way through the mud, handling so awkwardly his umbrella, speaking of his miserable income and stumbling through a proposal of marriage, exists in a way that Mrs. Woolf's Mr. Ramsay never does, because we are aware that he exists not only to the woman he is addressing but also in a God's eye. His unimportance in the world of the senses is only matched by his enormous importance in another world.

So the novelist, taking "refuge in the subjective novel," found that he had "lost yet another dimension": "the visible world for him ceased to exist as completely as the spiritual." Mauriac accordingly was rated as belonging to "the company of the great traditional novelists: he is a writer for whom the visible world has not ceased to exist, whose characters have the solidity and importance of men with souls to save or lose, and a writer who claims the traditional and essential right of a novelist, to comment, to express his views."

But if Greene gave his highest honors among modern novelists to James ("it is in the final justice of his pity, the completeness of an analysis which enabled him to pity the most shabby, the most corrupt, of his human actors, that he ranks with the greatest of creative writers. He is as solitary in the history of the novel as Shakespeare in the history of poetry")', to Conrad (for his instinct of " 'the mental degradation to which a man's intelligence is exposed on its way through life': 'the passions of men shortsighted in good and evil': in scattered phrases you get the memories of a creed working like poetry through the agnostic prose"), and to Mauriac ("if Pascal had been a novelist, we feel, this is the method and the tone he would have used"); if he granted his secondary respects to writers like Corvo ("he cared for nothing but his faith . . . if he could not have Heaven, he would have Hell"), Ford Madox Ford ("he had never really believed in human happiness"), and de la Mare ("no one can bring the natural visible world more sharply to the eye"); if he denied the authentic creative virtue alike to the agnostic Butler ("the perpetual need to generalize from a peculiar personal experience maimed his imagination") or Havelock Ellis ("invincible ignorance") and to the believing Eric Gill ("as an artist Gill gained nothing from his faith . . . his rebellion never amounted to much") or the angry mystic Léon Bloy ("he hadn't the creative instinct . . . the hatred of life . . . prevented him from being a novelist or a mystic of the first order"), it appeared that there was another order of talent that had conditioned Greene's own imagination from its earliest workings. He responded to it in the adventure tales of John Buchan ("Now I saw how thin is the protection of civilization") and Conan Doyle ("think of the sense of horror which hangs over the laurelled drive of Upper Norwood and behind the curtains of Lower Camberwell. . . . He made Plumstead Marshes and the Barking Level as vivid and unfamiliar as a lesser writer would have made the mangrove swamps of the West Coast"), but its mark had been laid on him long before he encountered these writers: in childhood when "all books are books of divination." Its masters then were the literary heroes of his boyhood: "Rider Haggard, Percy Westerman, Captain Brereton, or Stanley Weyman." But vividly as these ignited his imagination, much as *King Solomon's Mines* "influenced the future," it "could not finally satisfy"; its characters were too much "like Platonic ideas: they were not life as one had already begun to know it." The "future for better or worse really struck" when he discovered *The Viper of Milan* by Marjorie Bowen. "It was," says Greene, "as if I had been supplied once and for all with a subject."

"Why?" he asks, and gives his answer. Here for the first time he learned that while "goodness has only once found a perfect incarnation in a human body and never will again," evil "can always find a home there"; that there is a "sense of doom" that "lies over success"; that "perfect evil walk[s] the world where perfect good can never walk again." And he acknowledges that it was Miss Bowen's Italian melodrama that gave "me my pattern—religion might later explain it in other terms, but the pattern was already there"; and after "one had lived for fourteen years in a wild jungle country without a map . . . now the paths had been traced and naturally one had to follow them."[2]

It is apparent from these disclosures that Greene, whatever his sense of human and moral complexity or his sophisticated insight into the riddled situation of his time, early decided to address himself to a primitive order of fiction. But since the social and political conditions of the age had likewise reverted to primitive forms of violence, brutality, and anarchy, he found his purpose matched in the events of the historic moment. For that moment the thriller was an obvious and logical imaginative medium, and Greene proceeded to raise it to a skill and artistry few other writers of the period, and none in English, had arrived at. His novels between 1930 and 1945 record the crises and confusions of those years with an effect of atmosphere and moral desperation perfectly appropriate to the time. If their expert contrivance often seems to descend to sleight of hand; if the surrealism of their action and settings can result in efflorescences of sheer conjuring; if the mechanics of the thriller— chases, coincidences, strokes of accident, and exploding surprises

---

[2] All these quotations are from Greene's collection of essays, *The Lost Childhood*.

—can at times collapse into a kind of demented catastrophe, these were not too remotely at odds with the possibilities of modern terrorism, police action, international intrigue, and violence. His superiority to the convention in which he worked was clear; if at times it ran uncomfortably close to the jigsaw-puzzle manipulation which entertainers like Ambler, Hammett, and Raymond Chandler had made so readable and finally so trivial, there was always working in it a poetry of desperation and an instinct for the rudiments of moral conflict that lifted it to allegoric validity. It was apparently at such validity that Greene was aiming in these books. "What strikes the attention most in this closed Fagin universe," he has said in writing on *Oliver Twist*, "are the different levels of unreality"; and of Mauriac's novels he has said that "One is never tempted to consider in detail M. Mauriac's plots. Who can describe six months afterwards the order of events, say in *Ce Qui Était Perdu?* . . . . We are saved or damned by our thoughts, not by our actions."

In fiction of this kind, action itself becomes less real or representative than symbolic. Disbelief is suspended in acceptance of the typical or the potential; incredulity yields to imaginative recognition; and since the events of modern politics and militarism had already wrenched the contemporary imagination out of most of its accepted habits and disciplines, Greene's plot found the thriller fully conditioned to his purpose. If a writer like David Cecil could say, to the charge that John Webster's plays are "extravagant, irrational, and melodramatic," that "the battle of heaven and hell cannot be convincingly conveyed in a mode of humdrum everyday realism" and that "the wild and bloody conventions of Elizabethan melodrama provided a most appropriate vehicle for conveying his hell-haunted vision of human existence," a similar defense could be argued for Greene's melodrama—the more so because the battle of heaven and hell and the hell-haunted vision had become part of the European and contemporary experience.

Moreover, in tales of this kind (to which the adjective "operatic," used by Lionel Trilling to describe certain features in the novels of Forster, applies) character itself tends to reduce to primary or symbolic terms. The tests of average consistency or psychological realism are not of the first importance. A more radical appeal acts to suspend them. The novel refers to something more than the principles of temperament; the "humors" become not only moral but philosophic. At times, in books like *It's a Battlefield* and *England Made Me*, Greene worked in terms of Freudian or abnormal character types and so brought his characters into an uncomfortable but effective relation with his melodrama. At others—*This Gun for Hire* and *The Confidential Agent*—the psychic pathology submitted openly and conveniently to the claims of political violence and so left the story to rest at the level of the historical or political parable (hence "an entertainment"). In *Brighton Rock* the fable became explicitly religious; in *The Power and the Glory* it perhaps became "metaphysical" as well. The last-named novel is certainly one of Greene's finest achievements, possibly his masterpiece. In it the action and milieu are not only invested with a really convincing quality of legend. The fable itself, and the truth it evokes, are believably enacted by the two central characters—the priest with his inescapable vocation, the police lieutenant with his—in a way that is not pressed to exaggerate or simplify their primitive and symbolic functions in the drama. The book is sustained from first to last by a unity of atmosphere that harmonizes its setting, characters, moral values, and historic reference into a logical consistency of effect, and the result is one of the most haunting legends of our time.

Greene's ambition was not, however, content to rest with this kind of result. His more serious books had already aimed at being more than fables or parables. He had before him the examples of Mauriac and Faulkner, both of whom he has acknowledged as major influences in his work. *It's a Battlefield*, *Brighton Rock*, and *The Power and the Glory* pointed the way to a fiction of full-bodied and realistic substance, and in *The Heart of the Matter* in 1948 he undertook to write a complete and consistent novel. (His "entertainments" since that time have been frankly written for film production—*The Third*

Man and *Loser Takes All*.) This brought him squarely up against the problem of reconciling his religious and didactic premises to the realistic and empirical principles of the novel form; of harmonizing an orthodoxy of belief (however personal or inquisitive) with what George Orwell once called "the most anarchical of all forms of literature." ("How many Roman Catholics have been good novelists? Even the handful one could name have usually been bad Catholics. The novel is practically a Protestant form of art; it is a product of the free mind, the autonomous individual.")[3]

Greene certainly had no intention of conforming to the conventions of religious-literary sentimentalism. In this at least he shared what has been called "one major objective of young English Catholic writers"—"not to resemble Chesterton." On the other hand, he was by conviction committed to a belief in the efficacy and sufficiency of grace as the final test of value in character and conduct. Now that he committed himself equally to the demands of psychological and moral realism which the novel imposes, he met for the first time the tests a novelist faces when he joins the human claims of his art with the theological claims of his faith. And grace is bound to become a question-begging premise on which to rest the arguments of psychic and moral realism. ("The greatest advantage of religious faith for the artist," Gide once noted in his journal, "is that it permits him a *limitless* pride.")[4] The instinctive or lifelong believer—Mauriac, O'Faolain, Eliot, whatever their crises of "conversion" or re-conversion—usually finds a means of harmonizing orthodoxy with experience, dogma with moral inquisition. The voluntary or deliberate convert—Claudel, Greene, Waugh, perhaps Bloy and Bernanos—seems never to arrive at such reconciliation, at least not easily or convincingly. Experience and faith refuse to come to natural or practical conjunctions; in fact, it is implied that they were never intended to.

---

[3] *Inside the Whale and Other Essays* (London: Gollancz, 1940), p. 173.
[4] "*Le plus grand avantage de la foi religieuse, pour l'artiste, c'est qu'elle lui permet un orgueil* incommensurable." *Journal 1889-1939*, p. 191 (5 décembre, 1905).

Faith becomes for such men the most deadly-serious "vested interest" of their existence. If it does not assert itself in the form of a didactic or inflexible logic, it does so in the form of a perversely ingenious one. There has always been a visible gap between the writer or poet of inherited or habitual faith and the one of converted belief (the same difference shows up in writers of political dogmatism), and it is not lessened by the convert's acquaintance with unbelief. He usually conveys "the perpetual need to generalize from a peculiar personal experience," and his imagination is seldom left unmaimed, however much it may also have been stimulated.

Greene's plots from the first showed a tendency to enforce absolutes of moral judgment—a kind of theological *vis inertiae* —which resulted in the humors to which his characters tended to reduce. The "sanctified sinner" who appears in most of Greene's books is the most prominent of these. The type has become a feature of modern religious literature. Baudelaire, Rimbaud, and Bloy (*Une Femme Pauvre*) seem to have combined to give it its characteristic stamp and utility in literary mysticism, and since their day it has become a virtual cliché of religious drama and symbolism. The idea has been put bluntly by its critics: "vice is defined as the manure in which salvation flowers."[5] Orwell made a critical issue of it when he reviewed Greene's *The Heart of the Matter*.[6] It was not only the frivolity of the cult he found suspect: its suggestion "that there is something rather *distingué* in being damned" and its hint of a "weakening of belief" ("when people really believed in Hell, they were not so fond of striking graceful attitudes on its brink"). It was also its results in dramatic artistry: "by trying to clothe theological speculations in flesh and blood, it produces psychological absurdities." The cases of both Pinkie in *Brighton Rock* and Scobie in *The Heart of the Matter* were taken as showing its liabilities for a novelist: that of Pinkie by presup-

---

[5] Kenneth Tynan, reviewing the dramatic version of *The Power and the Glory* in *The Observer* (London), April 8, 1956, p. 11.

[6] *The New Yorker*, July 17, 1948, pp. 61-63.

posing "that the most brutally stupid person can, merely by having been brought up a Catholic, be capable of great intellectual subtlety"; that of Scobie "because the two halves of him do not fit together." ("If he were capable of getting into the kind of mess that is described, he would have got into it earlier. If he really felt that adultery is mortal sin, he would stop committing it; if he persisted in it, his sense of sin would weaken. If he believed in Hell, he would not risk going there merely to spare the feelings of a couple of neurotic women.")

In other words, the arguments which such characters enact tend to become increasingly "loaded" as they advance toward explicit theological conclusions. And the fiction that embodies such arguments soon runs into the difficulty which all tendentious or didactic fiction sooner or later encounters. It no longer "argues" the problems and complexities of character in terms of psychological and moral forces; it states, decides, and solves them in terms of pre-established and dictated premises. Grace is always held in reserve as a principle of salvation, a principle which soon becomes too arbitrary and convenient to find justification in conduct or purpose. It descends like a Christianized *deus ex machina* to redeem its vessels when they have driven themselves into the impasse or sacrilege that would, on moral grounds alone, be sufficient to damn them. Greene of course shirks nothing in presenting his men and women as psychically complex and morally confounded. But as he advances out of parable into realism, out of the tale of violence into the drama of credible human personalities, he still keeps an ace up his sleeve, and grace is called upon to do the work that normally would be assigned to moral logic and nemesis. "O God," says Scobie after he has taken communion in a state of mortal sin and is beginning to plan his suicide, "I am the only guilty one because I've known the answers all the time." This admission of his damnation is also his plea for salvation ("I think," says the priest afterward to his widow, "from what I saw of him, that he really loved God"); and what it implies is the kind of presumption or arrogance that has become a feature of recent religious fiction: namely, that neither conduct nor morals are of final importance to the believer. *Corruptio optimi pessima*: it is not only a case of the corruption of the best being the worst. It is by their capacity for corruption or damnation that the best—the believers—qualify for redemption. "The others don't count."

What accompanies this premise in Greene's later novels is likely to take a form which, whatever its theological tenability, can be as repugnant (intentionally repugnant, no doubt) to normal religious feeling as it is to aesthetic judgment. "O God, I offer up my damnation to you. Take it. Use it for them," Scobie murmurs at the communion rail; and when, presently, he contemplates future repetitions of his sacrilege, he has "a sudden picture before his eyes of a bleeding face, of eyes closed by the continuous shower of blows: the punch-drunk head of God reeling sideways." On such passages it is difficult not to agree with the critic who acts in revulsion: "a stern theological dogma [is] grossly degraded into melodrama, to an extent which allows even a nonbeliever to speak of blasphemy. . . . It is intolerable. Whether we accept the dogma or not, it is intolerable that it should be expressed in such luridly anthropomorphic terms as these . . . a hotting-up of religious belief for fictional purposes, a vulgarization of the faith."[7] Greene has made a repeated point of indicating pity as a sin of presumption. Rowe, Scobie, and Bendrix are all made to suffer the consequences of assuming a divine prerogative. It is, however, hard to believe that a similar presumption does not underlie the special pleading that accompanies Scobie's catastrophe. "A priest only knows the unimportant things," says Father Rank to Mrs. Scobie. "Unimportant?" "Oh, I mean the sins," he replies impatiently. "A man doesn't come to us and confess his virtues." To reasoning as conveniently circular as this no practical moral appeal is possible.

The Heart of the Matter is Greene's most ambitious book thus far, but in spite of its advance beyond the schematic pattern of its predecessors, it is not finally his most convincing

---

[7] Philip Toynbee, *The Observer* (London), December 4, 1955.

one. Its excessive manipulation keeps it from being that. *The End of the Affair* in 1951 showed an important development. It was Greene's first novel to put aside entirely the devices of intrigue, mystery, and criminal motivation. Its scene is modern London, its drama is intimately personal, and though the action takes place in wartime, war does not figure in the events except accidentally. Its plot shows a radical simplicity, and its characters, if tormented to the point of abnormality, remain recognizable as people of credible moral responsibility. It develops a story of secret passion between a modern novelist of brilliant sardonic talent and self-possessed agnostic egotism, Maurice Bendrix, and Sarah Miles, the surburban wife who loves him and suffers his selfish claims to the point of immolating herself destructively to save him from death in a bombing. Sarah makes a bargain with God: she will give up her love for Bendrix if his life is saved. Her sacrifice brings on her the sufferings of a religious atonement and finally results in the event of a miracle which reveals to Bendrix the nature and consequences of his selfish corruption. Greene's epigraph here comes from Bloy: "Man has places in his heart which do not yet exist, and into them enters suffering in order that they may have existence."

The tale is closely and powerfully developed, and its three principal characters are perhaps the most subtly drawn and intimately created of any in Greene's gallery. It is true that here again, especially in the final section of the book, they assume a disembodied abstraction of conduct which recalls the cases of Pinkie and Scobie, and the introduction of the miracle, shrewdly handled though it is, risks the dissolution of the entire conflict in an arbitrary conclusion. The symbolic effect that might make such an event convincing is weakened by the realistic basis on which the drama is built; it ends as the later, more schematized novels of Mauriac do, in an unprepared shift from realism to didacticism, an arbitrary change of moral (and consequently of dramatic) premises which has the effect of detaching the characters from their established logic as personalities and forcing them to serve a function outside themselves. The result is an effect of metaphysical contrivance which it would take the powers of a Dostoevski to justify. But if Greene here resorts to an artificiality of argument that has weakened a share of Mauriac's later work, he also invites in this novel a comparison with Mauriac's psychic and moral insight. By applying himself to an intimate human conflict and laying aside the melodramatic historical framework of his earlier work, he achieves a substance that brings him to a point of renewal and fresh departure in his fiction.

He remains significant, however, because of what he has done to recreate and reassert the moral necessity in his characters, and to project its reality, by symbolic means, into the human and social crisis of his time. He has used guilt and horror for what they have signified in every age, Elizabethan, Gothic, Romantic, or Victorian—as a mode of exploring the fears, evasions, and panic that confuse men or betray the dignity of reason to violence and brutality, but which must always, whatever the historic situation in which they appear, be faced, recognized, and mastered if salvation is to escape the curse of self-deception. The identity Greene's heroes seek is that of a conscience that shirks none of the deception or confusion in their natures. If the "destructive element" of moral anarchy threatens them, it is their passion for a moral identity of their own that redeems them. It is by that passion that they give his work, to quote one of its most acute critics [Donat O'Donnell, in *Maria Cross*]—whatever "its intellectual dishonesty, its ellipses of approximation and selective omissions, as well as its fragmentation of character"—its "sense of history." The drama he presents, "with its evasions and its apologia, is part of our climate of fear and guilt, where it is hard for a man of goodwill, lacking good actions, to see straight or to speak plain. The personal tragedy is in the womb of the general one, and pity is their common bloodstream."

It is because he dramatizes the hostile forces of anarchy and conscience, of the moral nonentity with which nature or history threatens man and the absolute tests of moral selfhood, that Greene has brought about one of the most challenging combinations of historical allegory and spiritual argument that have appeared in the present dubious phase of English fiction. His style and imagery can be as melodramatic as his action, but he has made of them an instrument for probing the temper and tragedy of the age, the perversions that have come near to wrecking it, and the stricken weathers of its soul. It still remains for him to get beyond its confusions, negative appeals, and perverse standards—not to mention the tricky arguments by which these are too often condemned in his books and which are too much left to do the work of the honest imagination—to become a fully responsible novelist in his English generation. This is a role to which his acute sense of history and his remarkable gifts in moral drama have assigned him. His skill already puts him in the descent of the modern masters—James, Conrad, Joyce—in whom judgment and imagination achieved their richest combination, as well as in the company of the few living novelists—Mauriac, Malraux, Hemingway, Faulkner—in whom their standard survives. He is one of the few contemporary English talents who insist on being referred to that standard and who give evidence that it means to persist.

R. W. B. LEWIS

THE "TRILOGY"

. . . The three novels published between 1938 and 1948 are sometimes taken together as a trilogy; but the word should be enclosed in quotation marks, for the trilogic pattern, if it existed in Greene's awareness, took hold only belatedly. But it is worth juxtaposing the three books, to observe several striking aspects of Greene. All three show his affection for the primitive; like Silone, Greene often turns away from the relatively civilized to inspect human life in its cruder and more exposed conditions: in a dark corner of Brighton, the jungles and prisons of Tabasco, the coast of West Africa—all places where, as Scobie tells himself in *The Heart of the Matter*, "human nature hasn't had time to disguise itself"; places where there openly flourished "the injustices, the cruelties, the meanness that elsewhere people so cleverly hushed up." In these primitive scenes we encounter the *dramatis personae* of Greene's recurring drama and of his troubled universe: the murderer, the priest, and the policeman, who are the heroes respectively of the three books. All three figures, in different embodiments, appear in all three novels; and they tend more and more to resemble each other. The murderer Pinkie is knowingly a hideously inverted priest; the policeman Scobie becomes involved with crime and criminals; the lieutenant in *The Power and the Glory* has "something of a priest in his intent observant walk," while the priest in turn has queer points of resemblance with the Yankee killer whose photograph faces his in the police station. The three figures represent, of course, the shifting and interwoven attributes of the Greenean man: a being capable of imitating both Christ and Judas; a person who is at once the pursuer and the man pursued; a creature with the splendid potentiality either of damnation or salvation. The actualities of their fate exhaust, apparently, the major possibilities. If one can be sure of anything in the real world or in Greene's world, Pinkie Brown is damned—it is his special mode of triumph; the Mexican priest is saved—sainthood gleams at last through his bloodshot eyes; and the final end of Major Scobie is what is precisely in doubt, as difficult to determine as his own ambiguous last words, "Dear God, I love . . ." Pinkie is a proud citizen of hell; Scobie's suffering is that of a man in purgatory; and the laughter in *The Power and the Glory* celebrates, perhaps, the entrance of a soul into paradise. The three careers are presented to us in three very different kinds of fiction: *Brighton Rock* just manages to escape melodrama and becomes a work *sui generis; The Power and the Glory* is, in its way, a divine comedy; and *The Heart of the Matter* is a tragedy in the classical tradition. These novels are, respectively, Greene's most strenuous, his most satisfying, and, artistically, his most assured.

Brighton Rock in particular is the most harrowing of Greene's stories about children; and Pinkie, the seventeen-year-old gangster (he is usually referred to simply as "the Boy"), is "the most driven and 'damned'" of all Greene's characters, to quote his own words about the evil forces in that other fearful tale about children, James's *The Turn of the Screw*. There is, to be sure, a superficial movement in the novel from death to life: the narrative begins with the revenge-murder by Brighton race-track hoodlums of Hale, the man who is working a publicity stunt for a newspaper among the holiday crowds; and it closes with the pregnancy of Rose, the wan underage wife whom Hale's killer, Pinkie, has been forced for protection to marry. So far there is a momentary likeness to Moravia's *Woman of Rome*, which similarly concludes with the heroine's pregnancy by a now dead murderer. Moravia's novel quite definitely suggests the painful victory of life over death. But Greene's artistic and intellectual purposes are almost always dialectically opposite to those of Moravia, and in *Brighton Rock* not only is the death legally avenged, the birth itself will be altogether darkened by Rose's discovery of Pinkie's true feeling about her—via the "loving message" he has recorded by phonograph and which, "the worst horror of all," she is on her way to hear as the story ends: "God damn you, you little bitch, why can't you go back home for ever and let me be?" The implied denouement in *Brighton Rock* is as disagreeable as anything in modern fiction. But *Brighton Rock* is deliberately pitiless, and partly because it aims, by moving beyond human pity, to evoke the far faint light of an incomprehensible divine mercy. . . .

Brighton Rock could have been a kind of disaster, two different books, between the same covers only by mistake. But it emerges as an original and striking work: for the relation between the detective story and the tragedy expresses exactly what *Brighton Rock* is finally all about. It is a relation between modes of narrative discourse that reflects a relation between two kinds or levels of reality: a relation between incommensurable and hostile forces; between incompatible worlds; between the moral world of right and wrong, to which Ida constantly and confidently appeals, and the theological world of good and evil inhabited by Pinkie and Rose. It is, in short, the relation that Greene had formulated for himself in Liberia, between the "sinless empty graceless chromium world" of modern Western urban civilization and the supernaturally infested jungle with its purer terrors and its keener pleasures. The abrupt superiority of *Brighton Rock* to anything Greene had yet written comes from the fact that for the first time he had separated the mystery from the mystery and confronted the one with the other.

Here, of course, the confrontation takes the form of deadly warfare: "[Ida] stared out over the red and green lights, the heavy traffic of her battlefield, laying her plans, marshalling her cannon fodder." That sense of the universal drama is both ancient and modern; for *Brighton Rock,* to put the case in perhaps exaggerated and misleading theological terms, belongs with the early and late medieval tradition, the tradition now again in fashion: the tradition of Tertullian and the dark, negative, and incorrigibly paradoxical theology wherein everything supernatural stands in implacable hostility over against everything natural and human; and for the most part, vice versa. This is the view Albert Camus has identified and attacked as *the* Christian tradition. But in another tradition, in so-called theocentric humanism, there are intermediate ends, intermediate goods, and intermediate explanations: because there is an intermediate figure, the God-man Christ, who reconciles the realms and makes sense out of human history. But about Pinkie and his small explosive world there is nothing intermediate—here everything is sudden and ultimate. Pinkie has no great involvement with the things of this world, with money or with sexual love or even with Brighton. His Brighton is not a town or a "background" but a Fury-driven situation; and he is involved immediately with evil and catastrophe.

He is deeply implicated, too, of course, with good—with the forlorn waitress Rose, who has just enough information about Hale's murder to make Pinkie decide savagely to marry her in order to keep her quiet; and who is as doomed to salvation (that is how Greene prefers to describe it) as Pinkie is to damnation. He sees her as his necessary counterpart. "What was most evil in him needed her; it couldn't get along without her goodness. . . . Again he got the sense that she completed him." Their world, too, is a battlefield, but with a difference:

> Good and evil lived together in the same country, spoke the same language, came together like old friends, feeling the same completion, touching hands beside the iron bedstead. . . . [Their] world lay there always, the ravaged and disputed territory between two eternities. They faced each other as it were from opposing territories, but like troops at Christmas time they fraternized.

In *Brighton Rock* the theme of companionship, which takes so many forms in the fiction of the second generation, appears as the reluctant fellowship between good and evil and is symbolized in the illegal marriage of Pinkie and Rose and the uncertain sexual union of the two virgins on their wedding night. There, touching hands beside the iron bedstead, they peer out together at the "glare and open world," the utterly alien world of Ida Arnold. "She was as far from either of them as she was from Hell—or Heaven."

In Ida's world the religious impulse is softened into a comfortable moralism, but in Pinkie's world the human impulse shrivels and looks ugly. Pinkie sees only extreme alternatives— not even sacred and profane love, for example, but the supernatural and the obscene. Normal love is reduced to the pornographic and is opposed only by fidelity to supernature; here, as in *England Made Me*, religion becomes a substitute for or even a heightened form of pornography. Pinkie quotes venomously from the cheap literature, "the kind you buy under the counter. Spicer used to get them. About girls being beaten." But in choosing the alternative, in submitting to the supernatural, Pinkie attaches himself primarily to supernatural evil. *"Credo in unum Satanum"* is the violent admission elicited on the same page by the outburst against pornography; and though he tells Rose scornfully, "Of course there's Hell," about heaven he can only say "Maybe."

As Pinkie pursues his dream of damnation, the tragic dimension of *Brighton Rock* turns into a sort of saint's life in reverse. The seven sections of the book dramatize one by one an inversion of all or most of the seven sacraments, dramatize what we might call the seven deadly sacraments: as Pinkie is confirmed in the habit of murder ("Hell lay about him in his infancy. He was ready for more deaths"), is ordained as a priest of his satanic church ("When I was a kid, I swore I'd be a priest. . . . What's wrong with being a priest? They know what's what"), performs the act of matrimony (which here is a mortal sin), and receives the vitriolic unction in the moment of his death. The entire reversal accomplished in *Brighton Rock*, haphazard though it is, manages to dignify the repellent protagonist on the principle indicated to Rose, at the very end, by the sniffling old priest: *Corruptio optimi est pessima.* The worst is the corruption of the best; only the potentially very good can become so very evil, and only the sacraments that save can so effectively become the sacraments that blast.

Despite its singularly uninviting character, accordingly, the narrow and oppressive world of Pinkie Brown is clearly to be honored—in the terms of the novel—over the spiritual bourgeoisie of Ida Arnold. Her world, for all its robust good humor, is increasingly represented as sterile, and she as a hollow, heartless menace. Ida with her big breasts and her warm enveloping body, remains childless; it is the angular, nearly sexless Rose who conceives at once, after a single sexual venture. And the final worldly victory of Ida, her destruction of Pinkie, coincides with a hidden defeat of her own world: a repudiation of it, accomplished relentlessly by the rhetoric of the book. That rhetoric aims at separating out and then destroying the moral domain, in the name of the theological; the conventional values of right and wrong are lured into prominence and then annihilated. This is done by a series of seeming contradictions that sometimes appear strained and perverse but often make arresting similes. A remark about Pinkie—"his virginity straightened in him like sex"—aptly suggests the colliding opposites that animate his experience. Oxymorons are employed in the account of Ida and her behavior, and with the intention of transforming or "transvaluating" our judgment of her. When allusion is made to Ida's "remorseless optimism" or her "merciless compassion," the aim is to negate the familiar human attributes—in this case, cheerfulness and pity—by stressing their remoteness from the religious virtues: in this case, penitent humility and mercy. The adjective, from its higher plane, denies all value to the nouns on their lower human level. And the whole process culminates in the epilogue when the priest, coughing and whistling through the grille in that unattractive and seedy way that Greene's priests almost always have, says to Rose about Pinkie—destroyed now by the ferocious pity of Ida Arnold—that no human being can conceive "the appalling strangeness of the mercy of God." ...

The motto of [the English edition of] *The Power and the Glory* is from Dryden: "Th' inclosure narrow'd; the sagacious power/Of hounds and death drew nearer every hour." The lines could apply to *Brighton Rock* and with a little stretching to *The Man Within*, as well as to most of Greene's entertainments; they summarize Greene's settled view of human experience. But they are peculiarly appropriate to *The Power and the Glory*, which is, one could say, Greene's most peculiarly appropriate novel and which comprises the adventures of a hunted man—the last Catholic priest in a totalitarian Mexican state—whom the hounds of power catch up with and to whom death does come by a firing squad. There is no complication of genres here: the novel has a single hero and a single action—and both are strikingly representative of the special kind of hero and heroic adventure that characterize the fiction of the second generation.

According to the laws of the godless Mexican state, the priest is an outlaw simply because he carries on his priestly duties; but he has also broken the laws of his Church. He is a rogue, a *pícaro*, in several kinds of ways; his contradictory character includes much of the comical unpredictability of the traditional *pícaro*; and the narrative that Greene has written about him is perhaps the most patently picaresque of any we are considering —the lively story of the rogue on his travels, or better, on his undignified flights from and toward the forces of destruction. In no other novel of our time, moreover, are the paradoxes of sainthood more expertly handled. The priest—who is a slovenly drunkard and the father of a devilish little child, who giggles a good deal and is often helplessly weak at the knees—is also a potential, perhaps finally an actual saint. He feels at the end that he has failed: "It seemed to him at that moment that it would have been quite easy to have been a saint. . . . He felt like someone who had missed happiness by seconds at an appointed place." But other evidence throughout the book suggests that all unwittingly he had kept his appointment with beatitude. *The Power and the Glory* stands beside Silone's

Bread and Wine. And the so-called "whisky priest," disguised as a layman and fumbling his way toward disaster, is, if not the twin, at least a brother of Pietro Spina, a layman (a revolutionist) disguised as a priest, and similarly the last lonely witness to truth in his own neighborhood, who is equally pursued by the forces of oppression and who is likewise the attractive, incompetent, and saintly source of damage and of death to almost everyone involved with him. These two novels give the most revealing account in second-generation fiction of the hero as outlaw, fleeing and transcending the various forms that power currently assumes.

In terms of Greene's artistic and intellectual development, however, another motto in place of Dryden's might be drawn from the book itself: when the priest, heading bumpily into the hills of Tabasco on muleback, daydreams in the imagery of a "simplified mythology"—"Michael dressed in armour slew a dragon, and the angels fell through space like comets with beautiful streaming hair because they were jealous, so one of the fathers had said, of what God intended for men—the enormous privilege of life—this life." *This life*. In this novel, by a refreshing contrast with *England Made Me* and *Brighton Rock*, the religious impulse no longer denigrates and undermines the human but serves rather to find in it or to introduce into it a kind of beauty and a kind of goodness. "I tell you that heaven is here," the priest cries out to the vacant-faced peasants gathered dumbly in a hut on the mountainside at dawn. It is, of course, characteristic of Greene that in *The Power and the Glory*, where the divine image for once irradiates and redeems the human, it is seen doing so only to the most squalid, repellent, and pain-racked of human conditions—just as omens of sanctity are seen only in an unshaven brandy-bibber. Natural beauty is not enhanced, but natural ugliness is touched by grace.

[. . .] at the centre of his own faith there always stood the convincing mystery—that we were made in God's image—God was the parent, but He was also the policeman, the criminal, the priest, the maniac, and the judge. Something resembling God dangled from the gibbet or went into odd attitudes before the bullets in a prison yard or contorted itself like a camel in the attitude of sex. He would sit in the confessional and hear the complicated dirty ingenuities which God's image had thought out: and God's image shook now, up and down on the mule's back, with the yellow teeth sticking out over the lower lip; and God's image did its despairing act of rebellion with Maria in the hut among the rats. [. . .]

Characteristically, too, it is less the splendor than the almost ridiculous *mystery* of the thing that Greene wants to dramatize. But let him do so in his own manner: in *The Power and the Glory*, a compassionate and ultimately a very charitable manner. For it is by seeking God and by finding Him in the darkness and stench of prisons, among the sinners and the rats and the rascals, that the whisky priest arrives at the richest emotion that second-generation fiction has to offer: the feeling of companionship, and especially the companionship of the commonly guilty and wretched. Arrested for carrying brandy, crowded into a pitch-black cell, crushed between unseen odorous bodies, with a woman on one side hysterically demanding to make her trivial confession and an unseen couple copulating somewhere on the floor, announcing their orgasms with whimpering cries of pleasure, the priest is touched suddenly "by an extraordinary affection. He was just one criminal among a herd of criminals: . . . he had a sense of companionship which he had never received in the old days when pious people came kissing his black cotton glove."

To appreciate this scene—it is the whole of Chapter Three of Part Two, and in my opinion the most effective scene Greene has yet written—we should locate it in the structure of the novel. It begins a few pages beyond the mathematical center of the book; but it constitutes the center as well of an action that has its clear beginning and its firmly established end. The basic unit in the structure of *The Power and the Glory* is the encounter: as it is in so many other novels of the second generation with their picaresque tendency and their vision of man as an outlaw wandering or hastening through an anarchic and hostile world. In *The Power and the Glory*, as in *Bread and Wine*, the plot is episodic and consists of a succession of en-

counters between the harried protagonist and a number of un-
related persons—while within that succession, we observe a
pattern of three dominant and crucially meaningful encounters.

We first see the priest when, in disguise, he sips brandy in
the office of Mr. Tench, the morose expatriate dentist. We
follow him, episode by episode, as he is hidden and given food
by Coral, the precocious daughter of an agent for a banana
company, Captain Fellows, and his miserable death-haunted
wife; as he arrives in the village which is the home of the
woman, Maria, by whom he has had the child Brigida; as he
travels onward in the company of a mestizo, the yellow-toothed
ignoble Judas who will betray him to the police; as he is arrested
and released and fights his way over the mountains to freedom
in a neighboring state and the comfortable home of Mr. Lehr
and his sister, German-Americans from Pittsburgh in charge of
a mining operation; as he is enticed back across the border of
Tabasco to attend the death of James Calver, an American murderer who has been fatally wounded by the police; is arrested
again by the police lieutenant, taken back to the capital city,
and executed. Mr. Tench, Coral, Maria, the Lehrs, Calver: these
are all strangers to each other. The episodes with each of them
thicken and expand the novelistic design (Coral, for instance,
is the priest's good spiritual daughter while Brigida is his evil
actual daughter). But the design itself is created by the three
encounters between the priest and the lieutenant.

These occur at carefully spaced intervals, about one-third and
two-thirds through the book, and then at length in the climax.
The first time, the lieutenant—whose whole energy and authority are directed exclusively to capturing this last remaining
agent of the Church—sees the priest and interrogates him; but
he neither recognizes nor arrests him. The second time, the
priest is arrested, but he is not recognized: the charge is carrying liquor. The third time, recognition is complete and the
arrest final. But these encounters are mere indicators of a carefully constructed plot; the action is something different and
more telling, and we are made conscious of it from the outset

when—in separate, successive views of them—paradoxical resemblances are registered about the two men. The priest disappears wearily into the interior, giving up a chance to escape in order to minister to a sick peasant woman and feeling "like the King of a West African tribe, the slave of his people, who may not even lie down in case the winds should fail." On the next page, the lieutenant marches by with a ragged squad of police, looking as though "He might have been chained to them unwillingly: perhaps the scar on his jaw was the relic of an escape." Later, as he walks home alone, dreaming of a new world of justice and well-being for the children of Tabasco, "There was something of a priest in his intent observant walk— a theologian going back over the errors of the past to destroy them again." The exhausted and sometimes drunken soldier of God, the chaste and fiercely dedicated priest of the godless society: each one enslaved to his mission, doomed to his role and its outcome: these are the beings, the systole and diastole, between whom the force of the novel is generated.

Readers of Dostoevski or of the Book of Revelation will easily identify them. They are the "hot" and the "cold" bespoken by the angel in lines quoted twice in *The Possessed*: "These things saith the Amen . . . I know thy works, that thou art neither cold nor hot: I would thou wert cold or hot. So then, because thou art lukewarm, and neither cold nor hot, I will spue thee out of my mouth" (Revelation III, 14-16). The lieutenant has had the chilling vision of absurdity: "He was a mystic, too, and what he had experienced was vacancy—a complete certainty in the existence of a dying, cooling world, of human beings who had evolved from animals for no purpose at all. [. . .] he believed against the evidence of his senses in the cold empty ether spaces." With a devotion only to the reality of the here and now, he is a rebel against all the misery and injustice and unhappiness he associates with the rule of a greedy Church and its insistence on the unimportance of the human lot in this world. He watches the children in the street, his love for them hidden beneath his hatred of the Church and its priests: "He would eliminate from their childhood everything which had made him miserable, all that was poor, superstitious, and corrupt."

The lieutenant, in a word, is *l'homme révolté* of Albert Camus, seen—with respect—in the unorthodox religious perspective of Graham Greene. François Mauriac was right, in his preface to the French edition of *The Power and the Glory*, to call the novel an answer in narrative terms to the widespread European sense of absurdity—to that sense as somehow the one necessary prerequisite to the struggle for social justice. *The Power and the Glory* is not perhaps *the* answer; but it does contain, among other things, a potent allegory of one of the major intellectual debates of our time. Greene, too, it should be said, gives fairer and more substantial play to what he regards as the opposition—embodied in the lieutenant—than Camus gives to *his* opponent, the crudely drawn cleric Paneloux in *The Plague*. Camus contrasts Paneloux, and his helpless appeal to divine irrationality, with the rational and dignified Rieux and Tarrou; while Greene joins the upright police officer in a contest with the wavering and incompetent whisky priest. Yet the nameless priest, consecrating moistly amidst the unspeakable heat and the detonating beetles of Tabasco, sweating his way toward a sort of befuddled glory, is of course the representative of the "hot," and the lieutenant's proper adversary.

These two are the persons of stature in the universe of *The Power and the Glory*, and eventually they acknowledge each other. "You're a good man," the priest says in astonishment when, at the moment of his release from prison, the lieutenant gives him five pesos. And: "You aren't a bad fellow," the lieutenant concedes grudgingly during the long conversations after the final arrest. Most of the other characters, those whom Greene calls "the bystanders," are the lukewarm, and their artistic purpose is, by a variety of contrasts, to illuminate the nature of the hunt. A good many of the more "regular" members of the Church, in fact, both in the past and now in the pleasant safety of another state, appear as lukewarm; *The Power and the Glory* may be a religious novel, but it is decidedly not an ecclesiastical one. The priest himself had been lukewarm in the old days, going smugly on his parochial rounds and attending the meetings of the guilds. It is only in his moment of degradation, arrested not even for being the last priest with the courage to remain in Tabasco but only as a common citizen carrying contraband, that the priest reveals the "hot," the heroic side. He does so unconsciously, out of humility and a conviction of his own unworthiness and an irrepressible sense of humor. We return to the prison scene mentioned above: it occurs just before the second of the three major encounters.

The whole of it should be studied, from the entrance into the cell to the departure next morning and the sudden sense of companionship even with the lieutenant. But perhaps the following fragments can suggest the remarkable interplay—not, in this case, the remote opposition—of sacred and obscene love, of beauty and extreme ugliness, of comedy and deadly peril: all of which gives the scene a rich multiplicity of action beyond anything Greene had previously achieved. Just as the key moment in *Bread and Wine* occurs in the darkness of a squalid hut, so here the "epiphany" takes place in the blackness and stench of a prison.

Among the furtive movements came again the muffled painless cries. He realized with horror that pleasure was going on even in this crowded darkness. Again he put out his foot and began to edge his way inch by inch away from the grille. [. . .]

"They'll shoot you, father," the woman's voice said.
"Yes."
"Are you afraid?"
"Yes. Of course."
A new voice spoke, in the corner from which the sounds of pleasure had come. It said roughly and obstinately: "A man isn't afraid of a thing like that."
"No?" the priest said.
"A bit of pain. What do you expect? It has to come."
"All the same," the priest said, "I *am* afraid."
"Toothache is worse."
"We can't all be brave men."

The voice said with contempt: "You believers are all the same. Christianity makes you cowards."

"Yes. Perhaps you are right. You see I am a bad priest and a bad man. To die in a state of mortal sin"—he gave an uneasy chuckle—"it makes you think." [. . .]

A long train of thought began, which led him to announce after a while: "They are offering a reward for me. Five hundred, six hundred pesos, I'm not sure." Then he was silent again. He couldn't urge any man to inform against him—that would be tempting him to sin—but at the same time if there was an informer here, there was no reason why the wretched creature should be bilked of his reward. To commit so ugly a sin—it must count as murder—and to have no compensation in this world . . . He thought simply: it wouldn't be fair.

"Nobody here," a voice said, "wants their blood money."

Again he was touched by an extraordinary affection. He was just one criminal among a herd of criminals . . . he had a sense of companionship which he had never received in the old days when pious people came kissing his black cotton glove.

The pious woman's voice leapt hysterically out at him: "It is so stupid to tell them that. You don't know the sort of wretches who are here, father. Thieves, murderers . . ."

"Well," an angry voice said, "why are you here?"

"I had good books in my house," she announced, with unbearable pride. He had done nothing to shake her complacency. He said: "They are everywhere. It's no different here."

"Good books?"

He giggled. "No, no. Thieves, murderers . . . Oh, well, my child, if you had more experience, you would know there are worse things to be." [. . .]

[*The reader is here referred to an extended passage from the text of the novel—page 176, line 2 ("Somewhere against the far wall . . .") to page 177, line 12 (" '. . . to hear I'm alive.' ").*]

Pinkie Brown and Major Scobie, the protagonists of *Brighton Rock* and *The Heart of the Matter*, are never seen to smile, much less to laugh; the former is in a constant state of fury, the latter of apprehension. It is the laughter, almost more than anything else, that distinguishes *The Power and the Glory*:

laughter based on the recognition of God's image in man, evoked by the preposterous incongruity of it and yet leading naturally to a warmth of fellow-feeling. Here again, a similarity may be noted with the comedy and the companionship of *Bread and Wine*; and perhaps Silone was not wrong, after all, to turn the ridiculous Sciatàp of that novel into the treacherous figure of *The Seed beneath the Snow*. In this particular comic vision, even the traitors—even the Judases—have a clownish aspect. Contemplating the mestizo (in another passage) and recognizing him as a Judas, Greene's priest remembers a Holy Week carnival where a stuffed Judas was hanged from the belfry and pelted with bits of tin: "it seemed to him a good thing that the world's traitor should be made a figure of fun. It was too easy otherwise to idealize him as a man who fought with God— a Prometheus, a noble victim in a hopeless war" (the very archetype, in short, of Camus's rebel). But the force of the comic consciousness in *The Power and the Glory* is indicated, properly enough, at the end, when the lieutenant, having completed his mission and arranged for the priest's execution, sits down at his desk and falls asleep. "He couldn't remember afterwards anything of his dreams except laughter, laughter all the time, and a long passage in which he could find no door." It is the lieutenant, Greene suggests, who is the trapped man, the prisoner; and the laughter he hears is like that laughter recorded by Dante on the upper slopes of purgatory, the chorus celebrating the release of a captive human soul from punishment and its entrance into paradise.

The priest himself hears none of that laughter and goes to his death persuaded of practical and spiritual failure. "I don't know a thing about the mercy of God," he tells the lieutenant, in the phrase that also rounds out *Brighton Rock* and *The Heart of the Matter*; ". . . But I do know this—that if there's ever been a single man in this state damned, then I'll be damned too." [. . .] "I wouldn't want it to be any different." It never occurs to the priest that if he should so far honor the mestizo as to call him a Judas, he might himself appear as a version of the man Judas betrayed. The book has been hinting as much all along, in the pattern and style of the priest's adventures. The relationship is far more pressing and elaborate here than in *Brighton Rock* or *The Heart of the Matter*, where the vigor of supernature is hardly sweetened by the figure of intermediary and reconciler. The priest, accordingly, preaches to the poor and the meek and downtrodden across the hilly countryside; is tempted in the wilderness; is betrayed, tried, and executed. Toward the end, he too is juxtaposed with a common criminal—the Yankee killer whose name, James Calver, echoes two syllables of the mount on which Christ was crucified, and opposite whose picture in the prison office there is a picture of the priest, grinning within the halo someone had inked around the face for identification. There is even a kind of resurrection in the little epilogue —about which one has mixed feelings—when a new, frightened priest arrives in town and is greeted with reverence by the boy Juan, who, prior to the martyrdom, had been a disciple of the lieutenant. That epilogue, offering presumably the first of the priest's miracles after death, insists perhaps too much. But if the priest is associated not only with Christ but with non-Christian divinities—the god-king of an African tribe, and the surrogate for the god, the bull that was slaughtered in the early Greek ritual of sacrifice and rebirth ("Then there was a single shot . . . the bull was dead")—the entire pattern is nevertheless artistically redeemed by a full awareness of the grotesque disproportion between the model and its re-enactment. "The priest giggled: he couldn't stop himself. He said: 'I don't think martyrs are like this.'" It is the giggle that saves both the priest and the novel Greene has written about him. For it is when he laughs that we know this slovenly rogue, this unshaven *pícaro*, to be also a saint; and we know that here for once—as in only one or two other novels—the paradoxes have held firm and the immense delicate balance has been maintained.

The Heart of the Matter is the most traditional of Greene's novels, in both content and construction. As such, it is obviously less representative than *The Power and the Glory*; and as such, it has a special appeal for those who mean by the word *novel* the kind of work that was typical in the nineteenth century. We note a major paradox about second-generation writers: they are developing a rather new sort of fiction—the novel as an act of inquiry or of rebellion or of expiation, rather than as a direct and unprejudiced impression of life; but at the same time, most of them turn for support not to the experimental achievements of the first generation but to the literary forms of the nineteenth century.

The paradox is further strained in the case of *The Heart of the Matter*. Here, for example, is the careful delineation, not altogether unworthy of Trollope, of various discordant elements in a multicolored society, the society of the coastal city in West Africa that Greene had known on his journey in 1935 and again as a government official during the war in 1942-43, the date of the novel's action. In *The Heart of the Matter* there is no savage eruption out of animal holes into the glare and open world that characterized *Brighton Rock*, and none of the rhythmic peregrinations through anarchy of *The Power and the Glory*. The incidents take place very much *within* the society of the book and involve, not proscribed outlaws, but persons of significance and authority whose intimate knowledge of each other provides much of the hero's tragic dilemma. Here too there is a narrative pace, leisurely but never slack, reminiscent of Greene's distant relation, Robert Louis Stevenson. Greene may not be a master of all the elements of fiction, but that he is a master of narrative can be doubted only by those too little interested in storytelling to be capable of discrimination; *The Heart of the Matter* is very handsomely told. And here too is an array of characters in the old tradition—and including one especially, the merchant Yusef, whose fat and candid dishonesty would have pleased Dickens and, even more, Wilkie Collins. Here, in short, is a traditional, almost a conventional *novel* that is yet a novel by Graham Greene, and something the nineteenth century could scarcely have imagined. For what the action serves to expose is not the habits of a society or the nature of the human heart (no one, says Father Rank in the epilogue, knows "what goes on in a single human heart"), but, going beyond all that, the absolute mystery of the individual destiny.

"Why, why did he have to make such a mess of things?" This is the hopeless and embittered question raised on the last page by Major Scobie's wife, Louise: not "Why did he?" but "Why did he *have to*?" That Scobie, the late Assistant Commissioner of Police, had made an appalling mess of things cannot be denied. *The Heart of the Matter* is the progressive account of it, from the first moment when he is passed over for promotion, through the disappointment of his restless, vaguely artistic wife —a disappointment so great that Scobie makes a dubious if not illegal transaction with the diamond-smuggler Yusef to get enough money to send her on a trip to South Africa; through the adulterous affair with the schoolgirlish widow Helen Rolt, on which he embarks during his wife's absence; through the now rapid deterioration of his public and private life; through the agony—for a Catholic of his temperament—of receiving the sacrament in a condition of mortal sin; to the still graver sin of despair and suicide by which Scobie ends his career. The mess is so great and Scobie's talent at every turn for making bad matters worse is so remarkable that the novel has occasionally been dismissed as implausible. George Orwell once wrote to the effect that no one who could get into such deep trouble so quickly could ever have had the honorable career Scobie is alleged to have had in the first place. In the sane and skeptical humanism of Orwell, the contention is reasonable, but it is a point made outside the world of the book; within that world, the issue of plausibility does not arise.

As a matter of fact, the novel offers a definite though still typically mysterious answer to Louise Scobie's question. It would not have satisfied Orwell, for it is not drawn, finally, from psychology: that, Greene thinks, is not where the real mystery lies. But, before we approach the real mystery, it should be said that *The Heart of the Matter* does also offer clues for a purely psychological explanation of Scobie and his conduct. He has the ingredients of a genuine tragic hero. He is presented as a good man, rather better than most, with an inviolable sense of justice irritating to some of his colleagues, "You're a terrible fellow, Scobie," the commissioner tells him affectionately. "Scobie the Just." He is an able man and within limits a forceful one; and he is a strong Catholic with that special religious intensity that only Greene's Catholics (not, that is, the Catholics one thought one knew) betray. And he has a fatal flaw: but it is not arrogance or any normal form of pride; Scobie calls down ruin on himself, plainly and articulately, but not through hubris. His flaw is an excess of the quality Greene calls pity—an inability to watch disappointment or suffering in others—with this portion perhaps of pride (in Greene's view), that he feels it peculiarly incumbent upon himself to relieve the pain. In *The Ministry of Fear*, the entertaining trial run for *The Heart of the Matter*, Arthur Rowe's troubles begin when he commits a mercy killing—or, to stick to Greene's verbal distinctions, a "pity-killing"—to end the intolerable physical suffering of his wife. Scobie kills no one, though he feels himself implicated in several deaths; like some other heroes of second-generation fiction, it is his misfortune to harm most of those he longs to help or even to save.

Scobie's troubles begin with his attempt to alleviate the painful disappointment of his wife. His feeling of guilt about her is due partly to his failure to be promoted; but it is rooted more deeply in another failure, an inability any longer to love his wife; and it goes back, too, to the moment when Scobie was unable to be present at the death of his child. He is a man clearly given to self-accusation, and the pattern of it thickens as the story moves forward. It might well be that the suicide, a third of the way through, of Dick Pemberton—an assistant district commissioner at Bamba who hangs himself and whose mode of death affects Scobie enormously—may have released in Scobie a congenital self-destructive impulse. Pemberton's name, Dicky, with which he signed the suicide note, and the nickname that Louise has coyly pinned on her husband—Ticki (his real name is Henry)—blur in Scobie's mind while he lies ill with fever after the Pemberton affair; and from then on the pace of his decline grows more rapid. Scobie, in summary,

is an affecting human being, whose sorry career is all too understandable. He is burdened by his own habit of pity for others.
But we can ally ourselves with him in that other kind of pity
that Aristotle called one of the two emotions properly evoked
by tragedy. Still, it is the second of the emotions named by
Aristotle—the emotion of tragic terror—that is the more deeply
aroused in us by this novel, according to Greene's intention.
Tragic pity (to borrow Joyce's definitions of these ancient
terms) associates us with the human sufferer during his grave
and terrible experience. Tragic terror springs rather from our
stimulated awareness of the secret cause of the suffering; and
in *The Heart of the Matter*, as traditionally, that secret cause
is the action of God.

The "heart of the matter," as a phrase, occurs after the opening of the novel's second part when Scobie, momentarily alone
and looking up at the stars, wonders whether "If one knew . . .
would one have to feel pity even for the planets? if one reached
what they called the heart of the matter?" Less than ten
minutes later, unknowingly—though he does suddenly feel
cold and strange—Scobie reaches the heart of the matter and
gives up the peace of his own soul. Coming in from his reverie,
into the resthouse where they have brought the stretcher-cases
from a torpedoed ship, Scobie is asked to stand watch over two
victims who lie unconscious on two beds divided by a screen.
One is a six-year-old girl. Looking at her, Scobie thinks again
of his own dead daughter, and he begins to pray. "Father . . .
give her peace. Take away my peace for ever, but give her
peace." We are to understand, I believe, that God does exactly
that. He gives the child the peace of death and a release from
suffering, and Scobie's peace is taken away for the remainder
of his earthly career. This is the book's major turning point,
when pity deepens into terror. And the human agent through
whom God acts is the patient on the other side of the screen,
"the young woman lying unconscious on her back, still grasping
the stamp album." It is Helen Rolt, whom pity and loneliness
will drive Scobie to make love to, in an affair that so torments

Scobie's Catholic conscience that only an overdose of tablets can rescue him. . . .

Greek classical tragedy customarily ended by a choral acknowledgment of the unsolvable mystery and the purgatorial terror. Father Rank performs a similar function in *The Heart of the Matter*, in the epilogue that Greene has characteristically added to ensure our befuddlement over the exact meaning of the events. "For goodness' sake, Mrs. Scobie, don't imagine you—or I—know a thing about God's mercy. . . . The Church knows all the rules. But it doesn't know what goes on in a single human heart." Again, the institutionalized Church is opposed in the name of the religious mystery; and again, the sheer incomprehensibility of God's mercy and grace is the aspect insisted upon. Again, too, the hero, moving doggedly toward disaster, is oddly associated with the figure of Christ: in the manner of *Brighton Rock* rather than *The Power and the Glory*, for we are once more in a universe without intermediaries. The role of Judas is played out by the English government spy Wilson, who covets Scobie's wife as well as his reputation for integrity; and Scobie tries desperately to condone his act of despair by seeing in it an imitation of Christ: "Christ had not been murdered: Christ had killed himself: he had hung himself on the Cross as surely as Pemberton from the picture rail"—a notion that turns up again after the suicide in *The Living Room*. All these items provide the reader, as planned, with a full measure of uncertainty about Scobie's conduct in this world and his chances in the next. It is suggested in the last lines that Scobie may really have loved God; and it is suggested that God may be the only being he did love. The night before he encounters the dying child and Helen Rolt, we hear Scobie murmuring the incomplete phrase as he falls asleep, "O God, bless—," and later, another incomplete phrase as he falls senseless and dying: "Dear God, I love . . ." Not even the reader, who knows more about Scobie than anyone else, can be sure of the objects of those verbs.

Psychology thus yields to a dark theology, the pity to the

terror, the human sufferer to the secret cause. All we are meant to know is that we know nothing; that is the answer to Louise's question. Pinkie Brown *almost* certainly is damned, and he was without any doubt a vicious and wicked young man. The Mexican priest is almost certainly saved, and he was one of the most curiously sympathetic figures in modern fiction. We conclude, about Henry Scobie, in a purging sense of the unguessable nature of human conduct and divine intervention. Insofar as they do constitute a trilogy, Greene's three novels reverse the direction of the greatest religious trilogy, *The Divine Comedy*. Dante's poem moves from ignorance to knowledge, from discord to harmony, from unspeakable darkness to overwhelming light. Greene's "trilogy" moves stealthily deeper into the darkness, moves through the annihilation of our confidence in human knowledge to an awareness of impenetrable mystery, moves from the deceptive light to the queerly nourishing obscurity. All the truth of things, for Greene, lies hidden in the darkness: whether of slum-ridden Brighton, of a squalid prison cell, or of a West African night of wonder and despair. Scarcely less mysterious is Greene's achievement of making visible in that darkness, and exactly by means of it, the unforgettable dramas of extraordinarily living human beings.

LAURENCE LERNER

Laurence Lerner has written on Shakespearean drama as well as
modern fiction. Among his publications are *George Eliot and Her
Readers*, *Thomas Hardy and His Readers*, and *Truthtellers: Jane
Austen, George Eliot, D. H. Lawrence*. Mr. Lerner is also the author
of two volumes of poetry, *Domestic Interiors* and *The Directions
of Memory*.

GRAHAM GREENE

There is a scene in *The Quiet American* in which Fowler,
the narrator, goes on a bombing raid with a French pilot.
Their target is a Vietnamese village. After fourteen dives, each
one terrifying but "free from the discomfort of personal
thought," they leave the village burning, destroy a small sampan
on the river, then turn for home, "adding their little quota to the
world's dead":

I put on my earphones for Captain Trouin to speak to me. He said,
"We will make a little detour. The sunset is wonderful on the
calcaire. You must not miss it," he added kindly, like a host who
is showing the beauty of his estate, and for a hundred miles we
trailed the sunset over the Baie d'Along. The helmeted Martian
face looked wistfully out, down the golden groves, among the great
humps and arches of porous stone, and the wound of murder ceased
to bleed.

I happened to hear Mr. Greene read this episode on the radio,
before the book was published. I can still hear his voice grating
on "the wound of murder ceased to bleed." On paper, the
paragraph is coolly ironic: the incongruity between the captain's
aesthetic sensibility and his indifference to war, between his

---

This essay appeared in the British *Critical Quarterly* V (1963). ©
Laurence Lerner 1963.

civilized behaviour (skillful craftsman, gracious host) and the barbarity of what he is doing, is given without comment— or rather with the one implied comment that the world which crowns a raid with such glory cares only for beauty, not for the suffering. But under this lies a deeper implication, that of anger that the world should be like that. This is implied only remotely, perhaps only by the context of the whole book; but it was this anger, compassionate, moving, and noble, that I heard in Mr. Greene's snarling voice.

That was the moment when I decided that Mr. Greene was not merely a skillful craftsman, but a writer with a vision. To say this is to suggest that I needed convincing; and I have begun with this testimony because I think many of his readers need convincing, including those who most admire his superb technique. It's not just that such great competence makes them suspicious (though I think it often does); it's also because of the nature of the technique itself. Mr. Greene does not quite belong in the central tradition of the English novel, that of realism and individual character-drawing. His characters tend to simplify into Humours; his plots (even outside the enter-tainments) are constantly tugged in the direction of thrillers. He has all the realistic surface detail of an ordinary novelist, but the techniques of farce and melodrama lurk not far below the surface. And to most readers these techniques suggest faking —skillful faking, but faking all the same. We are too used to the novel of individual, unbiased characterization not to assume it as a norm.

Mr. Greene has written a fascinating essay on *The Young Dickens*. "It is a mistake," he says, "to think of *Oliver Twist* as a realistic story: . . . we no more believe in the temporal existence of Fagin or Bill Sikes than we believe in the existence of that Giant whom Jack slew as he bellowed his Fee Fi Fo Fum." He sees the world of *Oliver Twist* as a Manichean world, where only Fagin, Monks, and Sikes are real: "we can believe in evil-doing, but goodness wilts into philosophy, kindness, and those strange vague sicknesses into which Dicken's young women so frequently fall." This is to make it sound like a novel by

Graham Greene—which, in parts, it almost is. Certainly this essay offers the best critical account of Mr. Greene's novels that I know: it is a mistake to think of *Brighton Rock* as a realistic story. Sean O'Faolain speaks of his novels as miracle plays, but the parallel with Dickens seems to me even more illuminating: if these are miracle plays they are disguised as novels, and convincingly. Dickens, too, does not quite belong in the central tradition of the English novel. Mr. Greene's essay concludes:

Is it too fantastic to imagine that in this novel, as in many of his later books, creeps in, unrecognized by the author, the eternal and alluring taint of the Manichee, with its simple and terrible explanation of our plight, how the world was made by Satan and not by God, lulling us with the music of despair?

In the case of Mr. Greene, since he is so much more sophisticated, the taint is recognized by the author—even with a kind of delight.

The technique of Mr. Greene's novels fits their philosophy, since both are (one presumes) the result of an obsession. There is clearly a link between individual characterization and the humanist tradition: before we promoted the individual to be the touchstone of our moral values, we did not make him the unit of literary creation either. Graham Greene rejects both—though one must add that the rejection is never simple, nor perhaps, as we shall see, total. Sean O'Faolain is wrong when he writes: "Greene, Mauriac, and Bernanos return us to the medieval world as if the great humanist tradition had never happened." Greene returns us there knowing quite well that it did happen.

Medieval man divided the next world into three—Heaven, Hell, and Purgatory. If we had asked him which of the three most resembled this world, he would surely have answered Purgatory. Like Purgatory, this world is temporary, a place of suffering and of preparation. But modern man will give a different answer: we no longer—and this includes Christians as well as atheists—think of this world merely as preparation, but as where we belong. Those who believe this world as Heaven are the humanists. Of course to believe that simply in 1963 would demand an impossible naïveté, but humanism must at least claim that the only heaven we can have (will have, if it's optimistic) is down here, and that it must be built of human values: that the materials for it are present, however damaged, however rudimentary, in the heart of man. But the humanist who despairs, who finds that the heart of man is a heart of darkness, may come to believe that the world is Hell: not simply a place of trial, but a place of intrinsic evil. Is not that what Mr. Greene believes?

> Down a slope churned up with the hoofs of mules and ragged with tree-roots there was the river—not more than two feet deep, littered with empty cans and broken bottles. Under a notice which hung on a tree reading: "It is forbidden to deposit rubbish . . ." all the refuse of the village was collected and slid gradually down into the river. When the rains came it would be washed away. He put his foot among the old tins and the rotting vegetables and reached for his case. [. . .] (*The Power and the Glory*)

That is a landscape of Hell—a parody of some innocent rural scene, a fit setting for the black passions of the story. It is not even a landscape of the pathetic fallacy, for everything decaying and filthy in it is man-made, the product of the corrupt and filthy humans who enact the story. The rubbish, we notice, has accumulated under a notice reading "It is forbidden to deposit rubbish." Why this cheap irony, played on the book by the author, or on mankind by some ironic spirit? It reads like Hardy: does Mr. Greene too believe in the Spirit Ironic, perversely enjoying its jests at our expense?

Graham Greene, as everyone knows, is a Roman Catholic (it's the one thing, in fact, that one can be sure *everyone* will know). Can he believe that the Christian God is ironic and perverse, and deliberately made the world into Hell? It seems that he does believe it, and it may not be such a crazy belief either.

Why, he wondered, swerving the car to avoid a dead pye-dog, do I love this place so much? Is it because here human nature hasn't had time to disguise itself? Nobody here could ever talk about a heaven on earth. Heaven remained rigidly in its proper place on the other side of death, and on this side flourished the injustices, the cruelties, the meanness that elsewhere people so cleverly hushed up. Here you could love human beings nearly as God loved them, knowing the worst: you didn't love a pose, a pretty dress, a sentiment artfully assumed. (*The Heart of the Matter*)

"This place" is West Africa, but it could be the world: for the West Africa where Scobie lives is simply a geographically apt location for Greeneland. I expect Mr. Greene would agree that people aren't wickeder there than elsewhere, it's simply that their wickedness is more apparent to the European eye—not only the eye of the *colon*, but also that of the just policeman, Scobie. Scobie is close to Mr. Greene's heart because he loves men as they are: anyone can love a pose or a pretty dress. To love knowing the worst is to make your love a shadow of that one perfect act of love, the love of Christ for mankind: "it needed a God to die for the half-hearted and the corrupt."

How proper then, is it not, for Mr. Greene to be so fascinated by dustheaps, filth, rotten teeth, pimples, obesity, lust, leprosy; and by moral filth—egoism, malice, and (worst and most fascinating of sins) betrayal. He depicts the world as Hell, since that is the first step of the argument to faith: if there is Hell, must there not be Heaven? Mr. Greene, who knows himself better than most novelists, always turns out to have anticipated one's best points about him; and he says just this in the remarkable opening pages of *The Lawless Roads*. It has been a common argument in our time, this path from humanism through disillusion to belief.

I will not try to trace the long history of this argument, literary and theological; but here is another specimen of it:

In the middle nineteenth century, an age of bustle, programmes, platforms, scientific progress, humanitarianism and revolutions which improved nothing, an age of progressive degradation, Baudelaire perceived that what really matters is Sin and Redemption. . . . The possibility of damnation is so immense a relief in a world of electoral reform, plebiscites, sex reform and dress reform, that damnation itself is an immediate form of salvation—of salvation from the ennui of modern life, because it at last gives some significance to living. (T. S. Eliot: *Baudelaire*)

How true this is of Baudelaire is arguable: I do not find in the *Fleurs du Mal* much sign of *relief* at the possibility of damnation, but a mixture of elegant gloating and a compassion that is more human than religious. I do not want to step too far outside the bounds of literary criticism, but I will at least suggest that such glib welcoming of the idea of sin is quite as facile as the bustle and humanitarianism it is meant to replace. True or untrue of Baudelaire, the opinion is surely true of Mr. Eliot, as it is of Graham Greene: true as a summary of their views, that is: the glib tone of Mr. Eliot's prose is, happily, unjust both to his own poetry and Mr. Greene's best novels. But Mr. Greene's, like Mr. Eliot's, is a religious vision without religious joy.

The pattern of characterization in a Greene novel follows from this view of the world. Without too much distortion, we can divide most of his characters into four: the pious, the sinners, the innocent, and the humanists. Mr. Greene detests piety more than anything: he once called it "that morbid growth of religion." His pious characters—his "smug, complacent, successful" characters—are surely the most unsympathetic of all: Aunt Helen in *The Living Room*, Milly in *Our Man in Havana*, Father Thomas and Rycker in *A Burnt-Out Case*, and (for liberalism has its piety as much as religion) Pyle, the quiet American. The sinners, on the other hand, are those he most likes: there is great variety among them, but all have certain features in common, the necessary nature of a Greene hero: they have imagination, they make mistakes, they are tempted by pity, they suffer. Their essentials can be seen simplified, even parodied, in the heroes of the thrillers—Dr. Czinner in *Stamboul Train*, D. in *The Confidential Agent*, Arthur Rowe in *The Ministry of Fear*—for these books not only popularize the material of the central novels, they make it explicit. They are Mr. Greene's literary criticism—of his own work. In the novels proper, these essentials are given flesh, most of all perhaps in the whisky priest of *The Power and the Glory* and Scobie of *The Heart of the Matter*, perhaps his two finest creations. The priest is his sad, grim portrayal of a saint, crudely but effectively contrasted with the tuppence coloured saint's life that is being read to the two pious little girls. Scobie I want to discuss in more detail.

Scobie, it will be remembered, finds himself with a wife and a mistress, both of whom he pities; that he loves the mistress and not the wife is, for once, not important: for compassion means more to Scobie than sexual love. It is compassion that prevents him doing what he knows is right. Since he is a Catholic, what is right is what God commands—to leave his mistress, to save his soul. But Helen Rolt, widow at nineteen, survivor of a torpedoed ship, has nothing but him. Their whole relationship seems to be contained in his first glimpse of her, carried on a stretcher: "her arms as thin as a child's lay outside the blanket, and her fingers clasped a book firmly." The book is a stamp album: "when this damned war started," says the officer, "she must have been still at school."

Helen recovers, but only to depend helplessly on Scobie. Their love, when they become aware of it, "proved to have been the camouflage of an enemy who works in terms of friendship, trust and pity." Scobie does not need to be told by his confessor that he must break with her: he wants to but can't. When they quarrel he longs to take the quarrel at its word:

An awful weariness touched him, and he thought: I will go home: I won't creep by to her tonight: her last words had been "don't come back." Couldn't one, for once, take somebody at their word? . . . He thought: I'd go back and go to bed, in the morning I'd write to Louise and in the evening go to Confession: the day after that God would return to me in a priest's hands: life would be simple again. He would be at peace sitting under the handcuffs in the office. Virtue, the good life, tempted him in the dark like a sin.

But he has to resist, because he cannot sacrifice Helen. She has no one else, not even God, in whom she doesn't believe. He ought of course to leave her to the wisdom and mercy of God, but he doesn't trust God. There is an extraordinary inner dialogue between God and Scobie which shows us what a superb casuist Mr. Greene would have made.

I have been faithful to you for two thousand years. All you have to do now is ring a bell, go into a box, confess . . . the repentance is already there, straining at your heart. It's not repentance you lack, just a few simple actions: to go up to the Nissen hut and say goodbye. Or if you must, continue rejecting me but without lies any more. Go to your house and say goodbye to your wife and live with your mistress. If you live you will come back to me sooner or later. One of them will suffer, but can't you trust me to see that the suffering isn't too great?

The voice was silent in the cave and his own voice replied, hopelessly: No, I don't trust you. I love you, but I've never trusted you. If you made me, you made this feeling of responsibility that I've always carried about like a sack of bricks. I'm not a policeman for nothing—responsible for order, for seeing justice is done. There was no other profession for a man of my kind. I can't shift my responsibility to you. If I could, I would be someone else. I can't make one of them suffer so as to save myself. I'm responsible and I'll see it through the only way I can.

The Greene hero never finds it easy to trust; for mistrust implies imagination. And trust, perhaps, implies selfishness, a willingness to leave to others what you should worry about yourself. Scobie mistrusts God because he cannot shrug off his part in Helen's happiness: the selfish action and the right action would, in his case, be the same, and he has to do the wrong compassionate action, even if it means giving up salvation. "I can't make one of them suffer so as to save myself." In fact, Scobie fails: he doesn't keep the knowledge from his absent wife, so he doesn't manage to spare her suffering, and Helen loses him. I can't make up my mind whether Mr. Greene wants us to believe that God, if he had been trusted, would have looked after them any better. We can't, in Greeneland, assume that he would have.

Nor, of course, can we assume that Scobie did give up his salvation. If Mr. Greene could be his judge, Scobie would certainly be saved; and though he can't be, he reminds us that no one else can be either, not even the church.

Pity is the terrible temptation of the Greene hero—"that sense of pity which is so much more promiscuous than lust." It is pity which undoes Querry in *A Burnt-Out Case*. Querry is not religious: so what he has to give up is not his salvation but his peace of mind, his success in escaping from the world's pestering. Nor is Querry naturally unselfish: he would not have helped Marie Rycker, and compromised himself, if he'd seen where it would lead to. The world of *A Burnt-Out Case* is radically ironic in a way that that of *The Heart of the Matter* isn't. Querry had behaved badly to women all his life and got away with it: now he behaves well and it ruins his life. (It is like the irony of the true and false murder in *The Ministry of Fear*: Mr. Greene often seems to play with a point in one of the entertainments before using it seriously in a novel.) By "behaves well" I don't, of course, mean that he doesn't seduce her: in his "burnt-out" state he is not even tempted by that. But the selfish act would have been the prudent one—to leave her alone, to ignore her plea for a lift to town, her need to be treated maturely by having her immaturity recognized.

Marie Rycker is one of Mr. Greene's innocents: one can usually recognize these by the amount of harm they do. Often they are minor figures, like young Pemberton, the District Commissioner in *The Heart of the Matter*, who hangs himself, leaving a note to his father:

Dear Dad,—Forgive all this trouble. There doesn't seem anything else to do. It's a pity I'm not in the army because then I might be killed. . . . It's a rotten business for you, but it can't be helped. Your loving son. The signature was "Dicky." It was like a letter from school excusing a bad report.

Mr. Greene despises Pemberton. "If you or I did it," says Scobie, "it would be despair." But Pemberton, who has not grown up, is not yet capable—one is tempted to say not yet worthy—of damnation. Pemberton harms only himself (unless we blame Father Clay's hysterical self-reproaches on his action), but this action is, for Mr. Greene, the type of those that do the greatest harm. This is the main theme of *The Quiet American*.

Two Greene types meet in Pyle, the pious and the innocent. He is a starry-eyed college boy from Boston who blunders into an international situation, eating Vit-health sandwich spread and talking about a third force. He has got his ideas from reading too many worthy books before he came, and when he finds his third force it is a ruthless general with a private army: the main result of his interference is a lot of unnecessary civilian deaths. Marie Rycker doesn't operate on so large a scale, but she destroys Querry's happiness as thoroughly as Pyle destroys the crowd.

Innocence always calls mutely for protection when we would be so much wiser to guard ourselves against it; innocence is like a dumb leper who has lost his bell, wandering the world, meaning no harm. (*The Quiet American*)
God preserve us from all innocence. At least the guilty know what they are about. (*A Burnt-Out Case*)

Invincibly unimaginative, Pyle and Marie Rycker both conceal the true nature of what they have done under a casuistry of phrases that they believe in, and whose ingenuity can cause us only fury or helpless, ironic laughter. "In a way you could say they died for democracy," says Pyle of his victims; "I didn't want him," says Marie to Querry. "The only way I could manage was to shut my eyes and think it was you. . . . So in a way it is your child."

Innocence has nothing to do with intelligence (Pyle is very intelligent, Marie Rycker very stupid) nor with selfishness (Marie is selfish, Pyle isn't): essentially, it means lack of imagination. The suffering which the innocent cause as they pursue their purposes with such pure intensity is something that never comes to life in their emotions.

The case is so plausible that one does not at first notice the trick. But there is a trick: it is that Mr. Greene has not, in these two characters, simply presented innocence: he has presented innocence that interferes. Pyle's belief in the third force (let us for the moment grant, with Fowler—perhaps with Greene—that a third force was not viable in Indochina in 1955) may be naïve, it may come from books, it may really contrast with the wise realism of Fowler and the Communists, but it did no harm until Pyle went in for politics. The image of the leper is not fair: a leper can't keep out of being infectious. Marie Rycker was unimaginative and immature from the beginning, but neither this nor the pity which Querry felt would have undone him if she hadn't told her lies, if she hadn't gone out looking for him. Of course Mr. Greene could reply that it isn't possible to be a spectator of life, that we are committed to interfering and need therefore to outgrow our innocence, and in a profound sense this is true. But there is a more superficial sense that we need for passing particular judgments and making practical decisions, and it is on this level that Pyle interferes and Pemberton—let us say—doesn't. Pemberton is ultimately responsible for the suffering his death may cause, since no man is an island; Pyle is immediately responsible for the explosion in the square, since he gave General Thé the bombs. It is not coincidence that Pemberton causes less suffering, and even that in an ambiguous sense of "cause": Father Clay was almost in pieces anyway.

Finally, the humanists. Here there is the greatest variety of all, and we might wonder if there's any worth in a classification that links Ida (of *Brighton Rock*) with, say, the lieutenant in *The Power and the Glory*. What they have in common is that both represent the alternative to the religious vision: sensual in the case of Ida, rational in that of the lieutenant. Both are ignorant of good and evil, which they replace by right and wrong. "Right and wrong," says Ida (it is one of her favourite phrases); "I believe in right and wrong." Everything that might be religious is turned by Ida into merely moral terms: she goes to Hale's funeral because it "shows respect." Against Ida are set Pinkie, who is evil, and Rose, who is good; they live their moral lives on a plane to which she has no access (that is why we should not call Rose "innocent": though she has no knowledge of evil in herself, she understands it, and her goodness does not cut her off from experience). The contrast comes to the surface in the scene in which Ida follows Rose up to her bedroom, trying to persuade her to tell the truth and incriminate Pinkie—who comes in while she is talking:

He smirked at the pair of them, nostalgia driven out by a surge of sad sensuality. She was good, he'd discovered that, and he was damned: they were made for each other.

"You leave her alone," the woman said. "I know all about you." It was as if she were in a strange country: the typical Englishwoman abroad. She hadn't even got a phrase book. She was as far from either of them as she was from Hell—or Heaven. Good and evil lived in the same country, spoke the same language, came together like old friends, feeling the same completion, touching hands beside the iron bedstead. "You want to do what's Right, Rose?" she implored.

Rose whispered again: "You let us be."

"You're a Good Girl, Rose. You don't want anything to do with Him."

"You don't know a thing." [. . .]

"You're a good girl, Rose," the Boy said, pressing his fingers round the small sharp wrist.

She shook her head. "I'm bad." She implored him: "I want to be bad if she's good and you—"

"You'll never be anything but good," the Boy said. "There's some wouldn't like you for that, but I don't care."

"I'll do anything for you. Tell me what to do. I don't want to be like her."

"It's not what you do," the Boy said, "it's what you think." He boasted. "It's in the blood. Perhaps when they christened me the holy water didn't take. I never howled the devil out."

"Is *she* good?" She came weakly to him for instruction.

"She?" The Boy laughed. "She's just nothing." (*Brighton Rock*)

This passage seems the very heart of Graham Greene: obsession and cunning, his two great qualities, mingle and blur here, and to great advantage. It is built round the contrast between good and evil, and right and wrong: or, since the very tones of Ida and the Boy reveal so much, between good and Good. It is made quite plain here that Pinkie has a spiritual dimension that Ida lacks: hence the hint of a pun in "instruction." Some of

the images that haunt Mr. Greene's writing have forced themselves in here: the wholly apt image of the traveller without a
phrase book, and the image that he put to such splendid use
in *The End of the Affair* of the holy water not "taking."

"What really matters," Mr. Eliot said, "is Sin and Redemption. The possibility of damnation . . . at last gives some
significance to living." Leaving aside any objections we may
have to this doctrine in itself, we must surely agree it has been
dangerous for literature, encouraging the writer with a taste for
profundity and spiritual gimmicks. Perhaps this doctrine lies
behind that brilliant piece of gimmickry, *The Third Man*;
most certainly it lies behind the critics who took *The Third
Man* seriously as a spiritual drama and/or archetypal myth. Thus
Mr. Lawrence Alloway, writing in *World Review* for March
1950, calls Harry Lime "an inverted Christ-figure" and claims
"though evil and ruthless . . . Lime is a better man than Holly
with his sentimentality and vague ethic." Remembering that
Lime betrayed his girl for his own interests, sold watered peni-
cillin for use in hospitals, and never seems to have any motive
except making money, I ask myself what earthly meaning (or
even what heavenly meaning) can be attached to the word
"better." Now the best way I can praise that passage from
Brighton Rock is to say that it does what the gullible critics
claimed that *The Third Man* did—it really gives body to the
doctrine that damnation gives significance to living. I continue
to find it pernicious, but I can no longer find it contemptible.

The humanism of *The Power and the Glory* lies only on the
periphery of the book. Although in some ways this is Mr.
Greene's most serious novel, it is also the most like his entertainments: everything is fitted into the pattern of the Hunt.
It is necessary, therefore, for the pursuer to remain shadowy and
menacing, always on the priest's heels, never catching up. To
keep the intensity, Mr. Greene has the priest's viewpoint all
through the central episode: when he varies it (Mr. Tench, the
children listening to the saint's life) it is for aesthetic contrast,
not to present us with another interpretation of the hunt. No one
can deny that the result is very powerful: but it necessarily makes

the book one-sided. The Communist case never has a chance. The police officer, never seen from within, exists only as a threat.

In view of Mr. Greene's prewar political novels (*It's a Battlefield* and the thrillers), I cannot think this was his intention; indeed, we can see from one scene in *The Power and the Glory* itself that it wasn't. When the priest is released from prison he is taken before the lieutenant, wondering if he will be recognized. For a moment the conversation hovers in the direction of identification, then veers away.

It was almost as if the lieutenant had something on his conscience, as he sat with his dark Indian-blooded hands restless on the pages, brooding. . . . He said: "Where are you going?"

"God knows."

"You are all alike, you people. You never learn the truth—that God knows nothing." Some tiny scrap of life like a grain of smut went racing across the page in front of him: he pressed his finger down on it and said: "You had no money for your fine?" and watched another smut edge out between the leaves, scurrying for refuge: in this heat there was no end to life.

"No."

"How will you live?"

"Some work perhaps . . ."

"You are getting too old for work." He put his hand suddenly in his pocket and pulled out a five-peso piece. "There," he said. "Get out of here, and don't let me see your face again. Mind that."

The priest held the coin in his fist—the price of a Mass. He said with astonishment: "You're a good man."

This is not only evidence of Mr. Greene's intention—that he did not want the Communists to make a merely negative impression—it is also very effective, coming when it does. We realize (and we share the priest's shock as he realizes) that for all he has learned through suffering, his imagination is still bounded: he had not known what the lieutenant was like. Yet to put it this way is to show not only what makes it effective, but also what limits it. We are concerned here with the priest's consciousness and with the lieutenant only as part of that; our view of what the lieutenant stands for has not, in any positive sense, been enlarged. Indeed, since we have only seen him as pursuer and destroyer, Mr. Greene has chosen his details badly: "You never learn the truth—that God knows nothing"—this is realistic enough, and touching in its tired sadness, but it is still negative. What of the positive beliefs of which all this is the corollary? Because we remain external to the lieutenant we remain external to his cause; and the last sentence, powerfully as it conveys the priest's shock, does not take us anywhere into the case and the motives of the other side.

How strong a contrast is Dr. Colin, the atheist of *A Burnt-Out Case*. Mr. Greene is so scrupulous in giving him a fair run that Dr. Colin emerges as the most attractive figure in the book. Even that seems to put it too mechanically: Mr. Greene appears to *like* Dr. Colin, even to sentimentalize him.

> "Swimming on your wave," Querry said with envy. "Do you never need a woman?"
> "The only one I ever needed," the doctor said, "is dead."
> "So that's why you came out here."
> "You are wrong," Colin said. "She's buried a hundred yards away. She was my wife."

This closes the conversation in which Dr. Colin has been explaining to Querry his rather old-fashioned belief in progress. Everything works in the doctor's favour in this scene, including his admission that his rationalism is just as superstitious as what the fathers believe. ("Who cares? It's the superstition I live by.") Perhaps no humanist claim annoys the Christian more than the claim to have transcended the need for a faith based on the irrational; here Mr. Greene is doing the best he can for Dr. Colin, he is giving him humility. And if that were not handsome enough, he closes the scene with this glimpse of him as devoted husband; and since we learn virtually nothing more about his wife, it doesn't seem too much to call it sentimentalizing.

Has Mr. Greene grown fonder of the humanists? *Our Man in Havana* certainly tempts us to say yes. Mr. Wormald is wholly engaging and wins our esteem not least by his devotion to his spoilt, selfish Catholic daughter, whose religion is simply a way of dressing up her desires. I would defy anyone to read *Our Man in Havana* without knowing the author and not conclude that it was by a wry and gently pessimistic humanist who disliked Christianity.

Returning to *A Burnt-Out Case*, I must say that there is another side to the penny we have been looking at. Not only is there more warmth towards the humanist, but the area of religion that is considered morbid has grown. Father Thomas is the one priest who suffers from piety, and the content of his disagreements with his fellow-priests is startling.

Father Thomas said, "I do not think Querry minds much about his food." He was the only priest in the leproserie with whom the Superior felt ill at ease; he still seemed to carry with him the strains and anxieties of the seminary. He had left it longer ago than any of the others, but he seemed doomed to a perpetual and unhappy youth; he was ill at ease with men who had grown up and were more concerned over the problems of the electric-light plant or the quality of the brickmaking than over the pursuit of souls. Souls could wait. Souls had eternity.

Is that really the conception of "growing up" that we are being offered? Yes, it is. We can't lay too much stress on the word "pursuit," since there doesn't seem to be any less voracious, more acceptable way of being concerned with souls that is offered to us. Mr. Greene shows us very well what is wrong with Father Thomas, who projects his own neurosis on to the problems he deals with, but he is curiously negative about what a priest should be like. "I don't look for motives," says the Superior; and we are meant to contrast this wise and generous attitude ("I hope I accept what he does with gratitude") with the morbid probings of Father Thomas's piety.

"We'll have air-conditioning in our rooms yet," Father Jean said, "and a drug-store and all the latest movie-magazines including pictures of Brigitte Bardot." Father Jean was tall, pale, and concave with a beard which struggled like an unpruned hedge. He had once been a brilliant moral theologian before he joined the Order and now he carefully nurtured the character of a film fan, as though it would help him to wipe out an ugly past.

Father Jean has grown up, and we are to like him the better for it. The passage is startling but not really ironic: a past in moral theology, we are being told, *is* ugly. When Father Thomas is going off the deep end at the crisis of the book, Father Jean tries to calm him by suggesting that what's going on is like a Palais Royal farce; this makes Father Thomas more indignant and dangerous than ever:

"Sometimes I think God was not entirely serious when he gave man the sexual instinct."
"If that is one of the doctrines you teach in moral theology . . ."
"Nor when he invented moral theology."

In the leproserie (and the leproserie, like Scobie's West Africa, is a figure for the world) moral theology and looking for motives are part of the morbid growth of religion. This is nearer to Hemingway than to *The Heart of the Matter*.

And where, in this dichotomy, does Querry come? Father Thomas and Rycker probe into Querry's motives with dangerous and obstinate stupidity; have we nothing to set against them but the assertion that motives are less interesting than Brigitte Bardot, or is there another version of Querry? There is, of course: it is indicated in the title. The book is built on a sustained analogy between the condition of Querry and that of a leper. Pain and mutilation are alternatives in leprosy: the leper who loses his fingers no longer suffers, and is known as a burnt-out case. Querry is burnt-out spiritually: emotionally maimed, he no longer suffers. The novel tells the story of how he regains the capacity to feel. The analogy (brilliant and utterly Greenelike) is worked out in discussion with Dr. Colin, in introspection, in dream, and we can see from Dr. Colin's remark

—You want to be of use, don't you? . . . You don't want menial jobs just for the sake of menial jobs? You aren't either a masochist or a saint—

that what we have really to reject is motive-hunting as a substitute for right action. Querry's self-analysis at the beginning is morbid because it is defeatist, not because it is wrong or uninteresting. The true substitute for moral theology need not be Brigitte Bardot and hard work, it can be sympathy and a mastery of metaphor.

But (and this is a terrible "but," poised to hit us between the eyes) to ask what view of Querry ought to replace Father Thomas's is to assume that his is wrong. This seems as safe an assumption as any and—therefore, since this is Greeneland, we must distrust it. Ought we perhaps to be turning the whole book on its head? There is, after all, *The End of the Affair*.

The End of the Affair is (surely) the most disliked of Mr. Greene's major novels. His intellectual *jusqu'au boutisme** (the happy phrase is—I think—Donat O'Donnell's) may go further theologically in other books, but nowhere else does it go so far artistically. A novel with miracles—how outrageous can one get? Yet if miracles can ever be justified in a novel, this is the sort of novel it must be.

It is a story of several love-triangles. There is Henry-Sarah-Bendrix: husband-wife-lover. Then there is Bendrix-Sarah-Smythe: Sarah really belongs to Bendrix, Smythe wants her. Slowly we realize that behind these two triangles is another, Bendrix-Sarah-God. God is a lover, having an affair with Sarah, using the dirtiest tricks he can to wind her from Bendrix. God has the sense to see that Bendrix is his real rival now, not Henry. God's methods are more underhand than Bendrix's ever were: bringing Bendrix back to life for her, if she will promise never to see him again; carrying Sarah off (i.e., killing her) when she's in danger of relapsing. (The only parallel I can think of to all this is the bargain made with God in *The Potting Shed.*) And then the miracles—poor Bendrix hasn't a chance. God not only seduced Sarah, he seduced Smythe too, and at the end of the book we realize that he is starting on Bendrix. Bendrix has also realized it, and reacts in helpless fury. We see that the blas-

---

* "Going to the furthest limit."—Ed.

phemer is very close to God; blasphemy is a kind of fury, not needed when God is leaving you alone. Smythe had always been closer to God; for he, of course, had never been one of Mr. Greene's humanists, his atheism had been a religious passion all along. When the book ends, another book is just beginning: Bendrix is being caught. It was the only way to catch him: "Hatred of God can bring the soul to God." The worst thing of all about God's dirty tricks is that they succeed.

The End of the Affair can only be read this way. If it isn't a religious novel, it's nothing; and if it is a religious novel, it's one which makes no bones about God's methods. But if Mr. Greene went the whole hog in this book, does that not mean that it's the type of a Greene novel: that concealed in every other book is a book like this? If this is true of *A Burnt-Out Case*, we have to conclude that Querry is a saint after all. Father Thomas's interpretation that he was going through the phase of aridity is then right, Rycker's unctuous, distasteful and unstable adulation is justified, Parkinson's spiteful attempt to ruin Querry's peace and build him up as a saint is justified because Querry *is* a saint. The attractiveness of Dr. Colin is not anything spontaneous, it is part of Mr. Greene's cunning, loading appearances in favour of the wrong side; and considering what God stooped to in *The End of the Affair*, we need not be surprised that he here elects to work through the three most unpleasant characters in the book.

And now it is time to protest. If *A Burnt-Out Case* is ironic in this sense, then anything is ironic. There are no clues planted in *A Burnt-Out Case* that correspond to the miracles in *The End of the Affair*, that force us to accept the religious reading or dismiss the book. There are not even half-clues: Father Thomas, for example, is always wrong about details. If this book had been written by a humanist who simply wanted a way out— a private joke, an excuse to stay in the church, a sop to his conscious beliefs—I cannot see that it would be any different from the way it is.

The Quiet American and *Our Man in Havana* seemed to suggest that Mr. Greene was no longer so clearly writing from a Catholic position. A *Burnt-Out Case* looks like a return—or relapse—but I am not sure that it is more than a return in subject matter. To make it a return in position we have to turn it on its head. Now no book can ever be defended against the assertion that it must be stood on its head: nothing can ever be proved to be unironic. Just as no argument against Christianity can ever be proof against the assertion that God left all that evidence lying around to mislead us.

I will end with what I hope is an unnecessary warning. It is hard to discuss a writer like Mr. Greene without seeming to pry into his most intimate beliefs, since he so obviously writes out of these. But the only Graham Greene who ought to interest us is the writer, not the man, and though that writer must be a version of the living Graham Greene, he may be a distorted and partial version. The distortions are not our concern, and to reconstruct his biographical self from his literary self may interest the man's friends, but should not engage his critics. It is hard to imagine a living writer with whom this warning is more needed than Mr. Greene, for he is strongly committed, fond of irony, and the finest novelist now writing in England.

BARBARA SEWARD

Miss Seward received her Ph.D. from Columbia University and taught English there until her death in 1958. She was the author of several critical articles and a book, *The Symbolic Rose*.

GRAHAM GREENE: A HINT OF AN EXPLANATION

Graham Greene and his British publishers have declared that *The Quiet American* marks a great alteration in his work. Although this is far from true, we do find in the new book surface changes which help us to uncover the source of a complex vision of life that has been Greene's from the beginning. For what Greene has actually done is to simplify his material by removing from it most traces of explicit Catholicism. The familiar obsessions—good and evil, death, pain, violence, pity, and innocence—still form the novel's emotional focus; the familiar protagonist—Greene's seedy, sensitive individual trapped in an impossible moral dilemma—still carries the novel's theme. But since the Catholic question of sin is not at issue in this book, guilt in our usual, secular sense is thrown into sharp relief as its chief motivating force, as the force that underlies the obsessions and determines the hero's behavior. "We have so few ways in which to assuage the sense of guilt," says Fowler; and we as readers suddenly realize that he has crystallized in an instant the dominant theme not only of this but of almost all Greene's novels to date. Re-examining the range of these novels in the light of insight gained from the latest, we see that guilt, though often hidden beneath despair or pity, has been the most

This essay appeared in *The Western Review*, Vol. 22, No. 2 (Winter 1958). Copyright *The Western Review*, 1958. Reprinted by permission of John P. Seward and Georgene H. Seward.

basic ingredient in Greene's central characters; that the fierce conscience driving these tormented heroes also drives their tormented author; that it goes a long way toward explaining the few unpleasant biases which limit Greene's vision and the virtues of sympathy and tolerance which give to that vision much of its strength.

Guilt is of course not a simple emotion. It is generally entangled with a sense of worthlessness and often results in a need to suffer retribution. In Graham Greene both components are present. Through his novels and entertainments from earliest to latest can be traced variations upon a single, central fantasy, resembling in outline the familiar pattern of crime and punishment, but betraying through notable deviations the attitudes and insights of a man oppressed with guilt. For where guilt is commonly presented as a consequence of crime, in Greene's self-distrusting characters it is often a cause of crime as well; where punishment is commonly a deserved but dreaded eventuality, in Greene's characters it is often self-sought or self-inflicted. Furthermore, the whole journey from guilt through retribution, which is commonly reserved for doers of evil, becomes in Greene's novels the prerogative of good men and the chief differential between the good and the deficient. Assuming that corruption is inescapable and that suffering is man's sole means of expiation, Greene repeatedly favors his redeemable characters with a sense of guilt so overwhelming that it exists with or without precipitating situations and demands for its appeasement an appalling price of pain.

Before the development of these attitudes in the moral design of Greene's novels is examined more specifically, it is important to consider their relation to Catholicism. Since Greene's point of view is in many ways consistent with Catholic doctrines of sin and atonement, one might be tempted to attribute his concern with sin to his religious persuasion. However, within a structure as broad as Catholicism, a man's choice of emphasis is significant, especially so if the man is known for distorting what he stresses. Moreover, Greene himself has most explicitly stated that his awareness of sin was not the result but the predecessor of his faith: "Religion might later explain it to me in other terms, but the pattern was already there—perfect evil walking the world where perfect good can never walk again" (*The Lost Childhood*). On the other hand, while the Church is not accountable for Greene's sense of guilt itself, it is accountable, to an extent, for the form and structure given that guilt. The Catholic faith has provided Greene with a traditional pattern of belief supporting and augmenting his particular convictions and saving him perhaps from Kafkaesque extremes of tormented hypersubjectivity. And not only has the Church provided a universal, objective background for his concern with sin and suffering, but, on the more hopeful side, its allowance that evil itself may be a possible source of good has provided him with a means of finding in the sin-sick human world an ultimately affirmative vision.

For Greene good is invariably filtered through evil. Mankind for him has so fallen from grace that good cannot exist in a pure state, cannot exist unmixed with sin. In the beginning there was innocence, and still in primitive areas of the world (such as the Africa of *Journey without Maps*), or in sheltered children or childlike adults, we can find fading traces of our lost heritage. But such traces are no longer cause for joy. Sin is our present condition and guilt alone points the way to redemption. Although it is commonly believed that Greene equates innocence with goodness, there seems little real evidence for this opinion in his novels. It is true that he expresses nostalgia for the lost state of the individual and the race, nostalgia for a time when one was free of guilt because one was free of the knowledge of sin. It is true that this nostalgia colors his treatment of every innocent child or semiadult in his novels. It colors, for example, Scobie's feelings for Helen Rolt, whose innocence heightens his sense of pity and duty toward her; it colors the whisky priest's affection for the child Coral, whose innocence links her in his mind with his own no longer innocent daughter; it colors the whole contrast between childhood's

natural happiness and maturity's consciousness of contamina-
tion that is one of the dominant motifs throughout *The Ministry of Fear*; and it colors Fowler's grudging but real affection for
Pyle, who is because of his innocence the one truly principled
person in *The Quiet American*. Yet Greene does not view innocence as either an ideal or a desirable condition.

Innocence is paradoxically undesirable for the very reason
that it evokes nostalgia. For innocence, being free of all knowledge of evil, is unconsumed by the agony of guilt. But the world
the innocent person must exist in is our fallen world of evil,
pain, and guilt; and in order to achieve the prime virtue of
love, he must sooner or later become aware of bleak reality.
"Happiness should always be qualified by a knowledge of
misery," says Arthur Rowe, thinking back with some distaste on
the "rather gross, complacent, parasitic stranger" he had been
during his amnesic period of innocence (*The Ministry of
Fear*). And the whisky priest, remembering his own innocent
past, thinks further along identical lines: "What an unbearable
creature he must have been in those days—and yet in those days
he had been comparatively innocent. . . . Then, in his innocence,
he had felt no love for anyone: now in his corruption he had
learnt" (*The Power and the Glory*). Personal corruption and
the suffering it entails are essential to the attainment of love,
for love in Graham Greene involves pity or compassion, and
unless one has experienced pain and guilt in one's own life,
one can feel no compassion for the pain and guilt of others.
Innocence, being ignorant of good and evil, is as incapable of
love as it is of sin, is in fact a morally negative condition unin-
volved in the struggle of our latter-day life.

Worse still, the innocent person, being ignorant, can become
an actual menace to the world he cannot understand. Pyle,
serving democracy with plastic bombs, and Helen, destroying
Scobie's life with love, are dangerous because of the naïve
idealism which blinds them to the realities around them and
because of the response their innocence evokes in whatever
feeling people their lives become entangled with. "Innocence
must die young if it isn't to kill the souls of men," says Scobie

(*The Heart of the Matter*); and Fowler enlarges on Scobie's point: "Innocence always calls mutely for protection, when we would be so much wiser to guard ourselves against it: innocence is like a dumb leper who has lost his bell, wandering the world meaning no harm." Coming too late upon corruption-ridden days, innocence is then no longer durable or desirable. Nostalgia for the guilt-free state of innocence must be tempered by awareness of its limitations; the guilt-tormented man must recognize that it is in his very torment that his salvation lies. Although innocence serves a definite purpose in Greene's novels, its purpose is not that of exemplifying ideal good. Rather, the innocent characters, being themselves outside the realm of good or evil, are able to serve as accurate measures of the good and evil in those around them. Those capable of good respond to innocence with a mingled sense of pity and protective, if often tragically misdirected, duty toward an evanescent, rare, and vulnerable condition. Those incapable of good respond with anything from callous exploitation to unmitigated sadism. In either case the innocent person plays an important but nonetheless secondary role, the role of agent in exposing the forces of good and evil which are the primary subject of Graham Greene's novels.

Since goodness stems not from innocence but from guilt, Greene must comb the realms of evil for redeeming hints of virtue. Invariably these hints are to be found in men of anguished conscience, while unredeemable ugliness exists in men who bear no load of guilt. The latter group in Greene's novels takes in the whole ordinary world, all of those who seek and find success and happiness in life. "Point me out the happy man," says Scobie, "and I will point you out either egotism, selfishness, evil—or else an absolute ignorance." From absolute ignorance to evil the range is great. Pious, church-going women in *The Power and the Glory*, harmless but complacent in their uncharitable self-righteousness, are among the invincibly ignorant. Ruthless, successful exploiters of others for personal gain, such as Colleoni in *Brighton Rock* or Cholmondely in *This Gun for Hire*, are among the insidiously evil. And between these two extremes lies the "great middle law-abiding class," peopled by plump, self-satisfied individuals such as the American government workers in the background of *The Quiet American* or sensual, fun-loving Ida in the foreground of *Brighton Rock*. But whether harmless, vicious, or a little of both, all of these types have in common one fundamental quality which marks each alike as an object of Graham Greene's contempt. Too old or too worldly to be excused as innocent, they are able to be happy in the fallen world because they are insensitive both to the spiritual evil that pervades our era and to the personal corruption that each of us bears within.

These characters are in fact condemned because they fail to be overwhelmed by feelings of guilt and self-contempt. They can laugh and enjoy life, can enjoy food and drink and sex, because they neither despise nor have to lacerate themselves. While Cholmondely is also an underhanded killer, Ida Arnold is nothing worse than warm-hearted, jolly, and well-meaning. Yet she and Cholmondely receive a like degree of scorn, and both are made disgusting at least as much through their sensuality as through the hurt they bring to others. "He was fat, he was vulgar," writes Greene of Cholmondely, "but he gave an impression of great power as he sat there with the cream dripping from his mouth." And of big-breasted Ida he writes with comparable contempt: "She bore the same relation to passion as a peep show. She sucked the chocolate between her teeth and smiled, her plump toes working in the rug, waiting for Mr. Corkery—just a great big blossoming surprise." Food is all right, sex is all right, but the thing that is not all right is enjoyment. Greene's sympathetic characters are not often presented eating, but when they are it is such a meal as the whisky priest's starved gnawing at a dying dog's fly-covered bone. They are more often shown in love, but the price of love is always as tragic as that between Helen and Scobie in *The Heart of the Matter*, that between Sarah and Bendrix in *The End of the Affair*, or that between Phuong and Fowler in *The Quiet American*. The things of this earth are acceptable, can even be tinged with a kind of beauty, but always with the one proviso that they give rise to pain and not to joy.

To an extent this masochistic outlook fits in with Greene's Catholicism. If sin is the cause of a whole world's misery, and suffering is the one means to atonement, the happy or self-satisfied can be seen as spiritually obtuse. But the Catholic faith is not incompatible with a love of human life, nor can it be held accountable for the extremes to which Greene carries his horror. For, going beyond passive disgust, Greene shows an active desire for violence to destroy complacency and success. In *The Lost Childhood* he looks with favor on "the sense of doom that lies over success—the feeling that the pendulum is about to swing," explaining that "only the pendulum ensures that after all in the end justice is done." And in the same volume's concluding essay, he links this pendulum clearly to violence, whose manifestations in World War II he finds remarkably welcome: "It [violence] had to be there to satisfy that moral craving for the just and reasonable expression of human nature left without belief." Furthermore, in the novels themselves violence is often the key note, and the dealers of violence as often as not are regarded with sympathy. Fowler, for example, is largely exonerated for the betrayal of Pyle because Pyle is the dangerous dupe of American complacency. And still more significant is the fact that Greene's two most criminally violent characters, Raven in *This Gun for Hire* and Pinkie in *Brighton Rock*, appear as relatively sympathetic counterparts to his two most self-satisfied, Cholmondely and Ida. Clearly, success and self-satisfaction are so antithetical to Greene that even murder is preferred, provided the murderer hates himself.

With the help of Péguy and T. S. Eliot, Greene is able up to a point to force this antisocial preference into his Catholic framework. From Péguy he derives the idea that the sinner is second only to the saint in depth of spiritual vision, and from Eliot comes the opinion that the most contemptible of all men are those not big enough to be damned, the spiritually unconscious who people the wasteland of the world. "It wasn't evil," writes Greene of our vast, ordinary, secular society, "it wasn't anything at all, it was just the drugstore and the Coca-Cola, the hamburger, the sinless empty graceless chromium world" (*The Lawless Roads*). Since our reality is spiritual, and in the human world spiritual evil seems more pervasive than spiritual good, those who are evil and aware of their evil, those who knowingly damn themselves, have at least an awareness of truth though they may use it in the wrong way. But a loathing for worldliness, happiness, and success even when they are relatively harmless, and a preference for suffering, sin, and failure even in homicidal forms, can hardly be laid at the door of the Church. Greene is pushing his religion farther than it will go when he uses it to vindicate an essentially un-Catholic preference for conscious spiritual evil over unknowing secular veniality.

Not Catholicism, then, but a strong inner sense of identity with the criminal outcasts of the earth determines Greene's preference for the suffering sinner over the satisfied average person. This sense of identity, generally seen in his sympathy with all sufferers no matter how culpable they may be, is specifically seen in his treatment of Pinkie, the most culpable he has created. For Pinkie is given childhood memories from Greene's personal store (the pregnant girl with her head on the tracks, the cement playground at school); he is given to an extreme the sadistic desires that Greene felt as a child ("Like a revelation, when I was fourteen, I realized the pleasure of cruelty . . ." *Journey without Maps*); and he is honored with the same phrase that Greene applies to his own early years: "Hell lay around him in his infancy." Pinkie is not Greene, but he is what Greene might have been, and he reveals the self-distrust that colors Greene's outlook on the world. For a man who feels that he and a murderer are brothers beneath the skin, and who goes beyond sympathy to empathy with the hell in which such a murderer walks, is a man whose terrible awareness of his own fallibility is as deep as his moral being. Pinkie with his intense, religious sense of evil, Pinkie who as a child had sworn he would be a priest, Pinkie with the world's horror "like infection in his throat" is Greene's most terrifying reminder to himself and to us all of the fragility of the barrier that separates us from the damned.

If Greene makes up in charity for the sinful what he loses in uncharity for the complacent, it is because the former experience what to him is the truth about our world, while the latter exist in an unreal, blind, smug, alien condition. But he does not go so far as to exonerate Pinkie; more is needed for salvation than a knowledge of life's horror. Pinkie has reached the first stage of awareness, has had his vision of evil which must precede any vision of good, since good in a fallen world can only evolve from evil: "One began to believe in heaven because one believed in hell, but for a long while it was only hell one could picture with a certain intimacy" (*The Lawless Roads*). But Pinkie can never believe in heaven nor ever see beyond evil because he is lacking the sympathy vital to spiritual growth. "He couldn't see through other people's eyes or feel with their nerves," writes Greene. And beneath his failure in sympathy lies the cardinal sin of pride, the complete absorption in one's own ego which creates hate of the very materials that humility uses to create love. For good and evil in Greene are determined by the manner in which a man handles pain. The proud man will resent it as a terrible wrong to himself, and will, like Pinkie, turn it outward in sadistic vengeance on God and man. But the humble, acutely aware of his guilt, will accept pain as his due and will develop from self-knowledge the tremendous virtue of pity for the entire tainted world.

A sense of guilt is then prerequisite to the attainment of true virtue. Just as the innocent and happy fall short because they lack real awareness of evil, and the wholly sinful fall short because they are blinded by pride to their own blame for evil, those characters in Greene who do attain some measure of stature attain it because they accept their share in the universal taint. Seeking for factors that would distinguish Christian from pagan civilizations, Greene once suggested that "all we can really demand is the divided mind, the uneasy conscience, the sense of personal failure" (speech to the "Grande Conférence

Catholique" at Brussels, 1947); and in his novels he has given to each of his sympathetic protagonists a sharply divided mind, a more than uneasy conscience. Intensely aware of encompassing evil, each is perpetually confronted with the impossibility in this world of performing a sinless act. Arthur Rowe, guilty of murder in the mercy killing of his wife, would have been guilty of her anguish had he allowed her disease to run its course; the whisky priest, guilty of pride in remaining in Tabasco, would have been guilty of desertion had he fled with the other priests: Fowler, guilty of complex treachery in his betrayal of Pyle, would have been guilty of Pyle's massacres had he done nothing to prevent them; Sarah, guilty of adultery in her love affair with Bendrix, was guilty of his suffering when she renounced his love for God's; and Scobie, guilty of almost everything in his affair with Helen, would have been guilty of her desolation had he refused to give her love. Conscious of guilt wherever they turn and faced with inescapable choices between corruption and corruption, the truly good men in Graham Greene's world are men sufficiently close to God to be appalled by their distance from Him.

The depth of a man's sense of sin, then, becomes the measure of his moral worth, and the depth of his sense of failure the measure of his moral success. For if the human world is remote from God and from perfection, it follows that those who strive hardest for goodness will be those most aware of their failure to reach it. It also follows that pain will pursue the good man in this life, for pain inevitably accompanies feelings of worthlessness, failure, and guilt. Oppressed by their own imperfections, Greene's more admirable characters regard pain as their natural state, in fact are uneasy if happiness threatens what they feel is their due retribution. Scobie, for example, expresses "the loyalty we all feel to unhappiness—the sense that that is where we really belong"; the whisky priest, over the border, feels in the terrain of peace that "he had no right to such luxury"; Fowler declares that always he is "afraid of losing unhappiness," that death is in fact "the only absolute value in my world." And going beyond passive acceptance, Greene's characters actually often seek out the punishments that alone can relieve their overwhelming feelings of guilt. The priest abandons peace for death, Scobie ruins himself for those he has injured, Fowler becomes involved in the human struggle he dreads, and Sarah prays for Bendrix: "I pressed my nails into the palms of my hands until I could feel nothing but the pain, and I said, I will believe. Let him be alive, and I *will* believe. . . . But that wasn't enough. It doesn't hurt to believe. So I said, I love him and . . . I'll give him up forever" (*The End of the Affair*).

This is the way of atonement. It is also the way of ordinary, secular guilt. But in Greene atonement is important because it makes possible positive beauty wrung from the rag of human pain. Regarding self-laceration as a means to spiritual purgation, Greene sees guilt's torments not as lamentable but as the only road to pity, which itself is his road to God. For pity requires conscience. Neither the innocent nor the complacent nor the evil can approach it. Without a knowledge both of sin and of one's own terrible fallibility, one cannot feel the responsibility for the unhappiness of others that forms a great part of Fowler's pity for war's innocent victims, of Scobie's for Louise and Helen, of the priest's for his tainted daughter, of Rowe's for his dying wife. Without a knowledge both of anguish and of one's own appalling inadequacy, one cannot feel the enormous sympathy for the world's brothers in failure that forms the remaining part of pity in Greene's conscience-stricken men: "And he saw," writes Greene of Scobie, "the body of Ali under the black drums, the exhausted eyes of Helen, and all the faces of the lost, his companions in exile, the unrepentant thief, the soldier with the sponge. Thinking of what he had done and was going to do, he thought, with love, even God is a failure."

While love is the greatest virtue in the orthodox Catholic view, pity is only one form of love. But in Greene's view pity remains the one adequate form that is left us in a world undone by human corruption. Feeling that sin and consequent suffering are our only reality, he cannot conceive of a lasting love based on admiration or joy. Admiration is out of the question because corruption is so universal that those who appear the most successful are simply the most obtuse. And joy is out of the question because pain is so much a part of life that the more one loves a person, the more one fears for his peace or safety. "I love failure: I can't love success," says Scobie, and again: "When we say, 'I can't live without you,' what we really mean is, 'I can't live feeling you may be in pain, unhappy, in want.'" Further, pity in a guilty world is to Greene not only the most likely but the highest possible form of love. It is in the first place uninfected with sensuality, selfishness, or happiness, all of which he finds incompatible with the attainment of virtue. And in the second place pity is our feeble but nonetheless closest approach to the vast, merciful compassion that God must feel for sin-sick man: "It was too easy to die for what was good or beautiful, for home or children or a civilization—it needed a God to die for the halfhearted and the corrupt" (*The Power and the Glory*).

Pity, then, being compounded with pain, not only evolves from guilt but serves as a form of atonement. Reflecting in a small way Christ's great act of atonement for man, pity is the one virtue that still can save us from damnation. But such salvation is not simple. In fact, Greene's pity at first glance seems to pull its possessor around full circle, swinging him from guilt through a suffering arc to a new-old starting point in guilt. For it is pity in Arthur Rowe that drives him to kill his wife, pity in Scobie that drives him to damn his soul for others, pity in the whisky priest that drives him to set his child above God, and pity in Fowler that drives him to betray his dearest friend. In reconciling the sins of pity with its great soul-saving power, Greene stretches the bounds of Catholic doctrine beyond the breaking point to maintain a view consistent with his own guilt-motivated universe. While the Church teaches that man's first duty is the salvation of his own soul, Greene presents such men as the priest and Scobie, who are willing to damn their souls for others, as approaching the Christlike love that lays down its life for its brother. While the Church teaches that despair and suicide are forms of mortal sin, such men as the priest and Scobie, who commit these sins for others, again reveal that Christlike love: "Christ had not been murdered: you couldn't murder God: Christ had killed himself: he had hanged himself on the Cross" (*The Heart of the Matter*).

In other words, since Greene sees sin as omnipresent in human life, and since he therefore feels sympathy only for those who both know and suffer from knowing their sin, he must find an opening in his faith whereby a man can possess sane reason for feeling terrible guilt and yet at the same time possess sufficient virtue for salvation. In the way of Christ Greene finds that opening. If God's pity for man was so great that He was willing to sacrifice Himself for us, surely a man who pursues a like path, however falteringly and darkly, will be in some part exonerated: "And then against all the teaching of the Church," says Scobie, "one has the feeling that love—any kind of love—does deserve a bit of mercy." This is not to say that Greene goes so far as to deny the Church's precepts. Scobie and the priest are both shown as committing the sin of pride in not trusting God to provide for the well-being of those they love and in setting their own imperfect judgments above the judgment of God. But though in their pride they become immersed in sins like adultery, murder, despair, their very sins paradoxically become their virtues if the roots of sin are guilty love.

There is after all a vast difference between the sin that grows out of love and the sin, such as Pinkie's, that grows out of hate. If Scobie and the priest place man above God, they at least do not make the error of placing themselves above man and God. Moreover, since evil is omnipresent in the human world, our only possible hope of heaven is in such sins as are mixed with love. Even Sarah, who alone of Greene's characters is able to renounce corrupt human love for divine, finds her God in the beginning through the sin of adultery. And the others, who never succeed in wholly abjuring sin, are nevertheless, like Sarah, started out on their journey to God through sin itself. For firstly, all love of man is an indirect love of God: "We were made in God's image—God was the parent, but He was also the policeman, the criminal, the priest, the maniac, and the judge" (*The Power and the Glory*). And secondly, love for man, based on pity for his failure to reach God, leads in the end to pity for God who also suffers for man's guilt. The priest, about to be shot in what he believes is a state of mortal sin, feels "only an immense disappointment that he had to go to God empty-handed"; and Scobie, about to die through the sin of suicide, "had a sudden picture before his eyes of a bleeding face, of eyes closed by the continuous shower of blows: the punch-drunk head of God reeling sideways."

In the end these men attain divine love not despite but because of their guilt, for pity that begins and ends in guilt leads them ultimately to God. Even Fowler, the nonbeliever, closes his saga of guilt and pity with words intended to show that he too is approaching final truth: ". . . how I wished there existed someone to whom I could say that I was sorry." But the road from guilt through pity to glory is anything but direct. Although pity is a kind of love, it is not, for example, the kind of love that either Dante or the saints that formed his vision wrote of. It is a love that emerges from pain and from a conviction that human reality has no share in peace or joy or glory, from a conviction that one must love weakness and ugliness and failure because in all human existence there can be no real purity, beauty, success. While Dante was led to heaven by those qualities in Beatrice that reflected the light of ultimate Good, Greene's heroes are led by pity for man's loss of so much of that heavenly light. While in Dante love grows from admiration for the Godliness of Beatrice to a vaster admiration for the essence of God Himself, in Greene love grows from pity for man in suffering the loss of God to a vaster pity for God in suffering the loss of man. Since either view finds a place within the broad Catholic framework, the choice of views must be determined not by creed but by temperament. Greene's sin-stricken, suffering path of pity is clearly the choice of a man whose vision of existence is suffused throughout with a terrible guilt.

We have seen that pity is only one of Greene's many guilt-laden obsessions. Childhood and innocence, success and enjoy-

ment, evil and violence are also obsessions that find their ultimate source in guilt. In fact, at the heart of Greene's markedly
subtle and complex moral vision lies an essential simplicity:
those who know that they are guilty alone possess true virtue,
those who know that they are failures alone possess success.
The view is paradoxical and involves a certain inversion of our
usual human values. Not only are happiness, pleasure, and
self-satisfaction regarded with distrust but our more common
conception of tragedy is in a significant sense reversed. The
suffering and downfall of an admirable human being becomes
in the Greene universe not a cause for ultimate grief; the elevation that is felt at the close of a Greene novel exists not in
spite of but because of the hero's collapse. This inversion, of
course, prevails only on the temporal plane, but the temporal
plane is surely important. Although Greene too holds peace and
happiness as eventual spiritual goals, he presents such goals as
attainable only through their own earthly opposites because he
perceives sin as pervasive and guilt as the sole way of atonement.

On the surface, Greene's upside-down outlook with its emphasis on pain appears decidedly negative. Although most
Catholic writers in our distracted modern world approach God
not through present manifestations of human glory but through
the now more clamorous manifestations of human evil, they
seldom if ever demonstrate Greene's total identification of life,
success, and goodness itself with overwhelming failure. Even
Mauriac, who comes perhaps closest to Greene's own view of
the human condition, shares with him a vision of guilt as man's
chief instrument of virtue, but departs from him in presenting
that virtue as an ultimate triumph over evil rather than as a
love that can only reveal itself in further sin. In fact, because
of Greene's singular obsession with inescapable evil, critics of
his writing tend to fall into one of two groups: Catholic critics
who stress and interpret the religious meanings in his books and
non-Catholic critics who discover that fundamentally he hates
life.

To an extent the latter are justified. The novels are certainly in large part a litany of suffering and failure, and the happier aspects of life, when presented at all, are treated with a contempt equaled among modern Catholic writers by T. S. Eliot alone. Furthermore, the avowed childhood origin of Greene's several attitudes, the observable departures from Catholicism which have disturbed his more orthodox Catholic critics, and Greene's own statement that "the novelist's task is to draw his own likeness" to his characters (*Why Do I Write?*), make indisputable the opinion that his prejudices stem not from his religion but from a wholly subjective source. That the personal source of these prejudices is a consuming sense of guilt is perhaps by now also apparent. Obsessed with his own worthlessness, projecting this outward to include the whole race through the doctrine of man's fall, and making a virtue of self-flagellation through the doctrine of atonement, Greene does present a conception of life that is strongly infused with private horror.

But this is by no means the whole of the story. Greene's anguish, however private its sources, has objective and positive meaning for the world he happens to live in. If often he seems to invert or reverse our usual humanistic ideals, his inversion is not destructive in either intent or final effect. Unlike the decadent writer, with whom he has been unjustly compared (E. Sewell, *Thought*, 29, 1954, 51-60), Greene denies our accepted values not for denial's sake but rather to emphasize values that he feels are more adequate. Certainly in our age his reversals are often distinctly in order. When man, having torn down much, is considering tearing down all, the complacency that Greene attacks with bias merits at least unbiased attack; when horror has assumed the frightening aspect of every day, the stress that Greene places on guilt and on universal responsibility is more than appropriate. Furthermore, horror in Greene's writings is not an end but a beginning. Just as in the lives of his characters awareness of guilt is the first step toward glory, so in his novels awareness of nightmare is the first step toward affirmation. Humanizing the moral laws by which most men would stand condemned, he finds at the heart of our guilty darkness the redeeming virtues of pity and tolerance, as applicable to our times as the evil they partly atone for. If these virtues are marred by uncharity toward satisfied, sensual people, he nonetheless gives to the lost, tormented, sin-ridden men of the world a depth of understanding and sympathy that transcends all else in his work. Out of a vision of horror founded on personal guilt, he creates what is in the last analysis a deeply positive vision of love.

SEAN O'FAOLAIN

The Irish writer Sean O'Faolain has published two dozen books of fiction, biography, criticism, and translation, among them *The Great O'Neill*, *An Irish Journey*, and *The Heat of the Sun*. Mr. O'Faolain was Director of the Fine Arts Council of Ireland from 1957 to 1959.

GRAHAM GREENE:
"I SUFFER, THEREFORE I AM"

The two most striking things about the novels of Graham Greene are their preoccupation with evil and their intellectual *jusqu'au-boutisme*. As for the latter, one is reminded of Camus's declaration that it is not sufficient to live, we must have and perceive a destiny that does not wait on death: man, that is, wants to anticipate his own destiny, and every writer wants to express in terms of this world the mortal destiny of man. It is a modern attitude among novelists. They were formerly satisfied to bring their novels to an intermediate destination rather than to expound an ultimate destiny. Marriage, love, domestic happiness, self-completion, self-fulfillment, self-perfection are in one way or another the themes of Balzac, Scott, Dickens, Stendhal, and Tolstoy; whereas it has been well said that Greene, Mauriac, and Bernanos return us to the medieval world, as if the great humanist tradition had never happened. Where Dante saw the totality of human destiny as a vision outside the flaming ramparts of the world, men like Greene bring the other world into this present life. If this has, as I intend to suggest, the effect of disintegrating his characters, of liquefying them, possibly of dehumanizing them, it also has the fine effect of enlarging the imaginative and visionary content of his work. It explains, at any rate, his extremism, his reckless courage in taking an idea to the limits of its implications. (He does this nowhere more fully than in *The Heart of the Matter.*) It is something which fills the sensitive reader with apprehension. "Whither next?" one asks, and wonders when he will come up against a stone wall, or a chasm.

His obsession with the ugly and evil side of life is equally troubling. More than occasionally one feels that he is not merely outraging nature but that he is taking a perverse pleasure in rubbing its face in its own ordure. One feels that in concentrating on a restricted set of themes he has implied that no matter what subject he may choose to paint—childhood innocence, mother love, a first kiss—he could make it look just as grim. Not, of course, that anybody has the least right to object to grimness, and every writer is entitled to wear whatever spectacles he pleases. But one may, indeed must, if necessary, draw attention to the limitations of an artist's palette, or of his human sympathy, or of his intellectual interests. One may, if necessary, draw a distinction between an intellectual approach and a pathological obsession. I feel that more than a few of Greene's books justify our apprehension on all these counts; that his attitude to life exists, like the mental world of Pascal, so close to the border line of the morbid and corrupt as to be saved from both only by the utmost delicacy and restraint; and much of Greene's work, to my mind, shows small signs that he is sufficiently aware of the importance of these sanitary precautions.

It must be clear to us all by now—he has made it clear—that his attraction to evil and ugliness was originally instinctive or emotional, and that he has gradually built about it an intellectual scaffolding. It is the natural way of the artist: first feeling, then perception. Evil and ugliness inspire him. They are the compost of his flower garden. Faith, for him, is not a gift; it is won from despair. Love relies on the validity of hate. His hope of heaven depends on the reality of hell. He believes in God because he believes in Satan. That it is an uncomfortable and not very attractive approach does not invalidate it; and it is not entirely alien to the English tradition—one thinks at once of Bunyan.

Indeed, there is nothing absolutely startling or new about it. Man has always cried to the Lord *de profundis*, and moralists have frequently observed that the most direct road to godliness may be the road that seems to lead the other way. Pierre Emmanuel said it simply in his *Autobiography* when he declared that it is not morality but immorality (ugliness and evil) that brings us to God—the nauseating experience of finding ourselves face to face with our own naked shame and stale self-disgust. Yet few writers have found so much positive satisfaction, even comfort, in the sight of evil as Greene has. Joyfully he reverses Browning. God's in his heaven, all's wrong with the world. He *has* to be in his heaven. Conversely, whenever Greene sees people happy in their vulgar, cheery, beery way he is filled with gloom. No good, he seems to say, can possibly come of happiness.

He has been explicit about this in the opening pages of *The Lawless Roads*, that entirely dreary book about Mexico which, in passing, is as good an illustration as any of his less successful books of the danger of sticking too rigidly to a narrow point of view. The first two pages of the book will suffice.[1]

It is fascinating, and it is frightening. Thereafter will the boy ever be able to do without "hell"? Will it become: "One believes in heaven only because one believes in hell"? Will everything that it is not heaven have to become hell? It begins to seem so. For from there the memory goes on to give us a strange picture of a little country town in Hertfordshire set in pastoral country within a crescent of the Chiltern hills. I must have passed through or paused at this rather pleasant-looking town a dozen times before. One afternoon, halting at one of the pubs for a drink, and observing a couple of men who were obviously schoolmasters chatting amiably over a beer, I realized that this was the hideous town anathematized in the opening pages of *The Lawless Roads*. Everything in Greene's description of it is in the manner of Joyce's impressions of a Dublin slum. Our attention is directed to a shabby shop

---

[1] The passage that Mr. O'Faolain cites here is reprinted on pages 453-55.—Ed.

selling *London Life*, with the usual "articles about high heels, corsets, and long hair" (for men, one presumes); to the fake Tudor Café where four one-armed men dine together, "arranging their seats so that their arms shouldn't clash"—which, one may observe, most two-armed people also do; we are told about "Irish servant girls making assignations for a ditch"—and one wonders how Greene could know. The most seemingly innocent things are made to seem cheap or sinister. When a girl is observed cutting some branches off a tree, she does so "with an expression abased and secretive." The saw "wails" through the wood. The photographs in a shop window became "yellowing faces," and they "peer out" at passersby. When somebody pushes in the door of the Plough Inn, it chimes; ". . . ivory balls clicked, and a bystander said, 'they do this at the Crown, Margate'—England's heart beating out in bagatelle to her eastern extremity." He quotes newspaper reports about a murder; about the suicide of a girl of fifteen, pregnant with a second child that might have been the child of any one of fourteen youths; which is the first really shocking thing, apart from *London Life*, that has been mentioned. Even the game of Monopoly, very popular hereabouts, we are told—as if it were not popular at the time in a dozen languages—is presented as a sign of a grasping, selfish world without any sense of responsibility for seduced children, early divorces, or the ancient soil abused by new bungalows. "You couldn't live," we are told, "in a place like this: it was somewhere to which you returned for sleep and rissoles by the 6.50 or the 7.25."

Obviously, common sense tells us, all this exists, or for hell's sake is made to exist, only in his own lacerated imagination. One sympathizes sincerely. The place is evidently associated with some deep, unhealed traumatic wound. But one suspects that when he sets off for the wilds of Mexico (to which this is the prologue) he will find everything just as squalid and heartless. He does. All he has to do is to change the names and the circumstances: the impression is in the same color, a general rot-green light. The only important difference is that he implies, not very persuasively, that if the Mexican people were allowed to practice their old religion in complete freedom, life there would be less squalid. To which one can only reply that nobody is hunting down Catholics with police dogs in Hertfordshire. But it would be pointless to argue rationally about all this, since the man is clearly not talking about objective conditions at all. We must agree, however, that it is an achievement to be able to see the devil in unlikely places, for he doubtless is everywhere. Mauriac has not a finer nose for Satan. Pascal had not a finer ear when he heard the voice of Beelzebub among the Jesuits than Greene hearing the authentic whisper of eternal corruption in the chiming doorbell of the Plough Inn and the innocent flick of billiard balls. This is real tin-chapel stuff. Bunyan suffered the same agonies in the Bedford pubs.

We can understand so much without difficulty; but two puzzles suggest themselves. It is good to see evil on many sides if it helps to remind us constantly that good and godliness are just around the corner. Why, however, must they always be around the corner, never walking down the High Street? It is also good to be able to show, if one persuasively can, that there is no real essential difference between native and foreign forms of evil: that nobody living in the home counties has the right to be smugly horrified by the affairs of Chiapas or Tabasco, with priests hiding in swamps and being shot when found there, hotel lavatories ankle-deep in ordure, flies that produce a hideous form of blindness, dead beetles lying on the floor being devoured by long processions of hungry ants, buzzards on tin roofs, and so forth and so on. But, if wherever one goes—London, Brighton, Mexico, Stockholm, Vienna, Stamboul, Indochina—one will always find the same story, why stir at all? The answer evokes what may be the essential question: that although it is true that whenever a moralist writes he describes a *voyage autour de son âme*, why does no other moralist bring back such a consistently identical story? Greene must then be some special sort of moralist; whereupon the essential questions arise: What is his sort? What is his tradition?

I suggest that the only comparable modern analogy is with Pascal and Jansenism. It is a literary tradition which has exercised a much more far-reaching influence on the course of modern literature than we commonly realize. Essentially its challenge has been felt as a challenge to the humanists to deny, and prove, that there is not an impassable gulf between pleasure and the virtuous life, between the weakness of human nature and its possibilities of greatness, between all that we like to enjoy and most of the things we pretend to admire. In its heyday it provoked a profound opposition, and when Port-Royal fell, it might all seem to have been no more than a flash in the pan. But Pascal did not come out of nothing, and when one is discussing the French nature, it is still one of the more agreeable problems to ask what in the French nature produced him. Perhaps it is enough to say that the pessimism of Jansenism is endemic in human nature in general. We may think back to Saint Augustine and the Manicheans, to go no further. What is more to our purpose is to observe how persistently it recurs; the power of an appealing literary form—every French writer must have read and admired Pascal—to keep ideas alive; and the historical fact that the rise of Jansenism coincided with the beginnings of the whole modern high-minded disapproval of aristocratic irresponsibility.

I do not suggest that many writers swallow Pascal whole. But he does seem to offer something to a great many types of writers—the ascetically minded Catholic, the natural skeptic with no interest in religion (La Rochefoucauld was of the type), the soured hedonist, the frustrated romantic, the earnest social reformer, the topical satirist. The list of candidates for the title of neo-Pascalians in our time is long: Bernanos, Julian Green, Mauriac, Céline, Marcel Aymé, Camus, Faulkner, Moravia, George Orwell, Graham Greene—all of them antihumanist, antiheroic, highly skeptical about man's inherent dignity, which the great humanist tradition took as the cornerstone of all its beliefs, full of misgivings as to the nature of free will.

We had here better redefine our terms, since Jansenism is one of those words that has been so loosely used—almost as a term of common abuse without any precise meaning, like Pink, or Liberal, or Left, or Romantic—that anybody using it as a term of literary criticism is under an obligation to say what precisely he means by it. The word, we will recall, originated quite simply out of an exchange of ideas between the Abbé Saint-Cyran and Jansen, Bishop of Ypres, with a view to a reform within the Catholic Church. The main documents are *Augustinus*, which is a sort of anthology of relevant Augustiniana—Saint Augustine being taken as a representative of the more extreme, though orthodox, view on the doctrine of Grace, which was the cardinal point involved; various records of the imprint the doctrine left on the convent of Port-Royal; the writings of Pascal, especially the *Lettres provinciales*, that highly entertaining book in which one may watch the fight between the Jansenists and the Jesuits as close up as in television; and the continuing marks of its influence well on into the eighteenth century in La Rochefoucauld, Racine, Boileau and others.

From these we gather that the central Jansenist doctrine was that man cannot be saved by his own efforts. Alone he is helpless. He depends for salvation on the arbitrary, if not actually capricious, gift of Grace, which he can neither achieve of his own efforts nor, if it is granted to him, resist. [. . .]

With so much by way of definition let us now turn back to Greene's novels and observe four of their cardinal characteristics.

1) *The obsessive theme*. It has been said frequently that his obsessive theme is the Hunted Man. This is true only if we take the phrase in the sense of a man hunted by himself: the sense of the epigraph to his first novel *The Man Within*: "There's another man within me that's angry with me." In the literal sense, the hunted man is not the subject of *The End of the Affair*, *The Heart of the Matter*, *Brighton Rock* (not the subject, though it is a thread in the story), *It's a Battlefield*, *Stamboul Train* (unless one strains a point to make Czinner the central character), or *Rumour at Nightfall*. He is the subject of *A Gun for Sale* and *The Power and the Glory*. In any case he is never the theme of Greene's novels.

His persistent theme is betrayal under one form or another: treason, unfaithfulness, the double cross, the letdown, the broken trust. This may be why there is such a strong suggestion of a sense of grievance in all his work, a certain sulkiness in his attitude to life which reminds one of Claude Edmonde Magny's remark about Hemingway, that behind the mask of the hero there is the face of a *pauvre petit garçon*, a little boy whose bun was stolen by somebody when he was very young. Somebody has said that there is no use in playing a game where everybody cheats. Everybody cheats Greene in Greene's world.

Let us test this suggestion that betrayal is his central theme. In *The Man Within* a smuggler betrays his best friend and his fellow smugglers. In *Rumour at Nightfall* two journalists, Crane and Chase, are attracted to the same woman. Crane betrays Chase to her. Chase then betrays Crane to the authorities. The woman thereupon, having married Crane only a few hours before, takes Chase to her heart. The bitter moral of *Stamboul Train* is that faithfulness never pays. Czinner the idealist revolutionary is shot. The honest little trollop Coral Musker is overnight swapped by the businessman Myatt for the quondam Lesbian Janet Purdoe, who thereby betrays her former friend Mabel Warren, who now takes on Coral Musker, after being instrumental in bringing about Czinner's death. In *It's a Battlefield*, where everybody lets down everybody else and gets nothing much out of it, the only conclusion open to us is that unfaithfulness does not pay either. Here Jim Drover, a Communist, is under sentence of death. His wife betrays him, his brother betrays him; Condor, a journalist, betrays his pals; his sister-in-law is unfaithful all round; Surrogate the writer is unfaithful to his dead wife; and the Assistant Commissioner of Police decides in his devotion to the law that he must not be overloyal to justice. In *Brighton Rock* the whole central story of Rose and Pinkie turns on betrayal or the fear of betrayal. Pinkie murders Hale for having betrayed the gang, then betrays Spicer, then seduces Rose lest she should betray him. *The Ministry of Fear*, a war story, is specifically concerned with traitors. In *England Made Me* we are in the world of international finance, where Kate Farrant is the only really reliable character: the central figure, Tony Farrant, might truthfully be described as the sort of charm-dispensing liar who would double-cross his sister, since that is precisely what he does. In *A Gun for Sale* the hare-lipped assassin is double-crossed by his employers, and any pity we may feel for this murderous maniac comes from his vain hope that Anne, the detective's girl, will not give him away to the police, which she has to do. In *The Heart of the Matter* Scobie is unfaithful to his wife, lets his mistress down, and his servant, and one may fairly hold the view that his final gamble for salvation is on the border line of a double cross on God. But we are given to understand that God is treated poorly by most of the characters in these stories. Raven, seeing the infant Christ in the crib, thinks: there He lies waiting "for the double cross, the whip, the nails." This general unfaithfulness is symbolical of mankind's eternally renewed Judas kiss.

2) *The denial of free will.* All these characters, we are made to feel, are coping with circumstances beyond their power, the dice loaded against them. They are fissurated by self-interest, self-distrust, self-pity, ambition, lust, greed, fear, hate, weak longing for peace at any price, and, most dissolvent weakness of all, human respect. They are, indeed, permitted to have glimpses of the Good Life, but the battle that takes place within their consciences—where the act of treason takes place—is a foregone conclusion. It is true that when we first come to these grim novels we have hopes that somebody will rise superior to the brute. Once we have become familiar with the obsessive theme we know that these brief spurts of gallantry will soon die. For example, one might, if one did not know the line of fate as Greene sees it, have, for a while, high hopes that Myatt, in *Stamboul Train*, will delight us by sticking pluckily to the chorus girl Coral. And Greene tries hard to be fair to Myatt, or seems to be trying, though since Myatt, like everybody else in the novel except Czinner, collapses in the end, one cannot avoid feeling that Greene has given only so that he may in the end take away. Or we might hope that Conrad Drover in *It's a Battlefield* will at least succeed in shooting the police commis-

sioner. Knowing the foreordained line of fate, we are sardonically gratified when he merely succeeds in shooting at the commissioner with blank cartridges. Nobody in Greene's novels stands a dog's chance.

Greene was not always so hopeless of humanity. He had a romantic period at the start of his career represented by three novels of which he has since suppressed two. In this period his men were, to be sure, just as prone to evil, but he did allow to some of them gestures of real self-perception, self-truth, and final regeneration. I think he may still have hoped at this period that man could save himself. There is a curious passage in *Rumour at Nightfall* which suggests that if he could then see this hope for man it was because he was still seeing life as a conflict of a purely human order. Crane has found out that his beloved Eulalia had previously been the lover of a Spaniard. The discovery pains him, but he nourishes this pain in the belief that without pain truth is of an inferior quality. In pain one discovers oneself. Descartes's "I think, therefore I am" becomes "I suffer, therefore I am." Crane expressed this by calling painless truth "comfortable," whereas those who suffer when they see the truth will not be comfortable, will desire virtue and admiration and courage, even though they may actually in their weakness choose "lies, evasions, compromises, fears and humanity." So Crane by honestly recognizing his own cowardice and suffering achieves a final act of courage.

It would be interesting to know what happened in Graham Greene's mind around 1931, for in that year the romantic-humanist period closed with a bang, as if something that had been gnawing at the foundations of his belief in man's power of self-purification brought down the wall separating him from an almost total despair of human nature. In that year he wrote *Stamboul Train*, and after that the road is clear. The romantic style vanishes. Decorous expression, reticence, the note of human idealism give way, with those nineteenth-century smugglers and Carlists, to the modern scene painted with all that ruthless brutality, brassiness, brilliance, cruelty, sexiness, tartness, satire, and so on which he would finally justify so magnificently in *The Power and the Glory*—though, as we shall note, with the new addition of a mystical escape into final optimism.

It is interesting, possibly revealing, that only two types are permitted to engage our sympathy from *Stamboul Train* on-ward: priests and trollops. Each of these is outside the battle: the priest because he is sold to heaven, the trollop because she is at least undeceived, knows that she is what she is—Greene loathes all forms of pretense, fake, sentimentality, as the surest paths to the Judas kiss—and, knowing herself, may one day re-enter the battle. See also *The End of the Affair*.

Why does Greene load the dice so completely against his characters? It is the old Jansenist reason that man, of himself, can do nothing. Only God can do it. He was already groping towards this idea in his early romantic period. There, in *Rumour at Nightfall*, we come on a frightening observation that "if Judas betrayed God, God betrayed Judas by waiting for his coming." Sin appears to be coercive. People are so caught in the net that even when they would do good they do harm—it is the theme of *The Quiet American*—and if they are godless, must do harm: as when Ida in *Brighton Rock* by her pity for Hale starts a chain of circumstances that brings disaster all round, or when Rose by her human pity for Pinkie drives him still deeper into evil. In *Brighton Rock* he allows us at least the chance of godly help, but it is only a chance, and it remains only a chance thereafter—if it is permissible to think of a last-minute miracle as a chance. Pinkie's only hope is expressed in the far from hopeful verse: "Between the stirrup and the ground he mercy sought—and mercy found." Scobie's gamble in *The Heart of the Matter* seems like a million-to-one chance. He cannot stop desiring Helen; his wife insists on his receiving Communion; his priest can give him no loophole; rather than go on offending God he kills himself. His only hope is that God will forgive self-murder because it was done through love of God. [. . .]

3) *His belittlement of human nature.* It inevitably follows that Greene tends to reduce man's stature and all his works. It must be unnecessary to give illustrations. I must again insist,

however, that we have no right to complain about this. A writer, given a certain *manière de voir*, can only do with it what he can. But we are entitled, and obliged, to consider the resultant technical and moral coercions.

One of these is that Greene by deliberately reducing man's stature, and impugning his free will, for the purposes of his theme, must always be in grave danger of making his people so subservient to his theme that they become its puppets. It must be left to each reader of *Brighton Rock*, for example, to say whether Pinkie strikes them as a human being or as a puppet. I find him entirely unpersuasive except as something strayed out of a mental home. I suggest that the same is true of Raven in *A Gun for Sale*. Everybody in *It's a Battlefield*, with the exception of the boy Jules, is coerced to play a foreordained role. So are the main characters in *England Made Me*: they are credible only as examples of that form of semipathological egotism so neatly intimated by the epigraph from Walt Disney, "All the world owes *me* a living." They are all, like Scobie, vehicles of a preconceived idea. Insofar as they come alive they come alive *after* they have been conceived as symbols.

We are forced again and again to the conclusion that Greene is not primarily interested in human beings, human problems, life in general as it is generally lived; that what he is writing is not so much novels as modern miracle plays. It is one of his great achievements that so many people can nevertheless read his novels on the naturalistic level, and be persuaded by them on that level; for he has enormous invention, a graphic eye, one of the quickest minds working in fiction today, and an inflammable and infectious imagination. I can only say that I do not believe that he is interested in the matter of his novels one-tenth as much as in their message. In fact, I go so far as to doubt if he is in the least interested in human nature except insofar as he can put it into some weird-looking cabinet, saw it up in bits, stick swords into it, fire shots at it, draw the curtain, and show us that it has suddenly been transmogrified magically, or miraculously, if one prefers, into an angel.

One constant coercion that follows from his treatment of mankind is that their power of intelligent thought is gravely impaired: that faculty which lifts us above the limitations of our natures and our circumstances. Nearly all his people are forced therefore to act violently, and to come to disaster. His people feel rather than think. In this he reminds me of Faulkner, whose people are so dominated by an overpowering weight of fate from the past that they can only struggle wildly, violently, and disastrously. It was not so much Greene who began to write thrillers in 1931 as his characters, who ran away with him.

4) *The mystical escape from nature.* There is a second watershed in Greene's career, after 1931. It occurred somewhere around 1938 when, in *Brighton Rock*, he had taken the ordinary thriller technique to the limit. Around that year he became involved by an act of God or chance in a libel action concerning Miss Shirley Temple, then a child actress. While acting as film critic for a humorous paper called *Night and Day*, most unfortunately for himself but fortunately for literature, he chose to intimate that Miss Temple was not so much the darling of her coevals as the *femme fatale* of elderly gentlemen gone a little beyond their sexual prime. Mr. Greene retired to Mexico, wrote *The Lawless Roads*, and found the theme of *The Power and the Glory*.

It is interesting that the first of these books, a factual record, was extremely dull, and the second, a play of imagination on fact, was to prove one of the finest novels of our time in any language. He saw there that far from being a pessimist in his sensitiveness to the omnipresence of evil he had all along been a supreme optimist. He had tortured himself unnecessarily with the squalor of the world's underground annexes—the furtive love-making in suburban back lanes or under mud-spattered iron bridges in the shadow of sweet evil-smelling gasometers, the savageries of race-course gangs, the painted madam, the exhausted whore, the cigarette butt disintegrating in the lavatory bowl, the dead gangster in his coffin at a peep show, the smutty postcard passed around under school desks—all the tawdry viciousness of which not merely the scum of humanity but each one of us, but for the grace of God, is capable. He saw that what he must do with all this was to magnify it more and more until it exploded, and there at the center of the foul explosion would shine the unsullied face of God. Everything for the best in the worst possible world. So, the priest in *The Power and the Glory*, when dogged by the Judas of the book and forced to listen to his sordid confession, thinks:

Man was so limited: he hadn't even the ingenuity to invent a new vice: the animals knew as much. It was for this world that Christ had died: the more evil you saw and heard about you, the greater glory lay around the death; it was too easy to die for what was good and beautiful, for home or children or a civilization—it needed a God to die for the half-hearted and the corrupt.

Indeed, the corruption of mankind is a sort of backhanded tribute to God; it is even a form of godliness to be corrupt; or at least to be corrupt does not deprive us of a form of godliness, as the priest argues in a striking and daring passage in which he looks down at the dirty, yellow-fanged, half-caste traitor jogging on a mule at his side and realizes the implications of the Christian belief that man is made after God's image and likeness:

But at the centre of his own faith there always stood the convincing mystery—that we were made in God's image—God was the parent, but He was also the policeman, the criminal, the priest, the maniac, and the judge. Something resembling God dangled from the gibbet or went into odd attitudes before the bullets in a prison yard or contorted itself like a camel in the attitude of sex. He would sit in the confessional and hear the complicated dirty ingenuities which God's image had thought out: and God's image shook now, up and down on the mule's back, with the yellow teeth sticking out over the lower lip. . . . He [. . .] pressed his hand with a kind of driven tenderness upon the shoulders of God's image.

It is superbly irrational. It is even illogical. Because a maniac is made in God's image, that does not make God a maniac. Since God has no body, it would be anthropomorphic to suggest that his image is bodily. The essence of man's likeness to God is intellectual and spiritual, so that a maniac or a fornicator ceases to act in God's "image" by his behavior. But such a daring and finely imaginative passage is not to be shredded to pieces. It is a sort of poem. It is not to be thought about. It is to be felt with. To be rational about such things is to be either vulgar or satirical. Mr. Evelyn Waugh could invent a delightful character who had read too much Graham Greene and ended up as some sort of specially obscene heretic.

All Graham Greene's best work can only be read as "a sort of poem," an exciting blend of realism as to its detail and poetry as to its conception. It is not only the brainless and predestined quality of his characters that makes them move so fast: they have been conceived under the emotional pressure of poetic inspiration which flies them as high as maddened kites. In this sense, Greene's characters really are hunted men, the hounds of heaven at their heels. It is one significant reason why they are least interesting when they pause. Then they come down to earth, to common life, and common life is a range of experience beyond Greene's powers, since it is outside his interest.

In *The Power and the Glory*, it will be remembered, the priest halts in his flight when, in a moment of weakness, he decides to dodge his fate. It is the one section of the novel in which he fails to hold us. The mystical escape from common human nature has been, so to speak, switched off. When the priest resumes his journey to his Gethsemane, the voltage of the novel at once comes up again. So, one of the finest scenes in the novel occurs when he is, while trying to buy wine for the Mass, arrested as a bootlegger and thrown into jail. That night scene in the jail, stinking with moral and bodily ordure, when, in the foul darkness among criminals, he at last publicly admits that he is a priest, and they, the lowest of the low, do not betray him, is one of the finest scenes in all fiction.

In Greene as in much of modern fiction the hero has given place to the martyr. Greene lives vicariously the broken lives of the betrayed ones of the earth. We, with whatever degree of misgiving as to his ideas about betrayal, partake in this general martyrdom, very much as we do also when we read Faulkner, or Hemingway, or Aymé, or Joyce, whose heroes are broken, or "betrayed," by a more human sort of enemy than Greene's Jansenistic invention of innate evil. In a strange and deeply moving sense Greene suffers crucifixion for his characters' sakes. Not that he can hope to redeem them. Within his philosophy the redemption of man by Christ is perpetually thwarted by innate evil. All he can give to us is a final hope, not intense, far from heartening, that our immortal destiny may be greater than our mortal deserts; but that we have small hope of release or even relief from the bondage of sin and the devil here below, the whole burden of his work gloomily asserts. Sweetness and light are hereafter, or not at all. Pascal would have sympathized with this sad message, however shocked by the author's method of presentation.

I have not attempted to conceal that, over the years, I have grown a little weary both of Greene's message and his methods. If one compares his work with Mauriac's, one will see that he has sacrificed too much to both. All Mauriac's best work keeps a fine balance between his humanity and his beliefs. He knows that if his beliefs do not demonstrate themselves in the ordinary world of ordinary people they cannot demonstrate themselves persuasively at all. So, the mental and emotional processes of the husband in *A Knot of Vipers* are purely human processes. They are recognizable and persuasive in proportion as they are human and normal processes. His characters are ridden by fierce passions, but they deal with their own passions, succumb to them or surmount them, as apparently fully rounded human beings. (In his weaker later novels, the puppet master's fingers are sadly visible.) His work has a corresponding variety. I do not find this variety in Greene's characters or themes; I find variety only in his brilliant inventiveness of incident, which seems to be inexhaustibly fertile. All Greene's novels are as subject to the tyranny of the last page as a railway train is subject to its destination. They lack autonomy. In Charles du

Bos's words about a certain type of Catholic novelist, "*il se mue soi-même en un Deus ex machina*."* I think the reason Mauriac never did this in his best work is that he retained his detachment towards his own church, and the only work of Greene's in which I wondered whether Greene might not be capable also of this detachment was that which pleased me least, his play *The Living Room*, where there were suggestions of impatience with Catholics' goodness, and piety, and pat answers. (The title could have a satirical ring if there had been any character in the play strong enough to represent a denunciation of those unco guid people who virtually smothered the unfortunate heroine to death by their appalling goodness.)

In his latest novel to date, *The Quiet American*, we see this habit of simplifying characters, in order to force them to illustrate a point, carried over to a story about a purely political problem. We are as oppressed as ever by a sense of inevitability. The character of the young American is so close to caricature that nothing but disaster can be expected from his ingenuous zeal; gradually we realize, in dismay, that the author has rigged the story in this way for the purposes of a political pamphlet very much as, earlier, he has rigged his stories to make a philosophical or theological observation. I find this particularly distressing in *The Quiet American*. After all, in the "religious" novels the theme, or point, was a general one. Here the point is particular, local, and historical; we are, in fact, on the borders of the historical novel. If we lay the book to one side while reading it, to consider what our attitude would be to a novel about the theme of the "white man's burthen," or the theme of the liberation of the Russian peasant by the Communist revolution, we will further realize that we are here on the borders of the propagandist novel: for this young American is not just any young foreigner anywhere—he is specifically a representative figure in a given place at a given time. If this be a just comment, it follows that *The Quiet American* is a novel in the class of *Uncle Tom's Cabin* and is open to a double

---

* "He transforms himself into a *Deus ex machina*."—Ed.

form of criticism—literary and factual. Simplification, or caricature, whether favorable or unfavorable, is thereby a double fault. I could not, in reading this novel, help thinking back several times to *For Whom the Bell Tolls*, in which another American comes to Europe to take part in another war, and on almost every count I found the comparison between Hemingway's theme, indicated by the title and the epigraph—generous, general, and humane—and Greene's misanthropy both informative and depressing.

I admit, gratefully and admiringly, that Graham Greene has expanded our view of human nature by his constant insistence on divine pity and divine mercy, and he must, in doing this, have brought courage and consolation to a great number of readers. It is hard to believe that the consolation can outlive the discovery that he has not—outside that triumphant book *The Power and the Glory*—wedded the pity and the mercy to the complexity of our common day. It is discouraging that in this latest novel, where the *deus ex machina* is literally out of a machine, he has so little pity of a purely human nature for human nature. "Thy will be done in heaven as it cannot be on earth" is a prayer, and an attitude, that leaves a novelist and his readers very little breathing space or living room.

❖❖❖

III

Analogies and Perspectives

GRAHAM GREENE

Another Mexico is Greene's account of his journey through Mexico
in 1938; in his introduction to *The Power and the Glory* (pages
1-5) Greene tells the circumstances in which the trip was undertaken.

Part of the strength of *Another Mexico* is that Greene's entire
Mexican experience was absorbed into a pattern of religious thought
that began to take shape in his mind early in his youth. That pattern
is hauntingly recalled and described in the first pages of the prologue. The book, in addition, provided a number of sources for
The Power and the Glory, and the reader may enjoyably pick out
the originals for Mr. Tench, the Lehrs—the German-American
brother and sister who give the priest refuge—the mestizo, and
perhaps other characters. There seem to be at least three sources for
the priest himself: Father Pro; a nameless priest who survived for
ten years by hiding in the jungles of Tabasco; and a Chiapas priest
known as a "whisky priest" who was asked by the nervous peasants
to move on and leave them alone.

THE SOURCE: SELECTIONS FROM
ANOTHER MEXICO

From Prologue

I was, I suppose, thirteen years old. Otherwise why should I
have been there—in secret—on the dark croquet lawn? I could
hear the rabbit moving behind me, munching the grass in his
hutch; an immense building with small windows, rather like
Keble College, bounded the lawn. It was the school; from
somewhere behind it, from across the quad, came a faint sound
of music: Saturday night, the school orchestra was playing
Mendelssohn. I was alone in mournful happiness in the dark.

Two countries just here lay side by side. From the croquet

---

lawn, from the raspberry canes, from the greenhouse and the tennis lawn you could always see—dominatingly—the great square Victorian buildings of garish brick: they looked down like skyscrapers on a small green countryside where the fruit trees grew and the rabbits munched. You had to step carefully: the border was close beside your gravel path. From my mother's bedroom window—where she had borne the youngest of us to the sound of school chatter and the disciplinary bell—you looked straight down into the quad, where the hall and the chapel and the classrooms stood. If you pushed open a green baize door in a passage by my father's study, you entered another passage deceptively similar, but none the less you were on alien ground. There would be a slight smell of iodine from the matron's room, of damp towels from the changing rooms, of ink everywhere. Shut the door behind you again, and the world smelt differently: books and fruit and eau-de-Cologne.

One was an inhabitant of both countries: on Saturday and Sunday afternoons of one side of the baize door, the rest of the week of the other. How can life on a border be other than restless? You are pulled by different ties of hate and love. For hate is quite as powerful a tie: it demands allegiance. In the land of the skyscrapers, of stone stairs and cracked bells ringing early, one was aware of fear and hate, a kind of lawlessness— appalling cruelties could be practised without a second thought; one met for the first time characters, adult and adolescent, who bore about them the genuine quality of evil. There was Collifax, who practised torments with dividers; Mr. Cranden with three grim chins, a dusty gown, a kind of demoniac sensuality; from these heights evil declined towards Parlow, whose desk was filled with minute photographs—advertisements of art photos. Hell lay about them in their infancy.

There lay the horror and the fascination. One escaped surreptitiously for an hour at a time: unknown to frontier guards, one stood on the wrong side of the border looking back—one should have been listening to Mendelssohn, but instead one heard the rabbit restlessly cropping near the croquet hoops. It was an hour of release—and also an hour of prayer. One became aware of God with an intensity—time hung suspended—music lay on the air; anything might happen before it became necessary to join the crowd across the border. There was no inevitability anywhere . . . faith was almost great enough to move mountains . . . the great buildings rocked in the darkness.

And so faith came to onc—shapelessly, without dogma, a presence above a croquet lawn, something associated with violence, cruelty, evil across the way. One began to believe in heaven because one believed in hell, but for a long while it was only hell one could picture with a certain intimacy—the pitch-pine partitions in dormitories where everybody was never quiet at the same time; lavatories without locks: "There, by reason of the great number of the damned, the prisoners are heaped together in their awful prison . . ."; walks in pairs up the suburban roads; no solitude anywhere, at any time. The Anglican Church could not supply the same intimate symbols for heaven; only a big brass eagle, an organ voluntary, "Lord, Dismiss Us with Thy Blessing," the quiet croquet lawn where one had no business, the rabbit, and the distant music.

Those were primary symbols; life later altered them; in a midland city, riding on trams in winter past the Gothic hotel, the super-cinema, the sooty newspaper office where one worked at night, passing the single professional prostitute trying to keep the circulation going under the blue and powdered skin, one began slowly, painfully, reluctantly, to populate heaven. The Mother of God took the place of the brass eagle: one began to have a dim conception of the appalling mysteries of love moving through a ravaged world—the Curé d'Ars admitting to his mind all the impurity of a province, Péguy challenging God in the cause of the damned. It remained something one associated with misery, violence, evil, "all the torments and agonies," Rilke wrote, "wrought on scaffolds, in torture chambers, madhouses, operating theatres, underneath vaults of bridges in late autumn. . . ."

Vaults of bridges: I think of a great metal bridge by the railway-station of my old home, a sense of grit and the great reverberation of plates as the trains went by overhead and the nursemaids pushed their charges on past the ruined castle, the watercress beds, towards the common, past the shuttered private entrance which the local lord had not used for a generation. It was a place without law—I felt that even then, obscurely: no one really was responsible for anyone else. Only a few walls were left of the castle Chaucer had helped to build; the lord's house had been sold to politicians. I remember the small sunk almshouses by the canal and a man running furiously into one of them—I was with my nurse—he looked angry about something: he was going to cut his throat with a knife if he could get away from his neighbours, "having no hope, and without God in the world."

I returned to the little town a while ago—it was Sunday evening and the bells were jangling; small groups of youths hovered round the traffic lights, while the Irish servant girls crept out of back doors in the early dark. They were "Romans," but they were impertinent to the priest if he met them in the high street away from the small, too new Catholic church in one of the red-brick villaed streets above the valley. They couldn't be kept in at night. They would return with the milk in a stranger's car. The youths with smarmed and scented hair and bitten cigarettes greeted them by the traffic lights with careless roughness. There were so many fish in the sea : . . . sexual experience had come to them too early and too easily. [. . .]

In July 1926, Father Miguel Pro landed at Vera Cruz. He was twenty-five years old and a Jesuit. He came back to his own country from a foreign seminary much as Campion returned to England from Douai. We know how he was dressed when a year and a half later he came out into the prison yard to be shot, and he may well have worn the same disguise when he landed (the equivalent of Campion's doublet and hose): a dark lounge suit, soft collar and tie, a bright cardigan. Most priests wear their mufti with a kind of uneasiness, but Pro was a good actor.

He needed to be. Within two months of Pro's landing,

President Calles had begun the fiercest persecution of religion anywhere since the reign of Elizabeth. The churches were closed, Mass had to be said secretly in private houses, to administer the Sacraments was a serious offence. Nevertheless, Pro gave Communion daily to some three hundred people, confessions were heard in half-built houses in darkness, retreats were held in garages. Pro escaped the plainclothes police again and again. Once he found them at the entrance to a house where he was supposed to say Mass; he posed as a police officer, showing an imaginary badge and remarking: "There's a cat bagged in here," and passed into the house and out again with his cassock under his arm. Followed by detectives when he left a Catholic house and with only fifty yards' start, he disappeared altogether from their sight round a corner—the only man they overtook was a lover out with his girl. The prisons were filling up, priests were being shot, yet on three successive first Fridays Pro gave the Sacrament to nine hundred, thirteen hundred, and fifteen hundred people.

They got him, of course, at last (they had got him earlier if only they had known it, but they let him go). This time they made no mistake, or else the biggest mistake of all. Somebody had thrown a bomb at Obregón's car in Chapultepec Park—from another car. The evidence since then points to Government complicity. All the assailants escaped but the driver, who was shot dead. A young Indian called Tirado was passing by, fled at the explosion, and was arrested. He was tortured without effect: he persisted in declaring himself innocent. The police pounced on those they feared most—Pro and his two brothers, Humberto and Roberto, and Luis Segovia Vilchis, a young engineer and Catholic leader. No evidence was brought against them; they were not tried by the courts. The American ambassador thought he could do more good by not intervening and left next day with the President and Will Rogers, the humorist, on a Pullman tour; one South American ambassador intervened and got a reprieve—timed too late to save any but Roberto. Pro was photographed by the official photographer, praying for his enemies by the pitted wall, receiving the *coup de grâce*; the photographs were sent to the press—to show the firmness of the Government—but within a few weeks it became a penal offence to possess them, for they had had an effect which Calles had not foreseen.

For Mexico remained Catholic; it was only the governing class—politicians and pistoleros—which was anti-Catholic. It was a war—they admitted it—for the soul of the Indian, a war in which they could use the army consisting mainly of Indians attracted by a dollar per day. (The individuals who composed the army too were Catholic, but it is quite easy to keep an uneducated soldier in ignorance of what he is doing.) By the time I left for Mexico, Calles had been gone some years—flown over into exile by his rival, Cárdenas. The antireligious laws were still enforced except in one state, San Luis Potosí, but the pressure from the Catholic population was beginning to make itself felt. Churches—now Government property—were allowed to open in most of the states, except for the hundreds that had been turned into cinemas, newspaper offices, garages. A proportion of priests calculated according to the size of the population was allowed to serve by the state governments. The ratio was seldom more favourable than one priest to ten thousand people, but the law, particularly in the Federal District of Mexico City, was slackly enforced. But in some other states the persecution was maintained. In Vera Cruz the churches remained closed until the peasants rose when a child was shot, early in 1937, in Orizaba; in Tabasco, the tropical state of river and swamp and banana grove, every church was believed to have been destroyed by the local dictator, Garrido Canabal, before he fled to Costa Rica—there wasn't a priest in the state; in Chiapas no church was open for Mass, the bishop was in exile, and little news came out of that mountainous untravelled region where the only railway-line runs along the coast to Guatemala. Nowhere were priests allowed to open schools. Educational programmes everywhere were laid down by the Government on dusty rationalist lines—nineteenth-century materialism reminiscent of Herbert

Spencer and the Thinkers' Library, alpaca jackets and bookshops on Ludgate Hill. . . .

The rabbits moved among the croquet hoops and a clock struck: God was there and might intervene before the music ended. The great brick buildings rose at the end of the lawn against the sky—like the hotels in the United States which you can watch from Mexico leaning among the stars across the international bridge.

From Chapter I: The Border

The border means more than a customs house, a passport officer, a man with a gun. Over there everything is going to be different; life is never going to be quite the same again after your passport has been stamped and you find yourself speechless among the money-changers. The man seeking scenery imagines strange woods and unheard-of mountains; the romantic believes that the women over the border will be more beautiful and complaisant than those at home; the unhappy man imagines at least a different hell; the suicidal traveller expects the death he never finds. The atmosphere of the border—it is like starting over again; there is something about it like a good confession: poised for a few happy moments between sin and sin. When people die on the border they call it "a happy death." [. . .]

From Chapter V: Voyage in the Dark

We arrived at Frontera at two-fifteen, forty-one hours from Vera Cruz, in an appalling heat. Only, I think, in Monrovia had I experienced its equal, but Frontera like Monrovia is freshened a little by the sea. To know how hot the world can be I had to wait for Villahermosa. Shark fins glided like periscopes at the entrance to the Grijalva River, the scene of the Conquistadores' first landing in Mexico, before they sailed on to Vera Cruz. Frontera itself was out of sight round a river bend; three or four aerials stuck up into the blazing sun from among the banana groves and the palm-leaf huts: it was like Africa seeing itself in a mirror across the Atlantic. Little islands of lily plants came floating down from the interior, and the carcasses of old stranded steamers held up the banks.

And then round a bend in the river Frontera, the frontier. So it will remain to me, though the Tabascan authorities have renamed it Puerto Obregón: the Presidencia and a big warehouse and a white blanched street running off between wooden shacks—hairdressers and the inevitable dentists, but no cantinas anywhere, for there is prohibition in Tabasco. No intoxicant is allowed but beer, and that costs a peso a bottle—a ruinous price in Mexico. The lily plants floated by; the river divided round a green island half a mile from shore, and the buzzards came flocking out, with little idiot heads and dusty serrated wings, to rustle round the shrouds. There was an election on: the name Bartlett occurred everywhere, and a red star. The soldiers stood in the shade of the Presidencia and watched us edge in against the river bank.

This was Tabasco—Garrido Canabal's isolated swampy puritanical state. Garrido—so it was said—had destroyed every church; he had organized a militia of Red Shirts, even leading them across the border into Chiapas in his hunt for a church or a priest. Private houses were searched for religious emblems, and prison was the penalty for possessing them. A young man I met in Mexico City—a family friend of Garrido's—was imprisoned three days for wearing a cross under his shirt; the dictator was incorruptible. A journalist on his way to photograph Tabasco was shot dead in Mexico City airport before he took his seat. Every priest was hunted down or shot, except one who existed for ten years in the forests and the swamps, venturing out only at night; his few letters, I was told, recorded an awful sense of impotence—to live in constant danger and yet be able to do so little, it hardly seemed worth the horror. Now Garrido is in Costa Rica, but his policy goes on. . . . The customs officers came on board, their revolver holsters creaking as they climbed the rotting rail. I remembered a bottle of brandy in my suitcase.

Their search was not a formality. They not only went through the cargo but the captain's cabin: you could see them peering under his bunk. They felt in the lifeboat and insisted on having unlocked the little cupboard where the plates and knives were kept. Presently the passengers were summoned below to open their boxes; I allowed myself to forget all my Spanish. People came and explained things with their fingers. I could hold out no longer and went down. But the customs men had come to the end of their tether; the heat in the cabin was terrific; everybody was wedged together—I slipped quietly away again and nobody minded. On the quay they were unloading beer—it was our main cargo: a hundred and fifty dozen bottles, to be sold only by Government agents. Puritanism pays.

I went for a walk on shore; nothing to be seen but one little dusty plaza with fruit-drink stalls and a bust of Obregón on a pillar, two dentists' and a hairdresser's. The buzzards squatted on the roofs. It was like a place besieged by scavengers—sharks in the river and vultures in the streets.

One introduction I had here, to the merchant who owned the warehouse on the quay, an old man with a little pointed beard who spoke no English. I told him I wanted to go to Palenque from Villahermosa. He tried to dissuade me—it was only a hundred miles, but it might take a week. First, as there were no roads for more than a few miles outside the capital I should have to return to Frontera, then I'd have to wait till I could get a barge up another river to Montecristo—or Zapata, as it was now called. There I could get horses. But the river journey would take two or three days and conditions would be—horrible. After all, I said, I had endured the *Ruiz Cano*. The *Ruiz Cano*, the old man said, was a fine boat. . . . I went back to the ship discouraged. They were still unloading beer; they wouldn't be moving that night, for it was still ten hours to Villahermosa and they needed daylight for the passage.

At sunset the mosquitoes began—a terrifying steady hum like

that of a sewing-machine. There were only two choices: to be eaten on deck (and probably catch malaria) or to go below to the cabin and the appalling heat. The only porthole was closed for fear of marauders; mosquito-nets seemed to shut out all the air that was left. It was only eight o'clock. I lay naked under the net and sweated; every ten minutes I tried to dry myself with a towel. I fell asleep and woke again and fell asleep. Then somewhere I heard a voice talking English— hollow overcivilized English, not American. I thought I heard the word "interpreter." It must have been a dream, and yet I can still remember that steady cultured voice going on, and the feel of my own wet skin, the hum of mosquitoes, and my watch saying 10:32.

I went for a walk with one of the sailors and we drank sweet unpleasant fruit drinks at a stall in the market and he tried— rather hopelessly—to sell me his second-hand crocodile-skin notecase for three pesos, about the price you pay for a whole crocodile. Then at nine-thirty we got under way up the monotonous, not unbeautiful river, shaking and rattling into the interior. There is always something exhilarating about moving inward from the sea into an unknown country. All the way along, the low banks were lined with bananas or coconut palms; sometimes a tributary stream ambled muddily off to God knows where.

A sailor came and told me there was a second gringo on board: he was sitting on the bench the other side of the smokestack. The boat was crowded now with passengers from Frontera, where he had come on board sick, unshaven, in an old black greasy hat. He wasn't very good to look at, sitting there with his mestizo wife and two blond washed-out little boys with transparent eyelids and heavy brown Mexican eyes. I couldn't foresee that I was to spend, oh, days in his company.

He was a dentist, an American, Doc Winter, and he hadn't been out of Frontera to Villahermosa for five years. But yesterday a long sickness had reached its climax; he said: "If I don't get away, I guess I'll die." He had tried to walk the two hundred yards to the ship to take his passage, but he couldn't make it. He had to send his wife, and this morning, well, he'd just struggled down and reached the bench, and he guessed he wouldn't move from there for an hour or two. In Villahermosa there was an English doctor—he didn't talk much English and he'd never been out of Mexico, but he was English all right— Dr. Roberto Fitzpatrick, and he would fix him up. It was the stomach, but what he most wanted was just a change of air, and the big stubbly western face sniffed for a breeze on the hot listless river.

I couldn't help wondering what had landed him in Frontera, the only foreigner there, and how he made a living in that dreary little river port. The answer to the second problem was, of course, gold fillings; I might have guessed that: they flashed at you from every face, like false *bonhomie*. He had the best practice, he said, in Frontera, for apparently that tiny town supported at least three. The people preferred to come to him rather than go to their own countrymen, who treated them like dogs. So his colleagues hated him. They wouldn't have hesitated, he said, at murder—if they had had the guts. Once a gunman did play for him—came to his consulting-room and instead of sitting down in the chair pulled a gun. Doc Winter was younger in those days: he'd kicked the man in the stomach and sent his gun flying and landed him on the point of the jaw. He groaned slightly as the engines rattled, and sniffed greedily for air. He was like the tough case of something labelled fragile.

What a country! he kept on exclaiming. God, what a country! He had to get Japanese drills from Mexico City because they were cheap, and they never lasted—sometimes they broke down after a single use. How he longed to get out, but what a chance! Every time you made money there was a revolution. And now this oil business and the exchange falling —he heard you could get five pesos for a dollar in Mexico City. Oh, things had been all right once in Tabasco—in the days when people still used mahogany furniture. There were a lot of American traders then—in timber. That was why you

had names like Bartlett among the Mexicans. They came down
after the Civil War from the South and intermarried and forgot their own tongue and took Mexican citizenship. But now
there was no money left in Tabasco: everything was just rotting
into the rivers.

"Well," I said, "I suppose things are better than in Garrido's
time."

Not on your life, he said. There was discipline in those days.
. . . Garrido was all right, only his friends went too far. "Why,"
he said, "that woman there, my wife, she's his niece. I was Garrido's dentist in Villahermosa. He never went to anyone else."

"Did he pay you?"

"I never sent a bill," he said. "I wasn't that crazy. But I got
protection." All that was wrong with Garrido was he went
against the Church. It never pays, he said. He'd be here now if
he hadn't gone against the Church.

"But he seems to have won," I said; "no priests, no
churches . . ."

"Oh," he said illogically, "they don't care about religion round
here. It's too hot."

That was incontestable—the heat increased not only as the
day advanced, but as the boat screwed further in to Tabasco.
"Frontera's nice and fresh," the dentist said, "not like Villahermosa." At about two o'clock in the afternoon we went aground
—backed furiously, swung this way and that, driving right up
against the bank, slid off and landed—hopelessly—on sand.
Our luck was in: we had chosen the only place in the whole
river where there was another ship to help us. We hadn't been
there twenty minutes when she came chugging round a bend,
dragging a chain of barges laden with bananas. It had been
intolerably hot, motionless there on the shoal, and we cried
out to them to let us have some bananas; and casually, as you
might throw feed to chickens, they threw great bunches on
board—a hundred or more fruit to a bunch—as if they were
weeds. Then they attached a chain and dragged us off. "Comrades," the captain called, raising his fist.

With the dark, the early hasty tropic dark, the fireflies came out—great globes of moving light, like the lamps of a town, flickering over the banana trees. Sometimes a canoe went by paddled by Indians—white and silent and transparent like a marine insect, and the oil-lamps in the bow and stern gave a sharp theatrical appearance to the sabre leaves on the bank. The roar of the mosquitoes nearly extinguished the sound of the engines; they swarmed across from the banks and shrivelled against the oil-lamps. I wondered nervously what would happen if we went aground now, with no hope of release till daylight and nearly fifty passengers on board and the mosquitoes drumming in. And then, of course, we did begin to go aground. Somebody shone an electric torch on a man in the bows taking soundings; the ship moved backwards and forwards, swung this way and that—inches at a time. Cries came up to the little dark bridge—naming the soundings—*"seis, siete,"* and then quickly down to *"tres."* Then the electric light would wane and die and a new bulb be fitted in. *"Seis, siete, cuatro."* For nearly half an hour we sat there in the river, swinging gently, before we got through.

And then suddenly, about eleven hours from Frontera, Villahermosa burst out at us round a bend. For twelve hours there had been nothing but trees on either side; one had moved forward only into darkness; and here with an effect of melodrama was a city—lights burning down into the river, a great crown outlined in electricity like a casino. All felt the shock—it was like coming to Venice through an uninhabited jungle—they called, triumphantly: *"El puerto, el puerto!"* and in the excitement we nearly ran aground for a third time—the bow swung round and dipped into the bank.

From Chapter VI: The Godless State

That effect of something sophisticated and gay in the heart of a swamp did not outlast the night—it was the swamp that lasted. I never, till the day I left, discovered what building had shone like a crown through the night—there certainly wasn't a casino, and the lights I had seen were not visible when once one was an inhabitant.

We tied up to a steep mud bank crowned by a high dark wall; under the shadow of Villahermosa—"the beautiful city" —the lights had all gone out. In the obscurity we could make out faces as the fireflies went by. A plank fifteen feet long bridged the mud river to the mud bank, and somebody switched on an electric torch to guide us. I began to slide on down the bank until a man took my arm and propelled me upwards. By the light of an electric torch I saw a policeman—or a soldier. He took my suitcase and shook it, listening for the clank of contraband liquor. It was like landing at the foot of a medieval castle: the ramp of mud and the old tall threatening walls and a sense of suspicion.

One came, as it were, through a crack in the walls to the only possible hotel, which stood in a small plaza on the main landing quay. An electric dynamo filled the hallway and the hotel itself began on the first floor at the head of a wide staircase, where an unshaved malarial creature sat rocking up and down in a wicker chair talking to himself. My room was a huge bare apartment with a high ceiling and a tiled floor and a bed put down somewhere in the middle. There was a private shower which put the price up by a peso a day, and it was only later that I found it didn't work; now, after the boat's dark cell, this room was luxury.

Somewhere music was being played: it came faintly down the hill to the riverside through the sticky night. I followed it—to the plaza. I was excited and momentarily happy: the place seemed beautiful. Under the trees of the little plaza the young men and women promenaded, the women on the inner circle, the men on the outer, moving in opposite directions, slowly. A blind man dressed carefully in white drill with a straw hat was led by a friend. It was like a religious ceremony going on and on, with ritualistic repetition—indeed it was the nearest to a religious ceremony you were allowed to get in Tabasco. If I had moved a camera all round the edge of the little plaza in a panning shot it would have recorded all the life there was in the capital city—a dentist's, with a floodlit chair of torture; the public jail, an old white-pillared one-story house which must have dated back to the Conquistadores, where a soldier sat with a rifle at the door and a few dark faces pressed against the bars; a Commercial Academy, the size of a village store; the Secretariat; the Treasury, a florid official building with long steps leading down to the plaza; the Syndicate of Workers and Peasants; the Casa de Agraristas; a few private houses with tall unshuttered windows guarded with iron bars, through which one saw old ladies on Victorian rocking-chairs swinging back and forth among the little statues and the family photographs. A public dance was going on with faded provincial elegance— you could see the couples revolving at a slant in the great brewery mirrors marked "Cerveza Moctezuma." At nine-thirty promptly all the main lights—the groups of four globes like balloons which stood at each corner of the plaza joined by ugly trailing overhead wires—went out. And I suppose the dance came to an end. For this was the puritan as well as the Godless state.

I went back to the hotel to bed and began to read *Dr. Thorne*: "There is a county in the west of England not so full of life indeed, nor so widely spoken of as some of its manu- facturing leviathan brethren in the north, but which is, never- theless, very dear to those who know it well. Its green pasture, its waving wheat, its deep and shady and—let us add—dirty lanes, its paths and stiles, its tawny-coloured, well-built rural churches, its avenues of beeches . . ." Trollope is a good author to read in a foreign land—especially in a land so different from anything one has ever known as this. It enables you to keep in touch with the familiar. A cockchafer came buzzing and beat- ing through the room and I turned out the light—the light went out all over Barsetshire, the hedges and the rectories and paddocks dropped into darkness, and as the cockchafers buzzed and beat one felt the excitement of this state where the hunted priest had worked for so many years, hidden in the swamps and forests, with no leave train or billet behind the lines. I remembered the confessor saying to me in Orizaba: "A very evil land." One felt one was drawing near to the centre of something—if it was only of darkness and abandonment.

Something went wrong with my watch in the night, so that I presented my only letter of introduction at seven-thirty in the morning when I thought it was ten-thirty. The man was away by plane, visiting a hacienda, but his wife received me with perfect courtesy as if she was used to foreigners arriving at that hour. We spoke of the Church in Tabasco (she was a Catholic), sitting in a little dark room out of the heat with her mother. There was no priest, she said, left in Tabasco, no church standing, except one eight leagues away, now used as a school. There had been one priest over the border in Chiapas, but the people had told him to go—they couldn't protect him any longer.

"And when you die?" I said.

"Oh," she said, "we die like dogs." No religious ceremony was allowed at the grave. The old people, of course, felt it most—a few weeks before they had smuggled the Bishop of Campeche in by plane to see her grandmother who was dying. They had money still . . . but what could the poor do? [. . .]

Of the old Dr. Fitzpatrick's Villahermosa—of St. Juan Bautista, as it was called then—very little remains: a few houses like the Hotel Tabasqueño, which must once have been lovely; a little classical plaza in pink stone with broken columns; the back wall of a church (what was the nave is a heap of rubble used—but rarely—for road mending). Of the cathedral not even that much remains—Garrido saw to that—only an ugly cement playground marks the site, with a few grim iron swings too scorching hot to use.

I said to Dr. Fitzpatrick, small bitter exiled widower, caged in his Victorian *sala*, with the vultures routing on his roof: "But I suppose *some* good came out of the persecution. Schools . . ."

He said the church schools were far better than those that

existed now . . . there were even more of them, and the priests in Tabasco were good men. There was no excuse for the persecution in this state—except some obscure personal neurosis, for Garrido himself had been brought up as a Catholic: his parents were pious people. I asked about the priest in Chiapas who had fled. "Oh," he said, "he was just what we call a whisky priest." He had taken one of his sons to be baptized, but the priest was drunk and would insist on naming him Brigitta. He was little loss, poor man, a kind of Padre Rey; but who can judge what terror and hardship and isolation may have excused him in the eyes of God?

The anonymity of Sunday seems peculiarly unnatural in Mexico: a man going hunting in the marshes with his dog and his gun, a young people's fiesta, shops closing after noon— nothing else to divide this day from all the other days, no bell to ring. I sat at the head of the stairs and had my shoes cleaned by a little blond bootblack—a thin tired child in tattered trousers like someone out of Dickens. Only his brown eyes were Mexican—not his transparent skin and his fine gold hair. I was afraid to ask his name, for it might have been Greene. I gave him twice what I usually gave (twenty centavos—say, five cents) and he returned me ten centavos' change, going wearily down the stairs with his heavy box into the great heat of Sunday.

Garrido has fled to Costa Rica and yet nothing is done. "We die like dogs." There were no secret Masses in private houses such as found in the neighbouring state, only a dreadful lethargy as the Catholics died slowly out—without Confession, without the Sacraments, the child unbaptized, and the dying man unshriven. I thought of Rilke's phrase: "An empty, horrible alley, an alley in a foreign town, in a town where nothing is forgiven."

There are, I suppose, geographical and racial excuses for the lethargy. Tabasco is a state of river and swamp and extreme heat; in northern Chiapas there is no choice between a mule and the rare plane for a traveller, and in Tabasco no choice between plane and boat. But a mule is a sociable form of transport—nights spent with strangers huddling together in the cold mountain air, talk over the beans and the embers; while in a boat you are isolated with the mosquitoes between the banana plantations.

And then there are no Indians in Tabasco, with their wild beliefs and their enormous if perverted veneration, to shame the Catholic into *some* action. Too much foreign blood came into Tabasco when it was a prosperous country; the faith with the Grahams and Greenes goes back only a few generations. They haven't the stability of the old Spanish families in Chiapas.

Nothing in a tropical town can fill the place of a church for the most mundane use; a church is the one spot of coolness out of the vertical sun, a place to sit, a place where the senses can rest a little while from ugliness; it offers to the poor man what a rich man may get in a theatre—though not in Tabasco. Now in Villahermosa, in the blinding heat and the mosquito-noisy air, there is no escape at all for anyone. Garrido did his job well: he knew that the stones cry out, and he didn't leave any stones. There is a kind of cattle-tick you catch in Chiapas, which fastens its head in the flesh; you have to burn it out, otherwise the head remains embedded and festers. It is an ugly metaphor to use, but an exact one: in northern Chiapas the churches still stand, shuttered and ruined and empty, but they fester—the whole village festers away from the door; the plaza is the first to go. [. . .]

From Chapter VII: Into Chiapas

The *finca* did exist. When the sun was low I allowed myself to be persuaded back onto the mule, and there beyond a belt of trees it lay, only a quarter of an hour out of Palenque—over a rolling down and a stream with a broken bridge, among grazing cows, and as we waded through the river we could see the orange trees at the gate, a tulipan in blossom, and a man and woman sitting side by side in rocking-chairs on the veranda—as it might be the States, the woman knitting and the man reading his paper. It was like heaven.

There was no beautiful daughter, though I think there must once have been one, from a photograph I saw in the *sala* (she had married, I imagine, and gone away), but there was this middle-aged brother and sister with an unhurried and unsurprised kindness, a big earthenware jar of fresh water with a dipper beside it, a soft bed with sheets, and, most astonishing luxury of all, a little clear sandy stream to wash in with tiny fish like sardines pulling at the nipples. And there were six-week-old copies of the New York papers and of *Time*, and after supper we sat on the veranda in the dark and the tulipan dropped its blossoms and prepared to bloom again with the day. Only the bullet-hole in the porch showed the flaw in Paradise—that this was Mexico. That and the cattle-ticks I found wedged firmly into my arms and thighs when I went to bed.

Next day I lay up at Herr R.'s—a bathe at six in the stream and another in the afternoon at five, and I should have felt fine if it hadn't been for the heat. My shirt was being washed and I had only a leather jacket lined with chamois to wear; the sweat poured down all day and made the leather smell, and the chamois came off on my skin. Like most Mexican things it was a bit fake. At the evening meal the lamp on the table made the heat almost unbearable; the sweat dripped into the food. And afterwards the beetles came scrambling up onto the porch. No it wasn't after all quite Paradise, but it contained this invaluable lesson for a novice—not to take things too seriously, not to attend too carefully to other people's warnings. You couldn't *live* in a country in a state of preparedness for the worst—you drank the water and you went down to bathe in the little stream barefooted across the grass in spite of snakes. Happy the people who can learn the lesson: I could follow it for a couple of days and then it went, and caution returned— the expecting the worst of human nature as well as of snakes, the dreary hopeless failure of love.

Herr R. had left Germany as a boy. His father wanted to send him to a military college, and he had told his father: "If you do, I will run away." He had run away and with the help of a friendly burgomaster had got papers and reached America.

After that he'd never gone back. He had come down to Mexico as agent for various firms, and now he was settled on his own *finca*. There had been revolutions of course—he had lost crops and cattle to the soldiers and he had been fired on as he stood on his porch. But he took things with a dry cynical Lutheran humour; he had a standard of morality which nobody here paid even lip service to, and he fought them with their own weapons. When the *agraristos* demanded land he gave them it —a barren fifty acres he had not had the means to develop— and saved himself taxes. There had been, I suppose, that beautiful daughter (his wife was dead) and there were two sons at school now in Las Casas. He said of Las Casas: "It's a very moral town." I promised to take them out when I arrived: I should be in time for the great spring fair.

Walking in to the village to send his mail, we talked of the Church and Garrido. Though R. was a Lutheran, he had no ill to say of any priest he had known here in the old days. Palenque had not been able to support a permanent priest, and the priests who came to serve Mass on feast days stayed usually with R. at the *finca*. He had an honest Lutheran distaste for their dogmas which took him to queer lengths. There was one priest who was so sick and underfed that R. insisted he should not go to Mass before he had breakfasted. To ensure this, when his guest was asleep, he locked him in, but when he went to call him he found the priest had escaped to church through the window. One felt that the Mexican priesthood in that politely unobtrusive act had shown up rather well. Another priest, one who sometimes came to Palenque, was an old friend of Garrido. He had great skill in brickwork, and Garrido invited him under safe conduct to come into Tabasco and undertake a building job. But friendship and safe conduct didn't save him—when the work was finished he was murdered, though possibly Garrido's followers had gone too far and the dictator may have had no hand in his friend's death.

Garrido's activities did not stop at the border. He sent his men over into Chiapas, and though in this state the churches still stand, great white shells like the skulls you find bleached beside the forest paths, he has left his mark in sacked interiors and ruined roofs. He organized an *auto-da-fé* in Palenque village, and R. was there to see. The evil work was not done by the villagers themselves. Garrido ordered every man with a horse in Tabascan Montecristo to ride over the fifty-six kilometres and superintend—on pain of a fine of twenty-five pesos. And a relative of Garrido came with his wife by private plane to see that people were doing as they were told. The statues were carried out of the church while the inhabitants watched, sheepishly, and saw their own children encouraged to chop up the images in return for little presents of candy.

It was six-thirty next day before we got properly started; the stiffness had been washed away in the shallow stream and my fever was gone, so we made far better time than when we rode from Salto. In less than five hours we reached the Indian huts where we had eaten on our way. After stopping for coffee, we pushed on three leagues more—distances in Chiapas are measured always in leagues, a league being about three miles. This time we intended to make the journey in two stages. Just short of our destination a sudden blast of wind caught my helmet and the noise of crackling cardboard as I saved it scared the mule. It took fright and in the short furious gallop which followed I lost my only glasses. I mention this because strained eyes may have been one cause of my growing depression, the almost pathological hatred I began to feel for Mexico. Indeed, when I try to think back to those days, they lie under the entrancing light of chance encounters, small endurances, unfamiliarity, and I cannot remember why at the time they seemed so grim and hopeless.

The old Indian woman (you cannot measure the age of the poor in years: she may not have passed forty) had a burnt pinched face and dry hair like the shrivelled human head in the booth at San Antonio. She gave us bad corn coffee to drink and a plate of stringy chicken to eat with our fingers. I lay all afternoon and evening in my hammock slung under the palm-fibre veranda, swinging up and down to get a draught of air, staring at a yellow blossoming tree and the edge of the forest and the dull dry plain towards Salto, striking with a stick at the pigs and turkeys which came rooting in the dust under my legs. I dreaded the night. For one thing, I feared the mosquitoes here in the open, and though I had my net with me, I hadn't the moral courage to go against the opinion of the inhabitants, who said there were no mosquitoes at all. And for another, I feared, unreasonably, but with a deep superstitious dread, the movements of the animals in the dark: the lean pigs with pointed tapir snouts, like the primeval ancestors of the English pig, the chickens, above all the turkeys—those hideous Dali heads, the mauve surrealist flaps of skin which they had to toss aside to uncover the beak or eyes. Suppose when night fell they chose to perch on the hammock? Where birds are concerned I lose my reason, I feel panic. The turkey cock blew out its tail, a dingy Victorian fan with the whalebone broken, and hissed with balked pride and hate, like an evil impotent old pasha. One wondered what parasites swarmed under the dusty layers of black feathers. Domestic animals seem to reflect the prosperity of their owners—only the gentleman farmer possesses the plump complacent good-to-live-with fowls and pigs; these burrowing ravenous tapirs and down-at-heel turkey cocks belonged to people living on the edge of subsistence. [. . .]

From Chapter VIII: A Village in Chiapas

[. . .] And now for the Norwegian lady. . . . A boy took my bag and led the way: a great square unused shattered church, weeds growing out of the bell towers where the buzzards perched; coffee laid out to dry all along the stone walks of the little plaza like yellow gravel; a little cobbed street between white bungalow houses, and the mountains terminating everything. The air after Salto even at noon seemed beautifully fresh: the village was two thousand feet up; I hadn't been so high since Orizaba. Through an open door in one of the little houses I came suddenly on a tall tragic woman with hollow handsome features and a strange twisted mouth—like an expression of agony—talking rapidly in Spanish. She broke off and stared at me. I asked rather stupidly if she could recommend a hotel.

Of course there was no hotel in Yajalon, but lodging could—sometimes—be got, she said, with a Señor Lopez. She sent her daughters with me—two thin little blond girls of fourteen and eleven, startlingly beautiful in a land where you grow weary of black and oily hair and brown sentimental eyes. The elder one disliked me on sight—I was the stranger breaking their narrow familiar life with demands—for lodging, conversation, company. They could both speak Spanish and an Indian dialect—the Camacho, I think—and a few words of English. I got a room—a wooden plank bed in a storeroom, behind the counter a few packets of candles, some empty tins, a few straw sombreros. I was to pay two pesos a day, and that included food.

At tea time I went up and called on Fru R. She had coffee ready and cake and we drank on and on under the porch of the patio where her coffee was drying. A separator hummed in a shed like a harvest engine in an English autumn. That was to become a daily routine for a week—I was to look forward to it from the moment I got up in the morning. Somehow I had to pass the days till five o'clock, and then all went well for two hours. It was a kindness impossible adequately to repay.

Poor lady, her position was tragic enough. Both she and her husband were Norwegian by birth, though they had both gone to the States to work. Her husband had bought a coffee farm in the mountains above Yajalon and they had prospered in a modest way—they had been happy, until first her eldest daughter had died and then her husband, and she had been robbed of all their savings by her *compadre* while her husband was dying. (A *compadre* meant a fellow god-parent, a spiritual relationship regarded in Mexico as a close one.) She was left with practically no money, two daughters, and two sons. She had sent the boys to the States to her mother, to be educated, and she hadn't seen them for four years and was unlikely to see them for many years more. She scraped enough money out of separating and drying coffee to keep them at high school, and one of them had gone on to an agricultural college and would soon have a job. Her dream was that one day he would have a good enough post to return and fetch them away from Mexico. Her daughters she taught herself—the small one was learning "The Charge of the Light Brigade"; she got the lessons by post from America, and held periodic examinations in the little darkened parlour. And all the time the elder one was growing up: in a year, by Mexican standards, she would be marriageable; it is difficult to conceive the pain and anxiety of this mother.

She was a Lutheran like my host at Palenque, but she too had watched without sympathy the sacking of the church. Men had ridden in from outside just as at Palenque; the whole *auto-da-fé* had been arranged by the Government people at Tuxtla. They had burned the saints and statues. There had been one great golden angel . . . the villagers stood weeping while it burned. They were all Catholic here . . . except the schoolmaster, whom I would meet at my lodging. Like all the school teachers now he was a politician. There had been a fiesta the night before at the school and he had made an impassioned speech on the oil expropriations (public affairs, which hadn't crossed the burning plateau to Palenque, had overtaken me now: I was not to hear the last of them). He had appealed to the people: "Get rid of the gringos," and of course, sitting there in a back seat, she knew she was the only gringo in the village —except for a German who kept a little store and did photography.

I asked if here in Chiapas there was any hope of a change (I had found such a sense of hopelessness in Tabasco) and I learned from her for the first time of the rather wild dream that buoys up many people in Chiapas: the hope of a rising which will separate Chiapas, Tabasco, Yucatán, and Quintana Roo from the rest of Mexico and of an alliance with Catholic Guatemala. All plots against the Mexican Government get somehow confused with this dream, so that she spoke as if Cedillo were behind it, and mentioned a Catholic general,

Pineda, of whom I was to hear more in Las Casas. German arms, she said, were being brought in by night from Guatemala and deposited in the mountains—by a German airman.

I went back in the dark to the hotel: there is no street lighting in a Mexican village, and the dark falls early and makes the nights very long. I saw my fellow-lodgers for the first time at supper, which we ate at a table under the veranda by the light of an oil-lamp—a stout white-toothed mestizo school teacher with an air of monotonous cheeriness (and one obscene English word which he repeated, with huge amusement, day after day), his pregnant wife, and his small son of a year and a half who ran up and down the floor of the *sala* every morning, admonishing in his father's manner the child nurse who with them occupied one room off the *sala*. And there were others who dropped in for meals only—a few grizzled friendly men, a young married couple with their baby, and a clerk I grew to loathe, a mestizo with curly sideburns and two yellow fangs at either end of his mouth. He had an awful hilarity and a neighing laugh which showed the empty gums. He wore a white tennis shirt open at the front and he scratched himself underneath it. I didn't know that first evening that I was to be stuck in the village for a week—an aeroplane for Las Casas was due in three days; I couldn't foresee how familiar those faces round the table were to become, so that I could go nowhere in the village without seeing one or other of them—the mestizo looking up from his typewriter in the Presidencia and showing his fangs as I went by, a grizzled man waving a hand from a doorway, the schoolmaster's rich powerful voice sounding all across the little plaza from his schoolroom, and the young married man pulling up his horse outside the cantina. It gave one the sensation of being under observation all the time. [. . .]

GRAHAM GREENE

"Creative art," Greene ventures in an essay on Somerset Maugham, "seems to remain a function of the religious mind." In the first of the following essays Greene recalls the moment in childhood when his own mind took a religious turn once and for all, and when, as a consequence, he determined to become a creative artist. The occasion was the reading of Marjorie Bowen's *The Viper of Milan*; and the pattern he found there—"perfect evil walking the world where perfect good can never walk again"—would constitute the essence of Greene's religious vision. It is a vision he has also discerned in other novels he admires: in *Oliver Twist*, for example, the world which he feels to be "a world without God," a world created perhaps by Satan and in which evil is always more compelling and believable than good. (One notes, incidentally, that Greene sees young Oliver as a hunted figure not unlike the priest in *The Power and the Glory*: "All London . . . belongs to his pursuers.") What religion contributes to the creative imagination, Greene contends in discussing Maugham, is a sense of the tremendous importance—"the heavenly and infernal importance"—of human characters and human acts. Greene, in writing about François Mauriac, maintains that the loss of the religious sense in the modern era has meant that the world as described by novelists like Virginia Woolf seems to have suffered a fatal loss of reality. In this he is directly at odds with Sean O'Faolain, who argued, in the essay which appears earlier in this book, that it is precisely Graham Greene's religious vision that undercuts the reality and importance of the human world as he projects it.

[CREATIVE ART AND THE RELIGIOUS MIND:] SELECTIONS FROM COLLECTED ESSAYS

The Lost Childhood

Perhaps it is only in childhood that books have any deep influence on our lives. In later life we admire, we are entertained,

---

we may modify some views we already hold, but we are more likely to find in books merely a confirmation of what is in our minds already: as in a love affair, it is our own features that we see reflected flatteringly back.

But in childhood all books are books of divination, telling us about the future, and like the fortune-teller who sees a long journey in the cards or death by water they influence the future. I suppose that is why books excited us so much. What do we ever get nowadays from reading to equal the excitement and the revelation in those first fourteen years? Of course I should be interested to hear that a new novel by Mr. E.M. Forster was going to appear this spring, but I could never compare that mild expectation of civilized pleasure with the missed heartbeat, the appalled glee I felt when I found on a library shelf a novel by Rider Haggard, Percy Westerman, Captain Brereton, or Stanley Weyman which I had not read before. It is in those early years that I would look for the crisis, the moment when life took a new slant in its journey towards death.

I remember distinctly the suddenness with which a key turned in a lock and I found I could read—not just the sentences in a reading book with the syllables coupled like railway carriages, but a real book. It was paper-covered with the picture of a boy, bound and gagged, dangling at the end of a rope inside a well with the water rising above his waist—an adventure of Dixon Brett, detective. All a long summer holiday I kept my secret, as I believed: I did not want anybody to know that I could read. I suppose I half consciously realized even then that this was the dangerous moment. I was safe so long as I could not read— the wheels had not begun to turn, but now the future stood around on bookshelves everywhere waiting for the child to choose—the life of a chartered accountant perhaps, a colonial civil servant, a planter in China, a steady job in a bank, happiness and misery, eventually one particular form of death, for surely we choose our death much as we choose our job. It grows out of our acts and our evasions, out of our fears and out of our moments of courage. I suppose my mother must have discovered my secret, for on the journey home I was presented for the train with another book, a copy of Ballantyne's *Coral Island* with only a single picture to look at, a coloured frontispiece. But I would admit nothing. All the long journey I stared at the one picture and never opened the book.

But there on the shelves at home (so many shelves for we were a large family) the books waited—one book in particular, but before I reach that one down let me take a few others at random from the shelf. Each was a crystal in which the child dreamed that he saw life moving. Here in a cover stamped dramatically in several colours was Captain Gilson's *The Pirate Aeroplane*. I must have read that book six times at least—the story of a lost civilization in the Sahara and of a villainous Yankee pirate with an aeroplane like a box kite and bombs the size of tennis balls who held the golden city to ransom. It was saved by the hero, a young subaltern who crept up to the pirate camp to put the aeroplane out of action. He was captured and watched his enemies dig his grave. He was to be shot at dawn, and to pass the time and keep his mind from uncomfortable thoughts the amiable Yankee pirate played cards with him—the mild nursery game of Kuhn Kan. The memory of that nocturnal game on the edge of life haunted me for years, until I set it to rest at last in one of my own novels with a game of poker played in remotely similar circumstances.

And here is *Sophy of Kravonia* by Anthony Hope—the story of a kitchen-maid who became a queen. One of the first films I ever saw, about 1911, was made from that book, and I can hear still the rumble of the Queen's guns crossing the high Kravonian pass beaten hollowly out on a single piano. Then there was Stanley Weyman's *The Story of Francis Cludde*, and above all other books at that time of my life, *King Solomon's Mines*.

This book did not perhaps provide the crisis, but it certainly influenced the future. If it had not been for that romantic tale of Allan Quatermain, Sir Henry Curtis, Captain Good, and, above all, the ancient witch Gagool, would I at nineteen have studied the appointments list of the Colonial Office and very nearly picked on the Nigerian Navy for a career? And later, when surely I ought to have known better, the odd African fixation remained. In 1935 I found my self sick with fever on a camp bed in a Liberian native's hut with a candle going out in an empty whisky bottle and a rat moving in the shadows. Wasn't it the incurable fascination of Gagool with her bare yellow skull, the wrinkled scalp that moved and contracted like the hood of a cobra, that led me to work all through 1942 in a little stuffy office in Freetown, Sierra Leone? There is not much in common between the land of the Kukuanas, behind the desert and the mountain range of Sheba's Breast, and a tin-roofed house on a bit of swamp where the vultures moved like domestic turkeys and the pi-dogs kept me awake on moonlit nights with their wailing, and the white women yellowed by Atebrin drove by to the club; but the two belonged at any rate to the same continent, and, however distantly, to the same region of the imagination—the region of uncertainty, of not knowing the way about. Once I came a little nearer to Gagool and her witch-hunters, one night in Zigita on the Liberian side of the French Guinea border, when my servants sat in their shuttered hut with their hands over their eyes and someone beat a drum and a whole town stayed behind closed doors while the big bush devil—whom it would mean blindness to see—moved between the huts.

But *King Solomon's Mines* could not finally satisfy. It was not the right answer. The key did not quite fit. Gagool I could recognize—didn't she wait for me in dreams every night, in the passage by the linen cupboard, near the nursery door? and she continues to wait, when the mind is sick or tired, though now she is dressed in the theological garments of Despair and speaks in Spenser's accents:

> The longer life, I wote the greater sin,
> The greater sin, the greater punishment.

Gagool has remained a permanent part of the imagination, but Quatermain and Curtis—weren't they, even when I was only ten years old, a little too good to be true? They were men of such unyielding integrity (they would only admit to a fault in order to show how it might be overcome) that the wavering personality of a child could not rest for long against those monumental shoulders. A child, after all, knows most of the game—it is only an attitude to it that he lacks. He is quite well aware of cowardice, shame, deception, disappointment. Sir Henry Curtis perched upon a rock bleeding from a dozen wounds but fighting on with the remnant of the Greys against the hordes of Twala was too heroic. These men were like Platonic ideas: they were not life as one had already begun to know it.

But when—perhaps I was fourteen by that time—I took Miss Marjorie Bowen's *The Viper of Milan* from the library shelf, the future for better or worse really struck. From that moment I began to write. All the other possible futures slid away: the potential civil servant, the don, the clerk had to look for other incarnations. Imitation after imitation of Miss Bowen's magnificent novel went into exercise-books—stories of sixteenth-century Italy or twelfth-century England marked with enormous brutality and a despairing romanticism. It was as if I had been supplied once and for all with a subject.

Why? On the surface *The Viper of Milan* is only the story of a war between Gian Galeazzo Visconti, Duke of Milan, and Mastino della Scala, Duke of Verona, told with zest and cunning and an amazing pictorial sense. Why did it creep in and colour and explain the terrible living world of the stone stairs and the never quiet dormitory? It was no good in that real world to dream that one would ever be a Sir Henry Curtis, but della Scala who at last turned from an honesty that never paid and betrayed his friends and died dishonoured and a failure even at treachery—it was easier for a child to escape behind his mask. As for Visconti, with his beauty, his patience, and his genius for evil, I had watched him pass by many a time in his black Sunday suit smelling of mothballs. His name was Carter. He exercised terror from a distance like a snow-cloud over the young fields. Goodness has only once found a perfect incarnation in a human body and never will again, but evil can always find a home there. Human nature is not black and white but black and grey. I read all that in *The Viper of Milan* and I looked round and I saw that it was so.

There was another theme I found there. At the end of *The Viper of Milan*—you will remember if you have once read it—comes the great scene of complete success—della Scala is dead, Ferrara, Verona, Novara, Mantua have all fallen, the messengers pour in with news of fresh victories, the whole world outside is cracking up, and Visconti sits and jokes in the wine-light. I was not on the classical side or I would have discovered, I suppose, in Greek literature instead of in Miss Bowen's novel the sense of doom that lies over success—the feeling that the pendulum is about to swing. That too made sense; one looked around and saw the doomed everywhere—the champion runner who one day would sag over the tape; the head of the school who would atone, poor devil, during forty dreary undistinguished years; the scholar . . . and when success began to touch oneself too, however mildly, one could only pray that failure would not be held off for too long.

One had lived for fourteen years in a wild jungle country without a map, but now the paths had been traced and naturally one had to follow them. But I think it was Miss Bowen's apparent zest that made me want to write. One could not read her without believing that to write was to live and to enjoy, and before one had discovered one's mistake it was too late—the first book one does enjoy. Anyway she had given me my pattern—religion might later explain it to me in other terms, but the pattern was already there—perfect evil walking the world where perfect good can never walk again, and only the pendulum ensures that after all in the end justice is done. Man is never satisfied, and often I have wished that my hand had not moved further than *King Solomon's Mines*, and that the future I had taken down from the nursery shelf had been a district office in Sierra Leone and twelve tours of malarial duty and a finishing dose of blackwater fever when the danger of retirement approached. What is the good of wishing? The books are always there, the moment of crisis waits, and now our children in their turn are taking down the future and opening the pages. In his poem "Germinal" A. E. wrote:

> In ancient shadows and twilights
> Where childhood had strayed,
> The world's great sorrows were born
> And its heroes were made.
> In the lost boyhood of Judas
> Christ was betrayed.

1947

The Young Dickens

A critic must try to avoid being a prisoner of his time, and if we are to appreciate *Oliver Twist* at its full value we must forget that long shelf-load of books, all the stifling importance of a great author, the scandals and the controversies of the private life; it would be well too if we could forget the Phiz and the Cruikshank illustrations that have frozen the excited, excitable world of Dickens into a hall of waxworks, where Mr. Mantalini's whiskers have always the same trim, where Mr. Pickwick perpetually turns up the tails of his coat, and in the Chamber of Horrors Fagin crouches over an undying fire. His illustrators, brilliant craftsmen though they were, did Dickens a disservice, for no character any more will walk for the first time into our memory as we ourselves imagine him and *our* imagination after all has just as much claim to truth as Cruikshank's.

Nevertheless the effort to go back is well worth while. The journey is only a little more than a hundred years long, and at the other end of the road is a young author whose sole claim to renown in 1836 had been the publication of some journalistic

"The Young Dickens" and excerpts from "Notes on Somerset Maugham" and "François Mauriac" from *Collected Essays* by Graham Greene. Copyright 1951, © 1969 by Graham Greene. Reprinted by permission of The Viking Press, Inc.

sketches and a number of comic operettas: *The Strange Gentle-man, The Village Coquette, Is She His Wife?* I doubt whether any literary Cortez at that date would have yet stood them upon his shelves. Then suddenly with *The Pickwick Papers* came pop-ularity and fame. Fame falls like a dead hand on an author's shoulder, and it is well for him when it falls only in later life. How many in Dickens' place would have withstood what James called "the great corrupting contact of the public," the popu-larity founded, as it almost always is, on the weakness and not the strength of an author?

The young Dickens, at the age of twenty-five, had hit on a mine that paid him a tremendous dividend. Fielding and Smollett, tidied and refined for the new industrial bourgeoisie, had both salted it; Goldsmith had contributed sentimentality and Monk Lewis horror. The book was enormous, shapeless, familiar (that important recipe for popularity). What Henry James wrote of a long-forgotten French critic applies well to the young Dickens: "He is homely, familiar and colloquial; he leans his elbows on his desk and does up his weekly budget into a parcel the reverse of compact. You can fancy him a grocer retailing tapioca and hominy full weight for the price; his style seems a sort of integument of brown paper."

This is, of course, unfair to *The Pickwick Papers*. The driest critic could not have quite blinkered his eyes to those sudden wide illuminations of comic genius that flap across the waste of words like sheet lightning, but could he have foreseen the second novel, not a repetition of this great loose popular holdall, but a short melodrama, tight in construction, almost entirely lacking in broad comedy, and possessing only the sad twisted humour of the orphan's asylum?

"You'll make your fortune, Mr. Sowerberry," said the beadle, as he thrust his thumb and forefinger into the proffered snuff-box of the undertaker: which was an ingenious little model of a patent coffin.

Such a development was as inconceivable as the gradual transformation of that thick boggy prose into the delicate and exact poetic cadences, the music of memory, that so influenced Proust.

We are too inclined to take Dickens as a whole and to treat his juvenilia with the same kindness or harshness as his later work. *Oliver Twist* is still juvenilia—magnificent juvenilia: it is the first step on the road that led from *Pickwick* to *Great Expectations,* and we condone the faults of taste in the early book the more readily if we recognize the distance Dickens had to travel. These two typical didactic passages can act as the first two milestones at the opening of the journey, the first from *Pickwick,* the second from *Oliver Twist.*

And numerous indeed are the hearts to which Christmas brings a brief season of happiness and enjoyment. How many families, whose members have been dispersed and scattered far and wide, in the restless struggles of life, are then reunited, and meet once again in that happy state of companionship and mutual goodwill, which is a source of such pure and unalloyed delight, and one so incompatible with the cares and sorrows of the world, that the religious belief of the most civilized nations, and the rude traditions of the roughest savages, alike number it among the first joys of a future condition of existence, provided for the blest and happy.

The boy stirred and smiled in his sleep, as though these marks of pity and compassion had awakened some pleasant dream of a love and affection he had never known. Thus, a strain of gentle music, or the rippling of water in a silent place, or the odour of a flower, or the mention of a familiar word, will sometimes call up sudden dim remembrances of scenes that never were, in this life; which vanish like a breath; which some brief memory of a happier existence, long gone by, would seem to have awakened; which no voluntary exertion of the mind can ever recall.

The first is certainly brown paper: what it wraps has been chosen by the grocer to suit his clients' tastes, but cannot we detect already in the second passage the tone of Dickens' secret prose, that sense of a mind speaking to itself with no one there to listen, as we find it in *Great Expectations?*

It was fine summer weather again, and, as I walked along, the times when I was a little helpless creature, and my sister did not spare me, vividly returned. But they returned with a gentle tone upon them that softened even the edge of Tickler. For now, the very breath of the beans and clover whispered to my heart that the day must come when it would be well for my memory that others walking in the sunshine should be softened as they thought of me.

It is a mistake to think of *Oliver Twist* as a realistic story: only late in his career did Dickens learn to write realistically of human beings; at the beginning he invented life and we no more believe in the temporal existence of Fagin or Bill Sikes than we believe in the existence of that Giant whom Jack slew as he bellowed his Fee Fi Fo Fum. There were real Fagins and Bill Sikeses and real Bumbles in the England of his day, but he had not drawn them, as he was later to draw the convict Magwitch; these characters in *Oliver Twist* are simply parts of one huge invented scene, what Dickens in his own preface called "the cold wet shelterless midnight streets of London." How the phrase goes echoing on through the books of Dickens until we meet it again so many years later in "the weary western streets of London on a cold dusty spring night" which were so melancholy to Pip. But Pip was to be as real as the weary streets, while Oliver was as unrealistic as the cold wet midnight of which he formed a part.

This is not to criticize the book so much as to describe it. For what an imagination this youth of twenty-six had that he could invent so monstrous and complete a legend! We are not lost with Oliver Twist round Saffron Hill: we are lost in the interstices of one young, angry, gloomy brain, and the oppressive images stand out along the track like the lit figures in a Ghost Train tunnel.

Against the wall were ranged, in regular array, a long row of elm boards cut into the same shape, looking in the dim light, like high shouldered ghosts with their hands in their breeches pockets.

We have most of us seen those nineteenth-century prints where the bodies of naked women form the face of a character, the Diplomat, the Miser, and the like. So the crouching figure of Fagin seems to form the mouth, Sikes with his bludgeon the jutting features, and the sad lost Oliver the eyes of one man, as lost as Oliver.

Chesterton, in a fine imaginative passage, has described the mystery behind Dickens' plots, the sense that even the author was unaware of what was really going on, so that when the explanations come and we reach, huddled into the last pages of *Oliver Twist*, a naked complex narrative of illegitimacy and burnt wills and destroyed evidence, we simply do not believe. "The secrecy is sensational; the secret is tame. The surface of the thing seems more awful than the core of it. It seems almost as if these grisly figures, Mrs. Chadband and Mrs. Clennam, Miss Havisham and Miss Flite, Nemo and Sally Brass, were keeping something back from the author as well as from the reader. When the book closes we do not know their real secret. They soothed the optimistic Dickens with something less terrible than the truth."

What strikes the attention most in this closed Fagin universe are the different levels of unreality. If, as one is inclined to believe, the creative writer perceives his world once and for all in childhood and adolescence, and his whole career is an effort to illustrate his private world in terms of the great public world we all share, we can understand why Fagin and Sikes in their most extreme exaggerations move us more than the benevolence of Mr. Brownlow or the sweetness of Mrs. Maylie—they touch with fear as others never really touch with love. It was not that the unhappy child, with his hurt pride and his sense of hopeless insecurity, had not encountered human goodness—he had simply failed to recognize it in those streets between Gadshill and Hungerford Market which had been as narrowly enclosed as Oliver Twist's. When Dickens at this early period tried to describe goodness he seems to have remembered the small stationers' shops on the way to the blacking factory with their coloured paper scraps of angels and virgins, or perhaps the face of some old gentleman who had spoken kindly to him outside Warren's factory. He had swum up towards goodness from the deepest world of his experience, and on this shallow level the conscious brain has taken a hand, trying to construct characters to represent virtue and, because his age demanded it, triumphant virtue, but all he can produce are powdered wigs and gleaming spectacles and a lot of bustle with bowls of broth and a pale angelic face. Compare the way in which we first meet evil with his introduction of goodness.

The walls and ceiling of the room were perfectly black with age and dirt. There was a deal table before the fire: upon which were a candle, stuck in a ginger-beer bottle, two or three pewter pots, a loaf and butter, and a plate. In a frying pan, which was on the fire, and which was secured to the mantel-shelf by a string, some sausages were cooking; and standing over them, with a toasting-fork in his hand, was a very old shrivelled Jew, whose villainous-looking and repulsive face was obscured by a quantity of matted red hair. He was dressed in a greasy flannel gown, with his throat bare. . . . "This is him, Fagin," said Jack Dawkins: "my friend Oliver Twist." The Jew grinned; and, making a low obeisance to Oliver, took him by the hand, and hoped he should have the honour of his intimate acquaintance.

Fagin has always about him this quality of darkness and nightmare. He never appears on the daylight streets. Even when we see him last in the condemned cell, it is in the hours before the dawn. In the Fagin darkness Dickens' hand seldom fumbles. Hear him turning the screw of horror when Nancy speaks of the thoughts of death that have haunted her:

"Imagination," said the gentleman, soothing her.
"No imagination," replied the girl in a hoarse voice. "I'll swear I saw 'coffin' written in every page of the book in large black letters —aye, and they carried one close to me, in the streets tonight."
"There is nothing unusual in that," said the gentleman. "They have passed me often."
"Real ones," rejoined the girl. "This was not."

Now turn to the daylight world and our first sight of Rose:

The younger lady was in the lovely bloom and springtime of womanhood; at that age, when, if ever angels be for God's good purposes enthroned in mortal forms, they may be, without impiety, supposed to abide in such as hers. She was not past seventeen. Cast in so slight and exquisite a mould; so mild and gentle; so pure and beautiful; that earth seemed not her element, nor its rough creatures her fit companions.

Or Mr. Brownlow as he first appeared to Oliver:

Now, the old gentleman came in as brisk as need be; but he had no sooner raised his spectacles on his forehead, and thrust his hands behind the skirts of his dressing-gown to take a good long look at Oliver, than his countenance underwent a very great variety of odd contortions. . . . The fact is, if the truth must be told, that Mr. Brownlow's heart, being large enough for any six ordinary old gentlemen of humane disposition, forced a supply of tears into his eyes by some hydraulic process which we are not sufficiently philosophical to be in a condition to explain.

How can we really believe that these inadequate ghosts of goodness can triumph over Fagin, Monks, and Sikes? And the answer, of course, is that they never could have triumphed without the elaborate machinery of the plot disclosed in the last pages. This world of Dickens is a world without God; and as a substitute for the power and the glory of the omnipotent and omniscient are a few sentimental references to heaven, angels, the sweet faces of the dead, and Oliver saying, "Heaven is a long way off, and they are too happy there to come down to the bedside of a poor boy." In this Manichean world we can believe in evil-doing, but goodness wilts into philanthropy, kindness, and those strange vague sicknesses into which Dickens' young women so frequently fall and which seem in his eyes a kind of badge of virtue, as though there were a merit in death. But how instinctively Dickens' genius recognized the flaw and made a virtue out of it. We cannot believe in the power of Mr. Brownlow, but nor did Dickens, and from his inability to believe in his own good character springs the real tension of his novel. The boy Oliver may not lodge in our brain like David Copperfield, and though many of Mr. Bumble's phrases have become and deserve to have become familiar quotations we can feel he was manufactured: he never breathes like Mr. Dorrit; yet Oliver's predicament, the nightmare fight between the darkness, where the demons walk, and the sunlight, where ineffective goodness makes its last stand in a condemned world, will remain part of our imaginations forever. We read of the defeat of Monks, and of Fagin screaming in the condemned cell, and of Sikes dangling from his self-made noose, but we don't believe. We have witnessed Oliver's temporary escapes too often and his inevitable recapture: *there* is the truth and the creative experience. We know that when Oliver leaves Mr. Brownlow's house to walk a few hundred yards to the bookseller, his friends will wait in vain for his return. All London outside the quiet shady street in Pentonville belongs to his pursuers; and when he escapes again into the house of Mrs. Maylie in the fields beyond Shepperton, we know his security is false. The seasons may pass, but safety depends not on time but on daylight. As children we all knew that: how all day we could forget the dark and the journey to bed. It is with a sense of relief that at last in twilight we see the faces of the Jew and Monks peer into the cottage window between the sprays of jessamine. At that moment we realize how the whole world, and not London only, belongs to these two after dark. Dickens, dealing out his happy endings and his unreal retributions, can never ruin the validity and dignity of that moment. "They had recognized him, and he them; and their look was as firmly impressed upon his memory, as if it had been deeply carved in stone, and set before him from his birth."

"From his birth"—Dickens may have intended that phrase to refer to the complicated imbroglios of the plot that lie outside the novel, "something less terrible than the truth." As for the truth, is it too fantastic to imagine that in this novel, as in many of his later books, creeps in, unrecognized by the author, the eternal and alluring taint of the Manichee, with its simple and terrible explanation of our plight, how the world was made by Satan and not by God, lulling us with the music of despair?

1950

From Some Notes on Somerset Maugham

[. . .] The nearest Maugham comes to a confidence is in the description of his religious belief—if you can call agnosticism a belief, and the fact that on this subject he is ready to speak to strangers makes one pause. There are signs of muddle, contradictions . . . hints of an inhibition. Otherwise one might trace here the deepest source of his limitations, for creative art seems to remain a function of the religious mind. Maugham the agnostic is forced to minimize—pain, vice, the importance of his fellowmen. He cannot believe in a God who punishes and he cannot therefore believe in the importance of a human action. "It is not difficult," he writes, "to forgive people their sins"—it sounds like charity, but it may be only contempt. In another passage he refers with understandable scorn to writers who are "grandiloquent to tell you whether or not a little trollop shall hop into bed with a commonplace young man." That is a plot as old as *Troilus and Cressida*, but to the religious sixteenth-century mind there was no such thing as a commonplace young man or an unimportant sin; the creative writers of that time drew human characters with a clarity we have never regained (we had to go to Russia for it later) because they were lit with the glare and significance that war lends. Rob human beings of their heavenly and their infernal importance, and you rob your characters of their individuality. ("What should a Socialist woman do?") It has never been Maugham's characters that we have remembered so much as the narrator, with his contempt for human life, his unhappy honesty.

1935-1938

From François Mauriac

After the death of Henry James a disaster overtook the English novel; indeed long before his death one can picture that quiet, impressive, rather complacent figure, like the last survivor on a raft, gazing out over a sea scattered with wreckage. He even recorded his impressions in an article in *The Times Literary Supplement*, recorded his hope—but was it really hope or only a form of his unconquerable oriental politeness?—in such young novelists as Mr. Compton Mackenzie and Mr. David Herbert Lawrence, and we who have lived after the disaster can realize the futility of those hopes.

For with the death of James the religious sense was lost to the English novel, and with the religious sense went the sense of the importance of the human act. It was as if the world of fiction had lost a dimension: the characters of such distinguished writers as Mrs. Virginia Woolf and Mr. E.M. Forster wandered like cardboard symbols through a world that was paper-thin. Even in one of the most materialistic of our great novelists—in Trollope—we are aware of another world against which the actions of the characters are thrown into relief. The ungainly clergyman picking his black-booted way through the mud, handling so awkwardly his umbrella, speaking of his miserable income and stumbling through a proposal of marriage, exists in a way that Mrs. Woolf's Mr. Ramsay never does, because we are aware that he exists not only to the woman he is addressing but also in a God's eye. His unimportance in the world of the senses is only matched by his enormous importance in another world.

The novelist, perhaps unconsciously aware of his predicament, took refuge in the subjective novel. It was as if he thought that by mining into layers of personality hitherto untouched he could unearth the secret of "importance," but in these mining operations he lost yet another dimension. The visible world for him ceased to exist as completely as the spiritual. Mrs. Dalloway walking down Regent Street was aware of the glitter of shop

windows, the smooth passage of cars, the conversation of shop-
pers, but it was only a Regent Street seen by Mrs. Dalloway that
was conveyed to the reader: a charming whimsical rather sentimental prose poem was what Regent Street had become: a
current of air, a touch of scent, a sparkle of glass. But, we
protest, Regent Street too has a right to exist; it is more real
than Mrs. Dalloway, and we look back with nostalgia towards
the chop houses, the mean courts, the still Sunday streets of
Dickens. Dickens' characters were of immortal importance, and
the houses in which they loved, the mews in which they damned
themselves were lent importance by their presence. They were
given the right to exist as they were, distorted, if at all, only
by their observer's eye—not further distorted at a second remove
by an imagined character.

M. Mauriac's first importance to an English reader, therefore,
is that he belongs to the company of the great traditional
novelists: he is a writer for whom the visible world has not
ceased to exist, whose characters have the solidity and importance of men with souls to save or lose, and a writer who
claims the traditional and essential right of a novelist, to
comment, to express his views. For how tired we have become
of the dogmatically "pure" novel, the tradition founded by
Flaubert and reaching its magnificent tortuous climax in England in the works of Henry James. One is reminded of those
puzzles in children's papers which take the form of a maze.
The child is encouraged to trace with his pencil a path to the
centre of the maze. But in the pure novel the reader begins at
the centre and has to find his way to the gate. He runs his
pencil down avenues which must surely go straight to the
circumference, the world outside the maze, where moral judge-
ments and acts of supernatural importance can be found (even
the writing of a novel indeed can be regarded as a more
important action, expressing an intention of more vital importance, than the adultery of the main character or the murder
in chapter three), but the printed channels slip and twist and
slide, landing him back where he began, and he finds on close

examination that the designer of the maze has in fact over-printed the only exit.

I am not denying the greatness of either Flaubert or James. The novel was ceasing to be an aesthetic form and they recalled it to the artistic conscience. It was the later writers who by accepting the technical dogma blindly made the novel the dull devitalized form (form it retained) that it has become. The exclusion of the author can go too far. Even the author, poor devil, has a right to exist. [. . .]

GRAHAM GREENE AND PHILIP TOYNBEE

Philip Toynbee is the author of several novels, among them *The Savage Days, The Garden in the Sun,* and *The Fearful Choice.* He has also been foreign correspondent of *The Observer* (London). The following conversation between Toynbee and Graham Greene first appeared in *The Observer* as the second in a series called "The Job of a Writer."

GRAHAM GREENE ON THE JOB OF THE WRITER: AN INTERVIEW

It was a sunny, rather quiet London day of early September, but the sudden cool and hush of the Albany arcade was an astonishing change from Piccadilly. Graham Greene received us in his bright, tidily-untidy upstairs room with every sign of extreme nervousness. He looked with dismay at the camera and the shorthand pad which my colleagues were carrying, gulped once or twice, and then made hastily for the fine array of bottles on top of a bookshelf.

Drinks put us both more at ease, and after a few preliminary courtesies Mr. Greene began to answer my questions with readiness and eloquence.

TOYNBEE: Shall we begin by taking the most appalling and least escapable event of our times, namely the extermination of the Jews? Do you think that this frightful crime and tragedy has had any direct effect on novels and poetry in England?

GREENE: Not direct, I should say, but certainly an indirect one. I rather think we were already living, before that, in a

---

From *The Observer* (London), September 15, 1957.

climate which made that kind of thing not only possible, but probable. After all, the thirties was the great period of engaged literature in this country.

I must admit that I was sitting next to an American woman in a plane the other day who said to me, speaking of Auschwitz, "Don't you think that all that was just propaganda?"

TOYNBEE: Yes, that's rather terrifying. I'm inclined to think, though, that there's a considerable difference between the climate of the thirties and the one we've been living in ever since the war. Twenty years ago writers like Auden and Spender deliberately set out to involve themselves in the public issues of the time. Nowadays, many young writers seem to be involved almost against their will—certainly not by any deliberate choice.

GREENE: That may be so. But the effect of this climate is very obscure. I don't see how the novelist can write about anything of which he hasn't had direct personal experience.

TOYNBEE: Well, let's take your own case, I suppose it would be possible to describe nearly all your novels as "engaged." But I very much doubt whether you ever set out deliberately to write a novel in defence of any particular political attitude.

GREENE: The nearest I came to it was in *The Quiet American*. But that was really only because I had seen so much of the country and got to know the issues over a period of years.

TOYNBEE: So you really feel that any deliberate decision by a writer to engage himself is rather nonsensical?

GREENE: It is to me personally. On the other hand, if anybody can write a good book by doing so, then I think he is thoroughly justified.

TOYNBEE: What I have been feeling is that this climate of which you speak is becoming, as it were, more and more powerful. Take the H-bomb for example. It would obviously be absurd for a writer to set out to write a novel for or against the bomb tests, but the existence of the bomb affects us all, I suppose, in all sorts of ways which we don't understand.

GREENE: Yet I think the climate in which I grew up was really just as powerful in its own way. The depression, unemployment, hunger marches, and then, from 1933 onwards, the inevitability of war.

TOYNBEE: I think you are about ten years older than I, so I suppose you had a few adult years before the depression.

GREENE: Yes, in that my generation was very lucky. I left Oxford in 1925, and the shadows didn't really begin to fall until 1930.

TOYNBEE: And would you say that, after the depression and the rise of Hitler, you were conscious of having to write in a new and different way?

GREENE: No, I wouldn't say that. I think most writers are far more interested in the technique of their job than in the atmosphere around them. But, of course, the effect of public events did somehow seep into our minds.

TOYNBEE: Well, can you envisage a young man nowadays writing like Firbank—who is, I suppose, about the most disengaged novelist one can think of?

GREENE: No, I can't. But I should be very glad if it happened.

TOYNBEE: Shall we take another example of your own work? It would be possible, though rather crude, to describe *The Power and the Glory* as a study of the conflict between church and state in Mexico.

GREENE: Yes, but I see that only as the background of the book. It is really an attempt to understand a permanent religious situation: the function of the priesthood. I was much more interested in the theological point of view than in the political one.

TOYNBEE: I suppose one might say that your religious convictions are themselves a form of involvement.

GREENE: I wonder. It wasn't until ten years after my conversion in 1926 that anyone noticed any trace of it in my novels. The reason for this is quite a simple one. I simply hadn't had sufficient experience of how Catholics think or behave, and therefore I couldn't write about them.

TOYNBEE: Of course, any book can be described in so many different terms. *Brighton Rock* was the first of your novels that specifically dealt with a Roman Catholic theme. Yet it could also be described as a study of juvenile delinquency.

GREENE: Yes, and the Catholic element in that book was really an afterthought. It grew up after I had begun the novel.

TOYNBEE: Let's get back to Firbank. You say that you wouldn't feel any offence if a writer of today wrote a good book in that sort of manner?

GREENE: No, I'd be delighted. I hate the idea that any sort of duty is imposed on the writer from outside. It savours of Communism. I see in today's paper that Mr. Khrushchev has just fulminated against Russian writers for not paying enough attention to collective farming and engineering projects.

TOYNBEE: Yet one might say that simply as a human being the man of today who was totally unconcerned about public tragedies would have something wrong with him. He would not be fully human, and I suppose one might say that good writers must be full human beings.

GREENE: A modern Firbank would certainly be a rather different Firbank. There would inevitably be a difference of tone in his books.

TOYNBEE: Perhaps a note of defiance?

GREENE: Or of despair. Or even of optimism.

TOYNBEE: Let's take a very extreme example. A Hungarian writer who had lived through the revolution of last October would really have to be a freak if that experience had had no effect upon him.

GREENE: I think the most likely effect of the Hungarian Revolution would be to drive writers to silence. After all, how much effect did the French Revolution have on French writers?

TOYNBEE: Very little direct effect, I suppose. Yet the Russian Revolution has proved a lasting inspiration to Russian writers and film directors. Of course, this was partly due to direction from above.

GREENE: I think it was. After all, you do get your disengaged writers in the Russia of the early 1920s. Books like *The Little Gold Calf* and *The Twelve Chairs*.

TOYNBEE: That was one of the natural reactions. Some writers wanted to forget the whole bloody business.

GREENE: Or was it an attempt to be anarchical in an over-organized society?

TOYNBEE: Very likely. And I think this raises an interesting new point. If you belong to a society—belong to it organically, I mean—you cannot rebel against it when the society is really threatened. For example, a great many anarchical writers became ardent French patriots during the occupation. On the other hand, when your society is really strong and healthy, it's a natural tendency to rebel against it.

GREENE: Which is what seems to be happening in Russia now. One example might be Dudentsev's novel *Not by Bread Alone*.

But I suppose we must also remember that there is such a thing as the good conformist writer. Someone like Trollope, or possibly Kipling. For all I know, there might be such writers in Russia today who genuinely thrive on following the Party directives.

TOYNBEE: What it perhaps boils down to is that unless the writer has a strong sense of pity he is bound to be in some sense a maimed writer.

GREENE: I prefer the word charity. Pity always sounds rather superior.

TOYNBEE: Well then, would you agree that lack of charity in a writer would be destructive?

GREENE: There are times when one would welcome a bit of destruction. Especially in a welfare state.

TOYNBEE: I mean destructive of literature. The lady in the plane who said wasn't it all propaganda about Auschwitz would probably have been a pretty bad novelist.

GREENE: Yes, I agree. And we were all guilty of the same thing after the First World War. We didn't want to think about all the horrors anymore.

TOYNBEE: Exactly. It wasn't until about ten years after the war that the public was willing to read about it. *Journey's End* was the first popular war play, and it was produced, I think, in about 1929. But wouldn't you say that it is one of the writer's jobs *not* to forget?

GREENE: Yes, it is. It's also the writer's job to try to engage people's sympathy for characters who are outside the official range of sympathy. For the traitor, for example.

TOYNBEE: And you have certainly succeeded in doing this in many of your novels.

GREENE: But not as a duty; simply from interest. To do this sets one a slightly more difficult task. It also makes people see something which they have failed to see. That the apparent villain is in fact human, and deserves more compassion than the apparent hero.

TOYNBEE: It is certainly a major function of the writer to make people experience emotions which they haven't experienced before.

GREENE: I rather feel that if one has anything direct to say about politics or society one should channel it into journalism. When I wrote about the Mau Mau in the *Sunday Times* it was quite obvious that my sympathies were engaged by the Africans and not by the white settlers.

TOYNBEE: And it didn't occur to you to write a novel about that issue?

GREENE: No, I had no wish to at all.

TOYNBEE: Yet *The Quiet American* was stimulated, clearly, by an equivalent journey?

GREENE: I knew the scene far better, I must have spent four winters there.

I should like very much to go to South Africa as a reporter. But the hero and villain of such nonfictional writing might well turn out to have their roles reversed in a novel.

TOYNBEE: You mean that, although you wrote with great sympathy for the African cause in Kenya in your capacity as a journalist, a novel on the same subject might well have had a British settler or official for its hero?

GREENE: Yes, exactly. It's in this way that one's function as a novelist seems to differ so much from one's function as a reporter of events.

TOYNBEE: Do you think this special sympathy you have always shown for the sinner, for the apparently unsympathetic character, is due to your religious belief?

GREENE: I don't know. To tell the truth I find it very difficult to believe in sin. Reviewers always talk about my sense of sin or evil, but doesn't that belong to some of my *characters*? Personally I find that I have very little sense of it. What it really adds up to is that I write novels about what interests me and I can't write about anything else. And one of the things which interests me most is discovering the humanity in the apparently inhuman character.

DALE WASSERMAN

TWO SCENES FROM THE TELEVISION
ADAPTATION OF
THE POWER AND THE GLORY

Greene on Screen and Stage

by R. W. B. LEWIS

In one of the selections from Another Mexico *included in the earlier part of this volume there appears the following passage from Greene's first view of Villahermosa:*

If I had moved a camera all round the edge of the little plaza in a panning shot it would have recorded all the life there was in the capital city—a dentist's, with a floodlit chair of torture; the public jail, an old white-pillared house . . . where a soldier sat with a rifle at the door and a few dark faces pressed against the bars; a Commercial Academy, the size of a village store; the secretariat . . .

and so on to further details, some old ladies on rocking chairs, a public dance in progress. Greene's cinematographic technique, which several critics have noticed and which he sometimes employs more surreptitiously, is there quite explicit. His journalistic eye moves about the square with the creative curiosity of a movie camera, bringing together the sharply observed objects and figures into a pattern that expresses the entire life of the place.

Greene's narrative method is often, in fact, so close to that of the cinema that his work has from the outset yielded easily to film treatment. One wonders if Greene himself remembers exactly how many films have been made from his novels and stories; the editors have counted about eighteen of them. Among these, the "entertainments" have been uniformly well conceived, well made, and well acted; the novels proper have had a more qualified success. The Heart of the Matter, for example, had a sort of somber excellence, with Trevor Howard perfectly cast as Major Scobie; The End of the Affair, the cast of which had best not be named, was appalling. It can be added that Greene is also the author of several impressive original film scripts, most notably that of The Third Man.

If Greene has, in the contemporary manner, adapted cinematic devices to valuable novelistic effect, his fiction is also strikingly dramatic in nature. His novels, that is, drive forward by their own inner compulsion from one "scene"—one human encounter or confrontation—to another, and the dialogue at each stage, far from being a static exchange of opinions, comprises rather a verbal struggle that pushes the action relentlessly forward. Each scene is a minor or major turning point, each adds its share to the total revelation; and nowhere is this so true as in The Power and the Glory. This phase of Greene's total style—his dramatism—derives in part, as it seems, from Henry James, the novelist whom Greene has always most admired and studied, and in part from the techniques of the modern stage. Like James, too, Greene developed a passion for the actual theater very early in life, but came to it with a production of his own relatively late.

In his preface to Three Plays (1961) Greene tells us that the first of his plays to be accepted—an exotic affair roaming as far afield as Samarkand—was written when he was sixteen. It never reached the stage, and indeed the whole incident, involving an overblown woman (the would-be producer) in a Knightsbridge flat and her escort who lay naked on the bed watching her interview the boy, might have been imagined by Greene himself. Greene attempted no more plays for two decades, but thereafter his life as a writer became "as littered with discarded plays as it is littered with discarded novels."

Three of Greene's plays have been staged to date, two of

them of the serious variety: The Living Room *and* The Potting Shed *(the latter taken over from one of the discarded novels); and one a species of "entertainment,"* The Complaisant Lover. Greene *agrees with most of his critics in considering* The Living Room *dramatically successful and* The Potting Shed *as lacking in unity and falling slightly apart in the last act. Both, however, are quintessential Greene:* The Living Room *with its atmosphere of death, its opposition of adultery and religion, its suicide, its painfully hopeful appeal to the unknowable mercy of God;* The Potting Shed *with its bleakly unbelieving priest, its miraculous resurrection, its concern with the fundamental human problem of coming into life and of feeling alive. It is interesting to see how Greene's congenitally taut and economic style fare on stage, where he is limited to dialogue and gesture; the original running time of* The Living Room *was only an hour and a quarter, and it had to be expanded to the conventional two hours by some skillful fakery. Greene's third play,* The Complaisant Lover, *came out of what he calls his manic side, as an escape from the extensive strain of serious writing; it is a comedy about adultery with not a whisper of religion; but Greene's depressive side, he believes, contributed more to it than he had expected. A rather poignant farce resulted, with the redoubtable Ralph Richardson as the cuckolded and oddly sympathetic dentist.*

The Power and the Glory *was made into a film (*The Fugitive*) in the late forties; it was dramatized in 1956; and it was produced on television in 1961, George C. Scott being especially memorable as the fiercely dedicated lieutenant. The editors have selected the TV version, rather than the play version, of the central episode in the story, the scene in the prison; the television treatment strikes us as closer in spirit and in rhythmic movement to the original. The student will want to compare this version to that in Chapter Three of Part Two in the novel.*

Scene 27

(Interior, the cell. In the dim light we see that it is a large common cell in which young and old, male and female, are confined together. Some are in rags, some in dirty drill, some in peon's clothes. The priest stumbles about, bewildered.)

A VOICE: Look out, can't you?

(The priest moves another way. A man sits up, furious.)

PRISONER: Get away from the bucket! D'you want to drown us?

PRIEST: I'm sorry. Is it water?

PRISONER: Are you thirsty?

PRIEST: Yes.

PRISONER: Try it.

(A snigger of laughter.)

Got any cigarettes?

PRIEST: No.

PRISONER: Anything to eat?

PRIEST: No.

PRISONER: Any money?

PRIEST: No.

PRISONER: Then lie down and shut up.

(The priest finds his way to a sitting space against a wall. Silence for a moment, then from the far side of the cell the low indrawn laughter of a woman in pleasure.)

SPINSTER (in tones of prim outrage): Imagine. Even in here. Like animals.

PRISONER: What's the matter, Your Majesty? Jealous?

SPINSTER: Disgusted! (Proudly): After all, I was arrested for wearing a holy medal.

(An old man next to the priest plucks at his sleeve.)

OLD MAN: Is that you, Caterina?

PRIEST: No, not Caterina.

OLD MAN: I didn't really think she'd come.

PRIEST: Is she your wife?

OLD MAN: What's that? No, I haven't got a wife.

A PRISONER (irritably): Why ask him questions, the old man is crazy.

PRIEST: Your daughter?

OLD MAN: Yes . . . but she'll never come.

PRIEST: If she loves you . . .

OLD MAN: It was the priests who did it.

PRIEST: The priests?

SPINSTER (impatiently): They took the child away from him.

PRIEST: Why?

SPINSTER: It was a bastard. They acted quite correctly.

PRIEST: Bastard . . . (with curbed passion): They had no right to make her hate him.

SPINSTER: They know what's right.

PRIEST: They were bad priests to do a thing like that. The sin was over. It was their duty to teach . . . well, love.

SPINSTER: You don't know what's right. The priests know.

(A pause.)

PRIEST: I am a priest.

(Silence for a moment.)

SPINSTER: What did you say?

PRIEST: I am a priest.

(There is a stir and a whispering in the cell: "A priest . . . He says he is a priest . . .")

SPINSTER (horrified): You shouldn't have told us. Father, there are all sorts here. Thieves . . . murderers . . .

A PRISONER (angrily): That doesn't make us informers.

PRIEST: There is no need for anyone to inform on me. When it's daylight they'll discover for themselves.

SPINSTER: They'll shoot you, father.

PRIEST: Yes.

SPINSTER: Are you afraid?

PRIEST: Yes, of course.

ANOTHER PRISONER (roughly): A man isn't afraid of a thing like that.

PRIEST: We can't all be brave men.

ANOTHER PRISONER (with contempt): You believers are all the same. Christianity makes you cowards.

PRIEST: No. Only I. You see, I am a bad priest. A bad man and a bad priest.

PRISONER (muttering): Anyhow, they haven't recognized you yet.

PRIEST: There is a reward. Seven hundred pesos.

(Reaction. They drew back.)

SPINSTER (aghast): Are you mad? Why did you tell them that?

PRISONERS (furious at her): What do you think we are? Just because we're in prison—! Let them keep their blood money!

FIRST PRISONER (kneels before the priest to examine him searchingly): Anyone would think you wanted to be caught.

(The priest shrugs.)

That's suicide, isn't it?

(A murmur of agreement.)

Even if you're the last priest in the country, it's still your duty to do your job. After all, most of us here have dangerous jobs.

PRIEST: In all this year I said three Masses and heard no more than twenty confessions.

SPINSTER: That's better than nothing.

PRIEST: Several men have been shot because of me. I'm supposed to help people and I have hurt them. Now I haven't even the wine to say Mass. Do you know what I'm here for? Drunk. I had a bottle of brandy.

SPINSTER: That's not so important. Once I knew a bishop—

PRIEST: Don't try and comfort me. Comfort's my job. And it's more than spirits I've been drunk with. I have a daughter.

SPINSTER: A daughter?

PRIEST: A bastard . . .

FIRST PRISONER (chuckles): So that's why you spoke up for that old lecher.

SPINSTER: There's always repentance.

PRIEST: I can't repent! I'm not sorry! I'm a bad priest, you see. I know . . . from experience . . . how much beauty Satan carried down with him when he fell. Nobody ever said the fallen angels were the ugly ones.

SPINSTER (coldly): Now I can see what kind of priest you are. If your Bishop could hear you . . .

PRIEST (giggles): He's a long way off.

FIRST PRISONER: And you're the only priest we have.

PRIEST (stands up, wildly): Seven hundred pesos! Don't you want money? You steal for it, you kill for it. Well, here it is with no trouble at all! Seven hundred pesos! Will nobody be my Judas?

FIRST PRISONER (after an embarrassed silence): You'd better be quiet, father. Soon it'll be morning.

(The priest slumps down against the wall and drops his head between his knees.)

Scene 28

(Entrance to the cell, morning. The sergeant is holding the door open as the prisoners file out.)

SERGEANT: Out! Out, all of you. Come on, into the yard.

(The prisoners shuffle past, eyes down. As the priest emerges, the sergeant reaches out and plucks him out of the line.)

SERGEANT: Did you sleep well, smuggler?

PRIEST: Not very well.

SERGEANT: Good. That'll teach you to like brandy too much.

PRIEST: Yes.

SERGEANT: You've got to work in return for your night's lodging, you know. Fetch the pails out of the cells.

PRIEST: Where do I take them?

SERGEANT (points): And don't spill any. This place stinks enough as it is. (Going off, bellowing): Get going, all of you. Start cleaning up the yard.

(The priest goes back into the cell and brings out the bucket, barely able to carry it. He sets it down outside the entrance. He plods along the wall to the next cell. The door stands open. There is one man in it, asleep and snoring with his legs sprawled atop the bucket. The priest bends down, removes the legs as gently as he can. He bends to lift the bucket, carries it toward the door.)

VOICE: Wait a minute.

(The priest turns to look at the man. It is the mestizo.)

Come here.

(The priest is frozen.)

Come here, I say. Do you want me to call for the guard?
(The priest sets the bucket down, comes back to stand obediently at the feet of the mestizo.)

What are you doing here?

PRIEST: They caught me with the bottle of brandy.

(The mestizo thinks about this. He chortles, then is silent, frowning as he thinks.)

Did they arrest you, too?

MESTIZO: Me? No. I'm a guest here. An *important* guest.

PRIEST: Why?

MESTIZO: Because I have information they need. But now everything's gone wrong. (Sitting up, indignantly): Why did you let them catch you? It looks crooked to me.

PRIEST: I'm sorry . . .

MESTIZO: It's my job, isn't it, to find you? Who's going to have the reward if they've got you already? The jefe, I suppose . . . or that bastard sergeant. (Brooding): You can't trust a soul these days.

PRIEST: There's also the soldiers.

MESTIZO: What soldiers?

PRIEST: The ones who caught me.

MESTIZO: Mother of God! They'll divide it up, and not a centavo for me!

PRIEST: I imagine they'll give you something.

MESTIZO: Something! Why shouldn't I have it all? (Rising, imploringly): They don't know who you are yet?

PRIEST: Not yet.

MESTIZO: Then don't tell them. Keep it quiet until the right moment, father. For my sake.

PRIEST: For your sake . . .

MESTIZO: You want to be taken, don't you? And I'm a man who's never had a chance. Please, father. You owe me that much.

PRIEST (backing away in horror): No.

MESTIZO: A poor man who's never had a chance . . .

PRIEST: Not by you! By anyone but you! (Shouting): Guard! Guard!

MESTIZO: No, father! Don't cheat me of it. I implore you—

PRIEST (running out of the cell): Guard!

(The sergeant comes on the run.)

SERGEANT: Here, what's the trouble?

PRIEST: I want to be . . . I want to see whoever's in charge.

SERGEANT: Well, *that* can be arranged.

(He exits with the priest. The mestizo's face is drawn in a snarl of fury and anxiety between the bars.)

Cut to:

(Interior, the jail office. The lieutenant is standing back to camera, looking at the posters on the wall behind the desk.)

LIEUTENANT: Well?

PRIEST (off): If you please, sir . . .

Cut to:

(Another angle including both men as the lieutenant turns abruptly. The priest stops short as he recognizes him.)

LIEUTENANT: Yes?

(A pause.)

Are you the drunk who came in last night?

PRIEST (trembling): Yes. . . . Lieutenant . . .

LIEUTENANT: All right, get on with it. What did you want to tell me?

(The priest is trembling and sweating, unable to speak. He puts his hand over his eyes, turns his head away.)

Well?

PRIEST (weakly, all resolution gone): I . . . I wasn't drunk, lieutenant . . . I . . . I . . .

LIEUTENANT: Look at me. Look at me, I said.

(The priest turns. They are face to face.)

I have seen you before.

PRIEST: You came to my village . . . you took a hostage.

LIEUTENANT: Yes. . . . I remember you now. What are you doing in the city?

PRIEST: I came . . . to buy tools.

LIEUTENANT: And you spent the money on drink?

(Priest nods.)

So you've nothing left to pay your fine.

PRIEST: No, lieutenant.

LIEUTENANT: What are you going to do?

PRIEST: God knows.

LIEUTENANT: God knows, God knows! You're all alike, you peasants! When will you learn that God knows nothing! (Controlling himself, pacing): Back home . . . have you planted your crops yet?

PRIEST: It's bad soil between the marshes and the mountains.

LIEUTENANT: Your daughter . . . I remember your daughter. You should be thinking of her future.

PRIEST: It's hard making a living out of stones.

LIEUTENANT: Then go across the mountains. In the next state the soil's good.

PRIEST: Always people tell me to go away.

LIEUTENANT: Take their advice.

PRIEST: Yes . . . I think I will try the other side of the frontier.

LIEUTENANT: How will you get food on the way home?

PRIEST: I've begged before now.

LIEUTENANT: We won't have beggars in this state. (Takes coins from pocket.) Take this—and if there's any over buy a piece of chocolate for your daughter.

PRIEST (looking at the money): You mean I can go?

LIEUTENANT: Get out of here and don't let me see your face again.

PRIEST (goes to the door, looking at the money): Lieutenant . . . (with astonishment): You're a good man.

FRANCIS THOMPSON

The English poet Francis Thompson (1859-1907) was educated in the Roman Catholic faith. His first book, *Poems*, which included "The Hound of Heaven," was published in London in 1893. He also wrote *Sister Songs* (1895) and *New Poems* (1897) and contributed prose pieces to *Academy* and the *Atheneum*. "The Hound of Heaven" is Thompson's most successful work, and it has proven his most enduring (it has been translated into a dozen languages).

THE HOUND OF HEAVEN

I fled Him, down the nights and down the days;
  I fled Him, down the arches of the years;
I fled Him, down the labyrinthine ways
  Of my own mind; and in the mist of tears
I hid from Him, and under running laughter.
      Up vistaed hopes I sped;
      And shot, precipitated,
Adown Titanic glooms of chasmèd fears,
  From those strong Feet that followed, followed after.
      But with unhurrying chase,
      And unperturbèd pace,
   Deliberate speed, majestic instancy,
      They beat—and a Voice beat
      More instant than the Feet—
"All things betray thee, who betrayest Me."

      I pleaded, outlaw-wise,
By many a hearted casement, curtained red,
  Trellised with intertwining charities;
(For, though I knew His love Who followèd,
      Yet was I sore adread
Lest, having Him, I must have naught beside).

But, if one little casement parted wide,
 The gust of His approach would clash it to.
 Fear wist not to evade, as Love wist to pursue.
Across the margent of the world I fled,
 And troubled the gold gateways of the stars,
 Smiting for shelter on their clangèd bars;
  Fretted to dulcet jars
And silvern chatter the pale ports o' the moon.

I said to Dawn: Be sudden—to Eve: Be soon;
 With thy young skyey blossoms heap me over
  From this tremendous Lover—
Float thy vague veil about me, lest He see!
 I tempted all His servitors, but to find
My own betrayal in their constancy,
In faith to Him their fickleness to me,
 Their traitorous trueness, and their loyal deceit.
To all swift things for swiftness did I sue;
 Clung to the whistling mane of every wind.
  But whether they swept, smoothly fleet,
 The long savannahs of the blue;
   Or whether, Thunder-driven,
  They clanged His chariot 'thwart a heaven,
Plashy with flying lightnings round the spurn o' their feet:—
 Fear wist not to evade as Love wist to pursue.
   Still with unhurrying chase,
   And unperturbèd pace,
  Deliberate speed, majestic instancy,
   Came on the following Feet,
   And a Voice above their beat—
 "Naught shelters thee, who wilt not shelter Me."

I sought no more that after which I strayed
  In face of man or maid;
But still within the little children's eyes
 Seems something, something that replies,
They at least are for me, surely for me!

I turned me to them very wistfully;
But just as their young eyes grew sudden fair
    With dawning answers there,
Their angel plucked them from me by the hair.
"Come then, ye other children, Nature's—share
With me" (said I) "your delicate fellowship;
    Let me greet you lip to lip,
    Let me twine with you caresses,
        Wantoning
    With our Lady-Mother's vagrant tresses,
        Banqueting
    With her in her wind-walled palace,
    Underneath her azured dais,
    Quaffing, as your taintless way is,
        From a chalice
Lucent-weeping out of the dayspring."
    So it was done:
I in their delicate fellowship was one—
Drew the bolt of Nature's secrecies.
    I knew all the swift importings
    On the willful face of skies;
    I knew how the clouds arise
    Spumèd of the wild sea-snortings;
        All that's born or dies
    Rose and drooped with; made them shapers
Of mine own moods, or wailful or divine;
    With them joyed and was bereaven.
    I was heavy with the even,
    When she lit her glimmering tapers
    Round the day's dead sanctities.
    I laughed in the morning's eyes.
I triumphed and I saddened with all weather,
    Heaven and I wept together,
And its sweet tears were salt with mortal mine;
Against the red throb of its sunset-heart
    I laid my own to beat,
    And share commingling heat;

But not by that, by that, was eased my human smart.
In vain my tears were wet on Heaven's grey cheek.
For ah! we know not what each other says,
    These things and I; in sound I speak—
Their sound is but their stir, they speak by silences.
Nature, poor stepdame, cannot slake my drouth;
    Let her, if she would owe me,
Drop yon blue bosom-veil of sky, and show me
    The breasts o' her tenderness:
Never did any milk of hers once bless
      My thirsting mouth.
      Nigh and nigh draws the chase,
      With unperturbèd pace,
    Deliberate speed, majestic instancy;
      And past those noisèd Feet
      A Voice comes yet more fleet—
"Lo! naught contents thee, who content'st not Me."
Naked I wait Thy love's uplifted stroke!
My harness piece by piece Thou hast hewn from me,
    And smitten me to my knee;
    I am defenseless utterly.
    I slept, methinks, and woke,
And, slowly gazing, find me stripped in sleep.
In the rash lustihead of my young powers,
    I shook the pillaring hours
And pulled my life upon me; grimed with smears,
I stand amid the dust o' the mounded years—
My mangled youth lies dead beneath the heap.
My days have crackled and gone up in smoke,
Have puffed and burst as sun-starts on a stream.
    Yea, faileth now even dream
The dreamer, and the lute the lutanist;
Even the linkèd fantasies, in whose blossomy twist
I swung the earth a trinket at my wrist,
Are yielding; cords of all too weak account
For earth with heavy griefs so overplussed.
    Ah! is Thy love indeed

A weed, albeit an amaranthine weed,
Suffering no flowers except its own to mount?
    Ah! must—
    Designer infinite!—
Ah! must Thou char the wood ere Thou canst limn with it?
My freshness spent its wavering shower i' the dust;
And now my heart is as a broken fount,
Wherein tear-drippings stagnate, spilt down ever
    From the dank thoughts that shiver
Upon the sighful branches of my mind.
    Such is; what is to be?
The pulp so bitter, how shall taste the rind?
I dimly guess what Time in mists confounds;
Yet ever and anon a trumpet sounds
From the hid battlements of Eternity;
Those shaken mists a space unsettle, then
Round the half-glimpsèd turrets slowly wash again.
    But not ere him who summoneth
    I first have seen, enwound
With glooming robes purpureal, cypress-crowned;
His name I know, and what his trumpet saith.
Whether man's heart or life it be which yields
    Thee harvest, must Thy harvest fields
    Be dunged with rotten death?

    Now of that long pursuit
    Comes on at hand the bruit;
That Voice is round me like a bursting sea:
    "And is thy earth so marred,
    Shattered in shard on shard?
Lo, all things fly thee, for thou fliest Me!
Strange, piteous, futile thing!
Wherefore should any set thee love apart?
Seeing none but I makes much of naught"
    (He said),
"And human love needs human meriting.
    How hast thou merited—

Of all man's clotted clay the dingiest clot?
    Alack, thou knowest not
How little worthy of any love thou art!
Whom wilt thou find to love ignoble thee,
    Save Me, save only Me?
All which I took from thee I did but take,
    Not for thy harms,
But just that thou might'st seek it in My arms.
    All which thy child's mistake
Fancies as lost, I have stored for thee at home:
    Rise, clasp My hand, and come!"

    Halts by me that footfall:
    Is my gloom, after all,
Shade of His hand, outstretched caressingly?
    "Ah, fondest, blindest, weakest,
    I am He Whom thou seekest!
Thou dravest love from thee, who dravest Me."

KATHERINE ANNE PORTER

For four decades Katherine Anne Porter has been regarded as one of America's most distinguished writers of fiction. Since the publication of *Flowering Judas* (a book of short stories) Miss Porter has written *Pale Horse, Pale Rider; The Leaning Tower; The Days Before;* and *Ship of Fools.* She has been guest lecturer at several colleges in the United States, and in 1954 and 1955 she was a Fulbright Lecturer at the University of Liège, Belgium. Miss Porter is a member of the National Institute of Arts and Letters and the Society of Fellows of the Library of Congress.

"Flowering Judas," which first appeared in 1930 (a decade before *The Power and the Glory*), is one of the unmistakable masterpieces in the short-story form. One reads it again and again, always aware of its extraordinary hypnotic power, always uncertain what the whole experience—one is tempted to say, the desolating absence of experience—eventually signifies. What is implied by the contrast, if contrast it is, between the American Laura, with her thin body and incomprehensibly full breasts, her queer premonitions of disaster, her baffling sense of betrayal (recall the story's title), and the hefty Braggioni, son of a Tuscan peasant and a Maya woman, with his boldness and vanity and cruelty, and his tear-stained wife to whom he is regulrly unfaithful and regularly returns?

But if "Flowering Judas" is endlessly absorbing in its own right, it can also be juxtaposed to *The Power and the Glory* with critical benefits for both works of fiction. The story and the novel are both set in Mexico during roughly the same period. Laura is a Roman Catholic at a time when it is at least a scandal, if not a serious crime, to practice her faith; stealthily "she slips now and again into some crumbling church," kneels, and says a prayer. As in *The Power and the Glory*, there is in "Flowering Judas" an atmosphere of constant danger, of persons driven to becoming outlaws, of jails and prisoners, of betrayal, of varieties of love and lovelessness.

FLOWERING JUDAS

Braggioni sits heaped upon the edge of a straight-backed chair much to small for him, and sings to Laura in a furry, mournful

---

voice. Laura has begun to find reasons for avoiding her own house until the latest possible moment, for Braggioni is there almost every night. No matter how late she is, he will be sitting there with a surly, waiting expression, pulling at his kinky yellow hair, thumbing the strings of his guitar, snarling a tune under his breath. Lupe the Indian maid meets Laura at the door, and says with a flicker of a glance towards the upper room, "He waits."

Laura wishes to lie down, she is tired of her hairpins and the feel of her long tight sleeves, but she says to him, "Have you a new song for me this evening?" If he says yes, she asks him to sing it. If he says no, she remembers his favorite one, and asks him to sing it again. Lupe brings her a cup of chocolate and a plate of rice, and Laura eats at the small table under the lamp, first inviting Braggioni, whose answer is always the same: "I have eaten, and besides, chocolate thickens the voice."

Laura says, "Sing, then," and Braggioni heaves himself into song. He scratches the guitar familiarly as though it were a pet animal, and sings passionately off key, taking the high notes in a prolonged painful squeal. Laura, who haunts the markets listening to the ballad singers, and stops every day to hear the blind boy playing his reed-flute in Sixteenth of September Street, listens to Braggioni with pitiless courtesy, because she dares not smile at his miserable performance. Nobody dares to smile at him. Braggioni is cruel to everyone, with a kind of specialized insolence, but he is so vain of his talents, and so sensitive to slights, it would require a cruelty and vanity greater than his own to lay a finger on the vast cureless wound of his self-esteem. It would require courage, too, for it is dangerous to offend him, and nobody has this courage.

Braggioni loves himself with such tenderness and amplitude and eternal charity that his followers—for he is a leader of men, a skilled revolutionist, and his skin has been punctured in honorable warfare—warm themselves in the reflected glow, and say to each other: "He has a real nobility, a love of humanity raised above mere personal affections." The excess of this self-love has flowed out, inconveniently for her, over Laura, who, with so many others, owes her comfortable situation and her salary to him. When he is in a very good humor, he tells her, "I am tempted to forgive you for being a *gringa. Gringita!*" and Laura, burning, imagines herself leaning forward suddenly, and with a sound back-handed slap wiping the suety smile from his face. If he notices her eyes at these moments he gives no sign.

She knows what Braggioni would offer her, and she must resist tenaciously without appearing to resist, and if she could avoid it she would not admit even to herself the slow drift of his intention. During these long evenings which have spoiled a long month for her, she sits in her deep chair with an open book on her knees, resting her eyes on the consoling rigidity of the printed page when the sight and sound of Braggioni singing theaten to identify themselves with all her remembered afflictions and to add their weight to her uneasy premonitions of the future. The gluttonous bulk of Braggioni has become a symbol of her many disillusions, for a revolutionist should be lean, animated by heroic faith, a vessel of abstract virtues. This is nonsense, she knows it now and is ashamed of it. Revolution must have leaders, and leadership is a career for energetic men. She is, her comrades tell her, full of romantic error, for what she defines as cynicism in them is merely "a developed sense of reality." She is almost too willing to say, "I am wrong, I suppose I don't really understand the principles," and afterward she makes a secret truce with herself, determined not to surrender her will to such expedient logic. But she cannot help feeling that she has been betrayed irreparably by the disunion between her way of living and her feeling of what life should be, and at times she is almost contented to rest in this sense of grievance as a private store of consolation. Sometimes she wishes to run away, but she stays. Now she longs to fly out of this room, down the narrow stairs, and into the street where the houses lean together like conspirators under a single mottled lamp, and leave Braggioni singing to himself.

Instead she looks at Braggioni, frankly and clearly, like a good child who understands the rules of behavior. Her knees cling together under sound blue serge, and her round white collar is not purposely nunlike. She wears the uniform of an idea, and has renounced vanities. She was born Roman Catholic, and in spite of her fear of being seen by someone who might make a scandal of it, she slips now and again into some crumbling little church, kneels on the chilly stone, and says a Hail Mary on the gold rosary she bought in Tehuantepec. It is no good and she ends by examining the altar with its tinsel flowers and ragged brocades, and feels tender about the battered doll-shape of some male saint whose white, lace-trimmed drawers hang limply around his ankles below the hieratic dignity of his velvet robe. She has encased herself in a set of principles derived from her early training, leaving no detail of gesture or of personal taste untouched, and for this reason she will not wear lace made on machines. This is her private heresy, for in her special group the machine is sacred, and will be the salvation of the workers. She loves fine lace, and there is a tiny edge of fluted cobweb on this collar, which is one of twenty precisely alike, folded in blue tissue paper in the upper drawer of her clothes chest.

Braggioni catches her glance solidly as if he had been waiting for it, leans forward, balancing his paunch between his spread knees, and sings with tremendous emphasis, weighing his words. He has, the song relates, no father and no mother, nor even a friend to console him; lonely as a wave of the sea he comes and goes, lonely as a wave. His mouth opens round and yearns sideways, his balloon cheeks grow oily with the labor of song. He bulges marvelously in his expensive garments. Over his lavender collar, crushed upon a purple necktie, held by a diamond hoop: over his ammunition belt of tooled leather worked in silver, buckled cruelly around his gasping middle: over the tops of his glossy yellow shoes Braggioni swells with ominous ripeness, his mauve silk hose stretched taut, his ankles bound with the stout leather thongs of his shoes.

When he stretches his eyelids at Laura she notes again that his eyes are the true tawny yellow cat's eyes. He is rich, not in money, he tells her, but in power, and this power brings with it the blameless ownership of things, and the right to indulge his love of small luxuries. "I have a taste for the elegant refinements," he once said, flourishing a yellow silk handkerchief before her nose. "Smell that? It is Jockey Club, imported from New York." Nonetheless he is wounded by life. He will say so presently. "It is true everything turns to dust in the hand, to gall on the tongue." He sighs and his leather belt creaks like a saddle girth. "I am disappointed in everything as it comes. Everything." He shakes his head. "You, poor thing, you will be disappointed too. You are born for it. We are more alike than you realize in some things. Wait and see. Some day you will remember what I have told you, you will know that Braggioni was your friend."

Laura feels a slow chill, a purely physical sense of danger, a warning in her blood that violence, mutilation, a shocking death, wait for her with lessening patience. She has translated this fear into something homely, immediate, and sometimes hesitates before crossing the street. "My personal fate is nothing, except as the testimony of a mental attitude," she reminds herself, quoting from some forgotten philosophic primer, and is sensible enough to add, "Anyhow, I shall not be killed by an automobile if I can help it."

"It may be true I am as corrupt, in another way, as Braggioni," she thinks in spite of herself, "as callous, as incomplete," and if this is so, any kind of death seems preferable. Still she sits quietly, she does not run. Where could she go? Uninvited she has promised herself to this place; she can no longer imagine herself as living in another country, and there is no pleasure in remembering her life before she came here.

Precisely what is the nature of this devotion, its true motives, and what are its obligations? Laura cannot say. She spends part of her days in Xochimilco, near by, teaching Indian children to say in English, "The cat is on the mat." When she appears in the classroom they crowd about her with smiles on their wise, innocent, clay-colored faces, crying, "Good morning, my titcher!" in immaculate voices, and they make of her desk a fresh garden of flowers every day.

During her leisure she goes to union meetings and listens to busy important voices quarreling over tactics, methods, internal politics. She visits the prisoners of her own political faith in their cells, where they entertain themselves with counting cockroaches, repenting of their indiscretions, composing their memoirs, writing out manifestoes and plans for their comrades who are still walking about free, hands in pockets, sniffing fresh air. Laura brings them food and cigarettes and a little money, and she brings messages disguised in equivocal phrases from the men outside who dare not set foot in the prison for fear of disappearing into the cells kept empty for them. If the prisoners confuse night and day, and complain, "Dear little Laura, time doesn't pass in this infernal hole, and I won't know when it is time to sleep unless I have a reminder," she brings them their favorite narcotics, and says in a tone that does not wound them with pity, "Tonight will really be night for you," and though her Spanish amuses them, they find her comforting, useful. If they lose patience and all faith, and curse the slowness of their friends in coming to their rescue with money and influence, they trust her not to repeat everything, and if she inquires, "Where do you think we can find money, or influence?" they are certain to answer, "Well, there is Braggioni, why doesn't he do something?"

She smuggles letters from headquarters to men hiding from firing squads in back streets in mildewed houses, where they sit in tumbled beds and talk bitterly as if all Mexico were at their heels, when Laura knows positively they might appear at the band concert in the Alameda on Sunday morning, and no one would notice them. But Braggioni says, "Let them sweat a little. The next time they may be careful. It is very restful to have them out of the way for a while." She is not afraid to knock on any door in any street after midnight, and enter in the darkness, and say to one of these men who is really in danger: "They will be looking for you—seriously—tomorrow morning after six. Here is some money from Vicente. Go to Vera Cruz and wait."

She borrows money from the Roumanian agitator to give to

his bitter enemy the Polish agitator. The favor of Braggioni is their disputed territory, and Braggioni holds the balance nicely, for he can use them both. The Polish agitator talks love to her over café tables, hoping to exploit what he believes is her secret sentimental preference for him, and he gives her misinformation which he begs her to repeat as the solemn truth to certain persons. The Roumanian is more adroit. He is generous with his money in all good causes, and lies to her with an air of ingenuous candor, as if he were her good friend and confidant. She never repeats anything they may say. Braggioni never asks questions. He has other ways to discover all that he wishes to know about them.

Nobody touches her, but all praise her gray eyes, and the soft, round under lip which promises gaiety, yet is always grave, nearly always firmly closed: and they cannot understand why she is in Mexico. She walks back and forth on her errands, with puzzled eyebrows, carrying her little folder of drawings and music and school papers. No dancer dances more beautifully than Laura walks, and she inspires some amusing, unexpected ardors, which cause little gossip, because nothing comes of them. A young captain who had been a soldier in Zapata's army attempted, during a horseback ride near Cuernavaca, to express his desire for her with the noble simplicity befitting a rude folk-hero: but gently, because he was gentle. This gentleness was his defeat, for when he alighted, and removed her foot from the stirrup, and essayed to draw her down into his arms, her horse, ordinarily a tame one, shied fiercely, reared and plunged away. The young hero's horse careered blindly after his stable-mate, and the hero did not return to the hotel until rather late that evening. At breakfast he came to her table in full charro dress, gray buckskin jacket and trousers with strings of silver buttons down the leg, and he was in a humorous, careless mood. "May I sit with you?" and "You are a wonderful rider. I was terrified that you might be thrown and dragged. I should never have forgiven myself. But I cannot admire you enough for your riding!"

"I learned to ride in Arizona," said Laura.

"If you will ride with me again this morning, I promise you a horse that will not shy with you," he said. But Laura remembered that she must return to Mexico City at noon.

Next morning the children made a celebration and spent their play-time writing on the blackboard, "We lov ar ticher," and with tinted chalks they drew wreaths of flowers around the words. The young hero wrote her a letter: "I am a very foolish, wasteful, impulsive man. I should have first said I love you, and then you would not have run away. But you shall see me again." Laura thought, "I must send him a box of colored crayons," but she was trying to forgive herself for having spurred her horse at the wrong moment.

A brown, shock-haired youth came and stood in her patio one night and sang like a lost soul for two hours, but Laura could think of nothing to do about it. The moonlight spread a wash of gauzy silver over the clear spaces of the garden, and the shadows were cobalt blue. The scarlet blossoms of the Judas tree were dull purple and the names of the colors repeated themselves automatically in her mind, while she watched not the boy, but his shadow, fallen like a dark garment across the fountain rim, trailing in the water. Lupe came silently and whispered expert counsel in her ear: "If you will throw him one little flower, he will sing another song or two and go away." Laura threw the flower, and he sang a last song and went away with the flower tucked in the band of his hat. Lupe said, "He is one of the organizers of the Typographers Union, and before that he sold corridos in the Merced market, and before that, he came from Guanajuato, where I was born. I would not trust any man, but I trust least those from Guanajuato."

She did not tell Laura that he would be back again the next night, and the next, nor that he would follow her at a certain fixed distance around the Merced market, through the Zócolo, up Francisco I. Madero Avenue, and so along the Paseo de la Reforma to Chapultepec Park, and into the Philosopher's Footpath, still with that flower withering in his hat, and an indivisible attention in his eyes.

Now Laura is accustomed to him, it means nothing except

that he is nineteen years old and is observing a convention with all propriety, as though it were founded on a law of nature, which in the end it might well prove to be. He is beginning to write poems which he prints on a wooden press, and he leaves them stuck like handbills in her door. She is pleasantly disturbed by the abstract, unhurried watchfulness of his black eyes which will in time turn easily towards another object. She tells herself that throwing the flower was a mistake, for she is twenty-two years old and knows better; but she refuses to regret it, and persuades herself that her negation of all external events as they occur is a sign that she is gradually perfecting herself in the stoicism she strives to cultivate against that disaster she fears, though she cannot name it.

She is not at home in the world. Every day she teaches children who remain strangers to her, though she loves their tender round hands and their charming opportunist savagery. She knocks at unfamiliar doors not knowing whether a friend or a stranger shall answer, and even if a known face emerges from the sour gloom of that unknown interior, still it is the face of a stranger. No matter what this stranger says to her, nor what her message to him, the very cells of her flesh reject knowledge and kinship in one monotonous word. No. No. No. She draws her strength from this one holy talismanic word which does not suffer her to be led into evil. Denying everything, she may walk anywhere in safety, she looks at everything without amazement.

No, repeats this firm unchanging voice of her blood; and she looks at Braggioni without amazement. He is a great man, he wishes to impress this simple girl who covers her great round breasts with thick dark cloth, and who hides long, invaluably beautiful legs under a heavy skirt. She is almost thin except for the incomprehensible fullness of her breasts, like a nursing mother's, and Braggioni, who considers himself a judge of women, speculates again on the puzzle of her notorious virginity, and takes the liberty of speech which she permits without a sign of modesty, indeed, without any sort of sign, which is disconcerting.

"You think you are so cold, *gringita*! Wait and see. You

will surprise yourself some day! May I be there to advise you!" He stretches his eyelids at her, and his ill-humored cat's eyes waver in a separate glance for the two points of light marking the opposite ends of a smoothly drawn path between the swollen curve of her breasts. He is not put off by that blue serge, nor by her resolutely fixed gaze. There is all the time in the world. His cheeks are bellying with the wind of song. "O girl with the dark eyes," he sings, and reconsiders. "But yours are not dark. I can change all that. O girl with the green eyes, you have stolen my heart away!" then his mind wanders to the song, and Laura feels the weight of his attention being shifted elsewhere. Singing thus, he seems harmless, he is quite harmless, there is nothing to do but sit patiently and say "No," when the moment comes. She draws a full breath, and her mind wanders also, but not far. She dares not wander too far.

Not for nothing has Braggioni taken pains to be a good revolutionist and a professional lover of humanity. He will never die of it. He has the malice, the cleverness, the wickedness, the sharpness of wit, the hardness of heart, stipulated for loving the world profitably. *He will never die of it.* He will live to see himself kicked out from his feeding trough by other hungry world-saviors. Traditionally he must sing in spite of his life which drives him to bloodshed, he tells Laura, for his father was a Tuscany peasant who drifted to Yucatán and married a Maya woman: a woman of race, an aristocrat. They gave him the love and knowledge of music, thus: and under the rip of his thumbnail, the strings of the instrument complain like exposed nerves.

Once he was called Delgadito by all the girls and married women who ran after him; he was so scrawny all his bones showed under his thin cotton clothing, and he could squeeze his emptiness to the very backbone with his two hands. He was a poet and the revolution was only a dream then; too many women loved him and sapped away his youth, and he could never find enough to eat anywhere, anywhere! Now he is a leader of men, crafty men who whisper in his ear, hungry men who wait for hours outside his office for a word with him, emaciated men with wild faces who waylay him at the street gate with a timid, "Comrade, let me tell you . . ." and they blow the foul breath from their empty stomachs in his face. He is always sympathetic. He gives them handfuls of small coins from his own pocket, he promises them work, there will be demonstrations, they must join the unions and attend the meetings, above all they must be on the watch for spies. They are closer to him than his own brothers, without them he can do nothing—until tomorrow, comrade!

Until tomorrow. "They are stupid, they are lazy, they are treacherous, they would cut my throat for nothing," he says to Laura. He has good food and abundant drink, he hires an automobile and drives in the Paseo on Sunday morning, and enjoys plenty of sleep in a soft bed beside a wife who dares not disturb him; and he sits pampering his bones in easy billows of fat, singing to Laura, who knows and thinks these things about him. When he was fifteen, he tried to drown himself because he loved a girl, his first love, and she laughed at him. "A thousand women have paid for that," and his tight little mouth turns down at the corners. Now he perfumes his hair with Jockey Club, and confides to Laura: "One woman is really as good as another for me, in the dark. I prefer them all."

His wife organizes unions among the girls in the cigarette factories, and walks in picket lines, and even speaks at meetings in the evening. But she cannot be brought to acknowledge the benefits of true liberty. "I tell her I must have my freedom, net. She does not understand my point of view." Laura has heard this many times. Braggioni scratches the guitar and meditates. "She is an instinctively virtuous woman, pure gold, no doubt of that. If she were not, I should lock her up, and she knows it."

His wife, who works so hard for the good of the factory girls, employs part of her leisure lying on the floor weeping because there are so many women in the world, and only one husband for her, and she never knows where nor when to look for him. He told her: "Unless you can learn to cry when I am not here, I must go away for good." That day he went away and took a room at the Hotel Madrid.

It is this month of separation for the sake of higher principles that has been spoiled not only for Mrs. Braggioni, whose sense of reality is beyond criticism, but for Laura, who feels herself bogged in a nightmare. Tonight Laura envies Mrs. Braggioni, who is alone, and free to weep as much as she pleases about a concrete wrong. Laura has just come from a visit to the prison, and she is waiting for tomorrow with a bitter anxiety as if tomorrow may not come, but time may be caught immovably in this hour, with herself transfixed, Braggioni singing on forever, and Eugenio's body not yet discovered by the guard.

Braggioni says: "Are you going to sleep?" Almost before she can shake her head, he begins telling her about the May-day disturbances coming on in Morelia, for the Catholics hold a festival in honor of the Blessed Virgin, and the Socialists celebrate their martyrs on that day. "There will be two independent processions, starting from either end of town, and they will march until they meet, and the rest depends . . ." He asks her to oil and load his pistols. Standing up, he unbuckles his ammunition belt, and spreads it laden across her knees. Laura sits with the shells slipping through the cleaning cloth dipped in oil, and he says again he cannot understand why she works so hard for the revolutionary idea unless she loves some man who is in it. "Are you not in love with someone?" "No," says Laura. "And no one is in love with you?" "No." "Then it is your own fault. No woman need go begging. Why, what is the matter with you? The legless beggar woman in the Alameda has a perfectly faithful lover. Did you know that?"

Laura peers down the pistol barrel and says nothing, but a long, slow faintness rises and subsides in her; Braggioni curves his swollen fingers around the throat of the guitar and softly smothers the music out of it, and when she hears him again he seems to have forgotten her, and is speaking in the hypnotic voice he uses when talking in small rooms to a listening, close-gathered crowd. Some day this world, now seemingly so composed and eternal, to the edges of every sea shall be merely a tangle of gaping trenches, of crashing walls and broken bodies. Everything must be torn from its accustomed place where it has rotted for centuries, hurled skyward and distributed, cast down again clean as rain, without separate identity. Nothing shall survive that the stiffened hands of poverty have created for the rich and no one shall be left alive except the elect spirits destined to procreate a new world cleansed of cruelty and injustice, ruled by benevolent anarchy: "Pistols are good, I love them, cannon are even better, but in the end I pin my faith to good dynamite," he concludes, and strokes the pistol lying in her hands. "Once I dreamed of destroying this city, in case it offered resistance to General Ortíz, but it fell into his hands like an overripe pear."

He is made restless by his own words, rises and stands waiting. Laura holds up the belt to him: "Put that on, and go kill somebody in Morelia, and you will be happier," she says softly. The presence of death in the room makes her bold. "Today, I found Eugenio going into a stupor. He refused to allow me to call the prison doctor. He had taken all the tablets I brought him yesterday. He said he took them because he was bored."

"He is a fool, and his death is his own business," says Braggioni, fastening his belt carefully.

"I told him if he had waited only a little while longer, you would have got him set free," says Laura. "He said he did not want to wait."

"He is a fool and we are well rid of him," says Braggioni, reaching for his hat.

He goes away. Laura knows his mood has changed, she will not see him any more for a while. He will send word when he needs her to go on errands into strange streets, to speak to the strange faces that will appear, like clay masks with the power of human speech, to mutter their thanks to Braggioni for his help. Now she is free, and she thinks, I must run while there is time. But she does not go.

Braggioni enters his own house where for a month his wife has spent many hours every night weeping and tangling her hair upon her pillow. She is weeping now, and she weeps more at the sight of him, the cause of all her sorrows. He looks about the room. Nothing is changed, the smells are good and familiar, he is well acquainted with the woman who comes toward him with no reproach except grief on her face. He says to her tenderly: "You are so good, please don't cry any more, you dear good creature." She says, "Are you tired, my angel? Sit here and I will wash your feet." She brings a bowl of water, and kneeling, unlaces his shoes, and when from her knees she raises her sad eyes under her blackened lids, he is sorry for everything, and bursts into tears. "Ah, yes, I am hungry, I am tired, let us eat something together," he says, between sobs. His wife leans her head on his arm and says, "Forgive me!" and this time he is refreshed by the solemn, endless rain of her tears.

Laura takes off her serge dress and puts on a white linen nightgown and goes to bed. She turns her head a little to one side, and lying still, reminds herself that it is time to sleep. Numbers tick in her brain like little clocks, soundless doors close of themselves around her. If you would sleep, you must not remember anything, the children will say tomorrow, good morning, my teacher, the poor prisoners who come every day bringing flowers to their jailor. 1-2-3-4-5—it is monstrous to confuse love with revolution, night with day, life with death—ah, Eugenio!

The tolling of the midnight bell is a signal, but what does it mean? Get up, Laura, and follow me: come out of your sleep, out of your bed, out of this strange house. What are you doing in this house? Without a word, without fear she rose and reached for Eugenio's hand, but he eluded her with a sharp, sly smile and drifted away. This is not all, you shall see—Murderer, he said, follow me, I will show you a new country, but it is far away and we must hurry. No, said Laura, not unless you take my hand, no; and she clung first to the stair rail, and then to the topmost branch of the Judas tree that bent down slowly and set her upon the earth, and then to the rocky ledge of a cliff, and then to the jagged wave of a sea that was not water but a desert of crumbling stone. Where are you taking me, she asked in wonder but without fear. To death, and it is a long way off, and we must hurry, said Eugenio. No, said Laura, not unless you take my hand. Then eat these flowers, poor prisoner, said Eugenio in a voice of pity, take and eat: and from the Judas tree he stripped the warm bleeding flowers, and held them to her lips. She saw that his hand was fleshless, a cluster of small white petrified branches, and his eye sockets were without light, but she ate the flowers greedily for they satisfied both hunger and thirst. Murderer! said Eugenio, and Cannibal! This is my body and my blood. Laura cried No! and at the sound of her own voice, she awoke trembling, and was afraid to sleep again.

TOPICS FOR DISCUSSION
AND PAPERS

Themes and Meanings

1. What is the significance of the title *The Power and the Glory*? There might be several explanations. François Mauriac, for instance, speaks of "the power and the glory of God" at work in the novel. What additional meanings can be discerned in this phrase?

In his introduction to this volume R. W. B. Lewis suggests the appropriateness of the novel's alternative title, *The Labyrinthine Ways*. Describe the correspondences between Francis Thompson's "The Hound of Heaven" (p. 515), from which the title was borrowed, and the novel.

2. *The Power and the Glory* has been considered a religious novel, both because the hero of the book is a Catholic priest and because the travel book which Greene calls the "source" of the novel, *The Lawless Roads*, is candidly and insistently pro-Catholic. Analyze the novel to determine whether or not it conforms to Catholic doctrine. To what extent does the meaning of the novel depend upon the reader's familiarity with Catholic teachings? Some Catholic critics have attacked Greene for "heresy," while the non-Catholic Barbara Seward argues that Greene's spiritual "cosmology" is not entirely compatible with that of the Catholic Church. How accurate, or important, are these charges of unorthodoxy?

3. What devices and techniques does Greene use to make his story universal? R. W. B. Lewis's introduction asks about the relevance of "an obscure Mexican priest who stumbled to his death through the wilds of Tabasco some forty years ago." How might this complaint be answered?

4. A symbol is a word or image, highlighted by stress and context, that conveys an extended meaning (in this novel usually a spiritual or moral meaning). For example, "Mr. Tench's father had been a dentist too—his first memory was finding a discarded cast in a waste-paper basket—the rough toothless gaping mouth of clay"

(p. 15). The discarded cast is a clear-cut symbol and is explained in context by Greene himself. What other symbols can be found in *The Power and the Glory*? Interpret them as completely as possible. To what extent is the meaning of the novel expressed through its symbolism?

5. In *The Lawless Roads* Greene repeatedly expresses his hatred for the tyrannical government of Tabasco, and especially for its persecution of the Catholic Church. How important are political considerations in *The Power and the Glory*? Trace the development of political satire through the novel.

6. In another of his novels one of Greene's characters says that when "the heart of the matter" is reached, one must feel pity, even for the planets. Both Barbara Seward and Richard Hoggart claim that Greene's sense of pity is essential to the meaning of *The Power and the Glory*. Do these two critics mean the same thing by the word "pity"? More important, how does Greene intend this notion to be understood?

7. Greene has been called a pessimist and *The Power and the Glory* a tragedy. Explain why such judgments are accurate or inaccurate. Compare the novel with acknowledged tragedies (for example, Shakespeare's).

8. Lewis's introduction to this volume states that "Greene shares many of the darkest apprehensions of those American novelists who, today, speak most urgently to our condition." Comment at length, using for comparison with Greene one or more of the novelists Lewis mentions—Ellison, Barth, Heller, Pynchon—or other writers, including American poets. (Greene himself has said that T. S. Eliot was an important early influence on his fiction.)

Style and Structure

1. Several critics have commented—some unfavorably—on Greene's use of conventional "thriller" devices, such as improbable coincidences and contrived events. Is this criticism justified? Deal specifically with the ending of the novel—the arrival of the new priest at the home of Luis.

2. Lila Rillo in her pamflet on *The Power and the Glory* (see Bibliography) notes that "it is rather strange that Graham Greene

drops Coral completely after presenting her with such vigour and humanity." How can Greene's strategy here be explained? Select another minor character and discuss his function in the novel. For instance, on his journey toward freedom in the second half of the novel the priest meets and follows an Indian who carries her dead child to the native burial ground. What purpose does this episode serve in the novel?

3. Beginning with a definition of "realism" as a literary convention, discuss realism—or lack of it—in *The Power and the Glory*. If the term realism does not adequately describe the technique of *The Power and the Glory*, what term does?

4. Lewis's introduction speaks of "Greene's strongly accented, highly individual and nearly indefinable style." Granted that the style cannot be completely defined, make an effort to describe it at length. In this connection, read the essays by Dominick P. Consolo and Richard Hoggart, noting especially what they say about such devices as recurring image patterns, abrupt verbal contrasts (the use of oxymoron is a good example), the use of the "catalogue," and reliance on cinematic techniques. Gather various examples of Greene's verbal habits and use them to formulate general conclusions about the method he follows in *The Power and the Glory*.

5. Greene's point of view in telling the story is primarily that of the hunted priest. From time to time, however, the focus shifts and he describes the action as it is seen by other observers. Why has Greene chosen this technique of multiple points of view? More specifically, working with individual episodes, try to explan why shifts in point of view occur when they do. (For example, why does the novel open and close with Mr. Tench?)

6. Karl Patten argues that *The Power and the Glory* is organized by different "structures" which operate simultaneously and interdependently. Comment on Patten's essay in detail.

7. Structural elements, of course, are quite closely allied with the thematic implications of the novel. In several of the essays included in this volume critics propose various symbolic or allegorical structures that serve, so they say, as principles on which the novel is organized. Choose one of these proposed structures (or offer still another) and discuss its thematic implication. For example, if the novel is a Christian allegory, how closely does the priest himself resemble Christ?

8. Kenneth Allott and Miriam Farris (see Bibliography) cite the prison scene as offering a stylistic contrast to other parts of the novel in its use of "dreams, reveries, quotations, and literary references . . . to suggest . . . a richness of central meaning." Explain why this is an accurate (or inaccurate) analysis. More generally, how is the content of any particular scene related to the style in which it is presented?

Characters

1. One of the major themes in modern fiction is that of alienation. Discuss Greene's priest as a character who exemplifies this theme. Compare Greene's protagonist with Camus's Meursault in *The Stranger*, who is often described as the archetype of the alienated modern man. Other comparisons might be with T. S. Eliot's Prufrock or Ellison's "Invisible Man." In terms of this theme, is Greene's priest a "special case" because of his religious faith? If so, how?

2. One of the questions that obsess the priest himself is his own "unworthiness." Aside from the divine implications of his priesthood, to what extent is he or is he not a worthy man? In what ways is the priest an example of the "antihero" of modern fiction? How well suited would he be to play the role of hero in a nonreligious story? Outline whatever development or growth you think the priest undergoes during the course of the novel.

3. The priest says to the lieutenant at one point that the latter is "a good man." How much sympathy and criticism does the lieutenant evoke? In what way does the reader's response to the lieutenant—and to the priest—result from the reader's own political and religious views?

4. Throughout the novel the priest and the lieutenant are elaborately compared and contrasted, often in terms of "traded" characteristics: the lieutenant, for instance, is described as if he were a priest (celibate and "monastic"), as opposed to the priest, who has lapsed sexually and alcoholically. What is the purpose of the general contrasts and of the specific oppositions? To what extent are they ironic? How is the final confrontation between these two men related to Greene's earlier, preparatory comparisons?

5. Greene carefully delineates the novel's three children, Luis,

Coral, and Brigida. What is the role of each in *The Power and the Glory*? What is the relation of each to the priest? How does the characterization of Greene's children break with the commonplace literary convention that "children represent both continuity with the past and hope for the future?"

BIBLIOGRAPHY

A Note on Greene and French Criticism

The French response to Greene's writings has been a phenomenon of contemporary literary history and deserves special mention. Though his work was vaguely known as early as 1929, it was not until twenty years later that he became suddenly and firmly established in the French world of letters. Armand Pierhal remarked, in the influential Paris periodical *Les Nouvelles Littéraires* in March 1950, that "the historians will have no doubt about it: the great event in French literary life in 1949 will have been the advent of Graham Greene, an English writer: a dozen books brought out in translation by half a dozen publishers; countless articles, two of them important studies . . .; two works, published one on top of the other, containing a first panoramic view of his production." The latter two volumes were by Paul Rostenne (with a letter from Greene about his method of working) and Jacques Madaule. Since 1950 the flow of translations and the flood of commentary have been unceasing.

The editors are especially grateful to Miss Marion Mainwaring for exploring the whole range of French criticism of Greene and for selecting and translating some of the best of it. These materials are available to any student seriously interested in pursuing this significant chapter in modern comparative literature and criticism. They include:

Selections from *L'Aventure intellectuelle du XXe siècle* ("The Intellectual Adventure of the Twentieth Century") by René-Marill Albérès (revised edition, 1963). Greene's central image of "the hunted man" and his theme of responsibility—paradoxical and useless responsibility, as Albérès sees it.

Selections from *Graham Greene*, by Victor de Pange (fourth edition, 1967). A thorough grappling with Greene's religious ideas, with a stress on the intricacies of the theme of freedom.

The final scene from *La Puissance et la Gloire*, a play in two acts by Pierre Bost, based on the adaptation of Greene's novel by Pierre Darbon and Pierre Quest. This dramatization is a valuable critique of the original novel and could be compared with the

English stage version and the American television screening. In Bost's play several cuts have been made; and the Chief of Police has been transformed and elevated into the role of sardonic mediator between the priest and the lieutenant.

Claude-Edmonde Magny, preface to the French translation of *Brighton Rock* (1947). A beautifully composed little piece by one of the most gifted French critics of our time, dealing with Greene's mastery in exploiting the genre of the thriller—a peculiarly self-enclosed form—to arrive at metaphysical drama.

Thomas Narcejac, preface to a later edition of *Brighton Rock* (1954). Another exceedingly suggestive discussion of Greene's use of the detective-story form and the way it permits him to expose his vision of a world from which God has withdrawn, and in which not only man but *things*—physical nature—are "corrupted by a sort of madness."

Armand Pierhal, "Romancier ou Theologien?" ("Novelist or Theologian?"), *Les Nouvelles Littéraires*, March 1950. The first survey of the French criticism of Greene.

Books by Graham Greene

Babbling April [poems]. Oxford: Basil Blackwell, 1925; New York: Doubleday, 1925.

The Man Within [novel]. London: William Heinemann, Ltd., 1929; New York: Viking, 1929; reissued, Viking, 1947; Heinemann Uniform Edition, 1952; Heinemann Library Edition, 1959.

The Name of Action [novel]. London: William Heinemann, Ltd., 1930; New York: Doubleday, 1931.

Rumour at Nightfall [novel]. London: William Heinemann, Ltd., 1931; New York: Doubleday, 1932.

Stamboul Train [entertainment]. London: William Heinemann, Ltd., 1932; New York: Doubleday, 1933 (under the title *Orient Express*); Heinemann Uniform Edition, 1948; Heinemann Library Edition, 1959.

It's a Battlefield [novel]. London: William Heinemann, Ltd., 1934, 1935; New York: Doubleday, 1934; New York: Viking, 1948 (revised); Heinemann Uniform Edition, 1948; Heinemann Library Edition, 1959; reissued, Viking, 1962.

England Made Me [novel]. London: William Heinemann, Ltd., 1935, 1937; New York: Doubleday, 1935 (under the title *The*

Shipwrecked); New York: Viking, 1953; Heinemann Uniform Edition, 1948; Heinemann Library Edition, 1960.

The Bear Fell Free [story]. London: Grayson and Grayson, 1935.

The Basement Room and Other Stories. London: The Cresset Press, 1935.

A Gun for Sale [entertainment]. London: William Heinemann, Ltd., 1936; New York: Doubleday, 1936 (under the title *This Gun for Hire*); Heinemann Uniform Edition, 1947; Heinemann Library Edition, 1960.

Journey without Maps [travel book]. London: William Heinemann, Ltd., 1936; New York: Doubleday, 1936; Heinemann Uniform Edition, 1950; New York: Viking Compass, 1961.

Brighton Rock [novel]. London: William Heinemann, Ltd., 1938; New York: Viking, 1938; reissued, Viking, 1948; Heinemann, 1968; Heinemann Uniform Edition, 1947; Viking Compass, 1956; Heinemann Library Edition, 1959.

The Lawless Roads: A Mexican Journey [travel book]. London: Longmans Green and Co., 1939; New York: Viking, 1939 (under the title *Another Mexico*); London: reissued, Eyre and Spottiswoode, 1950; Heinemann Uniform Edition, 1955; Heinemann Library Edition, 1960; Viking Compass, 1964.

The Confidential Agent [entertainment]. London: William Heinemann, Ltd., 1941; New York: Viking, 1939; Heinemann Uniform Edition, 1953; Heinemann Library Edition, 1960.

The Power and the Glory [novel]. London: William Heinemann, Ltd., 1940; New York: Viking, 1940 (under the title *The Labyrinthine Ways*); reissued, Viking, 1947 (under the title *The Power and the Glory*); Heinemann Uniform Edition, 1949; Viking Compass, 1958; reissued (with Greene's "Introduction"), 1963.

British Dramatists. Toronto: Collins, 1942.

The Ministry of Fear [entertainment]. London: William Heinemann, Ltd., 1943; New York: Viking, 1943; Heinemann Uniform Edition, 1950; Heinemann Library Edition, 1960.

Nineteen Stories. London: William Heinemann, Ltd., 1947; New York: Viking, 1949.

The Little Train [children's book]. London: Parrish, 1947; reissued, Parrish, 1957.

Why Do I Write? [with Elizabeth Bowen and V. S. Pritchett]. London: Percival Marshall, 1948.

The Heart of the Matter [novel]. London: William Heinemann, Ltd., 1948; New York: Viking, 1948; Heinemann Uniform Edition, 1951; Heinemann Library Edition, 1959; Viking Compass, 1960; reissued, Heinemann, 1968.

The Little Fire Engine [children's book]. London: Parrish, 1950; New York: Lothrop, 1950 (under the title *The Little Red Fire Engine*); reissued, Parrish, 1961.

The Third Man [entertainment]. New York: Viking, 1950.

The Third Man and *The Fallen Idol* [two entertainments in one volume]. London: William Heinemann, Ltd., 1950; reissued, 1959.

The End of the Affair [novel]. London: William Heinemann, Ltd., 1951; New York: Viking, 1951; Heinemann Uniform Edition, 1955; Heinemann Library Edition, 1959; Viking Compass, 1961.

The Lost Childhood and Other Essays. London: Eyre and Spottiswoode, 1951; New York: Viking, 1952; Viking Compass, 1962.

The Little Horse Bus [children's book]. London: Parrish, 1952.

Three by Graham Greene [*This Gun for Hire, The Confidential Agent, The Ministry of Fear*]. New York: Viking, 1952; Viking Compass, 1968.

The Living Room [play]. London: William Heinemann, Ltd., 1953; New York: Viking, 1954.

The Little Steamroller [children's book]. London: Parrish, 1953; New York: Lothrop, 1955.

Twenty-One Stories. London: William Heinemann, Ltd., 1954; New York: Viking Compass, 1962.

The Quiet American [novel]. London: William Heinemann, Ltd., 1955; New York: Viking, 1956; Viking Compass, 1957; Heinemann Library Edition, 1961.

Loser Takes All [entertainment]. London: William Heinemann, Ltd., 1955; New York: Viking, 1956; Viking Compass, 1957.

The Potting Shed [play]. New York: Viking, 1957; London: William Heinemann, Ltd., 1958; Viking Compass, 1961.

Our Man in Havana [entertainment]. London: William Heinemann, Ltd., 1958; New York: Viking, 1958; reissued, Heinemann, 1966.

The Complaisant Lover [play]. London: William Heinemann, Ltd., 1959; New York: Viking, 1961.

Three Plays [*The Living Room, The Potting Shed, The Complaisant Lover*]. London: Mercury Books, 1961.

A *Burnt-Out Case* [novel]. London: William Heinemann, Ltd., 1961; New York: Viking, 1961; Viking Compass, 1967.

In Search of a Character: Two African Journals [travel book]. London: Bodley Head, 1961; New York: Viking, 1962.

The Travel Books [*Journey without Maps* and *The Lawless Roads* in one volume]. London: William Heinemann, Ltd., 1963.

A Sense of Reality [stories]. London: Bodley Head, 1963; New York: Viking, 1963.

Carving a Statue [play]. London: William Heinemann, Ltd., 1964.

The Comedians [novel]. London: Bodley Head, 1966; New York: Viking, 1966; Viking Compass, 1970.

May We Borrow Your Husband? [stories]. London: Bodley Head, 1967; New York: Viking, 1967.

Collected Essays. London: Bodley Head, 1969; New York: Viking, 1969.

Travels with My Aunt [novel]. London: Bodley Head, 1970; New York: Viking, 1970.

An asterisk indicates a selection that has been reprinted in this volume in whole or in part.

Books on Graham Greene

Allen, Walter. *Reading a Novel*. London: Phoenix House, 1949, pp. 34-39. Brief and introductory essay on *The Power and the Glory*.

Allott, Kenneth, and Miriam Farris. *The Art of Graham Greene*. New York: Russell & Russell, 1963. Comprehensive thematic study of Greene's fiction through 1951.

Atkins, John G. *Graham Greene*. New York: Roy Publishers, 1957. Chapter Ten, "The Right to Suffer," is an attack on *The Power and the Glory*.

de Pange, Victor. *Graham Greene*. Paris: Éditions Universitaires, 1953. (Preface by François Mauriac.) "Redemptive love" as the key to Greene's fiction.

De Vitis, A. A. *Graham Greene*. New York: Twayne Publishers, 1964. Summary and study of Greene's fiction.

Evans, Robert O. *Graham Greene: Some Critical Considerations*. Lexington, Kentucky: University of Kentucky Press, 1963. Essays by various critics, most printed for the first time.

Graef, Hilda. *Modern Gloom and Christian Hope*. London: Henry Regnery Company, 1959, pp. 84-97. *The Power and the Glory* as an "existential" novel.

Karl, Frederick. *The Contemporary English Novel*. New York: The Noonday Press, 1962, Chapter on "Graham Greene's Demoniacal Heroes" argues that Greene has resurrected Greek tragedy in a Christian context.

Kohn, Lynette. *Graham Greene: The Major Novels*. Stanford University Honors Essays in Humanities #4. Stanford, California, 1961.

Kunkel, Francis L. *The Labyrinthine Ways of Graham Greene*. New York: Sheed and Ward, 1959. Discussion of Greene's theology.

Lewis, R. W. B. *The Picaresque Saint*. Philadelphia: J. B. Lippincott Company, 1961. Chapter on "Graham Greene: The Religious Affair."*

Lodge, David. *Graham Greene*. New York: Columbia University Press, 1966. Brief study of Greene's importance in modern British literature.

Madaule, Jacques. *Graham Greene*. Paris: Éditions du Temps Présent, 1949.

Maurois, André. *Points of View*. New York: Frederick Ungar Publishing Company, 1968, pp. 383-409. Biographical and critical chapter on Greene.

Mesnet, Marie-Béatrice. *Graham Greene and the Heart of the Matter*. London: The Cresset Press, 1954. Greene's major novels unified by his "spiritual intensity."

Moeller, Charles. *Silence de Dieu*. Tournai, Belgium: Établissements Casterman, 1958. Study of Greene's religious concerns along with those of Camus, Gide, Huxley, Simone Weil, Julian Green, and Bernanos.

O'Faolain, Sean. *The Vanishing Hero: The Hero in the Modern Novel*. New York: The Universal Library, Grosset and Dunlap, 1956, pp. 45-72.*

Pryce-Jones, David. *Graham Greene*. London: Oliver and Boyd, Ltd., 1963. Section on *The Power and the Glory* studies the novel's sources and allegorical significance.

Rillo, Lila. "The Power and the Glory." English Pamphlet #12, Buenos Aires, Argentina, 1946. Paraphrase of the novel with interpolated comment.

Rostenne, Paul. *Graham Greene: Témoin des temps tragiques.* Paris: Julliard, 1949. (Preface by Graham Greene.) A theological study.

Stratford, Philip. *Faith and Fiction: The Creative Process in Greene and Mauriac.* Notre Dame, Indiana: University of Notre Dame Press, 1964.

Turnell, Martin. *Graham Greene: A Critical Essay.* Grand Rapids, Michigan: Eerdmans Publishing Company, 1967.

West, Anthony. *Principles and Persuasions.* New York: Harcourt and Brace, 1951, pp. 195-200. The novels as expressions of "sexual guilt."

Woodcock, George. *The Writer and Politics.* London: Porcupine Press, 1958, pp. 125-153. Discussion of the "Catholic-humanist" paradox in Greene's fiction.

Wyndham, Francis. *Graham Greene.* London: Longmans, Green and Company, 1955. #67 in a series *Writers and Their Work.*

Zabel, Morton Dauwen. *Craft and Character.* New York: The Viking Press, 1957, pp. 276-296.*

Articles and Essays on Graham Greene

Allen, W. Gore. "Another View of Graham Greene." *The Catholic World,* 169 (April 1949), pp. 69-70. Greeneland as the Wasteland.

————. "Evelyn Waugh and Graham Greene." *Irish Monthly,* 77 (January 1949), pp. 16-22.

Allen, Walter. "The Novels of Graham Greene." *Penguin New Writing,* 18 (July-September 1943), pp. 148-60. An "interim" and favorable judgment.

Atkins, John G. "Altogether Amen: A Reconsideration of *The Power and the Glory.*" *Graham Greene: Some Critical Considerations* (see Evans, Robert O., above), pp. 181-87. Attack on the stylistic and theological ambiguity of the novel.

Barnes, Robert J. "Two Modes of Fiction: Hemingway and Greene." *Renascence,* XIV (Spring 1962), pp. 193-98.

Beary, Thomas John. "Religion and the Modern Novel." *The Catholic World,* 166 (December 1947), pp. 203-11. Uses *The Power and the Glory* as a key example.

Boyle, Alexander. "Graham Greene." *Irish Monthly,* 77 (November 1949), pp. 519-25.

————. "The Symbolism of Graham Greene." *Irish Monthly*, 80 (August 1952), pp. 98-102.

Boyle, Raymond M. "Man of Controversy." *The Grail* (July 1952), pp. 2-7. Brief portrait of Greene and his stormy relationship with the Catholic press.

Braybrooke, Neville. "Graham Greene as Critic." *Commonweal*, 54 (July 6, 1951), pp. 312-14.

Calder-Marshall, Arthur. "Graham Greene." *Living Writers* (critical studies broadcast by the B.B.C. Third Programme), ed. Gilbert Phelps. N.c.: The Sylvan Press, n.d., pp. 39-47. Greene's "conviction" of evil is the source of his intensity.

Chapman, Raymond. "The Vision of Graham Greene." *Forms of Extremity in the Modern Novel*, ed. Nathan Scott, Jr. Richmond, Virginia: John Knox Press, 1965, pp. 75-94.

Connolly, Francis X. "Inside Modern Man: The Spiritual Adventures of Graham Greene." *Renascence*, I (Spring 1949), pp. 16-24. Study of Greene's interpretation of Christian concepts.

Consolo, Dominick P. "Style and Stylistics in Five Novels." *Graham Greene: Some Critical Considerations* (see Evans, Robert O., above), pp. 61-95.*

Cosman, Max. "An Early Chapter in Graham Greene." *Arizona Quarterly*, XI (Summer 1955), pp. 143-47. Detailed speculations on Marjorie Bowen's influence.

Costello, Donald P. "Graham Greene and the Catholic Press." *Renascence*, XII (Autumn 1959), pp. 3-28. Includes an extensive bibliography of representative Catholic criticism.

De Vitis, A. A. "The Catholic as Novelist: Graham Greene and François Mauriac." *Graham Greene: Some Critical Considerations* (see Evans, Robert O., above), pp. 112-26. Both authors are "necessarily unorthodox" Christians.

————. "The Entertaining Mr. Greene." *Renascence*, XIV (Fall 1961), pp. 8-24. Greene's entertainments as "preliminary studies" for the novels that follow.

Dinkins, Paul. "Graham Greene: The Incomplete Version." *The Catholic World*, 176 (November 1952), pp. 96-102. Attack on Greene's fiction for aesthetic and philosophical "imbalance."

Ellis, William D., Jr. "The Grand Theme of Graham Greene." *Southwest Review*, XLI (Summer 1956), pp. 239-50. Title definition: the appalling mystery of love in a ravaged world.

Fytton, Francis. "Graham Greene: Catholicism and Controversy." *The Catholic World*, 180 (December 1954), pp. 172-75.

Gardiner, Harold C. "Graham Greene, Catholic Shocker." *Renascence*, I (Spring 1949), pp. 12-15.

Grubbs, Henry A. "Albert Camus and Graham Greene." *Modern Language Quarterly*, X (March 1949), pp. 33-42. Compares, among other works of both men, *The Power and the Glory* and *The Plague*.

Haber, Herbert R. "The Two Worlds of Graham Greene." *Modern Fiction Studies*, III (Autumn 1957, Special Greene Number), pp. 256-68. Study of *Brighton Rock* and *The Power and the Glory*.

Harmer, Ruth Mulvey. "Greene World of Mexico: the Birth of a Novelist." *Renascence*, XV (Summer 1963), pp. 171-82, 194. Detailed comparison of *The Power and the Glory* with its "source," *The Lawless Roads*.

Hesla, David H. "Theological Ambiguity in the 'Catholic Novels.' " *Graham Greene: Some Critical Considerations* (see Evans, Robert O., above), pp. 96-111.

Hoggart, Richard. "The Force of Caricature: Aspects of the art of Graham Greene with particular reference to *The Power and the Glory*." *Essays in Criticism*, III (October 1953), pp. 447-62.*

Hortmann, Wilhelm. "Graham Greene: The Burnt-Out Catholic." *Twentieth Century Literature*, X (April 1964-January 1965), pp. 64-76. Greene's later novels as aggressively heretical.

Hughes, Catherine. "Innocence Revisited." *Renascence*, XII (Fall 1959), pp. 29-34. Discussion of the theme of childhood in Greene's fiction.

Jerrold, Douglas, "Graham Greene: Pleasure-Hater." *Harper's*, CCV (August 1952), pp. 50-52. Greene as a "life-hating" genius.

Kenny, Herbert A. "Graham Greene." *The Catholic World*, 185 (August 1957), pp. 326-29.

Lees, F. N. "Graham Greene: A Comment." *Scrutiny*, XIX (October 1952), pp. 31-42. Detailed attack on Greene's style.

Lerner, Laurence. "Graham Greene." *Critical Quarterly*, V (1963), pp. 217-31.*

Lohf, Kenneth A. "Graham Greene and the Problem of Evil." *The Catholic World*, 173 (June 1951), pp. 196-99.

Marian, Sister I. H. M. "Graham Greene's People: Being and

Becoming." *Renascence*, XVIII (Fall 1965), pp. 16-22. Greene as a Christian existentialist.

Marshall, Bruce. "Graham Greene and Evelyn Waugh." *Commonweal*, (March 3, 1950), pp. 551-53.

McCarthy, Mary. "Graham Greene and the Intelligentsia." *Partisan Review*, XI (Spring 1944), pp. 228-30. An attack.

McLaughlin, Richard. "Graham Greene: Saint or Cynic?" *America*, LXXIX (July 24, 1948), pp. 370-71. Brief personality portrait.

Monroe, N. Elizabeth. "The New Man in Fiction." *Renascence*, VI (August 1953), pp. 9-12. Greene's whisky priest as a "modern hero."

O'Donnell, Donat [Conor Cruise O'Brien]. "Graham Greene." *Chimera*, V (Summer 1947), pp. 18-30. Discussion of Greene's "infernal" vision.

Patten, Karl. "The Structure of *The Power and the Glory*." *Modern Fiction Studies*, III (Autumn 1957, Special Greene Number), pp. 225-34.*

Peters, W. "The Concern of Graham Greene." *The Month*, X (November 1953), pp. 281-90. The theme of sin in Greene's major fiction.

Rolo, Charles J. "Graham Greene: The Man and the Message." *Atlantic*, CCVII (May 1961), pp. 60-65. Personality portrait.

Sackville-West, Edward. "The Electric Hare: Some Aspects of Graham Greene." *The Month*, VI (September 1951), pp. 141-47. Application of Greene's critical writings to his fiction.

Scott, Carolyn D. "The Witch at the Corner: Notes on Graham Greene's Mythology." *Graham Greene: Some Critical Considerations* (see Evans, Robert O., above), pp. 231-44.

Scott, Nathan A., Jr. "Graham Greene: Christian Tragedian." *Graham Greene: Some Critical Considerations* (see Evans, Robert O., above), pp. 25-48.

Seward, Barbara. "Graham Greene: A Hint of an Explanation." *Western Review*, XXII (Winter 1958), pp. 83-95.

Sewell, Elizabeth. "Graham Greene." *Dublin Review*, CVIII (First Quarter 1954), pp. 12-21. Greene as post-Romantic "decadent."

Simons, John W. "Salvation in the Novels." *Commonweal*, 56 (April 25, 1952), pp. 74-76.

Smith, A. J. M. "Graham Greene's Theological Thrillers." *Queen's Quarterly*, LXVIII (Spring 1961), pp. 15-33. Greene's fiction as "explorations of sin."

Stratford, Philip. "Master of Melodrama." *Tamarack Review*, XIX (Spring 1961), pp. 67-86. Approval of Greene's use of melodramatic devices.

Sylvester, Harry. "Graham Greene." *Commonweal*, 33 (October 25, 1940), pp. 11-13. Early praise for Greene.

Traversi, Derek. "Graham Greene: The Later Novels." *Twentieth Century*, CXLIX (April 1951), pp. 318-28.

Turnell, Martin. "The Religious Novel." *Commonweal*, 55 (October 26, 1951), pp. 55-57.

Webster, Harvey Curtis. "The World of Graham Greene." *Graham Greene: Some Critical Considerations* (see Evans, Robert O., above), pp. 1-24. Chronological survey of Greene's fiction.

Wichert, Robert A. "The Quality of Graham Greene's Mercy." *College English* (November 1963), pp. 99-103. Morality in Greene's fiction based on love and mercy.

Wilshere, A. D. "Conflict and Conciliation in Graham Greene." *Essays and Studies 1966*, ed. R. M. Wilson. London: John Murray, 1966, pp. 122-37.

Woodcock, George. "Mexico and the English Novelist." *Western Review*, XXI (Autumn 1956), pp. 21-32. Comparison of the "Mexican experience" of Huxley, Lawrence, and Greene.